THE
LONGEST
SPRING

P.D. SHERRARD

FOREST PRESS

Book Cover photography and design by Pete Sherrard.

Published by Forest Press.

1st Edition 2023

ISBN 978-1-7394790-0-8 (eBook edition)

ISBN 978-1-7394790-1-5 (Paperback edition)

Visit the author's website at http://pdsherrard.com

For Tiff & Forest

1

DAWN

30th June, 1916.

He's killed a lot of men this morning, but this one, if he does it, will be so much harder. He knows this man. He knows those hands, swollen now and dark with cuts, but he can remember how they held a pen or a cup of tea. That bruised mouth, creased with dried blood, still holds the remnant of a smile that he'd once courted. He reaches out to wipe the blood but stops himself; he mustn't wake him.

He looks at the clouds above the sandbags, warmed and made plump by a hint of dawn. It will be light soon. If he does it, he must do it quickly. He must be sure. If he does it, he must do it well.

He looks down at the pistol, turning it over in his hand. The little dents and scratches glint in the half-light. The wooden grip is marked with cross-hatched lines. He watches the pattern it makes in his palm; pinched white, then fading as the blood rushes back into his skin.

He can hear the soldiers coming along the trench. If he does it, he must do it now. But it's so much harder if you've known them. And this one, if he does it, will be murder.

2

THE MULE CART

4th March, 1916

'Any more for the war?' yells the cart driver, pulling hard on the reins. Hooves and cart wheels grind against wet cobbles.

Alex steps back, too late to stop mud spraying across his uniform.

The driver peers out from the hood of a rubber poncho. 'Where you off to, Son?'

'Neuve Chapelle,' says Alex. 'D Company, 12th battalion, Royal Sussex.'

'Then tonight's your lucky night! I'm going past exactly where you need to be.'

It's taken the whole day for the train to bring Alex the sixty miles from the coast to Hazebrouk. He's supposed to find his own way from here to the regiment. He's been outside the station, up and down the line of transport vehicles, covered supply lorries and officers' motor cars, but nothing is going in his direction. It's dark now and raining so hard he feels like he has to take deep breaths just to reach the air between the water. He's soaked and cold. He hoped there would be something a bit more comfortable than an open mule cart, something covered at least.

'There's nothing else going up that far tonight, Son,' says the driver, seeing Alex's expression. 'Go on, throw your valise in the back there.' He jabs his thumb towards a pile of wooden crates in the cart behind him. 'Just mind them bombs.'

Alex doesn't move.

The driver laughs. 'I'm joking with you, Son. Those are tins of stew! Climb up.'

Alex carefully places his valise in the back of the cart, making sure he doesn't touch the crates. Then he climbs up and sits on the bench next to the driver.

'Don't ever eat that stew,' says the driver, hunching over and snapping the reins. 'That's Maconochie stew in them tins. Eat your boots if you have to. But never that stew.' The mules ease out into the flow of traffic and plod along the muddy road. 'Just come off the ship, have you?'

'No, I've been training in Etaples for the last two weeks.'

The driver stares. He wears an eye patch, the good eye glimmers like a wet billiard ball. 'Training for what? How to shave?'

'Officer training, actually,' says Alex, lifting his chin and feeling for the epaulette under his top-coat. 'Second Lieutenant.'

The driver whistles and clicks his tongue as the mules, heads down, ears flicking, wet backs like black treacle, plod through the town.

Slowly, the red brick houses make way for flat, open fields and rows of poplar trees, swaying and hissing in the darkness. On the horizon, occasional blossoms of light, hazy behind the rain, hint at low rolling hills and woods that remind Alex of the South Downs. He thought everything would be more French, more foreign.

The driver glances at Alex. 'How old are you, Sir? If you don't mind my asking?'

'I've just turned twenty,' says Alex, although he doesn't see what that has to do with anything.

An eyebrow appears momentarily above the driver's eye patch. 'What were they thinking? An officer! You've got no experience.' He shakes his head, water spinning off his helmet. 'Sending young lads out here to lead men twice their age...'

Alex sighs. He'd had a very similar discussion with his father before he left England. He really didn't expect to be having it again with a uniformed soldier just a few miles behind the frontline.

What his father said was true; Alex has never seen a German or fired a gun at anything that wasn't made of straw. But that doesn't mean he can't lead. Leadership isn't about experience. It's about confidence and making the right decisions under pressure. It's something you're born with; you either have it or you don't. Alex thinks he has it. He was one of the first in his officer training corps to receive a commission. Although the pride of that had become disappointment when he was sent to defend Newhaven Harbour from nothing more menacing than storms and angry seagulls. But he'd been in charge of his own unit of men, to an extent, and his battalion commander had said he'd *done well*.

The driver is still talking. 'Can't expect *boys* to just come out here and lead. There's *men* in those trenches who've seen things you couldn't bear to imagine...'

'I won't be just walking into a battle, leading the men on my own. There's plenty of officers, to learn from as I go.' One of the reasons why Alex had chosen, and to his delight, been accepted by the 12th was that the company was led by two great Captains. 'Captain Kingsman is the commanding officer,' says Alex, despite himself.

'Kingsman,' says the driver, with a nod of approval. 'He's a good man. And who's second?'

'Captain Eden.' Alex waits for the driver to impart his opinion of Eden but all he does is grunt and mumble something into the rain.

Captain James Eden; the battalion's resident hero. Victoria and Military crosses for gallantry, countless mentions in despatches. He's famous in London and was once applauded by an audience at a musical he'd attended. Alex has read and reread newspaper articles about him.

The driver stands and yells something at a group of soldiers who are trying to cross the road. He swerves violently around them. 'If you was my son,' he says, settling back onto the seat. 'And at your age, you might be, me not knowing who your mother is... I would advise you to just keep your head down, avoid the enemy as best you can.' He leans across the bench towards Alex. ' You should have stayed at home with your mother.'

Alex shakes his head. He doesn't have a mother, and even if he did, he would have no intention of staying at home with her or keeping his head down. In fact, he intends to keep his head very much up. He'd spent a year, sitting in a pillbox, staring at the churning sea, listening to the dull crump of the guns drifting across the water and he had longed to be here in France; ached for it. 'How close are we going to the front?'

'I'll drop you off at the entrance to Liverpool Street trench, Sir. Your regiment is on the front line at the far end of that, I believe.'

'And how far away are the Germans?'

'You'll hear them pissing in the night.'

Alex pulls his coat tight around his legs. He leans back and breathes in the damp French air. He's finally here, just a few miles to go and he'll finally be where he should have been from the beginning.

As they roll through the darkness, towards the pulsing horizon, they pass villages that appear untouched. Then there are others where every house has lost its roof. Sandbags piled up against crumbling walls. Churches with broken spires. Heaps of rubble where the pavements had once been.

Something reaches out of the darkness and grabs Alex by the arm; an old woman, shawled, soaked, pleading, tapping her fingers to her mouth. Alex doesn't know what she wants; he doesn't speak French. He apologises in English and fumbles in his pockets for a coin.

The driver raises his hand, angrily. The mules flinch and the woman steps away.

They pass military tents in village squares, endless columns of horse-drawn cannon, trucks ploughing through the mud in each direction and, like monstrous centipedes, rows of tired, stone-faced soldiers marching quietly through the rain.

'Is that lightning?' says Alex, pointing to the flashes ahead of them.

'Lightning?' The driver laughs. 'No, Son, that's war.'

He realises now. It sounded like thunder on the English coast, but here it has a metallic, hollow sound. Howitzers, probably.

The driver pulls up on the reins and the wagon rolls to a halt by a crossroads. He nods towards a group of crumbling buildings by the side of the road. 'Just on the other side of that barn, Sir, there's a gate.'

Flares; giant parachuted fireworks, flood the now shell-holed landscape with a grotesque daylight.

Alex thanks the driver and climbs down, pulls his pack from the wagon and walks towards the buildings.

'Eden, did you say?' calls the driver.

Alex turns.

'Just remember,' says the driver. Yellow explosions silhouette him, beetle-like and black against the sky. 'The enemy isn't always in the direction that you think it is.' The reins crack, the cart trundles into the flow of traffic and disappears.

It's quieter away from the road, just the deep rumble of the big guns and the hiss of the rain.

A painted wooden board reads "LIVERPOOL STREET" in black letters. Below it is a ribbed-iron gate.

Alex pushes it open.

Wooden steps lead down into a sandbagged corridor. The walls curve away into the gloom.

He pauses for a moment, smiles, and climbs into the trench.

3

THE DUGOUT

A flare hisses in the strip of sky between the trench walls. Silver rain scratching across black clouds. Rows of sandbags loom like writhing scales of a dragon. As the flare splutters and falls, shadows stretch and dissolve into the darkness. The air smells acidic, smoky.

It's difficult to see. Alex slips on the wooden duckboards lining the trench floor. Shellfire now, closer and louder than anything he's ever seen in training. Someone yelling; crying out for help, or is that laughter? He stops and turns. No sign of anyone. He's alone. He's not sure if he should go back to the road. He can't go back. Where would he go? He has to keep going. He has to be calm. He breathes in, holds it, listens: a churning hum of activity and voices.

Following the sound, he feels his way along the rough walls: sackcloth, corrugated metal, wet wood. He turns a corner. Dim lamp light. Relief.

Men carrying boxes, satchels, rifles, food rations, rum rations, tarpaulins and barbed wire. A river of dripping helmets glistening in the light of the shellfire, and below them, mud-caked faces staring blankly ahead. A khaki procession winding through the mud.

He pushes into the throng of soldiers and allows himself to be swept along, until he sees a soldier standing by a doorway. A sign saying "D COMPANY HQ" is lit by an oil lamp behind his head.

He catches his breath, clears his throat. 'I'm Second Lieutenant Alexander Ryan. I'm supposed to report to Captain Kingsman?'

'Kingsman's unavailable,' says the soldier.

Rain sizzles on the lamp glass.

'Can I go in?' says Alex.

The soldier drags on a cigarette. The ember glows, lighting a face like a bag of stones.

'I think I should go in,' says Alex, trying to sound more like an officer.

The soldier drops his cigarette into the mud. 'Wait here,' he says, disappearing behind the door.

Faint voices from inside.

Something digs into Alex's back and slides under his arm. He turns and jumps as a mule nudges him to one side. There's four of them, unattended, plodding determinedly in a line, boxes of ammunition strapped to their backs.

He wonders if he should go in and introduce himself. He's been thinking of this moment for weeks. Sometimes he'd imagined a room full of dashing regimental officers, toasting his arrival with strong handshakes and champagne. Or perhaps he would be thrown straight into a raid on the enemy trenches; smiling introductions made through clouds of revolver smoke and a hail of shrapnel. Or—

The door swings open. A tall soldier comes out and pulls the lamp from the wall. He's dark-skinned and sinewy like an old olive tree. 'Lance Corporal Fenton, Sir, the junior officer's batman,' he says, smiling. 'I'll show you to your dugout. You'll be sharing with Lieutenant Collins.' He picks up Alex's valise, swings it onto his back and leads Alex around a corner, into a narrower, empty trench. A blinding flash and a thud like a kick from one of the mules. Alex falls sideways, thumping against the trench wall.

Fenton staggers, but doesn't drop the lamp or the valise.

Clumps of dirt and stones clatter on the duckboards.

'No harm done, Sir,' says Fenton, collecting Alex's hat from a puddle.

Alex places it firmly back onto his head. 'Are we being attacked?'

As if he hadn't noticed, Fenton looks up, listening. 'I don't think so, Sir. They're not aiming at anything in particular. Probably just letting off a bit of steam.' He shakes his head dismissively and walks on along the trench. 'We've had no casualties tonight. It's been quiet.'

'How many casualties do you normally have?'

'Depends. Five last night. But they were standing in the wrong place.'

Before Alex has a chance to ask where the wrong place is, Fenton stops at a canvas sheet, draped over a frame in the side of the trench. 'Lieutenant Collins?' he yells.

Slow footsteps. The sheet opens and a face appears in the doorway. 'I was asleep. What is it?' He sees Alex and smiles. 'Oh. Hello. Sorry, were you out here long?'

Leaving Fenton in the rain, Alex follows Collins down the three wooden steps of the dugout.

There are two narrow beds, a small desk between them with a book, some loose papers, an open bottle of something and a mug. It smells damp, not unpleasant, waxy and mossy. A rough bookshelf, halfway up the far wall, has a candle burning in a food tin that makes the little room feel cosy.

'Hang your coat over there, that's the *wet* area.' Collins points into the corner where his own coat is hanging from a nail in the wall. 'There isn't actually a dry area but...' He sits on one bed and gestures for Alex to sit on the other. 'The beds are terrible, but you'll get used to it. You'll be so tired most nights, you won't care.'

The bed creaks and twangs when Alex sits. Just chicken wire, stretched between two poles and blankets on top of that. But it seems comfortable enough. He didn't actually expect to have his own bed in a private room. He thought they would be sleeping in the open, in the trenches with the men.

A deep thud seems to shake the whole room. Grit sprinkles from the wooden roof beams that seem to barely hold back the bulging earth above them.

'Don't worry about the shelling,' says Collins. 'You'll get used to it.'

Alex laughs to show he isn't afraid. 'No, I was just—'

'We're a good five hundred yards from the front line,' Collins wipes dust from the little desk. 'I'll show you where everything is in the morning.' His hands are shaking. Seeing that Alex has noticed, he stretches out his fingers and runs them through his hair. 'It's been a very long day.' It's difficult to tell how old he is; he must be early twenties, but there are dark bags under his eyes, and a layer of dirt exaggerates the creases in his skin. His tunic is patchy with dried mud. It's been torn and repaired in several places.

'Have you been fighting?' says Alex, suddenly conscious of how new and clean his own uniform must look.

'Not today. Haven't for a while. We do go on raids sometimes, but us junior officers spend most of the time handing out clean socks to the men, rum rations, that sort of thing. It's mind-numbingly dull most of the time, thank God. Then, every now and again, things start happening and...' He shakes his head and folds back the blankets on his bed. 'In the morning, I'll take you over to meet Kingsman and Eden.' He yawns. 'They'll explain the important things.' The yawn turns into a smile. 'And I can show you how to inspect the men's feet.'

'I'm so sorry, I've kept you awake,' says Alex. 'I'll just wash and—'

'All right. I am very tired. You must be exhausted too, after your journey here. There's a water jug over there.'

Alex leans forward. 'What's Eden like?'

Collins laughs, knowingly. 'Well, you'll meet him tomorrow.'

'Yes, of course,' says Alex, standing. 'I'm sorry. It's just that I've read so much about him and—'

'You have to respect him,' says Collins, lying down and covering himself with the blankets. 'He's been a soldier for longer than any of them put together and he always...' He pauses, looking into the shadows for the word. '*Succeeds*. He always succeeds. And if you manage to come back from one of his raids, they'll almost certainly pin a medal on you.'

Alex frowns. 'What do you mean, *if you manage to come back?*'

A rat jumps down the steps, runs, tail lifted, across the floor and disappears under Alex's bed.

'You'll get used to those too, I'm afraid,' says Collin's, closing his eyes. 'You'll get the hang of things… In the morning we…'

Alex waits.

Collins breathing grows loud and slow. He's already asleep.

As quietly as he can, Alex walks across the room to get the wash pack from his valise. A noise startles him.

The rat is on the shelf and tugging at the candle with its teeth. The candle falls, hits the floor and the room snaps into darkness.

Alex can't see anything. His torch is at the bottom of the valise. He stands still, listening: soldiers laughing. They'll have matches. He feels his way to the steps, crawls up and out through the canvas door.

Outside, it's cold and stinks of rain and petrol. He walks along the trench and around the first traverse. There's a soldier sitting on the fire-step, smoking a cigarette. Alex goes over to him and smiles.

A tearing, metallic scream shreds the air around them; a shell falling.

The soldier looks up and gasps. Then, for a split second, a strange and utter silence. White and yellow flashes. A burning mix of sound and dirt flies up, kicks Alex in the back. He is on his knees, huddled, face pressed against the wall of the trench. Ringing in his ears. Muffled shouting around him. The soldier running. Alex gets to his feet. More men rushing past. Alex stumbles, staggers back towards the dugout. He thinks he's where the entrance was but there's just a pile of loose earth. Soldiers are pulling at the soil with their hands. Splintered posts stick out of the soil. Shreds of cloth flap in the wind and smoke drifts along the trench, lit intermittently by distant shellfire.

Someone finds a hand, and the soldiers pull a body from the soil. It's Collins. His head rolls as they lay him on the duckboards. His eyes are open, there's grit on them. He doesn't blink. Wet earth clings, black and blood-soaked to the side of his face.

Alex feels a hand on his shoulder. 'Let's get you a blanket, Sir.' Fenton's voice, vague behind the ringing in Alex's head. 'I'll ask the boys if they can find any of your things.'

Alex walks. He doesn't speak. Can't speak.

They take him to a shallow hole, scraped into the side of the trench. Canvas, cool against his face. He's lying down now, curled up on his side. There's straw and a blanket.

He listens to the canvas flapping in the wind, the soldier's feet sloshing in the mud and the muffled cracks of gunfire.

He sees a barn; his father's barn. Sees the flames behind the high windows. He hears the flames roaring and the snaps and cracks of the breaking glass and his mother calling his name.

4

THE TRENCH

The canvas sheet flies open and light floods in. Cold air wafts, rustling the damp straw. A boy, holding a candle in a glass jar, peers inquisitively in, then steps back, staring. Surrounded by a woollen balaclava, his large blue eyes look like eggs in a nest.

It's 6.30. Alex has slept through the night. He's in a *funk hole*; nothing more than a shelf scooped out of the trench wall, straw for a mattress and canvas to keep out the rain. The men sleep in these every night. How can they stand it? It's not even long enough to straighten your legs. He shivers, swings his legs out into the trench and sits up. He rubs his hands; blood on them. He must have fallen when the shell hit. He doesn't remember. He tries to speak but his throat is too dry so instead, he salutes.

The boy doesn't salute back. He looks confused. 'We've been told we're not to salute the officers, Sir.'

Alex clears his throat. 'Why not?'

The boy points above the sandbags. 'Snipers.' His uniform is baggy; sleeves hanging over thin and dirty hands. 'They see who we're saluting at and shoot them first.'

Alex must remember not to salute anyone. 'What's your name, Private?'

The boy blinks slowly. 'Private Percy Elphick, Sir.' He smiles triumphantly, as if he's just recited a difficult poem. Pink cheeks and teeth the colour of the straw. He's like a seal cub; shiny and soft and bright-eyed.

'How old are you, Elphick?'

Percy mouths something under his breath, pauses and smiles. 'I'm nineteen, Sir. But everyone says I look more like less.'

'More, like, less,' says Alex. 'Yes, I suppose you do.' The boy can't be any more than fifteen.

'Captain Kingsman has asked to see you, Sir. I'm to show you the firing trenches and take you along to the HQ dugout.'

As they move through the narrow passages, light from Percy's candle pulses across the sandbags. Tufts of dripping grass droop inwards along the wet walls. There are soldiers here, waking up, emerging from rubber capes, lighting cigarettes and standing in quiet groups. Tobacco smoke hovers above them.

Percy turns a corner. No sandbags here, just loose soil piled up and supported by planks of wood. The air feels thick; a pungent, rotting sweetness.

Percy holds his fingers against his nose. 'Stinks, doesn't it! Eddy Rowlands says it's a crouton.'

Alex tries not to gag. 'A crouton?'

Percy grins. 'A dead Frenchy, floating in a crater. I've seen him! He's just on the other side of the bags. There's another one on that side too!' He pauses, as if he's trying to remember something else he needs to say about the corpses, then hurries on.

Alex remembers standing in a corridor, forbidden to go into the room where they put his mother's body. He remembers creaking floorboards and the whispers of vague relatives. Death was an abstract idea. It meant someone stops being there, quiet church services and graveyards in the rain. Here, it seems, you can smell death, drag it out of the mud and make jokes about it. He's going to have to get used to that.

The trench grows deeper; sandbags again. Every few yards, soldiers climb onto a wooden step that runs along the side of the trench, place their rifles on the parapet, shoulder height, and face out into the dawn.

'This is the *stand-to*,' says Percy, proudly. 'We've to guard the line in case the dirty Hun decide to give it a go before breakfast.'

'Could I take a look?' says Alex.

Percy sticks his tongue out and grimaces. 'The first time Lieutenant Falkener looked, he got a bullet through the eye! His brains splatted out into Bob Dobson's breakfast!'

A calm-eyed soldier reaches out to help Alex up onto the step. 'That's cheerful. Thank you for that, Percy.' He winks and smiles. 'Private Henry Stubbs, Sir.' His hand is warm and compact. 'Look through here, Sir. Don't put your head up over the bags.' He steps aside and points into a square tube of wood that passes through the sandbags.

Alex, flinching as if that might stop a bullet, looks through the hole.

It's getting light. A carpet of mud leads out from the parapet for thirty yards. There's a hedgerow of snarled and twisted wire. From it, wooden posts and crosses grow. Beyond the wire is No Man's Land, as the papers call it now; three hundred yards of nothing. A brown field, scarred with circular ridges and banks of earth that must be shell craters. Occasional patches of grass flutter and dip in the rain. Puddles reflect a row of poplar trees; black against a colourless sky. Below the trees, hidden behind a mass of wire and bags, is the German army.

Alex catches his breath. He's finally here; the very front edge of the war. He wishes his father could see this; his son standing only a few hundred yards away from the enemy. He would write a letter, tell his father about everything that's happened, but the idea of his father having to sit down and awkwardly reply, or the idea of him not replying at all, makes Alex wince.

After his mother's death, Alex's father had sunk into himself. He began to move very slowly through the spaces that his wife had shared with him; like an old priest shuffling around an empty church. He still preached his opinions *at* Alex, but real conversations were so awkward, if either of them suspected they might be about to have one, they would back away like cats finding themselves accidentally standing in water.

As Alex was leaving for Falmouth, instead of words, his father had given him a folding knife. Later, on the train, folding and unfolding the blade, Alex caught his own reflection in the window and cursed himself; an officer, not even brave enough to embrace his own father.

'Right,' says Alex. 'I'd better go and find the CO. Come on, Private Percy Elphick. Show me the way.'

Percy has found a slug on a sandbag and is poking it carefully with a grubby finger. He flicks it over the parapet, jumps down off the fire-step and wanders away.

'He shouldn't be here. Just a kid.' Stubbs taps his temple with his finger. 'Younger even than his age.'

'He told me he was nineteen.'

Stubbs laughs. 'Nineteen! He gets a year older every week!'

'Elphick!' A tall sergeant is striding along the duckboards. Thick moustache quivering beneath metal-framed glasses. 'Elphick, why are you in the firing trench, young man?' He speaks playfully; rhythmically, as if he's thinking of a song. 'You are supposed to be emptying the latrine buckets, like I showed you.'

'No, I'm not, Sergeant.' Percy shakes his rifle towards Alex. 'I'm taking him to see Captain Kingsman.'

The sergeant pushes his glasses up his nose and blinks. '*Him?* Do you mean this lieutenant? Who, I would assume, is Second Lieutenant Ryan?'

'Yes, I'm taking... *Second Lieutenant Ryan...* to see Captain Kingsman!'

'No, you're not. You can't,' says the sergeant. 'The Captain's away on urgent business. Go and empty those latrines!'

Percy glares, then slumps back the way they came.

The sergeant turns to face Alex. 'Sometimes, Sir, it helps to think of Private Elphick as more of a mascot than an actual soldier.' He smiles. 'Welcome, Sir. I'm Sergeant Kemmell. The captain sends his apologies, and asks if you would lead the ration party this morning.

Bring the lunches up. There's nothing to it. The adjutant will give you a map. The boys have all done it before and can show you what to do.'

'Lunches?' says Alex. He'd hoped for something a bit more... exciting. But it is his first day... 'Yes, of course.'

'The boys found your valise, Sir. They've put it in the new dugout. You'll be sharing with Lieutenants Pope and Phillips.' Kemmell pushes his glasses up his nose again. 'Heard you had a bit of a scrape last night, Sir. You all right?'

Alex thinks of the pale body against the mud. The eyes. The grit. 'I'm fine, thank you. Just a bit shaken.'

'You get used to it, Sir.'

'Yes, so everyone keeps telling me. But I'm not really sure if I want to get used to something like that.'

Kemmell smiles a tired, knowing smile. He looks up, searching for the words in the rain, silver now in the dawn light. 'Well, it's like a forest isn't it? Come autumn, you can't cry over every leaf.'

5

THE COOKHOUSE

The rat is fat and heavy. It shivers, spraying little droplets back into the cascading rain. Ears twitching, blackberry eyes blinking, it watches Alex and his men from the shelter of an iron sheet that rattles in the wind above the cookhouse door.

When Kemmell had introduced Alex to the six-man team, they'd been welcoming enough. As they made their way through the warren of communication and support trenches, signalling stations, ammunition dumps, equipment stores; a muddy, medieval medina, he'd asked them questions, simple things, about their employment before the war, their families. They'd answered cautiously but politely. No one had asked him anything, but that was all right. That was to be expected.

They knew the way to the cookhouse, and he sensed that they'd allowed him to lead them, little map in hand. They wanted to see if he would get them lost. He hadn't, and by the time they arrived, two miles behind the frontline, despite the rain, and Percy shivering so badly that he couldn't speak, everyone seemed in fairly good spirits.

But they've been waiting for D Company's lunch rations for over an hour. Everyone is cold and disgruntled, apart from Percy, who is sitting inside the cookhouse, next to a stove, with a cup of tea.

Sergeant-cook Coles is standing outside the cookhouse, stirring a stew with a big wooden spoon. The lumpy brown liquid is boiling in a field kitchen; a huge coal-fired pot on cartwheels. The stove pipe leans precariously to one side and barely reaches above the soldiers' heads. The smoke, struggling to lift between the rain, swirls angrily around the trench.

The men swear, cough and grumble.

Coles points at the rat with his spoon. '*Rattus rattus*, that is. The black rat.'

'It looks brown to me,' says Alex.

'Everything's brown here, Sir. It's the mud! This stew would have delicate spring hues if it wasn't so full of mud.' Under his helmet, Coles has cut holes in the sides of his balaclava so his ears can stick through. With his shiny, pink skin, he looks like the rat. He sticks a powerful finger into the pot, pulls something out that isn't brown, sniffs it, and flicks it into the mud. 'You get brown ones too.' He waves the spoon. '*Rattus norvegicus*, they are, but that one is *Rattus rattus*.'

The rat stares. The rain falls harder.

Coles doesn't seem to mind the rain, he doesn't seem to notice it's raining at all. 'Did you know, the Romans thought that mice were just small rats?' he says cheerfully, shoving a log into the stove and slamming the door shut with his boot. 'They called both of them *mus*.'

'Mus?' says Alex, trying to sound interested.

'Yeah, *mus*.'

'I didn't know that.'

'Just *big mus* and *little mus*.'

'Fucking shut up and cook our lunch!' yells Private Edward Rowlands, who in better times, he'd told Alex, had been a waiter in a very good restaurant in Brighton. 'Then we might be able to get back before we either drown or starve!'

Coles stares at Rowlands. 'No fear of you starving, I shouldn't think.'

'What the fuck was that?' says Rowlands. He's plump and fitted so tightly into his uniform that the buttons look as if they're about to give up.

'We have an officer present,' says Wislawa, curling wiry fingers, trying to light a cigarette. 'No need for swearing.'

Alex doesn't mind the swearing; it's interesting. He's never heard anyone swear the way these men do. He'd no idea that so few words could mean so many different things.

'Food's ready now, Sir,' says Coles. 'Holmes! Get out here and help me dish this shit out!'

Holmes comes out of the Cookhouse. A stained chef's hat flops limply on his head. Percy follows, looking bird-like next to the two cooks.

'You feeling better, little Perce?' says Stubbs, squeezing the boy's shoulder.

Percy nods, dropping his helmet into the mud.

Stubbs bends down, plucks it out of the grime and sticks it back onto Percy's head with a tap.

The men line up as the two cooks ladle the stew into smaller tins and hand out sacks of bread. They know what they're doing but it's Alex's first day and he feels he should say... *something*. 'All right men, let's get this up to D Company before it gets too cold.'

'The comms trench is two-foot underwater, Sir,' says Wislawa. 'By the time we get back, this lot will be freezing.'

'It's not supposed to be hot,' says Coles. 'It's just supposed to be cooked.'

'Hot or cold, still tastes like shit,' says Rowlands, hoisting a tin onto his shoulder and making his way along the trench.

Coles aims his spoon carefully. It spins through the air and hits the back of Rowlands' helmet with a thud. Rowlands stops, puts his tin down and walks up to the cook. The two men stare, noses almost touching.

Alex has no idea what he should do if they start fighting. He looks at the other men. They don't seem to have noticed.

Rowlands and Coles blink at each other. Rain falls between them.

Alex should threaten them, give them an order. 'Rowlands, get back to that tin or...' He can't think of a threat. He should have thought of something before he started speaking. 'Or there will be... consequences.' He winces.

'How's Gladys?' says Rowlands.

'She's chipper, thanks for asking,' says Coles, with a smile. 'She sends her regards.'

'Lovely!' says Rowlands, winking. 'Send her my returns, if you'd be so kind.' He picks up his tin and heads off down the trench.

'I will!' says Coles. 'You look after yourself, Ed. See you in the Pelican!'

Alex, relieved, thanks the cooks and runs to catch up with the men.

They trudge through wet trenches, slipping on duckboards, scraping the tins against the narrow walls. As they turn a corner, a startled rat leaps into a tea-brown stretch of water that runs the whole length of a traverse. It swims across and clambers up the sandbags into the field above.

Stubbs wades in until the water is up to his armpits. 'We should form a chain, Sir.'

Carefully, they edge their way in, handing the rations from man to man. As they reach the firmer ground at the far end, two stretcher-bearers stagger around the corner carrying an unconscious man. 'Now we've had it,' says the bearer at the back, staring at the flooded trench. 'We won't get through that in time.'

Alex brushes the matted hair away from the injured soldier's closed eyes. His skin is the colour of an autumn leaf. 'Is he alive?'

'Not for long, Sir. Took us forty minutes to get here. That was only three hundred yards. Still got a mile to go.'

'What's he got?' says Rowlands.

'Sniper. Both legs. We put tourniquets on him, but if we don't get'em off soon, he'll lose the legs. If we take'em off before we get there, he'll bleed to death.'

'Can we help?' says Alex.

'Looks fucked,' says Nolan, a stocky, weather-beaten soldier. 'He won't make it. If he does, he won't walk again.'

'What if that was you?' says Rowlands.

'Then shoot me.'

'It's too far, Sir,' says the bearer. 'The field hospital's past the support trench. We won't get there in time.'

'There you go,' says Nolan. 'No time. No point hanging about here.'

'What if you took a short cut?' says Alex, taking out the map he'd been given. 'If we went up over the bags, here, could we cut diagonally across, into the support line? There's grass up there, it's not as muddy. It would only take ten minutes.'

The stretcher-bearers look at each other. 'It's broad daylight, Sir. They've got snipers all over this section.'

'But it's raining so hard,' says Stubbs. 'They might not see us.'

'We? Us? Come on!' Nolan laughs nervously. 'This is effing stupid, Sir. We wouldn't last a minute.' He starts to walk away. 'Let these lads do their job and we can do ours.'

Alex takes a deep breath. 'Private Nolan, if you move one more inch you will be on rations duty for two weeks.'

Nolan stops, turns around, then slowly places his tin onto the ground.

Alex needs to think. He should stay with his men, stick to the mission, but he'd only be gone for half an hour, and they know the way back better than he does. This man is dying. This is why he came here, to help people, isnt it? This has to be more important than lunch. There's nothing heroic about delivering soup. This could be his chance to show command what he's capable of. 'Wislawa, you're in charge of the men until I get back. I'll catch you up. If I don't, inform Sergeant Kemmell of my action.'

Wislawa nods and leads the men away.

Stubbs stays behind. 'You'll need a fourth man on the other corner of that stretcher, Sir.'

'Yes, of course,' says Alex. 'Thank you, Stubbs.'

'We've got red cross flags, Sir,' says the bearer. 'If we have flags, sometimes they don't shoot.'

'Sometimes?' says Alex.

The bearer shrugs.

Stubbs takes a flag and ties it to his bayonet, then fixes that to his rifle.

Alex climbs up the sandbags and slowly raises a flag that he's tied to the handle of a shovel. It flaps wildly as it opens into the wind.

He takes off his helmet and raises that, grimacing, waiting for the sniper's shot. It doesn't come. He climbs over the parapet and lowers his feet down into the grass. He breathes in deeply, trying to breathe into the space where the bullet will come. Is this his last breath? Is this? Or this?

A row of poplar trees hisses in the wind on his right.

No shot.

They lift the stretcher over.

'Go!' says Alex. 'Head for that big tree. Two hundred yards, just keep walking.'

With Alex at the front and Stubbs waving his flag at the back, they head out across the muddy field, through tufts of grass, around the shell holes. A mass of wood and wire, discarded cans, water bottles, helmets, puddles and broken trees. To their right, faded behind the rain, cross-hatched like an etching, is the German wire. It's close.

'If they fire, drop down. Just drop the lad,' says the bearer. 'Stay down in the grass.'

'Shouldn't we keep our voices down?' says Stubbs.

'They won't hear nothing in this wind,' says the other bearer, but he doesn't seem sure.

'We want them to hear us, don't we? So they know we're helping someone,' says Alex. 'That's why we're waving the flags.'

'We want them to see the flags, if they hear us,' says the bearer. 'But we don't want them to hear us if they can't see the flags.'

The ground becomes rocky and slippery. They have to steady themselves with their hands.

Stubbs, without a free hand, slips to his knees and has to lever himself up with the butt of the rifle.

The injured soldier groans.

'Watch your feet,' whispers Alex, as they reach a dead soldier, lying face down in the grass. As he steps over, he realises the soldier isn't lying face down; he's on his back, but his face is missing somehow, caved in, hollow; the cavity filled with rain water as clear and dark as a pond.

They push on, all of them slipping now in longer grass. No one speaks. Everyone stares ahead, away from the German line, as if looking that way might catch someone's eye.

A thousand Boche soldiers are behind the wire at the end of the field. Alex can feel them watching. He can feel their warm fingers pressing gently on the cold triggers. He can feel the bullets waiting in the darkness of the guns, waiting to be flung out into the silver light, across the field, through the rain, into his flesh, grinding against the bone.

They push on.

The wind picks up. The wet flags flutter. The rain stings.

'Nearly there, so nearly there!'

Ahead of them, the rain seems to curdle; swirling streaks of grey, forming into rows of sandbags and barbed wire.

'Almost made it!' says the bearer.

'That's the parapet!' says Stubbs.

They set the stretcher down in font of the wire and crouch as Alex looks for a way through.

'Who goes there?' yells a soldier from behind the sandbags.

'Lieutenant Ryan, Royal Sussex. We have a wounded man here!'

A soldier appears on the parapet, drops down into the grass and runs out, crouching. 'Come this way, Sir. Over here! Here's a gap in the wire!' He helps them through and takes the corner of the stretcher from Alex and the injured soldier is lifted up and over the parapet.

Men on the fire-step. Arms come up. The stretcher is lifted down, followed by Stubbs and the bearers.

Alex pauses on the parapet, steadying himself against the wind.

He grips the shovel, holding it high, just for a moment, letting the flag snap and writhe above his head. The poplar trees sway at the side of the field. The branches claw at the sky. Columns of rain dance like ghosts across the soldiers that lie still behind him in the grass.

There is so much death here, but as he drops down into the safety of the trench, he feels life searing through him in a way that he's never felt before.

6

CHICKEN STEW

Alex is standing outside the entrance to the officers' mess. He brushes dirt from the lapel of his top-coat. Sergeant Kemmell showed him how to scrape the mud off with the back of a knife and beat the dirt out with a stick. His hand is shaking; in a minute he will be sitting at the same table as the D Company captains.

A cook shuffles along the duckboards, balancing two steaming tins from a yoke across his shoulders.

'Is that bacon I can smell?' says Alex, brightly, trying to calm himself.

'Bully beef, Sir, but fried in a pan that might've had bacon in it a week ago. And this, Sir…' The soldier spins like a chorus girl. 'Is petrol flavoured tea!' He walks happily away along the trench. A trail of steam swirls up and merges with the drizzle.

Alex takes a deep breath, pulls back the canvas flap and steps inside.

Smells of candle wax, meat stew and whisky curl around him like a warm blanket. The low-beamed room is heated by a small iron stove. Light flickers from the grating, casting rippled shadows on the walls. A long wooden table takes up most of the room. Three places have been set with white enamel bowls and glasses.

A slender man with black, curly hair is writing at the table in a notebook. He looks up. 'Lieutenant Ryan?'

'Yes, Sir.'

'Excellent! Thought I'd check. The German army is just over there! Can't be too careful!' He smiles, crow's-foot wrinkles spreading out from dark, candle-lit eyes. 'I'm Captain Kingsman. Henry.' His hand-shake is tight and welcoming. 'What will we call you when we're alone, Mr Ryan?'

'Call me Alex, please, Sir. It's Alex.'

'You're very welcome here, Alex. We'll try to make your stay here as comfortable as possible. I'm sorry about the war. There's nothing we can do about it. But apart from that, anything you need, just let us know.' He gestures towards a bottle of whisky on the table. 'We've been celebrating. James has just been given *another* medal, would you believe, for something he did when he was with the 2nd. He'll show it to you if you behave. Won't you James?'

Eden is sitting away from the candlelight, at the end of the table, he leans forward into the light, grabs the bottle and pours out three whiskies. 'Hello Alex.' He's in his early thirties, handsome, angular, like an emperor on a coin.

Alex reaches out his hand. 'It's very good to meet you, Sir.'

'You look cold,' says Eden, pushing a whisky into Alex's palm. 'Get that wet coat off and drink this.'

Alex isn't cold. He suddenly feels hot. He gulps the whisky down and, not sure what to do with the glass, keeps hold of it, fumbling with the buttons of his coat.

Eden watches, smiling. There were photographs of him in the papers, but none could show the colour of his eyes; they are very blue.

'I heard about your first night,' says Kingsman, taking the glass and helping Alex with the coat. 'Beastly business with Lieutenant Collins. Are you all right?'

'Yes. Sir. I'm fine. I just wish I could have done something. I only—'

Kingsman lifts his finger. 'You mustn't think like that. Does no good. If your number's up, it's up.'

'Are you hungry, Alex?' says Eden. Without waiting for a reply, he leans towards a doorway at the back of the room and yells, 'Fenton, feed us!'

As they sit, an aproned Fenton appears, places a large pot on the table and lifts the lid. A plume of scented steam rolls up and hangs above them in the candlelight. 'Cocotte de poulet de Normandie,' he says, with no effort to sound French. 'Bacon, dried apple, sautéed shallots.'

Kingsman closes his eyes and inhales. 'Thyme?'

'Yes, Sir, fresh,' says Fenton, serving each officer. 'One of the lads found it growing up top when they were digging the latrines.'

Kingsman tries the soup and smiles. 'Remarkable, Fenton.'

Fenton nods. 'Thank you, Sir.'

Eden points his spoon. 'He's good. An actual Chef. The Grand Hotel wasn't it?

'For a while, Sir, yes.'

'He can make a turnip taste like a chicken and a potato look like a turnip. Can't you Fenton?'

Fenton looks away. 'Yes, Sir… I'll fetch the bread.'

As they eat, the two captains explain about the battalion's position here in Neuve Chapelle. And the role of D Company along this sector of the front line.

Alex listens carefully, his spoon hovering between his bowl and mouth. As he asks what he considers to be pertinent questions, he glances at Eden, who seems to be watching him intently.

'But now, with this rain,' says Kingsman. 'Apart from the odd trench raid to keep everyone on their toes, neither side has had a chance to move an inch.'

Eden grunts. 'This is precisely the time we should be making a push.'

'James, we've been over this. The mud is as deep as a horse in places. I can't risk—'

'That's why it's the perfect time. They won't be expecting it. If we…' Eden pauses as Fenton comes back into the room. 'Fenton, this *is* chicken isn't it?'

'Yes, Sir. If you like.'

The two Captains laugh.

To Alex, the food, whatever it is, tastes delicious. The flavours, the whisky, and the warm, humid air in the little underground room are soaking into him. He basks in it. And in the esteemed company he's now keeping, feeling his muscles soften for the first time since he arrived in France.

'They're expecting a cold spell by the end of the week,' says Kingsman. 'So hopefully some of this mud will freeze. Perhaps then...'

Eden doesn't reply, or even look up.

Kingsman shifts in his chair, swallows and turns to Alex. 'I've heard from Kemmell, that you seem to be getting along with the men?'

'Yes, Sir, I think so.' Alex had spent the day supervising the digging of a new communications trench. Everyone had worked hard and cheerfully, except one, who had sneered whenever Alex had given them a command. He felt sure the man had been making fun of him behind his back. 'It's difficult to lead them in a task that most of them probably know how to do better than I do.'

Eden gets up and shovels charcoal into the stove. 'Command with confidence. It doesn't matter if you don't know what you're doing, just act like you do. Then, when it comes to more important matters, a mission or a raid, where you will know,' He slams the stove door shut. 'They'll follow. Am I right, Henry?'

'Yes, I suppose so. But I think the most important thing is to never order them to do anything that you wouldn't do yourself. And let them see you doing the difficult things. You'll quickly gain their *respect*, and with *that*, their obedience.'

Eden laughs. 'Their respect!'

Kingsman is about to say something but Eden turns to Alex. 'You might also consider not wandering off and leaving your men to fend for themselves.'

Alex looks blank.

Kingsman raises an eyebrow. 'Yes, we heard about your little escapade with the stretcher bearers and the injured soldier.'

Alex swallows, feeling the blood rush into his cheeks.

Eden comes back and sits at the table. 'Your order was to collect lunch. Not lead a damn charge across No Man's Land!'

'I'm sorry, Sir. I—'

'I understand your intention,' says Kingsman. 'But you had other responsibilities. You were supposed to be caring for *your* men.'

'I'm really sorry. I rejoined them twenty minutes later and—'

'Never leave your men,' says Eden. 'You could be charged with abandoning your position.'

Alex feels sick. 'Yes, Sir.'

'It wasn't even one of ours, was it?'

Alex stares into his bowl of stew. 'I don't know, Sir. I'm sorry. I thought… because the casualty was dying—'

Eden grunts. 'Dying? Everyone is dying. It's a war.'

'It sounds awful,' says Kingsman, softly. 'But the rule is, you only help our chaps. We just don't have the resources to help every injured soldier that we see. We have to prioritise our own men.'

Alex clenches his fist against the table. 'I'm genuinely sorry. I thought I was doing the right thing. I can see now… It won't happen again.'

Eden pours everyone another drink. 'You enjoyed it though, didn't you?'

Alex looks up. 'Sir?'

Eden smiles. 'Your *daring daylight dash* across No Man's Land. Fun, wasn't it?'

Alex can't tell if Eden is teasing him. 'Well… actually… I think…'

Kingsman raises an eyebrow, tilts his head, and smiles.

Alex speaks slowly, cautiously. 'It was terrifying at first, Sir… But then I did find it… quite exciting.'

Eden drinks his whisky in one gulp, slams the glass down and grins at Kingsman.

'Your priorities should always be with D Company,' says Kingsman, ignoring Eden. 'But it was a brave thing and God knows, I do need brave men. So well done.'

Alex breathes again. 'Thank you, Sir.' He bites off a large chunk of bread to hide a relieved grin.

Kingsman turns to Eden. 'Have you selected the men for tonight?'

'I have. They'll be ready by ten.'

Kingsman nods, gravely, and finishes his soup.

'Is this a trench raid, Sir?' says Alex.

'Not exactly,' says Eden. 'While we were out last night, I thought I heard something. A hissing sound, scraping, to the left of our line.'

'What do you think it was?' says Alex, enthralled.

'The Boche could be digging a sap, with a listening post. Not sure. We're going to find out.'

Eden explains the mission, drawing out the plan on the table cloth with a butter knife. There's a scar on his cheekbone, a neat rectangle. Alex wonders if this is from the Battle of Loos. According to reports, he led a company of men across No Man's Land, through a hail of bullets and, despite being hit by shrapnel and choking on gas, with almost the entire platoon being killed, he made it to the German line. Then wiped out a machine gun team with nothing but his pistol, captured the gun and used it to hold off the Germans in their own trench until support arrived. 'From here, if it is a sap, we can drop in and work our way along—'

'That worries me,' says Kingsman. 'We've no idea how many Hun will be in that sap. More could come along from behind. Then we're trapped.'

'Not if you stay behind and guard the rear,' says Eden. 'I can take the men up. If anything happens, we simply get out and come home.'

'I don't want anyone going in until we know what they are doing,' says Kingsman. 'I'll take the men up and wait. You can go out before us, have a look around and report back on what you see. Then we can decide what to do.'

'It would be better if I took the men in,' says Eden, calmly.

Kingsman leans back, seemingly forcing himself to relax. 'This is my company, my men. So *you'll* go out, reconnoitre the sap and *I* will take the men up.'

Eden glares for a moment, then shrugs and pulls out a leather smoking kit from his tunic pocket. 'What did you do before the war, Alex?' He unrolls it, carefully laying out the pipe and tobacco.

'Nothing, Sir.' Alex winces. 'I mean, the war started before I graduated. I was studying art at Brighton.'

'Oh, an artist! What do you do, paint?' says Kingsman, pouring everyone more whisky and seemly avoiding Eden's eye.

'Yes, painting, watercolours mainly, I was hoping to be able to sketch while I was out here. But it all seems rather silly now.'

'The regiment's always looking for chaps who can draw,' says Eden, stuffing tobacco into the pipe with his thumb. 'I could talk to Major Babcock. See if they can find you a mapping job.'

'No, please don't do that, Sir. I'd rather be here, in the thick of things.'

Eden puffs a little blue cloud into the candlelight. 'If you were hoping for excitement and action, then I'm afraid you might have joined the wrong battalion. Things here are actually rather *thin*.' He glances at Kingsman. 'Nothing much ever seems to happen here. Apart from the occasional exchange of trench mortars, which is usually preceded by a polite warning and followed by an apology.'

'Thank God for that,' says Kingsman. 'I'd be happy if we never had to fire a single shot.'

'Well, I was in Sussex for a year before this,' says Alex. 'We didn't see any action at all. In the training, all we ever seemed to do was stab scarecrows!'

Kingsman laughs. 'They'll still make you stab scarecrows here!'

'But I've read a lot about this battalion. It seems to me quite a lot happens here.'

Eden looks bemused. 'Don't pay attention to what you read in the papers. Most of it's fiction.'

'Really?' says Alex.

'It might be *based* on truth, but it's simplified and exaggerated to make it easier for the politicians and housewives to understand. They think we're rushing around with knives in our teeth, leaping out of the smoke and cutting the throats of the evil Hun!'

Kingsman laughs. 'But that's *exactly* what *you* do, most of the time, James!'

Eden puffs loudly through his pipe. '*I* do, of course, but most of the regiment just plays cards, or tries to figure out new ways to cook potatoes in their helmets.' He sniffs. 'God prevent it, but if the women of England understood the boring truth, they would stop sending us cake!'

Kingsman laughs again and the captains finally smile at each other.

'Well, Sir,' says Alex. 'I hope to be a very active member of this battalion. I hope to make the regiment proud.'

Eden leans across the table towards Alex; eyes tight and sharp. 'Do you want to know how to make us proud, Lieutenant?'

'Yes, Sir. I do.'

Eden finishes his whisky stands. 'Come out with us and help us find who's making all these fucking scraping noises!'

Alex looks at Kingsman. 'Me? Tonight?'

Kingsman shrugs.

Eden grins. 'Yes, tonight. Now! You can be our support. Off you go. I'll meet you in the firing trench in half an hour. Don't worry about your coat!'

7

THE SAP

The firing trench is deserted. Mist curls around a low-flamed lamp; sinewy fingers feel along the sandbags, fading into the darkness in both directions.

It's cold without a coat, but at least the rain has stopped. Alex tightens the knot of his tie and fastens the top button of his tunic.

There's no sign of Eden. Kingsman and his men came past earlier, on their way to the ammunition store. Four excited soldiers and their Captain, all smiles and nervous banter. Like they could take on the whole German army if it came to it. Like they could win the war. One of them had offered him chocolate. He didn't take it. He wishes he had now.

He remembers a nighttime mission in the training corps. It was summer then and the warm air smelt of cowslips and cowpats. He was leading a platoon of schoolboys across the South Downs. Wooden rifles and pine cones for grenades. Hiding in the gorse bushes, they laughed so much the sergeant had to stop them, tick them off, remind them that war was a serious business.

He reaches for his revolver; heavy, oiled, loaded, *real*. He's ready. He takes a deep breath, savouring the moment. But should the gun be in his hand or in the holster? He should see what Captain Eden does with his. He kneels to check his boot laces.

'All right?' says Eden.

Alex stands; too fast, nearly slips. 'Yes, Sir.' Too loud.

Eden has changed his clothes. He's wearing a woollen pullover that can't be regulation, a satchel across his shoulder and a black balaclava pulled down around his neck. He looks like a mountaineer. Alex feels clumsy in his tunic; more like a postman.

Eden climbs onto the fire-step and points out across No Man's Land. 'Big shell hole about fifty yards out. We'll move out to that and listen.'

Alex can't see anything, just a hint of grey sky.

Eden swings his legs over the parapet and drops into the grass.

Alex follows, slipping on the way down and landing on his knees. 'What about the Captain and the men?' he says, to show he isn't hurt. 'Will they meet us in the hole?'

'It's just you and me for this bit.'

Alex smiles to himself in the darkness.

'Keep tight behind me,' Eden whispers. He moves out, bent double, fast and silent.

The ground is rough and slippery. Patches of long grass, gravel and soil that looks like it's been ploughed. The air smells of mushrooms and petrol.

Eden is already yards ahead; a dark shape against the dark earth.

Alex is running blind, hands out towards the black. He's out of breath. He must catch up. He stops. Where is Eden? Nothing but mud and darkness. A sting of panic, like a shard of glass in his throat.

'Down here. Hurry!' Eden is crouching against the far bank of the shell hole.

Relieved, Alex steps in. The sides are softer than expected, and steeper. He half-falls, half-runs down the gravelly bank, hits thick mud, tries to walk but falls head-first into the stinking water. It fills his mouth, freezing, tastes of iron and rivers. On the edge of panic again, but it's only knee-deep. He crawls out. Gasping, coughing.

'Keep it down for Christ's sake,' whispers Eden. His breath is warm and smells of whisky. 'Snipers!' He points a finger between his eyes and taps. 'Boche. Hundred yards.'

Alex nods, panting. He tries to breathe quietly. The mud, ice-cold, is soaking through his clothes. He shivers.

Eden raises one finger very slowly into the air; listening.

Alex listens: his own breathing at first, blood pumping. Eden's breathing; slower, calmer, the crackle of a machine gun, not too close, and the soft thud of big guns in the far distance.

'Hear that?' whispers Eden. 'There!'

A faint, rhythmic scraping.

Eden points. 'Twenty yards.'

'What are they doing?' whispers Alex.

'Stay here.' Eden crawls out, flat against the soil, still for a moment, then moving further into the night.

Suddenly Alex is alone. He takes out his revolver. Fingers, slow with cold. He didn't imagine it would be *this* cold. He crouches at the edge of the hole. His eyes are adjusting; treetops along the horizon. It's raining now. The silence shimmers. If something happens, is he supposed to stay where he is or move back to the main trench? He checks his watch: four minutes; feels like ten. What if Eden doesn't come back? What's the correct course of action? He can't stay out here, with soaking clothes, the whole night. Or is he supposed to do exactly that? He should have asked more questions. He's shivering so hard he can hardly hold the revolver. Eight minutes. He'll wait twenty minutes then go back and find Kingsman and the others.

Soil and gravel spray up, hitting Alex in the face. He nearly fires his gun. Feels like his heart will split. Blood thumping.

Eden, sliding into the shell hole, laughs. 'Sorry. Did I make you jump?' He's out of breath. 'Didn't mean to be so long. I went further than expected.' He's talking louder than before. 'There's three Hun. Up to something, not sure what, though. I managed to get in behind them. They had no idea I was there.' He's soaked, pullover sagging across his shoulders. It's freezing but he doesn't seem to notice.

'You were in their sap?' says Alex, still whispering.

'Sort of fell in. It's dark.'

'So, we're going back to report to the captain?'

Eden looks back across to the British line. 'No. We don't have time to wait for Kingsman to decide what we should do. I've just seen a Boche patrol, over there, in the middle of the field, so we have to do this alone and we have to move fast.'

'Move where?' says Alex, staring out at the black nothingness all around them.

'The Boche sap is only thirty yards away. We'll crawl out to it and drop in. You guard the rear. I'll sneak up, get rid of two, then we both grab the third and bring him in.'

'But shouldn't we tell Kingsman—'

'Don't worry about Kingsman. He'll be delighted when he gets a live prisoner to take up to Battalion HQ for questioning. I can explain everything to him later. Wait for my whistle and come up and help me. We'll have no time with that Boche patrol so damned close, but we should be able to get him back to our trench before they realise what's happened.' Eden points to Alex's revolver. 'Is that a Webley?'

'Yes, Sir.'

'I'll get you a Luger from one of the Hun. Much more reliable.'

'Yes, Sir.'

'Do you have enough ammunition?'

Alex feels for the pouch. 'Twelve I think.'

Eden digs in his pocket and hands Alex a fistful of bullets. 'Take these. I only need three.' It's too dark to see if he's joking. 'Make sure no one comes up behind us in that sap. It's narrow, they can only come one at a time, so you should be fine.' He pulls out two grenades from the satchel. 'Better have these, just in case.'

With shaking hands, Alex puts one into each of his tunic pockets.

'You all right?' says Eden.

'Yes, Sir, just a bit cold.' Alex makes fists to stop the shivering. 'What should I do if...' He steadies his voice. 'If it doesn't go as planned?'

'Run.'

As they crawl through mud and clumps of grass, icy grit splashing in their faces, Alex remembers a church somewhere. He can't have been more than four years old; sitting on a prayer cushion, crawling under the pews.

They reach the German sap and peer over the edge. It's like a ditch for laying drains, about four feet deep, curving sharply.

Eden drops down, silently, signals for Alex to follow.

Alex slides down, boots splashing.

Eden pulls a coil of wire out of his satchel, wraps it around both fists and is gone.

Alex points the revolver at where the Hun will be coming from. He's shaking so much, he has to aim with both hands.

Something, a noise, behind him. He turns around. Nothing; a gaping blackness. He moves up along the trench to see if he can see where Eden is; just more curving walls, looming. He shuffles back down the trench, then stops. This isn't the way he came. Or is it? There's nothing to recognise, just mud and tree roots. Perhaps he's gone too far. He turns back. No sign of anything in the field above, but it's raining so hard now, he can't tell. He doesn't know which way is the British line and which is the Hun.

A flare goes up, eerie and green. His own shadow, terrified, lurches out along the trench.

Darkness.

He waits for his eyes to adjust. He has to think, calm down.

Marks on the wall opposite. This must be where he slid into the trench with Eden. He knows where he is. Thank God. He breathes again, crouches down, faces towards the enemy.

Movement against the charcoal sky. Legs striding. Men, five, maybe more, moving fast towards him, coming from the German line. The rain thickens, details vanish.

He holds his breath, blinks the rain away, ducks down. What should he do? He only has six bullets then he'll have to reload. He could fire, run along the sap and try to get out further down. He lifts his head. They're close now, coming straight at him. They must know he's here.

He lifts his revolver. The barrel catches in the mud and the gun falls into the water at his feet. He scrabbles for it, pulls it out. It's thick with mud. Now he can't be sure if it will fire.

They're just yards away.

He remembers the grenades, pulls one out, pulls the pin, leans back and hurls it over the wall. It explodes. A white flash slams into his skull. Something flies through the air above him, thuds against the far wall of the trench and rolls into the mud at his feet. It's a man, face down.

Alex aims his revolver and waits. The soldier doesn't move. The back of the shirt is ripped and blood-soaked. There's something familiar. Officer's boots. British officer's boots. Alex is dizzy; might pass out. He slumps down, leans forward and turns the soldier over. A woollen cap falls off; black, curly hair... Looks like Captain Kingsman but it can't be; they came from the other side. This isn't Kingsman, but the face... *It is Kingsman!*

Alex chokes on vomit. Spits it out. He should get out. Skin prickling across his back, up into his head. He laughs. Cries. Cries out. *Hold it together!* Tries to breathe. Deep breaths. He has to do something; try to save them. Them! What about the others? He lifts his head above the wall of dirt. Shapes, soldiers, those young men, lying in the dirt. Now Eden is here. He's crouching over them. He sees Alex and jumps into the trench. Eden is talking. Alex can't hear the words; ringing in his ears. 'happened?... done?... Kingsman... grenade?'

Alex tries to speak. No words. He shakes his head, glaring at Eden.

'What did you do?' hisses Eden.

'I thought it was the Germans! I thought...' Alex is crying.

Eden grabs Alex by the collar. 'You've killed them all!'

Kingsman groans.

Alex pushes Eden out of the way and lifts Kingsman's head, cradles it in his lap. 'He's still alive! We have to save him!' He tries to wipe the mud from Kingsman's face. 'I'm so sorry, Sir! I didn't know it was you!'

'Let me look,' says Eden, pushing Kingsman onto his stomach, ripping at the clothes. Kingsman's back is torn and bloody; flaps of pale skin and dark raw muscle. He yells out.

'You have to be quiet,' whispers Eden. 'You'll bring the patrol right to us if you don't keep quiet.'

'He'll be all right, won't he?' sobs Alex. 'We just have to—'

'Shut up!' spits Eden. 'The Hun know we're here. They'll be swarming up this trench. We need to get out. We'll have to leave him here.'

'But we can't! We've got to help! Please, Sir.'

'He's had it, don't you see?'

'Please, can we just try?'

'You got morphine?'

'No. I didn't think we'd...'

Eden lifts his head and scans the field. 'We'll try to carry him, but if the Boche see us, we leave him. Do you hear?'

'Yes!'

Eden heaves Kingsman onto his back and, bent double, clambers up the muddy wall and into the field.

Kingsman groans loudly.

'Shut up!' says Eden.

'Will he be all right?' says Alex, stumbling to keep up. 'I thought they were the Germans. I thought—'

Kingsman yells out; spluttering, guttural.

Eden lowers him to the ground. 'Shut up! You have to shut up!'

Kingsman gasps loudly, gulping for air.

Eden puts his hand over Kingsman's mouth.

Kingsman grabs, tries to push, wet hands slipping.

Eden leans in. Rain dripping off his face onto Kingsman's. 'You'll bring them right to us if you don't shut up!'

Kingsman's fingers uncurl and both hands drop into the mud by his side. His body softens and falls still.

'Kingsman? Captain?' Eden stands, staggering a little.

He takes Kingsman's arms and drags the lifeless body across the field.

Alex follows, stumbling. The rain falls hard and steady between them.

When they're close to the British wire, Eden stops and turns to

Alex. 'You can't tell anyone what happened. If they find out, they'll shoot you, do you understand?'

'But it was... an accident!' Alex is struggling to push the words out, trying not to cry. 'I thought they were Germans!'

Eden stabs his finger into Alex's chest. 'You threw the grenade. That's all they'll care about.' He grabs Alex by the neck and pulls him close. 'Ryan, listen to me. The *Hun* patrol did this. *We* tried to save him. *You* tried to defend him. Yes?'

Alex nods.

'Yes?' says Eden, louder.

'Yes.'

When they reach the parapet, Eden calls out and suddenly a throng of soldiers is clambering over the bags and lowering the body onto the fire-step.

Kemmell leaps up and stares out into the darkness. 'What of the others, Sir? Are they on their way?'

'Dead,' says Eden. 'All dead.'

Kemmell is stunned. 'All of them, Sir? All my lads?'

Eden, staring at Alex, shakes his head. 'A Boche patrol. Ambush. Nothing we could do.'

The men gather round, staring in horror at Kingsman's limp, mud-soaked body.

Alex wants to beg for their forgiveness, to yell out that he didn't realise who it was! He thought they were Germans!

Eden, as if sensing that Alex is about to do something, pushes him forward. 'Until I arrived, Ryan here, managed to fight them off on his own. We tried to save the captain but it was too late. There was nothing we could do.'

Alex is disgusted. Bile wells up into his mouth. He pulls away from Eden and spits into the mud.

'Help me get the captain down to the field hospital,' says Eden. 'Kemmell, get HQ on the line. I need to speak to them, now!' He pushes through the men and marches away.

Soldiers lift Kingsman's body and slowly, reverently carry him away.

Alex doesn't move. He can't. He watches the procession of men disappearing into the darkness.

He's alone in the trench again. The same place he'd stood, excited and proud, only an hour before. But everything feels different now. The night is even colder. He lifts his face into the icy rain. He clenches his fists, feeling the grit between his fingers. He feels the darkness dragging damp across his back, swirling up into the wet black air.

8

SNOW

He's suspended in a white nothingness. The nothing becomes a space. He becomes heavy. He is lying on a bed, and for a moment it is his own bed at his father's farm. Then the air fills with the smells of charcoal soot and damp earth. He opens his eyes. He's in the junior officer's dugout in the communications trench and last night he... he... Something boils in his blood. Anger. Why the hell didn't Kingsman and his men say something, shout to him? They must have known that Alex was in the sap. Why didn't they call out and tell him who they were? The anger turns to shame. God, what has he done? Eden must think that Alex is such a fool. Guilt now, flooding. He turns over, grips the sheet into fists, bites into it and yells. When he feels calmer, he sits up.

A soft blue light is creeping around the edge of the canvas curtain at the top of the dugout steps. Footsteps outside are muffled.

He lights a candle.

Icicles, where drips had been coming through the dugout roof, glisten like glass pencils above his bed.

There are two other beds against the opposite wall. One belongs to Lieutenant Pope, who Alex hasn't met. The other is Lieutenant Phillips, who, last night, said well done to Alex, for defending the soldiers, for bringing in Captain Kingsman. *Well done!* Alex shakes his head.

What will they say when they find out the truth? They *will* find out. They'll collect the bodies of the four soldiers tonight. Then they'll know. There must be a way of knowing, from the wounds. The pattern of the wounds. Do the German grenades make a different mark? The rips in the cloth, the cuts in the flesh? They'll come and find him. He should pack his things.

He shivers and looks at his watch. It's only four hours since it happened. Since the beginning and the end. His feet are very cold and his socks are stiff and damp. He must have taken his boots off when he came in, but doesn't remember doing that. He pushes his feet into the boots and ties the frozen laces. Fenton must have brought his top-coat here; it's hanging by the stove. He puts it on. It's no comfort; colder than the dugout.

The canvas sheet flies open. Here they come. Alex is ready. An officer walks in, stomps down the steps and kicks snow off his boots. 'Oh good, you're up,' he says. And to Alex's surprise, removes his gloves and offers a hand. 'Charlie Pope. I was just coming to wake you.' His grip is warm and strong. 'Major Babcock is here. He wants to see you in the HQ dugout.' He smiles. 'What have you done?'

Alex opens his mouth but nothing comes out.

Charlie kneels by the stove and pokes the embers with a stick. 'On your way to HQ, you should check the sentries along the first three traverses. Then find Eden. He'll tell you what's to be done. He's had my lot fetching ammunition all night. Took us three hours to bring it from the depot. It snowed.' He puts a few pieces of coal inside the stove and shuts the door. 'My fellows were crying with the cold but they worked like engines. God knows what he'll ask you to do. Invade Berlin?' He laughs and stops when he turns to Alex. 'Are you all right?'

Alex hasn't moved since Charlie came in. He's still standing in the middle of the dugout, head bowed against the low beams. 'Captain Kingsman was killed.'

Charlie sits down on his bed. 'I know. I'm sorry. I was trying to make light of it. Stupid. What happened?'

'A grenade,' says Alex, carefully. He doesn't want to say anymore, not yet, not until he's spoken to the major. Then they can all know.

Charlie shakes his head.

'And four soldiers too,' says Alex. 'They were also killed.'

'I know. It's terribly sad. They were good men. And Kingsman, I liked him. Everyone did.'

'I was there,' says Alex. 'I thought it was a German patrol. I was in the sap. I was supposed to be guarding the rear. I was supposed to protect them but —'

'It wasn't your fault. It was dark. Those patrols appear out of nowhere. Eden told us what you did. You should be proud of that.' He stands and puts his hand on Alex's shoulder. 'You've had such a rough time of it. Collins on your first night and now this. You must be shaken to bits.'

Alex fights the urge to move away. 'I don't know.' He doesn't know.

'You'll be all right. Give it a few days and you'll be laughing.' Charlie smiles. 'You should go up. Don't keep the major waiting. Sorry old chap, that was a terrible introduction. Let's talk this afternoon. I need to get a few winks before Eden has me at it again.'

Alex straps on his revolver and climbs up the steps. He pauses, wants to go back down, say something. He pushes open the canvas and steps out into the trench.

The air bites into his skin. The duckboards are covered in grey slush and bootprints. He walks along the trench, passing cold, quiet soldiers.

'Cup of tea, Sir? Just boiled,' says one, holding a chipped teapot over a candle.

Alex shakes his head.

'Will Captain Eden be commanding now, Sir?'

'I don't know,' says Alex, moving away. He comes to the place where he'd gone out with Eden in the night.

Private Stubbs is standing on the fire-step. Frost has built up on

45

his scarf, under his chin.

Alex climbs up. 'You must be freezing.'

Stubbs puts his rifle onto the sandbags and tucks his hands under his armpits. 'I've been warmer, Sir. I won't lie.'

No Man's Land looks so different; the torn up, chalky earth and shell craters look brown now against the perfect white of the snow.

'Are you all right, Sir?' says Stubbs, looking out across the snow. 'We've all heard.'

Alex turns to the soldier. 'Am I all right?'

'Yes, Sir, we heard what happened. The captain gone. I can't believe it. We heard what you did, you and Captain Eden. I was friendly with Turner,' says Stubbs. 'His wife had just had twins. Proper chuffed he was about that. Showed us all the picture. That must be them there, poor buggers.'

Thirty yards away, perfectly black, as if bullet holes had been shot right through a painting of the landscape, is a mass of crows, huddled, fidgeting, pulling and scratching at four shapes lying in the snow. Dark strips, elastic and soft, rip and split against the grey sky.

Alex says nothing. The two men stand in silence looking out across the white field.

There are other dark patches all over No Man's Land; cloth-covered bundles the shape of men, the shape of young fathers, half-buried and already half-forgotten under the snow.

Stubbs picks up his rifle, aims towards the crows and fires.

Alex flinches.

The birds tumble and lurch into the air, squawking, chattering, drifting in a great heaving black arc, back to the snowy ground, hop and flutter and tug again at the corpses.

'You should get some breakfast,' says Alex, shivering and stepping down onto the duckboards. 'I'll send someone along to replace you.'

'Right oh. Thank you, Sir.'

The sky droops; iron heavy, pregnant; losing the last of its dawn blue. It is the colour of milk. It begins to snow. Thick, large snowflakes brush Alex's face and tap against his helmet. As he steps down into the HQ dugout, he can still hear the crows.

9

MAJOR BABCOCK

There's raised voices behind the canvas door. Alex pauses and listens.

'You would be frustrated if you were commanding, Eden. I know you. You wouldn't be able to go out. The brigadier doesn't want the commanders going out. Too risky.' This must be Major Babcock speaking. 'Can you honestly imagine yourself staying behind, stuck in a dugout, issuing receipts for, for clean underpants, while the men were up there, attacking the Germans?'

'I've done it before.' Eden's voice. 'I don't see why I can't command from the front like—'

'It's not about being at the front or the back.' Babcock sighs. He sounds tired. 'You just took too many risks. You can't expect your men to...' Shuffling. 'And after, after what happened in Loos, some people think you're lucky to still be a captain.'

'Just give me a few weeks, Sir. I'm sure once you see—'

'It's out of my hands, Eden. We've got a good man coming. Woodstone. He's not seen much action but his father's a fine chap and given me assurances. So we're giving him a go. This will allow you to do what you do best: fight the damned Boche! That's what you want isn't it?'

'I just think... that...' Eden's words trail off. He calls up the steps. 'Is there someone there? Is that you, Ryan?'

Alex pauses a moment then pushes through the canvas. 'Yes, Sir. I was just—'

'This him?' says Babcock, leaning against a desk at the side of the room. He stares at Alex as if he was expecting someone taller, more robust. He has a plump face like a boiled potato, with a grey and stiff moustache that swivels as he speaks. 'I've just read Captain Eden's report. Good effort with that Boche patrol. Shame about Kingsman. Can't be helped. Eden here said it couldn't be helped. You all right? We need a report from you. Get that to me as soon as you can.'

'Yes, Sir,' says Alex. He can feel Eden staring at him.

'You both did well,' says Babcock. 'Shame though about...' He shakes his head. 'Oh well, can't be helped. Well done. I've got to get back.' He picks up his gloves and hat from the desk and turns to Eden. 'So I'll leave things with you, just for a few days, until this chap arrives.' He waves a glove at Alex. 'New company commander on his way; Captain Woodstone. He'll need good men by his side.'

Alex stares at the floor.

As Babcock pushes through the canvas and out into the trench he says, 'Eden, remember they're men, not pawns.'

Eden squints for a moment and clenches his jaw. He opens a notebook. 'I need you to clear the snow from the comms trench, Ryan. Take four men.'

'I don't know what to do,' says Alex.

'You will clear the snow from the comms trench. That's what you do.' He doesn't look up. 'Get shovels from the quartermaster sergeant.'

'I don't mean that. I mean... I can't just carry on as if nothing happened.'

Eden looks up. 'You can. You will. Do the report for Babcock. Read mine. Then you will carry out your duties as normal.'

'But everyone thinks I did something brave, something good. It's a lie.'

Eden closes the notebook and pushes his chair away from the

desk. 'Ryan, let me tell you something that no one else in this battalion knows: a week ago, Field martial Haig wrote a letter to the brigadier. In it he said that he was worried about Kingsman's leadership. He was getting soft. Haig was concerned about the declining levels of discipline in this battalion. He said the men need to be given a signal, a warning, that things can't be allowed to deteriorate further. So the Brigadier, Babcock and the rest of HQ have been looking for someone to punish. And now you turn up and kill your commander and four of the company's best men. You, a junior officer, with no record of good behaviour, no redeeming battle history, would be exactly what they're looking for. They would court-martial you with much publicity. Then, in front of the whole battalion, they'd tie you to a post and shoot you.' He laughs. 'It doesn't matter what actually happened out there, they wouldn't understand and even if they did, they wouldn't care. Trust me, I know.'

Alex doesn't speak. He doesn't know what to say.

Eden's face softens. 'Look. In a way that no one expected, you've solved their problem...and now, if we can work with this, this... Woodstone chap, we might have an opportunity to sharpen this battalion into something that can really be useful out here. You just have to...' He waves his hand as if he's swatting a fly. 'I've dealt with it. As far as anyone needs to know, the Hun patrol killed Kingsman and his men. Do the report and it's finished. Understand?'

Alex nods and turns to go.

'Ryan? For now, I am the acting-commander of this company. Just remember that. I am your captain. You will always refer to me as Sir. Now get out.'

10

THE WIRING PARTY

Eggleton is tying a pile of corkscrew stakes into a bundle. He's wearing a new sheepskin jacket and pauses regularly to proudly run his fingers through the white fluff. He can't be more than thirty-five but he has dry, wrinkled skin. It looks like brown paper in the candle-light that flickers against the wall of the firing trench.

'You'll get fucked by a sheep if you wear that,' says Rowlands. He winks at Percy, who's sitting quietly between them. 'Or eaten by wolves.'

Eggleton thinks. The wrinkles on his forehead tighten. 'They don't have wolves in France.' Rowlands turns to Alex. 'Sir, do they have wolves here?'

'I think so... I don't know.' Alex is tired. His afternoon attempts at sleeping were interrupted, first by a bombardment that destroyed thirty yards of parapet and killed one man, then by a strange dream; Kingsman and the four dead soldiers, crouching like terrified wild animals, stuffing their faces with chocolate. He woke up with sweat freezing across his skin.

'They'll spot you a mile off, wearing that sheep,' says Rowlands.

'No they won't,' says Eggleton. 'There's snow on the ground.

Snow is white. If Fritz sends up a flare, I'll blend in. You, on the other hand, will be standing there, lit up like a fat opera singer.'

Rowlands looks down at his mud-stained tunic. 'Why would I be standing? We're to drop if a flare goes up. I'd be on the ground, hidden, like a rock or... or some mud.'

'No, not here,' says Eggleton, emphatically. 'We're supposed to freeze if a flare goes up.'

Rowlands turns again to Alex. 'Sir, are we supposed to drop or freeze?'

'The Boche look for movement,' says Alex, remembering his training. 'So, despite how uncomfortable it feels, you should freeze until the flare goes out.' Eden has ordered him to lead the wiring party, despite never having repaired any wire or even been trained to do so. But it will be a relief to be going up into No Man's Land again, away from the stagnant, rancid air in the trenches. He hands out wire cutters and pliers to Eggleton and Rowlands. He was only given one pair of leather gloves. He gives those to Percy. If only he could stop seeing the dead soldier's faces; the smiles as they walked past him in the trench.

Percy hasn't said a word, shivering on the fire-step with his knees up, staring at the sandbags. His helmet wobbles over his eyes.

Alex takes the helmet, tightens the strap and hands it back to Percy.

'You missed cake,' says Rowlands.

'When?' says Eggleton. 'When was there cake?'

'This afternoon. Mortlock's wife sent it. Ginger with currants. Where were you?'

'Bloody Eden put me on latrines. Again! I tell you, another week with him in command and I'll be dead from exhaustion. At least with Kingsman we got—'

Rowlands sees Eden marching along the trench and jabs Eggleton with his elbow. Eggleton drops the bundle of stakes onto the duck-boards. A rat, startled by the noise, falls off the sandbags and scurries away through the slush.

'Drop those up there and the Hun will have a bullet through your eye before you hear the shot,' says Eden.

'Yes, Sir,' says Eggleton, scrabbling to pick up the stakes.

Eden shakes his head and turns to Alex. 'There's a painted post where you can climb under our wire. Turn right, crawl out about a hundred yards until you reach the damaged section. It was cut and partly buried in the bombardment this afternoon. The Boche will be expecting you. So be quiet, and drop if you see a flare.'

'Drop, Sir?' says Rowlands with his nose in the air.

'Yes, drop. There's mist and long grass. So drop. You can crawl away and they won't find you.'

Rowlands looks smugly at Eggleton.

Alex turns away, clenching his jaw. He couldn't even get that right. If his men listen to him, they'll soon all be as dead as the others.

'Eggleton,' says Eden. 'You've done this before. Some of the men here have not. Show them how it's done.' He doesn't look at anyone when he says that, but Alex knows that Eden is talking about him.

Eggleton looks smugly at Rowlands.'Yes, Sir!'

Eden walks away without another word.

The four men crawl out, single file, along narrow, slushy tracks between the shell holes.

There's no moon but it's not very dark. Layers of smoke from the soldiers' tin-can stoves drift lazily across the snow. At the front, Eggleton's fleeced back arches out of the mist, sliding through the tufts of grass like a rabbit. Behind him, slow and heavy, crawls Rowlands. The rolls of barbed wire bounce against his back. 'Jesus,' he whispers, louder than most men's normal talking voice. 'My knees are so cold they don't feel cold anymore!'

They reach the carpet of wire with the painted post, crawl under and turn right to find the damaged section.

Wooden posts lie splintered and broken. Loose wire is coiled and twisted, running in and out of shell hole puddles and surprisingly long grass. Between the craters, the snow has drifted in humps, soft and curvaceous like sleeping seals.

Eggleton twists a corkscrew stake into the cold ground with an iron bar. Then takes the rolls of wire from Rowlands and gives one to Percy. 'Wind this out, quietly as you can,' he whispers, placing a finger across his lips and pointing dramatically into the darkness; No Man's Land spreads out, huge and flat and open, fading into a wall of grey mist. Somewhere in the mist, just a few hundred yards away, are the silent, listening Germans. Percy understands. He nods, wide eyed. He walks backwards, unwinding the wire as he goes. Rowlands twists more stakes into the ground and Eggleton wraps the wire around them, showing Alex how to hold and cut the wire with the pliers.

When they have filled the gap with a tangle of new wire, they collect up the tools and start to head back. A flare goes up, spitting sparks, bleaching the field to daylight. Alex drops into the snow. Ice crystals glisten on the edges of the blades of grass.

Percy, his uniform dazzling against the inky sky, is still standing upright next to the wire.

Eggleton and Rowlands have dropped. 'Perce! Get down you daft bugger!' hisses Eggleton from the grass.

The boy doesn't move. He's staring, stone-faced, up towards the flare.

'Elphick!' whispers Alex. 'Down! Now!'

A gunshot rushes across the snow, echoing back from the darkness. It thuds dully into the snow behind them.

'Snipers!' says Eggleton. 'They've seen him!'

Alex jumps to his feet but Eggleton grabs his leg and he falls back into the grass. 'Let go of me! I have to pull him down! Why doesn't he get down?'

'There's nothing you can do, Sir! If you get up, they'll shoot the both of you.'

'Percy! Get into the grass!' yells Alex.

The flare drifts behind trees at the edge of the field. Shadows of the branches crawl over Percy's face; frozen like marble.

Another gunshot and Percy falls, spinning sideways and landing in the grass. Powdered snow sprays up around him.

The flare splutters and dies.

Darkness.

Alex crawls over. The boy is lying on his back, eyes wide but not seeing. His body, rigid and trembling, still gripping the pliers.

Eggleton runs his hands over Percy's back. 'I can't find a wound. I thought he must be hit in the back. But I can't find a hole.'

Rowlands crawls over. 'What's happened? What's the noise?' He looks at the quivering boy. 'What the bloody devil? Whats happened to him?'

'We need to get his tunic off,' says Alex. 'Perhaps there's a wound we can't see.'

Suddenly, as if an electric switch has been flipped, the boy groans. The shaking stops and he yawns, rubbing his eyes.

'What happened?' says Alex 'Are you hit?'

Percy looks confused. 'No,' he says, patting his legs and chest as if searching for a match. He looks as if he might cry. 'Sorry.'

'For what?' says Rowlands, tapping the boy on the stomach. 'You scared us half to death, is all. We thought you was possessed!'

Percy blinks slowly, staring at the three men as if trying to remember who they are. 'I think I was asleep.'

'Asleep?' says Rowlands. 'What the...'

'Well, that's that then,' says Eggleton, laughing.

A bullet slashes through the grass above their heads.

Hidden by the mist, sliding on their chests through the snow, they inch their way back.

No Man's Land is quiet, just a silver murmur in the freezing grass and the muffled thump of distant guns.

11

BACON

Two tiny pink hands grip the edge of the canvas. Brown whiskers twitch and disappear. A rat-shaped indent works its way across the roof, squeezing between the sheeting and the beams.

It's strange how safe Alex feels in the dugout. How buffered from the tons of iron falling around him every hour. Above the rat are railway sleepers, two feet of earth and a layer of sandbags. Enough to stop shrapnel but if a shell hit, it would go right through. It's a matter of luck, whether you spend the rest of the night in a bed or a coffin.

'Get up. There's bacon,' says Charlie, frying something on the coal stove. He's bathed in a candlelight and woodsmoke haze.

Alex pulls the damp blanket tighter around his neck. 'Is it morning yet?'

'It's eight o'clock. Sixteen hours before we get relieved.' Charlie scrapes whatever it was that he was cooking onto two tin plates. 'Sixteen hours before hot baths, real beds and eggs! So get up! Make the most of your last day in the trenches for... well, at least a week.'

Alex sits. 'Eight? I've missed stand-to!' It's only been a few hours since he staggered into bed, soaking wet and fully clothed. His back feels like he can't have moved since he lay down. He swings his aching legs round and faces the little table between the beds. He's still wearing his boots. He should change his socks, they feel like wet seaweed between his toes.

'It's all right. Captain Eden said not to wake you,' says Charlie, placing a slice of bread on each plate. 'You were fast asleep when I came in. How did the wiring go?'

Alex scratches his head. His hair feels loose, like it doesn't fit his head. 'All right, I think. We closed the gap. One of my men, Elphick, had some kind of shaking fit.'

'There's so many diseases going round these trenches...' Charlie's words are muffled by a mouthful of bread. He chews. 'It could be anything... You should send him to the MO for a checkup if it happens again.' He points his fork at a thin strip of orange meat on Alex's plate. 'Eat your bacon. The snow's turned to rain and the mud's so deep now, I doubt they'll get anything else up here from the field kitchens today.'

Alex stabs the meat with a fork and slides it onto the bread. It flops flat, spraying oil into the candle flame with a hiss. 'Nothing personal Charlie, but I'm just wondering what happened to Fenton? I thought he was the officer's cook.'

'Fenton is the *captains'* batman. We eat with them by invitation only. The rest of the time us subalterns have to fend for ourselves. Most officers have food sent up. I prefer to eat what the men are eating. Doesn't seem fair to eat anything else when they're out there in the cold, eating this.'

Alex takes a bite. The 'bacon' feels like an old belt in his mouth.

Charlie laughs. 'You'll be amazed what some of the men can do with a bit of bacon, a carrot and a candle to cook it with. I'm not much of a cook. My wife used to do all of that.'

'Oh, you have a wife?' says Alex, smiling. 'I didn't know.'

Charlie nods. 'What about you?' He clears his throat. 'Wife, girl, parents? Someone who loves you? Someone to send you a Harrods hamper, so you don't have to eat my bacon?'

Alex laughs. 'A father, but not one who would send me a hamper!' He tells Charlie that there had been a girl, two summers ago. She held his hand at the back of a church and they had kissed under trees by a slow river. One afternoon, with such certainty, she told him that she loved him. If she had sounded less sure of the fact, he might have told her that he loved her too. But her certainty made him wonder if you should *know* that you're in love. He liked her very much, loved her company and thought about her all the time, but he just wasn't sure about how sure you should be. So he said nothing, and the next time he invited her to meet him, she was busy. After that they only met in the company of others. Then the war started and he was sent away.

A twinge of embarrassment flushes through Alex and he wishes he hadn't said anything. He's never talked to anyone about love before, but Charlie mentioned it so casually, they might as well have been discussing a shipment of lice ointment for the men.

Charlie is listening intently. He doesn't seem uncomfortable at all. 'I think,' he says, squinting in concentration. 'I think love is something that you don't understand when it isn't love, but when it is, you know. So if you had to think about it, probably, it wasn't.'

Alex leans forward; he wants to understand this. 'So, when you are with your wife, do you absolutely *know*, for certain?'

Charlie slowly brushes crumbs off his hand. 'My wife, Evelina, doesn't live in our home anymore. She left me.'

A loud explosion. A flash. Dirt flies down the dugout steps. Shouting.

Charlie stares at Alex for a moment, then the two of them leap up and climb the dugout steps.

12

TRENCH MORTARS

Outside, the trench is filled with swirling white smoke. It's dazzling. Soldiers stagger through it, coughing and yelling.

Eden, silhouetted against the smoke, is giving orders from the fire-step. 'Sergeant Kemmell, try to get a messenger to artillery. We need to silence that trench mortar! They've blown the parapet at both ends. I need men up there. We have to get it cleared, now!' He sees Alex. 'Go! Find shovels. Use planks of wood, your hands, anything.'

Alex takes a group of men as far as he can along the traverse. Sandbags have burst and collapsed, spilling soil over the fire-step. Sheets of ribbed-iron and wooden beams lie scattered and bent, blocking the way. Bullets slam into the bags as they try to climb over the rubble. The parapet is gone. There's nothing to protect them from snipers, no way to get into the next traverse.

'They might be about to attack,' says Eden, turning to Charlie. 'Get everyone standing-to on the fire-step. But keep their heads down! How are we doing with that messenger?'

'No luck, Sir,' says Kemmell. 'They've got snipers trained on the broken section. One lad's had his arm shot up trying to get over. Another's had a bullet through his hat. I'm not risking more and even—'

Eden glares. 'You'll risk whatever I order you to risk, Sergeant.'

'Yes, Sir. I meant, we're clearing as fast as we can, but even if we get through, it's still blocked all the way down.'

'We could climb over the parados behind us,' says Charlie. 'Run along the top until—'

Someone blows a whistle.

'Look up, lads!' yells Kemmell.

Everyone squints into the light.

White sky. Then a spot of darkness. Wings; a black angel, hurtling down towards them.

'There! Run to the left!'

Soldiers scramble, clambering through the traverse, tripping over each other, staring into the sky.

'Stay where you are!' Eden, fully upright, watches as the bomb falls. 'It's short,' he says. 'Stay where you are and crouch down!'

The men push themselves against the sandbags, arms above their heads, squinting against the coming bomb. It slams into the field above the trench and a wave of soil crashes over them.

Wislawa is scrabbling in the dirt. 'Higgit!' he yells. 'We'll get you out, son! Just hold on.'

Higgit is buried with only his head and shoulders showing above the rubble. He blinks, runs his tongue across his bloody lips.

Wislawa, gritting his teeth, drags Higgit out of the rubble.

Higgit's lower legs have gone. He runs his hands along his thighs, pulls at the shredded cloth of his trousers, tapping the soil where his legs should be, as if he's looking for something, but there's nothing there. He looks up at Alex, then to Wislawa and blinks slowly.

'Lieutenant Ryan!' Eden is on the fire-step again, scanning No Man's Land with field-glasses.

Higgit grabs Alex by the neck, pulling himself up until their faces are pressed together. 'Shoot me,' he says, swallowing between each breath. 'Please, for God's sake, shoot me!'

Alex tries to push him away. 'No! No. You'll be all right! We'll get you to the field hospital.' He pulls a field dressing from his pocket, rips it open and tries to wrap it around the stumps of Higgit's legs. The flesh hangs stringy and gritty with soil.

Higgit spreads his hands out towards Alex like a child asking to be carried. 'Shoot me,' he says again, crying now.

'Ryan! Get up here!' yells Eden.

Alex, furious, grabs Higgit with both hands. 'We'll get you out! Do you hear me? Just wait and we will get you out!'

'Ryan! Come here, this minute!'

'We have to get Higgit out, Sir,' says Alex, climbing onto the fire-step, next to Eden. 'He's lost his legs!'

'I can see where they're firing from,' says Eden, pointing. 'I saw a puff of smoke.' About one hundred yards, directly in front of where they're standing is a low wall, a few bricks high, the corner of an old farm building or shed.

Explosions further along the line. Soil sprays up like a rough sea.

Behind them, Wislawa is gripping Higgit in his arms. Higgit's body flops loosely, his pale hand dragging in the dark soil. Alex thinks of The Madonna cradling the dead Christ and he can't turn away, staring at the violent beauty of what he's seeing.

A shell slams into the sandbags.

Everyone drops, except Eden. 'I think I can get to them,' he says, stepping over Alex, who's crouched at his feet. 'Kemmell, I'm going out. Get me some bombs.'

'But it's broad daylight, Sir,' says Charlie. 'Why don't you wait? Artillery might have got a range on them by now.'

Eden tilts his head, theatrically listening. 'Do you hear any artillery, Lieutenant?' He takes off his tunic and hands it to Alex. 'I'll take my time going out. But they'll have noticed me by the time I start heading back, so have your chaps firing at that wall. That should keep their heads down long enough for me to get to our wire.'

Kemmell hands Eden a satchel of grenades.

'It's not my place, Sir,' says Charlie. 'But as the commanding officer, shouldn't you stay here? Perhaps one of us should go? I'm happy to do it.'

Alex looks at Charlie and steps forward. 'We could both go, Sir.'

Charlie glances at Alex and flashes a smile.

'No,' says Eden, rolling up his shirt sleeves. 'I'd rather mess it up myself than have to explain to Babcock that I sent you out. In fact, it's probably best if Babcock doesn't hear about this at all.' He climbs up the parapet, turns and grins. 'All right?' He drops over into the grass then crawls out until he reaches the British wire and goes out of sight.

Another whistle.

A mortar shell shoots up, slowing and hovering as if watching the men cowering in the trenches, before choosing where to fall. It curves through the thin light, closer, faster.

'Here it comes, lads!' yells Kemmell. 'Get to the sides!'

Everyone runs along the fire-step, pushing, yelling, falling over each other. 'Move along! Move!'

The shell explodes. Stones and shrapnel spin through the air, slicing into the sandbags. Shouting; someone in pain.

As the smoke begins to clear, they see Eden crawling, skirting around a low mound of earth in front of the wall. When he reaches it, he opens the satchel and takes out two grenades and, with his back to the mortar, throws them over his shoulder, over the wall.

A boiling plume of fire and black smoke rolls up into the white sky. Eden leaps forward, dropping flat into the ground and disappears into a shell hole before he and everything around him is engulfed in thick grey smoke.

The men cheer.

'Hold it!' yells Kemmell. 'Steady... Volley fire on my command!'

The smoke drifts. Eden is up and running with it, through it, back towards the British wire, then fully exposed in the sunlight.

'Fire, lads! Fire!'

The men fire, volley after volley. Filling the air with more smoke and brick dust.

'That's it lads!' Kemmell is firing too. 'I can't believe what I'm seeing!'

'How are the snipers missing him?' says Alex, firing his revolver.

Eden is half-way across the field; arms pumping like pistons, chin up, chest pushing through the smoke. He curves around the shell holes, leaps over tufts of grass. Running, running.

'He's fucking going to make it!' says Rowlands.

Charlie is laughing.

Eden reaches the British wire and disappears under it. He's up again and across the grass in no time, leaps over the parapet and falls to his knees on the fire-step.

Everyone is laughing and cheering.

'Never seen a thing like it,' says, Kemmell, shaking his head. 'Never in all my days.'

Two crumpled bodies lie either side of the brick wall. Thin smoke rises slowly from behind it. Something is burning. 'Put a sniper towards that,' says Eden, panting. 'In case Fritz tries to get the mortar back later.' He gets to his feet, looks for Alex and smiles. 'Do you have my jacket?'

Alex hands Eden the tunic and gives him water. He watches as Eden drinks.

'That explosion singed the back of my head,' says Eden, rubbing his neck, smiling at Alex. 'I'll have to get a hair cut in Vieille Chapelle.' He looks relaxed, like someone who's just come back from a good swim in the river. 'I want five men clearing the rubble at each end. As soon as they get through, carry the injured out and find stretcher-bearers. Everyone else, guns cleaned and standing-to. The Hun look like they're in the mood for a fight today.'

The men get up, clearing the debris, taking shovels and scraping the soil against the fire-step. Alex helps them fill sandbags with dirt and push planks of wood back into the trench walls.

A loud gunshot.

Alex spins around. Wislawa is standing over Higgit, holding a revolver loosely in his hand. Higgit is lying on his side. There's a neat hole in his temple. It glistens in the sunlight as blood rises gently up, fills his eyebrow and drips into the dirt.

'Let's get this all cleared,' says Eden, taking the revolver from Wislawa.

'Why did you do that?' says Alex, trembling. 'We should have tried to save him!'

Wislawa kneels and wipes the blood from Higgit's face with the side of his thumb. 'He didn't want us to, Sir.' He lifts what's left of Higgit's legs, gently folding the ragged cloth under them. 'He was a footballer. Played for Brighton and Hove. He was very good.'

13

CAPTAIN WOODSTONE

'With you in a moment,' says Captain Woodstone, without looking up. He's hunched behind a huge desk, reading from a neat pile of papers, mouthing the words and following along with a pencil.

Alex is standing in front of the desk; chin up, chest out, hands behind his back, waiting. He's been waiting for some time.

The dugout is new. On his arrival, Woodstone had been surprised to find that he had no office; Captain Kingsman had been content to use either his personal dugout or the officers' mess. Woodstone said it is essential for the CO to have an office. So the men dug him one, complete with side rooms for his servant and *equipment*. The walls smell of rotting vegetation and damp wood. The soil hasn't dried out and Kemmell says it never will.

It's dark in here. The light from the single oil lamp doesn't seem to reach any of the walls. Only Woodstone and the desk are in its cocooning flicker. His jet black hair shimmers. He's a slim man. Alex doesn't know why that surprises him. At thirty years old, there's no reason for Woodstone to be portly, but with the way the other officers had described his manner, Alex expected there to be more of him, more gravitas.

'Sit down,' says Woodstone, running his fingers carefully along his parting, stroking a few errant hairs back into position.

There are three chairs lined up against the wall. Alex sits on the nearest one, placing his helmet across his knees. The chair creaks and wobbles as it settles into the damp floor.

The legs of Woodstone's desk have been carved to resemble the limbs of a deer. Hooves and animal thighs morph into buxom young women, who stare disapprovingly at Alex. It must have been carried here through miles of trenches from one of the abandoned châteaux somewhere behind the lines.

Woodstone slowly circles a word with the pencil. His thin moustache twitches with concentration, as if he's deciphering an ancient text. He places the pencil on the table, adjusts it slightly until it's parallel to the documents and looks up. 'Where have you been?'

'I'm sorry, Sir,' says Alex. 'I was just talking to some of the men on the way here.'

'No, I mean, where have you come from? Just in from Sussex aren't you?'

'I've been with the company for almost two weeks, Sir.' Has it only been two weeks? It feels like a lifetime; not even *his* life. It was someone else who arrived in that rain, full of excitement, like a boy scout at the start of a camping weekend. 'I had two weeks training in Etaples before that, Sir.'

'So, you have been here for just a couple of weeks, and I have been here for just a couple of days. You know what that means, Ryan?'

'No, Sir.'

'It means you and I are the new boys.' Woodstone raises an eyebrow, waiting, as if this is supposed to mean something more important than it sounds.

'Yes, Sir,' says Alex, trying to make his answer not sound like a question, but failing.

Woodstone nods encouragingly. 'As the new boys we should have each other's backs, watch out for the school bullies, rely on each other. Can we do that, Ryan? Can you rely on me? Can I rely on you?'

Alex doesn't know what to say; they've only just met. 'Yes, Sir.'

Woodstone smiles. 'Good! Because there's a problem.'

Alex's chair creaks.

Woodstone stops smiling. 'D Company is short of officers. I've asked for new ones, but HQ said they're running out of good ones to send me. Some chap arrived from B Company; Lieutenant Halsall. Enthusiastic, but didn't seem to know his arse from his elbow. So I've sent him off on a course; machine guns. Talks a lot; his wife. What about you?'

'Er...' Alex blinks. 'I'm not married, Sir.'

'No.' Woodstone looks embarrassed. He strokes his hair again. 'No, that's not what I meant. You seem quiet. Are you?'

'I don't know, Sir.' Alex should say something else, but he can't think of anything.

Woodstone leans back in his chair. 'So, Captain Kingsman is dead.'

Alex tries to swallow and breathe at the same time and chokes on his own spit.

Woodstone brushes something off his desk until Alex recovers. 'Sorry. Never easy. Must have been shocking. Chin up. All right?'

Alex can feel sweat dripping into his eyebrow. There's a stove in the corner of the room. He hadn't noticed it before. 'Yes, Sir.'

'Nasty business. Not just the shock; admin. So much to be done. I've got to arrange the service.'

'Which service, Sir?'

'Kingsman's and the other fellow, the subaltern... Collins. But I was thinking we could wait, see if we get more. Do them all at once; more efficient. We can have it at the church in Vieille Chapelle, if it's still standing. I need to check.' He picks up his pencil and puts it down again. 'We could do them all together, later. Religious?'

Alex is leaning forward, trying to follow. 'Am I religious, Sir?'

Woodstone nods.

'I don't really think about it, Sir. I suppose I am, in some ways.'

'The men...' Woodstone points at the ceiling; presumably towards the soldiers in the trench above them. 'They find it comforting, but I think it's all rather confusing. Best to go along with it, though, for them; the men. Do you drink, Ryan?'

'Sorry, Sir?'

'Drink?'

'Sometimes, Sir.'

'Gibbons!' yells Woodstone, startling Alex.

A soldier wearing an apron comes in from the side room. He leans towards Woodstone as if he is expecting to catch a ball.

'Gibbons, Mr Ryan will have a whisky with water and I'll have my usual.'

Woodstone watches Gibbons leave the room then stands and crosses the room, adjusting his hair slowly with one hand. He sits down next to Alex. 'I'm supposed to write to his wife. We both are.'

Alex has to twist in his chair to face Woodstone. 'I'm supposed to write to his wife, Sir?'

'I hear you were with him when he died.'

Alex catches his breath. 'The captain, yes, Sir.'

'Then you'll need to write to his wife.'

'Why, Sir?'

'It's expected. You and Captain Eden were the last to see him alive. Get it done this morning if I were you. Get things out of the way.'

'But I didn't know him, Sir. We'd only just met.'

'I never even met him. I still have to write.'

'But I can't, Sir. Honestly I...' Alex is raising his voice. He has to calm down. 'I wouldn't know what to say.'

'Just tell her that he died heroically leading his men into battle. Bravely doing what he loved, etcetera. She'll love that.'

Alex can't write a letter. He won't do it. 'Yes, Sir,' he says, quietly.

Gibbons returns with two whiskies on a tray.

'Don't get used to this,' says Woodstone, handing a glass to Alex. 'I heard that Captain Kingsman used to drink with the officers, and now what? Dead.'

Alex is confused. 'He was killed by a German patrol, Sir.' There, he's said it now, said the lie.

'You should write that in the letter, to his wife. Shouldn't be hard. I heard he was a good fellow.'

Alex tries to look composed. 'I think he was very popular with the men.'

'I heard that.' Woodstone leans across the empty chair and glances behind him as if he's about to share a secret. 'I keep hearing how good they are, were; the captains. Kingsman and Eden. Both of them are, is.' He's staring into the darkness behind Alex. 'They've asked me to step in. Not sure how I... My father, you see...' For a moment Woodstone looks like a child, as if he might cry, then his face hardens and he sits up. 'I've heard good things about you, Ryan.' He leans across and gently touches Alex's knee with the tips of his fingers. 'Heard you've shown initiative, and you've been brave.'

'I'm not brave, Sir,' says Alex, tightening the muscles in his leg. 'I haven't done anything good.'

'Nonsense. I read your report, what you did for Kingsman. And Captain Eden has spoken very highly of you. You're too modest. That won't do. With a tweak in your attitude, I'm sure it won't be long before you have your own platoon.'

Alex stands. 'I don't think I want my own platoon and with your permission, I really must get on, Sir. I'm supervising the digging of the new supply trench. But before I go, I wanted to talk to you about one of my men. He's—'

'Nonsense,' says Woodstone. 'Everyone wants their own platoon. And I'm short of officers, as I said.'

'I just don't think I'm ready to be leading—'

'Beg' pardon, Sir,' says Gibbons, leaning into the room. 'Captain Eden is here to see you.'

'Ah! Show him in, Gibbons.' Woodstone drinks his whisky in one go, takes Alex's glass, winks and puts both glasses in a drawer behind the desk and sits.

'Captain, come in! I was just explaining to Lieutenant Ryan, here, that I'm keen to give him a go with his own platoon, but he seems to think he isn't ready. What do you think?'

'He's more ready than some people in this company,' says Eden, taking off his helmet and standing in the shadows next to Woodstone.

Woodstone places his hands neatly on the desk, either side of the pile of papers and leans towards Alex. 'You hear that, Ryan? Direct from the horse's mouth.' He turns to Eden. 'Is that the phrase? I didn't mean to imply... About the horse...'

Eden is leaning against the wall, smiling.

Woodstone has picked up his pencil and is pointing it at Alex. 'Perhaps Ryan isn't sure about real battles, up there, in No Man's Land. He's done the training at... at Edibles, or wherever it was, but training is one thing. Charging about while some idiot's throwing pine cones at you, is one thing. But it's quite a different matter when you're leading a platoon across No Man's Land, and you get your leg blown off, and you're being strafed by enemy machine guns. Isn't that right, Captain Eden?'

Alex isn't sure why Woodstone's saying this. Kemmell said that this is the first time Woodstone has even been near the front line. He's never been in combat. Is this supposed to impress Eden?

'I think Ryan has a fairly good idea about what it's like up there,' says Eden. 'I think he knows how confusing things can be, in the dark, the rain.'

'Good,' says Woodstone, tilting his head, as if he's not sure if he's missed something. He coughs and turns back to Alex. 'Anyway. Now, Captain Eden and I have... items to discuss. We're being relieved by the King's Royal Rifles tomorrow and I want this trench looking like...' He grimaces. 'Oh blast it, tip of my tongue... Something clean and tidy?' He waits for Eden to help.

Eden says nothing.

Woodstone looks disappointed. 'Anyway, off you trot, Ryan.'

'Before I go,' says Alex. 'One of my men, on the wiring party. A young chap. He had some sort of a fit and I wondered if it would be possible for the medical officer to take a look at him?'

Woodstone smiles. 'There you see, Captain Eden? You see what he just said? "One of *my* men." He thinks they're his men already. We'll have him charging across No Man's Land, waving his sabre, at the front of his own platoon in no time at all!'

14

THE BILLET

The regiment is relieved just before dawn and marches through drizzle to a village called Vieille Chapelle, a few miles West of the front line. It takes a long time to organise the billets and it's mid afternoon by the time D Company arrive at the Ferme du Boaze. Each platoon spreads out in one of four great barns. They're given blankets and make beds out of sandbags filled with straw.

A mile away is the Ferme du Berger, an old dairy farm where the officers are billeted. The red-bricked buildings, clustering around a flagstoned courtyard, seem held to the grey earth by clouds that hang like wet cloth.

Woodstone and Eden are in the main farmhouse and the lieutenants, in various outbuildings. Charlie and Alex share a shed that was a milking parlour when the farm had a full herd of cows.

Fenton has found a copper boiler in the cowshed. He prepares hot baths for each officer in turn. By the time Alex is called, it's almost dark.

The shed is open-sided. Stone pillars buckle against brick arches and moss-covered beams. An oil lamp lights the steam rising up from an old tin bath. Alex eases himself into the water and an almost painful pleasure ripples through him. He closes his eyes as the warmth soaks into his bones.

It's quiet here. Doves are settling on the roof. In the middle of the yard, a pump trickles water into a grate. Three skinny cows shuffle and snort in the shadows behind wooden stalls. Chickens, falling asleep on the beams, mumble quietly.

He turns the smooth soap over in his fingers, reverently scrubbing away the blood and dirt of the trenches, the way a priest would wash the dead. His body looks white and soft in the water. He thinks of the torn skin on Kingsman's back. Red flesh blooming beneath it. He pulls at his own skin and pushes a finger into his stomach, as hard as he can, like shrapnel from a grenade. He imagines the flesh parting, blood flowing out into the water. He's crying. He ducks his head under the water, lets out a bubbling scream, and climbs out of the bath into the cold air.

Charlie looks up from writing a letter and grins as Alex walks into the hut. 'This is the first time I've seen you clean! I hardly recognised you!' He looks different too, with a clean uniform and his hair combed back and smoothed with Brilliantine.

They stare at each other for a moment, like strangers again, smiling and admiring the cleanness.

'I grew up on a farm,' says Alex. 'I think I'm more comfortable being dirty.'

'Then you're in the right place. Despite Fenton's best efforts, I can still smell this shed's previous occupants.' Charlie looks under his bed. 'In fact, I'm wondering if they're somehow still in here.'

Alex hadn't noticed. He likes the smell of cows. 'Who are you writing to?'

Charlie shrugs. 'To my wife. Although… ' He stares into the distance, shakes his head and smiles again. 'What about you? I think we've got half an hour before dinner. You should write to someone.'

Alex hasn't written a single letter since he arrived in France. He should write to his father. He must. But now, after everything that's happened, it would be so difficult to know where to start. He must try... But not tonight. 'I'll just get dressed and go over. Is Fenton here? I need a clean tie.'

'He left you one over there. He's gone into the village.'

'Is he not making us dinner?'

'Apparently the farmer's wife and her rather pretty daughter will prepare all our meals while we're here,' says Charlie.

'We should probably go over then.'

Charlie laughs.

'Because I'm hungry!' says Alex.

'You go if you're ready. I want to finish this. I'll be over in a minute.'

Outside, retreating rain clouds stretch out dark and flat above the barn roofs. Alex crosses the courtyard and walks into the farmhouse kitchen. The humid air is rich with garlic, mutton, potatoes and herbs. There's a girl standing with her back to him, scrubbing a pan at the sink. Her hair, the colour of wet pine, is tied up in a knot on the top of her head. She pauses and turns around; grey eyes like storm clouds.

He tries to find words, French words. 'Bonjour, Madame,' he says, shaking her wet hand. Soap bubbles pop between their fingers.

'It's Mademoiselle,' she says, gently pulling her hand out of his. 'My mother has gone to fetch bread. I am Odette.'

'Oh good.'

'Good that I am Odette or that my mother is fetching bread?'

Alex's cheeks burn. 'It's good that you speak English. I don't.'

She looks confused.

'I mean, I don't speak French, so it's good that you do.' He winces. 'I mean, that you speak English.'

'What is your name?' she says, laughing.

'Sorry. It's Alex.'

'Your friends are through there. In the dining room,' she says, pointing.

Alex waves at Odette, turns and walks headfirst into the edge of the door.

In the dining room, Eden pours a whisky and hands it to Alex.

'Did you just walk into the door, old chap? You need to be more care-ful. Farms can be dangerous places.' He raises an eyebrow. 'Full of doors and… *beautiful mademoiselles!*'

'Are the men settled?' says Woodstone, warming the backs of his legs by a crackling fire. 'Room for everyone?'

'Yes, Sir. Four barns. We gave them an early dinner, bread and bacon. Everyone was asleep by the time we left.'

'They'll need a bit of a rest,' says Woodstone. 'But not too long. Don't want them going soft. Just a day. Then a week of training and route marches before we go into support. That should be enough time to give you and 4 Platoon a chance to get used to each other.'

'4 Platoon, Sir?'

'Yes, I'm giving you command of 4,' says Woodstone, putting on his coat. 'You'll have Sergeant Kemmell with you. He knows what's what. Hey Captain?'

'He's a good man,' says Eden, who seems to have found something floating in his whisky.

'But, Sir,' says Alex. 'I was hoping—'

'Good,' says Woodstone, buttoning his coat. 'See you both at breakfast.'

'Are you not dining with us?' says Eden.

'No, dinner at Battalion HQ.'

'But Madame Berger has been doing things in the kitchen for the whole afternoon,' says Eden. 'I don't think she'll be happy.'

'I know. I forgot,' says Woodstone, as the door closes behind him. 'Tell her it's an emergency, would you?'

Eden shakes his head at the closed door and turns to Alex. 'You should be pleased about the platoon. Some of the junior officers don't get anything for months.'

A clock ticks loudly on the mantlepiece. Alex crosses the room to examine it. 'Woodstone would never let me lead a platoon if he knew what happened.' He unclips the clock-glass and touches the delicate hands with his finger. He's shaking. He feels utterly ashamed but at the same time, something close to pride is surging in his chest. The two sensations make him feel lightheaded, numb. He should sit down. He doesn't turn around. He can feel Eden watching him.

'Everyone knows what happened, Ryan... The German patrol... You seem to be the only one who doesn't.'

Alex can hardly remember the truth now; all he can think of is the rain. He can't decide if he would rather go back to his room and lie down or run into the fields and yell. He pulls out a chair and sits at the table. Eden takes the whisky and sits opposite Alex. 'I've seen you leading. I've seen the way you handle the men.' He fills Alex's glass. 'You've already come up with some good ideas and implemented them in a way that's improved things in the trenches.'

'What? I replanned the layout of the latrines. Is that what you mean, Sir?' He's being complemented by the famous Captain Eden. He takes a long sip of the whisky to hide a smile.

Eden laughs. 'Yes, the latrines, the comms trenches and the other tasks. You're doing well! I can see that you have the potential to really make a difference here. But you have to stop this sulking, Ryan. Pull yourself together. Not just for your own sake but for the—'

The kitchen door flies open and a woman dressed in black storms in. She's holding a wooden spoon and waggles it as if she intends to crack someone's skull with it. She yells something in French. She looks strong, impressive, like she could out-kick a mule. Her weather-beaten face is beautiful.

The two officers stand and wait for her to finish shouting. Then Eden replies courteously to her in what seems to be fluent French. This calms her a little and she talks more quietly now, waving the spoon towards the window.

'It seems Woodstone didn't make it,' says Eden from the corner of his mouth. 'She spotted him crossing the courtyard.' He bows. 'Madame Berger, puis-je présenter Lieutenant Ryan.'

Alex also bows. 'Bonjour, Madam.'

Madame Berger stares at Alex, grunts and leaves the room.

Eden exhales loudly. 'I think we might be safer back in the front line.'

15

THE THIEF

The soldier stretches out his hands towards Alex, fingers splayed, chocolate dripping from them. He opens his mouth. Chocolate spews, splashing down his uniform. He begins to scream.

'What was that?' says Charlie.

Alex opens his eyes. He's in the milk shed, on the farm. He's drenched in sweat. 'I think… I must have been dreaming.'

'No. Outside. Someone was screaming.' Charlie grabs his revolver and runs out.

Alex follows. Bare feet. The courtyard is cold and wet.

Madame Berger, wrapped in a blanket and silhouetted in the kitchen doorway, is shouting.

Odette, holding a shotgun to her shoulder, is moving slowly towards the cowshed. 'Come out or I *will* shoot you!' she yells. Her nightgown flutters around her bare ankles.

Alex and Charlie, revolvers drawn, advance behind Odette.

'What's happening?' says Charlie.

'Who's there?' says Alex.

A round-faced soldier steps slowly out of the shadows. 'Don't shoot!' he says. He's holding a chicken.

Charlie steps forward. 'Price? What the hell are you doing?'

'You know him?' says Alex.

'Unfortunately, I do. He's in my unit.'

'They steal everything!' says Odette, angrily. 'Our chickens, the crops. Even a cow was taken!'

'Price, you're a fool. We could have shot you,' says Alex.

Price raises his arms towards Odette's gun, dropping the chicken. The bird squawks, flutters and runs in a zigzag back into the cowshed. 'Don't shoot, Madame. I was just off to bed. Must have got the wrong farm. I heard this chicken and I thought…' Price looks for the chicken, staggers, reaches out for something to support himself and misses. He hits the floor and ends up slouched against the barn wall.

'Are you drunk, Price?' says Charlie.

'Yes, Sir.'

'Where did you get the drink?'

'Estaminet…do Pelican, in the village,' says Price, with some difficulty. He fumbles through his tunic pockets and pulls out a card. 'I've got a pass.' Coins clatter onto the flagstones and roll away.

'Why do you steal from us?' says Odette. 'This farm, all the farms here, we are all here to feed you! How are we supposed to feed you if you take everything!'

Price shakes his head and points into the barn. 'I just…chicken.'

'Do they not feed you?' She looks at Alex. 'Do you not give your men the food that we grow for them. The eggs? The milk?'

Alex shrugs. 'We do our best.'

'Sometimes it's hard,' says Charlie. 'With the bad weather, to get fresh food up to the front line. But here, in the billets, they've been eating fairly well. We've made sure that they get extra rations to make up for what they've been missing in the line. No one's going hungry.'

'We don't have chicken,' says Price.

'Can I just say?' says Alex 'This is hardly the point, is it? Price tried to steal a chicken!'

Price kneels and places his hands together as if in prayer. 'I'm sorry.' He turns to Odette. 'I'm so sorry Madame. If I'd known this was your farm I would never have climbed over the fence.'

'It doesn't matter whose farm it is!' says Odette. 'You have no right!'

Price bows his head, sees a coin on the flagstones, starts to reach for it and gives up.

Odette lowers the gun. 'We are doing everything we can to give you what you need.' Her voice wavers and softens. 'But you still steal from us.'

Alex puts his hand on her shoulder and guides her away. Her skin feels warm in the cold air. 'I'm sorry,' he says to her, and means it. 'He'll be punished for this. He'll be arrested. We can't have them stealing animals.'

She shakes her head, brings her hand up and, just for a moment, touches Alex's fingers.

Madame Berger mumbles something and goes inside the house.

Charlie comes over. 'I think it might be better if we say nothing about the chicken. It might end very badly for him.'

'What do you mean?' says Odette.

Alex whispers. 'They can charge him for plunder, and he's drunk. He could end up getting shot for this.'

'Shot? For stealing a chicken? That is ridiculous!' she says. 'I don't want that.'

'I thought you were just about to shoot him yourself,' says Alex, smiling.

She looks upset. 'I would never do that. I just wanted him to think I would.'

'It was convincing,' says Charlie.

Price has retrieved the coin from the flagstones and is sitting with it cupped in his hands.

'He's a good man, a good soldier,' whispers Charlie.

'We should just say he was drunk,' says Alex. 'He'll get a field punishment and—'

'What's happening here? Why is there a soldier sitting on the floor?' Woodstone has arrived with Eden.

Alex stands to attention. 'I'm afraid he's drunk, Sir. Must have got

77

lost on his way back from the village and wandered in here by mistake.'

Charlie nods in agreement. 'He's one of mine, Sir. Private John Price.'

Eden walks over to Price. 'Get up for me would you?' he says quietly.

Price pushes himself up and stands awkwardly. He looks small opposite the captain.

'Where is your rifle?' says Eden.

Alex hadn't noticed; Price doesn't have his rifle.

Price looks around his feet. 'Must have left it leaned up against the fence, Sir.'

'Did I see you earlier, in the Pelican?' Eden is almost whispering.

'Yes, Sir. We had time off.' He fumbles in his pocket. 'I've got a pass.'

'And you've lost your rifle?'

Price looks over his shoulder. 'Not exactly, Sir. I think—'

'Look at me for a moment would you?'

As Price looks up, Eden slaps him hard across the cheekbone.

Price falls back, cries out, sprawling across the flagstones.

'Steady, Eden,' says Woodstone.

Alex looks at Charlie and shakes his head.

Odette runs over and stands between Eden and Price. 'What are you doing?'

'He's just drunk, Sir,' says Alex, stepping forward.

Eden stares coldly. 'He's drunk. He's trespassing and he's abandoned his weapon.'

'There is no need for that!' says Odette, firmly. 'You don't have to be violent. He was answering your questions.'

Eden smiles. 'I believe you're the one holding the gun.'

Woodstone laughs. 'You don't need your gun, Mademoiselle. You don't need to be afraid. We will look after you.'

'I am not afraid. And you think you will look after me? Is that what you think? The reason I need a gun at all is because of you.'

Woodstone looks around for support 'I'm sure you don't mean that. We are officers. You're quite safe with us.'

Odette laughs. 'I am not safe. No one is since you came here.'

'But we are here to protect you and your, your people,' says Woodstone. 'So perhaps, Mademoiselle, you should be more grateful.'

Odette glares at Woodstone. 'We didn't ask you to come here. None of us did. You are not guests on this farm. We are obliged to give you food and shelter. That is all. And since you came here, bad things have happened. Our animals and equipment have been stolen and... other things, with the soldiers... We are not safe.'

'I put it back. I'm sure I did,' says Price, starting to crawl away into the barn.

'Quiet, Price!' says Charlie. 'And stay where you are.'

Price looks confused and rubs his cheek, as if he's already forgotten what's happened.

'I think, what Captain Woodstone means,' says Eden. 'Is that we are here to protect you from the *Germans*. If we were not here, God knows what would have become of you and your farm.' He steps closer to Odette. She doesn't move away, she stares up at him.

Alex wants to step between them, push Eden away, but he doesn't move.

'The Germans will know you are staying here,' says Odette. 'We were safer before you came.'

Eden curls his fingers gently around Odette's arm. 'I don't think that's true. But these men, our men, are supposed to be protecting you, but they can't do that if they're drunk. Can they, Price?'

'No, Sir,' says Price, quietly.

'I'm sorry about this, Odette,' says Eden, 'I'm sorry about whatever has happened. These things shouldn't happen. They won't happen any more.'

Alex watches to see if Odette will move her arm away from Eden, but she stays quite still. 'So Price is here to protect me from the Germans,' she says. 'You are here to protect me from Price, but who will protect me from you?'

Eden takes a deep breath and smiles back at Alex. 'That's a good point, Mademoiselle! Perhaps you should keep that gun under your pillow.'

Odette yanks her arm away and glares.

'Where is Fenton?' says Eden.

'He went into the village, Sir,' says Charlie.

'Fetch him, would you? And bring Gibbons too. Have them escort Price to the billet guardhouse. We can deal with him in the morning.'

Odette stares at Eden, taking deep, slow breaths. She's still for a moment then storms into the house.

Eden smiles. 'Right. Bedtime. Early start. Goodnight, Gentlemen.'

'Well done, everyone,' says Woodstone, following Eden.

Charlie sighs. 'That could have gone a lot worse.'

'What do you think he'll get?'

'Field punishment number two probably. Tied up for a bit and lose some pay… Are you listening?'

'She touched my hand.' says Alex, staring at the kitchen door.

'My God,' says Charlie, walking away. 'When will this war be over? I'm surrounded by madmen.'

16

PARSNIPS

The sun has cleared the trees along the sides of the fields and it's already warm. Mist lingers in the hedgerows. Little birds cut through it, casting grey shadows against the gold. Cobwebs and wet grass quiver.

He reaches into his tunic pocket and feels the rough edges of his sketchbook. It hasn't been opened a single time since he's been in France. Not because he's been too busy; the officers have plenty of time to attend to their own, un-military, interests when they're behind the lines. But sketching has seemed so pointless, so trivial. Who would the sketches be for? Who would see them? He's never sold any. No gallery is hanging any of his paintings. And what would he draw? How could he even begin to describe what he's seeing here every day? If he looks in one direction, all he sees is trees and canals and sunlight shimmering on the backs of dairy cows. In the other direction: severed limbs and broken skulls oozing out of the blood-soaked mud. Each point of view would be dismissive of the other. It's the juxtaposition, the collision of this idyllic, pastoral life and the mangled horror of the trenches that he needs to express. He doesn't know how.

But last night, Alex lay in bed, staring up into the dark corners of the room, and he realised that he just needs to start sketching again. It doesn't matter what or where at the beginning; he just needs to start. And he thought about Odette; the place where she touched him, burning like a nettle, and he decided that the subject of his first sketches might as well be her. This morning, as she served breakfast, she hadn't looked at him, just a quick smile as she handed him a jug of milk. No touch; the tiny curve of porcelain between them was a chasm. But he felt that she had felt that too. And her not looking at him had been deliberate.

So he's striding along the lane towards her. Gravel twisting satisfyingly beneath his boots. He's going to tell her about his sketches and ask her if she'll sit for him. He wants to draw her in this light. Take her into the fields behind the farm, away from the others, away from Eden. She might be interested, flattered, even.

An officer's tunic is hanging on a fence post by the side of the lane. Voices are coming from the field. Eden is standing with Odette between rows of low, wilted plants. He looks strong in the sunshine; his shirt, tight across his chest and the sleeves rolled up. His voice is raised. He's pulling a basket away from her. It looks like they're arguing. Odette might even be crying.

Last night, when she stood up to Eden, Alex did nothing. He wished he'd said something to support her. But what could he have done? One word against a superior officer and Alex would probably have been tied right next to Price. He should go over to them and stand with her. He doesn't have to say anything. Eden can't punish him for that.

Alex ducks through a gap in the hedgerow, pushes through the grasses, breaking cobwebs, walking out into the soft soil and lines of wilted plants. As he gets closer, he realises Odette isn't angry, she's laughing.

He pauses in the sunlight, caught between them and the safety of the road. They both have their backs to him. They haven't seen him. He turns around, fists clenched, walks back along the furrows.

'Careful where you're treading, Lieutenant!' calls Eden.

Alex closes his eyes and breathes. He turns around and waves.

Odette waves back.

Eden walks over. 'I thought these crops were dead but they're parsnips.' He brushes soil off a thin white root and holds it out to Alex. 'Odette says the plants wilt after the first frosts, but they leave them in the ground the whole winter and pull them out as they need them. Stay fresh that way for the whole spring.'

Odette is pulling parsnips out of the dirt, twisting and snapping the soft leaves.

Alex takes the parsnip from Eden. 'I've been doing kit inspections, Sir. I saw you were in the field.'

Odette stands up and walks over with the basket. She's smiling, but no differently than she would at anyone who has just wandered off the road.

'Did Lieutenant Pope sort everything with Price?' says Eden.

'Yes, they tied him to the front gate.'

'Good. Two hours each day until we go back to the front. The men will see him each time they go to the village. Remind them to behave themselves.'

'How was he?' says Odette.

'A headache and feeling sorry for himself, I think,' says Alex.

'I told the Captain he mustn't be too hard on them. He has to be fair,' says Odette, waving her finger at Eden. She's pretending to be angry.

Eden wraps his hand around her finger. 'I'm always fair.'

She glances at Alex and pulls her finger away.

Alex feels his limbs grow heavy. He wants to turn around and walk back to the road.

'Have you come to help?' says Odette.

Alex doesn't know what to say. He doesn't know if she wants him to. 'I was walking back to the farm. I've got inventories to write up for the quartermaster.'

'Then you won't need that,' says Eden, taking the parsnip from Alex and throwing it into Odette's basket. It makes her jump. She scowls at him and walks back to the parsnips.

Eden grins and rolls his eyes. 'I'm riding out to take a look at the

83

new trenches near Richebourg. We're taking over that section from the 11th in a week and I want to get a feel for the land. Do you want to come along? It's a lovely day, I think the winter is finally over. We could pick up some wine and cheese on the way back. Make a picnic of it.'

'I'm supposed to be helping with musket training this afternoon,' says Alex. 'We lost our instructor and they haven't sent us a new one.'

'Sergeant Kemmell can do that. They won't need you. I'll tell Woodstone I need some sketches of the trench layout. He'll let you go if I tell him that.' Eden calls to Odette. 'Alex is an artist. He's going to be a great painter one day. Did he tell you?'

Odette smiles curiously. 'No, he didn't.'

Alex looks at his feet. 'It's not really...They're just sketches—'

'I'll find you a horse from somewhere,' says Eden, 'You ride don't you?'

'I do, Sir. I did. I haven't for a while.'

'Good. Eleven o'clock.'

'Yes, Sir.'

Eden turns away and goes back to Odette.

Odette says something that Alex doesn't understand.

Eden laughs.

Alex watches them for a moment. He mumbles a goodbye; too quiet for them to hear. And walks back to the farm.

17

MILK

A group of chickens is scratching in the corner of the yard. Their red backs shine in the sunlight.

Alex follows the plump curves with his pencil; circles, roundness, errant feathers. He doesn't want to, but he's waiting for Odette. He hopes she'll come back, alone. He keeps looking up towards the road. He should stop thinking about her. The way she had behaved with him is how she is with everyone; friendly, interested.

The chicken sketches are good. He'll keep this page open until she comes. He cross-hatches a shadow.

But the way she seems to be with Eden; it's different somehow, she's more... He needs to stop thinking about her. He closes the sketchbook.

The birds have wandered into the cowshed.

He follows them.

The cows are in the barn, chewing, shifting their weight. Dust sparkles above them. The nearest one is coloured like weathered sandstone. She watches him, the whole barn curving around her brown and glassy eye.

He kneels down next to her and strokes the flat, dusty jaw. She leans into him, presses her nose up against his hand and breathes out sharply with a satisfying hiss.

'She likes you.' Odette is behind him. She's carrying a stool and two buckets.

'I like cows,' he says, standing up too fast and almost falling against the cow. 'My father has a farm with cows.' He doesn't know what to do with his hands. He slaps the cow on the neck. Dust puffs out and fills the sunlight in the doorway. He tries not to cough.

'Can you milk?' she says.

'Yes.' He thinks he might be blushing.

'Then you can help me. Come and wash.' She holds Alex by the hand, pulls him outside to the water pump in the middle of the yard. He feels the coolness of her hand on his. She gestures towards his tunic. He takes it off and rolls up his sleeves. She works the pump. Air hisses in the pipe. It smells of moss and forests. Sunlight glistens as the water runs cold across his hands and falls into the damp darkness below the grate and he feels as if she's pumping laughter.

She leads him back into the barn, to a row of clothes that's hanging from hooks along the wall. 'These were my father's. I don't know why we haven't given them away.' She rifles through them: trousers, shirts, coats. She hands a jacket to Alex. 'Put this on so you don't ruin your shirt.'

The jacket smells of old sweat and dust. It's comforting; it reminds him of his own father.

She moves between the cows, pushing them apart, places the stool and bucket down, then stands back, smiling. Alex sits down, strokes the cow in a long arc from its back down to the ankle, grips the warm teats in his hands, pulls gently and squeezes, finger by finger, top to bottom. The milk squirts in. It smells sweet. He works carefully and calmly. The cow is calm too. She's a good cow.

Odette stands with her fists on her hips, watching as the bucket fills. 'Bon.' She gets a box from the corner of the barn, moves over to the next cow and starts to milk. Her shoulders rise and twist. Her neck muscles flex behind her collar bone. She moves the bucket lightly with her foot.

Doves coo softly somewhere on the roof. The cow's great ribs move in and out against Alex's face. He breathes with the cow, breathes into the shadowed spaces in the barn, breathes into the sunbeams and the sunlit dust between him and the cows and the French farm girl. He's happy.

When all three cows have been milked, they carry the full buckets into the kitchen.

'Where *is* your father?' he says.

'He's gone,' she says, dismissively, pouring the milk through a cloth into a metal urn. 'You said your father has a farm. Is your mother there too?'

He pauses, leaning back against the table in the middle of the kitchen, wondering if he should ignore her question and ask her more about her father. 'My mother died when I was a child,' he says.

'I'm so sorry.' She puts down the bucket. 'Was she ill?'

'It was a fire, in a barn at my parents' farm.'

She moves around the table and touches his arm.

His instinct is to flinch, to move away, but he breathes into it, feeling the warmth of her hand against his arm and suddenly he wants to tell her. 'She was feeding the horses and something, something happened, a lamp must have turned over, I don't know.'

Odette puts her hand over her mouth and squeezes his arm. 'How old were you?'

'I was eight.'

'Oh, Alex. You were so little.' She's rubbing his arm and looking so closely at him, he has to look away.

Something lurches in his lungs and he gasps. He turns it into a laugh. 'I'm sorry, I... This week, at the front, it's all been very... difficult.'

'Alex—'

Horses in the yard outside.

'Ryan!' Eden is yelling. 'Ryan. Come out! I stole you a horse!'

Alex goes to the kitchen window.

Eden, riding one horse and leading another, is circling around the water pump.

'I'm sorry,' says Alex. 'I have to go.'

She walks over to him and turns his face towards hers with the tips of her fingers. 'You can talk to me, if you need to.'

'Ryan! What are you doing in there?' Eden has ridden up to the window and is peering in. '*Oh*, I see!' He says, grinning.

18

THE PICNIC

Outside a little shop on the far side of the village, Alex is holding the horses. The sunshine warms their flanks. They smell of dust and leather. Eden is inside, buying food for the picnic. Food tins and wine bottles are set out on shelves behind the arched windows. In front of the window, an old woman sits at a table, hammering holes through a strip of leather that looks exactly like her own skin. She's a white bonneted, dried up apple. Each time she hits with the hammer, despite, or because of everything they endure, the horses flinch. She mumbles something to Alex, points at the horses and giggles like a child.

Eden comes out with cheese and bread and two bottles of wine. A young woman in a red bonnet follows him to the door. He says something to her and she laughs. 'Its harvest time,' he says to Alex, as he loads the provisions into the saddlebags.

'What do you mean?'

'Look at her. Look at the way she's looking at us.'

The girl is leaning against the doorframe, smiling at the two officers.

'I've seen it everywhere,' says Eden. 'These villages, the ones that haven't been bombed to powder, the men are away fighting or dead.

All the things the men used to do just don't get done. The tiles fall off the roofs, cartwheels fall off the carts and the crops don't get harvested.' He leans conspiratorially across the horse. 'And one of the crops, the women... are forgotten!'

The old woman slams the hammer down with a loud crack. The horses' heads fly up. She giggles.

Eden mounts. 'It may be spring but it's always harvest time here!' He smiles at the girl. She waves as he rides away.

Alex mounts and rides to catch up. 'I assume you don't have a girl back home, Sir?'

'Why do you assume that? Here and home are quite different places.'

They ride past a field with rows of horse-drawn cannon. Cavalrymen at the side of the road are backing a team of horses towards a gun. Alex's horse is nervous and skips sideways into the road. Eden reaches out, grabs the halter and the horse calms instantly.

'What about you, Ryan?' he says, as if nothing has happened. 'I haven't seen you writing any letters. You're a handsome enough chap. Is there no pretty little thing sitting sadly at her window, waiting for the postman?'

Alex has never understood this idea of feeling sad in the absence of someone you love. He's never felt it himself, but he's often thought that being apart from one's lover must feel like having a silver thread running through the air between the two of you; however far apart, you would feel its delicate pull. It would feel beautiful; a spider's silk connection that would stretch you both out from your own centres, towards each other. He thinks of Odette, tries to imagine that thread rushing out from his back, up over the fields and trees towards the farm. This tiny line, pulling against her skin under her blouse and wrapping around her heart. He struggles not to mention her. But he doesn't want to hear Eden talk about her in the same way he talks about these other girls. In fact, Alex hasn't been able to stop thinking about her, but he can't say that. Eden would laugh. 'I need to write to my father, but there's no one else back home.'

'Probably for the best, I would say,' says Eden, as they turn onto a grassy lane that runs through a wood.

'Why do you say that?' says Alex, not really wanting to hear the reply.

'Well, there's nothing more distracting than a lover. There's nothing worse, if you need a good night's sleep. But more importantly, officers who have... *attachments* are far less comfortable with the idea of dying than the rest of us, so they're more reluctant to take the risks.'

Alex winces to himself. 'But I thought we shouldn't be taking risks.'

'On the contrary. The risk-takers become either fools or heroes. We can ignore the fools; no one will ever hear about them. But if you take a risk and you succeed, it's good for the battalion; puts us on the map. It's good for morale, for the men and for everyone back home.' Eden slows his horse and turns to Alex. 'I've got hopes for you, Ryan. You need to stay focused and you'll be all right.'

The horses relax and soften as they move away from the road. Sunlight shines yellow through the backs of new leaves. They tie the horses and walk out to a place where they can see for a long way. Beyond the trees are broad, flat fields that lift gently up to a ridge on the horizon. Swathes of green and silver light move through the grasses. Birdsong drifts up, the trees sway in a soft breeze.

'We could be in Hampshire, about to wander down for a spot of cricket,' says Eden, filling his pipe. 'But look over there. That's the German trenches.' He points to a zig-zagged line that curves away ahead of them. It looks like an infected cut, puckered and swollen along either side. A grey gash running right through the landscape. 'And just on the other side of that hill, over there, is our line. Funny to think that somewhere at the end of this green and pleasant land there are men drowning in mud, screaming for their mothers.' He thumbs tobacco into his pipe.

'It looks so peaceful,' says Alex. 'I hardly even noticed the sound of the guns. The things that happen, in those trenches, it feels like a bad dream from up here.'

'Lunch!' yells Eden, pulling the wine out of the saddlebag.

'Are we safe here?' says Alex.

'Yes, of course. There's nothing for them to shoot at in this direction. I'll show you later, but I'm hungry. Let's eat.' Eden carries the food over to a low dry-stone wall at the edge of the trees.

Alex cuts the bread with the folding knife that his father gave him.

He thinks of his father's empty house; the smoothness of the walls and the silence in the hallways. 'Do you have family back home, Sir?'

'My parents are... *important* people,' says Eden, with a smile that fades quickly. 'I see them when I'm summoned. We're not close.'

'You have brothers or sisters?'

Eden shrugs. 'I... *had* a brother.' That's all he says. They eat the bread with the cheese and drink the wine from mugs that Eden has brought from the saddlebags.

'I lost my mother,' says Alex, feeling hopeful for something, he's not sure what, a connection between them, perhaps.

Eden chews, staring at Alex. 'What? Dead?' he says with a mouth still full of food.

'Yes, when I was a child. A fire.' Why has he told Eden this? Is he trying to prove to himself that Eden isn't interested?

A wood pigeon flaps out of the shadows and glides into the light. A column of ants is walking up the wall, collecting bread crumbs and returning into the grass.

'How old was your brother when he died?' says Alex.

Eden takes a gulp of the wine and shakes his head. 'No, I didn't mean he's dead. I chose to lose him, if you like, in Africa.'

'What happened?'

Eden looks away. 'He let me down.'

'Was this something to do with a woman?' says Alex, managing a smile.

Eden takes the knife, cuts off a chunk of cheese. 'No, we were always very forgiving with that. No, this was... We fought together, Henry and I, the same regiment. We'd attacked a camp, it had gone horribly wrong. We were withdrawing under heavy fire and I was on foot, injured, couldn't run. Thought it was the end, really. Then Henry

was there with his horse, saw me, but didn't stop. Rode right past.'
The wind gusts in the trees. Eden looks up, pauses, looking at something beyond the swaying branches. 'It took me a while to get back to
the regiment, quite a while.' He smiles. 'We haven't spoken since.'
He's talking softly as if he's alone. 'He was scared of course, but we
all were.' Eden places the knife across the line of ants that are walking
along the wall, watches them doubling back, circling, climbing over.
'So when even your own *brother*...' He jabs the knife towards his
chest. 'What I'm saying is, *I* got *myself* back. Do you see? No one else.'

Alex is fascinated. He stares at Eden; the hero, the man he'd read
so much about in the papers, now sitting a few feet away from him,
crossed legged in the grass, chewing a lump of bread and cheese.
There's one whisker from Eden's moustache that's longer than the
others. It droops down below the line of his top lip. He's subliminally
aware of it and touches it with his tongue occasionally as he talks. He
seems so human, so normal. 'Did you not say anything to your
brother when you got back?' says Alex.

Eden stares into the grass. 'The French, terrible trenches.' He
picks up the bottle and finishes the wine. 'Terrible trenches, but
splendid wine... if you know where to ask.'

Alex waits to see if Eden will come back to the subject of his
brother, then says, 'What's wrong with their trenches?'

Eden hurls the empty bottle into the trees. It spins, silver and
green flashes in the dappled sunlight. The sound of breaking glass
echoes through the wood. 'You'll see when we move into this new
sector. The French built everything. Shoddy, second-rate. Scrape a
bayonet along a wall and the damned roof caves in. They spend more
time on interior decorations than they do on their battlements.'

'Interior decorations?'

'You'll see. Pictures on the walls, curtains, even patterned wallpaper in one of them!' He takes a second bottle of wine, uncorks it
with his teeth and fills both mugs.

'Curtains? That's ridiculous!' Alex laughs awkwardly, pauses, 'But
I have actually been thinking about this.' He watches Eden, to see if
this is all right. 'I was thinking that, if we spent a bit more time

making better dugouts, I mean, warmer and better protected from the weather, then the men might sleep better, have fewer health problems.'

Eden drinks. 'You sound like Pope. He treats his men like women at the seaside.' He drinks again. 'Perhaps we could arrange to have fresh flowers in the dugouts, silk sheets and a couple of whores for each platoon?'

Alex feels a sting of panic. 'No, I mean, I just thought, if they were less tired and cold, they'd be able to think and act faster, they would be—'

'The men don't need to think. We do the thinking.' Eden pours the rest of the wine. 'I do like the way you're thinking now; how to make things better, more efficient, but don't worry too much about the men.'

'But they still have to go over the bags, and fight and face death, the same way we do.'

Eden laughs. 'How often do you think they actually fight? How many Germans have *you* even seen in the entire time you've been here?'

Alex hasn't actually seen a single *living* German. He shrugs.

'Exactly,' says Eden, smiling.

'But they still have to dig, and carry things all day.'

'They don't have to carry anything very far.' Eden points the knife at the column of ants. 'They're like these chaps. One man picks up a sack and if something happens to him, if a shell comes and cuts him in half...' He turns the knife on its side and carefully squashes one of the ants. Its legs twitch, the head thrashing from side to side until it slows and stops. 'Then another man will come from behind, pick up the sack and carry it a little further.'

Alex watches Eden; hunched over, gripping the knife, transfixed by the panic rippling through the ants that are crowding around the dead one.

Eden wipes the blade between his fingers. 'They don't need to carry the sack all the way. Just a bit further than the ant before them.'

'Is that why you killed Higgit? Because he wouldn't be able to carry any more sacks?' Alex is surprised by the strength of his own words but the wine feels like a visor, protecting them both from the confrontation.

'I didn't kill Higgit, Wislawa did. But that's a good example. That was a coup de grâce. He would never have made it.' Eden narrows his eyes. 'It takes a lot of resources to look after an injured man. Higgit knew that. He was a good soldier.'

'You sound like you think the sack is more important than the men,' says Alex.

Eden hands the knife back to Alex and stands up. 'Sacks, men; they're equally important. The *objective* is to get the sack where it's needed.' He's already walking away. 'Come on. We're supposed to be looking at these trenches. What do you think this is, a damn picnic?'

Alex takes a deep breath. He collects what's left of the food and follows Eden back to the horses.

19

COMPANY HQ

A little wooden gate opens onto a tranquil garden. A curving, flagstone path, slippery in rain that hasn't stopped for two days, leads past rose bushes to D Company headquarters; a delicate, red-bricked townhouse that seems to be surviving the worst of the war.

Alex shakes off his coat and walks into the wood-panelled drawing-room, where the officers sit drinking tea in china cups.

Charlie is slumped in a chair at the back. 'Where've you been? I was just nodding off,' he says, tapping an empty chair that he's saved for Alex.

A wrinkled old man, presumably the owner of the house, immediately appears and serves Alex a vibrating cup of tea. It tinkles against the saucer.

'I was undertaking a vital mission for Woodstone,' says Alex, sitting. 'Then I had to help Odette with the cows.'

Laughter bursts out from a huddle of officers at the end of the room. Eden seems to be enthralling them with an amusing story. There's a skinny man who Alex hasn't seen before, sitting upright and still, teaspoon poised above his tea like a heron on the edge of a lake. This must be Lieutenant Halsall, back from Vickers machine gun training.

Woodstone's adjutant, Lieutenant Lindsey, freckle-faced and bottle green eyes, is pointing to places on a map that's been rolled out on a table in the middle of the room. He's trying to explain something to Woodstone, but Woodstone is laying out his pencils and doesn't seem to be listening.

'Have I missed anything?' says Alex, sipping his tea.

'Shortbread,' says Charlie. 'But I think there'll be a second round.'

'Are we winning?'

'The war? I'm not sure. If they said, I must have been asleep.'

'Where were you all night?' says Alex. 'I didn't see you at breakfast.'

'Eden had me leading a working party, delivering a huge set of bellows up to the front-line. It'll eventually pump fresh air into a mine they're digging right under the Boche. Until last night, I had no idea the mine was even there. I had no time to wash before coming here. I'm still covered in half an inch of mud under this tunic. What was your vital mission for Woodstone?'

The old man returns with a plate of shortbread biscuits and rattles it loudly under Alex's chin. 'He ordered me to make a list of all the soldiers in the company who play musical instruments. So I spent the night gathering the information, and making a form. It was rather good. So is this shortbread! I laid out the names of each musician, the instruments they played, with levels from beginner to professional.'

'Whatever for?' says Charlie.

'I've no idea. When I proudly handed it to Woodstone at breakfast, he couldn't remember why he'd asked me to do it.'

'Excuse me Gentlemen!' calls Woodstone, tapping his cup with a spoon. 'Before we start. I'm sorry to inform you of the unfortunate death of Lieutenant Hartman.'

The officers look blankly at each other.

'Hartman, Sir?' says Charlie.

'Yes, new chap. Came in last night.'

'He didn't actually make it to us here at D Company,' says Lindsey. 'Hit by a five-nine on the outskirts of the village.'

'Of this village?' says Eden.

'Yes, very close to the church.'

Eden grunts. 'That's a shame. He sounds like he would have been exactly the kind of officer that this regiment needs; a good planner; dying right next to the cemetery!'

The officers laugh.

'Talking of... of such matters,' says Halsall, clearing his throat. 'When should we expect the memorial service for Captain Kingsman, Sir? It was a terrible shock for me to hear of his death. I was away when it happened. Such a fine commander, and a friend. I should very much like to pay my respects, as I'm sure would every man here.'

A soft mumble of agreement rolls around the room.

Alex's stomach tightens. He slides down into his chair.

'You all right?' says Charlie. 'You've paled.'

Alex nods and flashes a smile.

'Well, I think we have enough now, so we'll organise something,' says Woodstone.

'Enough what, Sir?' says Lindsey.

Woodstone coughs and turns the map around, so that it's facing out into the room. 'Shall we look at the plan?'

The officers gather, bringing their tea cups with them.

Printed in black: fields, woods, villages and farms. Hand-drawn in blue, down the west side of the map, like cracks in plaster, are the British trenches. To the east, looking dangerous in red, are the German trenches.

Woodstone, reading from his notebook, announces the raid: 'Reports suggest that several Boche battalions are forming in the area directly in front of the left sub-sector at Festubert.'

'How dare they!' someone shouts from the back. Everyone laughs.

Woodstone continues. 'Command has requested a full battalion raid with the objective of securing prisoners in order to ascertain the identity of the German regiments and their intention.'

The officers cheer politely and take out their notebooks.

Woodstone looks delighted, as if he's just announced a marriage.

'Finally,' says Halsall. 'Action!'

Lindsey takes over. 'At zero three hundred hours, an artillery barrage will cut the wire in front of the Boche line, here, and wipe out these machine guns, here and here.' He points to places marked on the map with arrows and crosses. '3 Platoon will advance across No Man's Land, under cover of a smoke screen laid down by artillery. In total silence. Centre, led by Francourt with Pope in second. 4 Platoon, left flank, led by Ryan with Sergeant Kemmell.'

Charlie catches Alex's eye and smiles. Alex tries to smile back. He can feel his heart beating in his throat. He loosens his tie.

'Then, 2 Platoon, led by Captain Eden, will advance to halfway and wait. 3 and 4 will enter the Boche trench, here, and here respectively. Once in, fire a green flare. On sight of that signal, 2 enter at the right flank. All units will then work their way along, capturing live prisoners and collecting any paperwork, maps, order books etcetera, before returning to our own line.'

The room erupts with excited chatter.

'Now gentlemen, settle down please!' shouts Woodstone. 'Captain Lindsey doesn't have much time.'

'Why is my platoon waiting before platoons 3 and 4 go in?' says Eden, taking out his smoking kit and unrolling it next to the map.

'No particular reason,' says Lindsey. 'I just allocated positions to each platoon.'

'Then, with my experience, wouldn't it be better if I went in first and have 2 wait for *my* signal?'

'Er, well. I've already—'

'I'm quite happy to have Captain Eden go in first, if that's better for everyone, Sir?' says, Alex, hopefully. He would much rather be at the back for this one. That way, it's less likely that anyone will accidentally die.

Lindsey looks at Woodstone.

'Lets keep things as they are for now shall we?' says Woodstone. 'See what Ryan can do with a bit of responsibility?'

Eden doesn't reply. He squints at Alex for a moment, lights his pipe and stares at the map.

Alex takes a deep breath. He knows he has to do this. It can't be avoided. He moves closer to the map. He must listen to every word, understand everything.

Lindsey explains how the ammunition and supplies will be brought up to the front, the positions of signallers, hospital field stations and where telephone lines have been laid.

'Excuse me, Sir. Where will I be?' says Halsall.

'Platoon 1, in reserve, I'm afraid, Richard,' says Lindsey, walking out the door.

Halsall looks despondent. The officers throw him sympathetic looks.

Woodstone coughs. 'Now, if you've all had enough tea—'

'What if the wire isn't cut?' says Eden.

Woodstone looks worried. 'There's no reason to think it won't be. I've been told the artillery have been getting excellent results. The Boche are going to get a hell of a show.'

'Of course,' says Eden, puffing out a cloud of smoke. 'But if it isn't?'

Woodstone blinks then stares at the map. 'If the wire is not cut then...' He shrugs. 'Cut it yourselves. The quartermaster will give you plenty of wire-cutters. Now, tea cups back on the sideboard, please.'

Coats are lifted from hooks on the back of the door and the officers begin to file out of the house, into the rain.

Eden is still standing by the table. 'If we're advancing along the trench from both ends to here,' he says, tapping the map with his pipe. 'Then we've effectively taken this whole section. One third of this trench. Why not bring in Halsall's platoon and hold it? We can then extend our line up from this sap, block this off, here, and we've cut off the Hun, turning this into a salient.'

Woodstone doesn't seem to be focusing. He slides his finger around the map as if he's imagining stirring the mud with a huge spoon. 'Quite.'

Eden waits. 'So?'

Woodstone continues to stir. 'Erm... That's more of a specific, strategy question.' He clears his throat. 'You should have asked Captain Lindsey when he was here.' He finds a shortbread crumb on the map and brushes it onto the floor. 'I think... This is not meant to be about gaining ground... More about raising the men's fighting spirit.'

'Fighting spirit!' says Eden, looking at Alex. 'You hear that, Ryan?'

Alex walks to the window. He doesn't want to get caught up in whatever this is between Eden and Woodstone. Rain splatters against the glass. In the garden a small brown bird is picking at something on the lawn.

Woodstone rolls up the map. 'Command said the men have done nothing but twiddle their thumbs and polish their bayonets for weeks. This will get them excited. There's nothing better for the morale of the troops than a damned good show.'

Eden walks to the door and puts on his coat. He turns to Alex. 'You see, Ryan? No one actually cares about how far the men carry the sack. It's all about how *excited* they are to be carrying it.' He slams the door behind him.

Woodstone looks at Alex. 'What does that mean? What sack?'

Outside the window, the bird tugs, and a worm is stretched until it snaps.

20

WAITING

He's making loose drawings in his sketchbook. There's hardly any light, just a smudge of brighter charcoal behind the barbed wire and wooden posts. He's feeling his way across the paper with the pencil, staring out over the sandbags, towards the ground they will run through when the time comes.

A young fox screams. Alex shivers.

The Hun must have heard it too; crouching in the cold behind their sandbags, staring out into the same darkness.

It's calming; focussing on something other than what's about to happen. The wire, the grass, the mud strewn with bully beef tins, the Maconochie stew tins, the Milkmaid milk tins, the Mörser shells, the bullet casings, the skulls in rusting helmets.

Below him, along the trench, dim lamplight illuminates pale faces. Alex's men wait, hunch-backed and huddled in the trench, reading, smoking, playing soft-voiced card games.

Earlier, the officer's mess was bursting with excited laughter, singing even. A nervous energy that reminded Alex of the dressing rooms at school before the Christmas play. He's not nervous, he's afraid. Sick with it. He couldn't eat a thing at dinner. He can't say that to anyone. And that seems to make it worse. If he shows any fear to his men, they won't trust him. He has to be strong. He has to be brave. He takes a deep breath and tries to breathe away the fear. He closes the sketchbook, climbs down and makes his way along the trench, marking off the names of his men. 'Good luck and remember to hold the formation.' He wants to say a few words to each one of them. 'Where are you from, Reginald?'

'Lewes, Sir.' A cigarette flaps limply on the edge of the soldier's lip. 'How long have we got before we go over, Sir?'

'The bombardment will start in about an hour. We go as soon as it lifts. Good luck.'

Percy is sitting away from the others, hugging his knees.

'How are you, Private Elphick?'

'All right, Sir. Bit nervous, I think.'

'Listen to Sergeant Kemmell, and to me, to our instructions. Watch what the others do. Stubbs will show you. Stay with him and if no one tells you to get up, stay down.' Alex manages a smile. 'Just do that and everything will be all right.' It sounds simple when he says the words. He needs to listen to his own words.

Percy nods, wide eyed.

'Lamps out!' yells Kemmell.

Lamp by lamp, the light fades until the platoon is in complete darkness.

'It's very dark,' says Percy.

'It's good that it's dark,' says Alex. 'The Boche won't see us. Your eyes will get used to it, then you'll be able to see again and then it will be dawn.'

A slow, sad song reaches them from far away along the trench.

'I had a letter from my Mum,' says Percy, when the song finishes. 'She fusses I'll get too cold. Stubbs tried to help me but I didn't know what to write back.'

'Just tell her that you're keeping warm. It's hard for them to understand. She doesn't need to know too much.'

Percy tugs his sleeves across his wrists. 'I am a bit cold though.'

'Do you not have gloves? I think we can get you some. Remind me tomorrow when we get back in.' Alex rolls up Percy's gas hood and fastens it. 'You need to fix this properly under your helmet, so it doesn't fall down over your face while you're running. And remember, if you have to use it, you must tuck it into the neck of your tunic.'

'I can't see when I'm wearing it. The goggles steam up.'

'You must wear it, if there's gas. You must, even if you can't see. Just sit down and don't move. But never take it off. Do you understand?' Alex tightens Percy's canvas straps. All his equipment is too big for him. It hangs off him like it's been thrown over a coat stand. 'When did you sign up, Percy?'

'October, 1914, in Brighton.'

'So you must have been what, fourteen, when you enlisted?'

'I signed up with my brother, David. He came over earlier. I came later. David wrote a letter to ask them if I could come be with him and they said I could.'

'David? Is he here, in this company? Have I met him?'

'I don't think so. He was killed at Loos on the 25th of September. Then they sent me to this battalion instead.'

Alex doesn't know what to say. He sighs. 'We'll be all right. I'm sure of it.' He squeezes Percy's arm and moves along the trench. He makes jokes with the men: about the cold, the waiting, the Hun, anything he can think of. Nothing he says is actually funny. The men are laughing to be polite, but they are as nervous as he is and probably have better things to think about than his bad jokes. He should stop making jokes.

'Albert Worthington, Sir,' says a soldier with skin like a lemon.

Alex ticks his name off the list.

Rowlands, standing nearby, offers Alex and then Worthington a cigarette.

'*Black Cat?*' says Worthington, indignantly. 'No thanks. *Muratti's Ariston* is my tobacco of choice.'

Rowlands laughs.

'My wife sends them to me, Sir,' says Worthington to Alex, ignoring Rowlands. 'She knows what I like. It's a superior cigarette. Everyone knows that.' He rests his rifle against the sandbags and stands straight, daintily clasping an imaginary cigarette in his fingers.

'Here we go,' mutters Rowlands.

Worthington clears his throat theatrically. *'Muratti's Ariston. With the full exotic aroma that one associates with shadow-bound mosques, spice laden breezes, strange, priceless perfumes and the alluring sweetness of the East!'*

Rowlands laughs.

Worthington lifts his chin and turns his back on Rowlands. 'I assume you are familiar with them, Sir? The packet says that it's the only cigarette that officers smoke.'

'I'm not familiar with any cigarette,' says Alex. 'I don't smoke and I've never asked what the other officers smoke.'

'Well, I'm certain that if you was to ask, Sir, you'd find they smoke *Muratti's Ariston*. They are *discerning*.'

Rowlands laughs louder.

'Rowlands smokes *Black Cat*,' says Worthington. 'That's why his wife left him. My wife would leave me if I smoked *Black Cat*.'

'Oh yeah?' Rowlands yells. 'The last time I was on leave, your wife didn't complain about me smoking *Black Cat*... In her fucking bed!'

Worthington grabs Rowlands by his kit straps and tries to pull him into the mud.

Sergeant Kemmell is a few feet away, adjusting the clips on a soldier's bayonet with a pair of pliers. 'Keep it down you idiots! Save some of that for the Hun. And Rowlands, use language like that again in front of an officer and I'll come over there and wash your dirty mouth out with my fist.'

The two soldiers stop fighting and, trying not to laugh, apologise to Alex.

'I wonder what the Hun smoke?' says Rowlands.

'Eckstein,' says Eden, startling Alex. He puffs a little cloud of smoke from his pipe. He's standing so close that Alex can feel the warmth from it. There's whisky in it too. 'The Hun smoke Eckstein.' He turns to Rowlands. 'If you make it through the wire, you should hunt for Ecksteins. They're rather good.'

Rowlands doesn't know where to look. 'I will, Sir,' he mumbles. 'Thank you, Sir.'

'Are they ready, Lieutenant?' says Eden, staring with an intensity that Alex hasn't seen before.

'Yes, Sir,' says Alex.

'Make sure they are.' Eden seems to be slurring his words. 'This is our first joint attack with the battalion. We need to show the other companies what we're made of. Show them what D Company can do. We have to get into that trench. No option.'

'We'll do our best, Sir.'

'No, you don't understand.' Eden leans closer, tobacco crackles in the pipe. 'I don't care about your best. We need to get into that trench. Whatever happens, I'm going in. If you take too long, I'll go in without you.'

'Sir? I thought you're to wait for our signal. Captain Lindsey said—'

'Fuck Lindsey, all of them,' Eden whispers. 'There's a chance of medals if we get this right. We have to get into that trench, whatever it costs. Do you understand?'

'Yes, Sir.' But Alex doesn't understand.

Eden takes a step back. 'And don't rely on Pope. Wouldn't be surprised if he gets lost and ends up attacking his own trench.'

Alex's face doesn't move, he makes sure of it. Why does Eden think that it's Charlie who will mess this up? Charlie didn't kill his own commanding officer.

Eden looks along the line of Alex's men, as if he's searching for something. Every one of them, Alex notices, has turned away, busying themselves with something. 'Just get on with it,' says Eden. 'It'll be cold out there. We don't want to catch our deaths waiting.'

Kemmell standing next to Alex, watches Eden walk away. 'We should get the men into formation now, Sir,' he says, shaking his head. 'It's almost time. Once the bombardment starts, the men won't be able to hear any commands.' He divides the men into groups and has each group line up in front of a ladder. 'Fix bayonets!' The knives are found with practiced fingers, unsheathed and clipped onto the rifles. 'You should go up the ladder now, Sir,' says Kemmell, touching the buttons on his tunic, one after the other; up, down, up. 'We'll wait for your signal.'

'Sergeant, what are you doing there?' says Alex. 'With your buttons?'

Kemmell smiles. 'In Africa, Sir, I was doing up my tunic, and a shell landed at my feet. Right between my feet. It never went off, so now, whenever... I'm sure there's nothing to it, but it does no harm, so...' He smiles again and shrugs.

Alex brings Percy up to the centre, placing the boy's shaking hand onto the ladder. 'It will be all right,' he whispers. Then he climbs halfway up and turns to face the men; shadows with rifles. They're waiting for him to say something. He breathes in. 'There will be a smoke screen but it won't last long. We should get to their wire before it runs out.' His voice is wavering. He clears his throat. 'We must be as quiet as we can. Good luck and... And watch for my signal.'

The men are silent. He can feel them staring.

'All right boys!' yells Kemmell, climbing up next to Alex. 'Right now those lazy Hun bastards are sleeping, but any minute now our artillery lads are gonna wake them up! As soon as that's done, off we go! You get up those ladders as if your sweetheart's husband is after you!' The men laugh. 'It's going to be hot, so when you get into those trenches, you cool those Hun bastards down with the icy steel of your bayonet!' He's waving his fist in the air. 'Then what do you do? You keep going is what you do! You keep going until you're in Berlin! And when you get there, you find those bastard Hun's wives and you show them why all the girls in England miss us!' The men cheer.

As the sound fades away, the cold, and the darkness folds around them.

21

THE FESTUBERT MISSION

The first shells whistle overhead, tuneful as a flock of birds. They hit the ground in front of the German wire. Rocks fly up. The whistle turns to wailing. The soil churns. Fire spurts in lurching flames. Flailing demons drifting across the field. Primordial. Nothing but smoke, fire and darkness.

The men climb the ladders, over the bags and spread along the parapet. Percy comes, slips on the last rung of the ladder and falls forward, knuckles and rifle buried in the grass. Stubbs pulls him up.

Alex signals for the men to move forward and they walk; through the grass, the littered soil, between the gaps in their own wire, out across the field, bayonets forward, steady.

Percy, walking next to Alex, looking straight ahead, long strides. Stubbs is with him. On they go, holding the line: Fenton, Eggleton, Rowlands. Charlie's out there and Francourt's men and Eden's. The whole battalion, hundreds of men, walking together on either side; silent, towards the Hun.

The smoke gets thicker; an eerie, green light. Rough ground; shell holes. Explosions pulsing in the puddles.

A soldier trips on something in the dark. Kitbag, satchel and rifle clattering. Swearing. Kemmell is there; slams his hand against the soldier's mouth. 'Silence!' On they go.

Air, thick and stinking; sulphur and a nauseating death-smell. Earth, rising up and falling away. Cloth-wrapped, mud-trapped bones float up; fleshless soldiers swimming through a dead and rotting sea. The smokescreen, held in the breeze, rears in front of them; an undulating wall. Behind it is the German wire.

Alex raises his arm and signals to the men. '*Stop. Find cover. Lie down.*' He moves into the smoke, finds the wire and walks along it, looking for a gap where the men can get through. Some of the posts have been buried by the bombardment, but the wire looks intact.

Kemmell grabs Alex by the back of the neck and pulls him to his mouth. 'We have to find a gap.'

'There are no gaps. Try to climb through?'

'Too much noise. We have to cut through,' says Kemmell, pulling wire cutters from his belt. He lies on his back and grips the wire above his head.

Worthington kneels down and holds the wire away from the post.

Smoke swirls; sulphurous and choking.

The wire clicks loudly.

German voices.

Kemmell freezes. He shakes his head, then tries again. 'Cutters won't cut! We should get back.'

Alex grabs the cutters from Kemmell and tries to cut the wire. They have to try; Eden's waiting for them. They can't give up! He squeezes and twists as hard as he can but the wire is too thick for the cutters and hardly even bends. Even if they could cut it, it would take an hour to get through. The wire fades into the smoke for thirty yards ahead of them; spiralling back towards the German trench, tangled, twisted; a rusting thorn thicket.

A burst of machine gunfire sends soil and stones singing around them. Worthington lets go of the wire and it flings back, twanging against the post.

'For Christ's sake, Worthington!' hisses Kemmell.

But Worthington doesn't hear. He's on his back, gulping, clutching at his stomach. He tries to stand, falls, kicking at nothing. He fumbles with his tunic, trying to cover part of his gut that's bulging and pulsing against the cloth.

'Give me a dressing!' says Kemmell.

Alex takes a field dressing from his pocket, struggles to open it.

Kemmell snatches it but fumbles too. 'Can't see!'

Alex unclips his torch and, cupping it in his fingers, shines it low towards Worthington.

Steam drifts through the torchlight as Kemmell presses the padding into the wound.

Worthington cries out, tries to pull the padding away. Then his hand relaxes and falls still. His eyes are half-closed. In the broken stillness of his expression, he looks disappointed and sad.

'We don't need the torch now, Sir,' says Kemmell, wiping the blood off his hands.

'He's the one who smoked the good cigarettes,' says Alex.

Beyond the wire, posts and sandbags come into view and, in a shellfire flash, something that looks like German helmets. The smoke rolls in again and they disappear.

Rifles join the machine gun and now there is gunfire all along the line. Eden will expect Alex to keep pushing forward, but he can't risk any more of his men; he won't. His fear softens and congeals into a gut-wrenching disappointment. But he knows what he has to do. 'All right,' he says, standing. 'Get everyone back.'

Kemmell signals the retreat.

The men climb out of their shell holes and run back across the field.

Bullets fly past. The air ripples.

A silhouetted soldier against the flashes. Smoke swirls around him. He's standing quite still and upright, close to the wire. It's Percy.

Alex runs. 'Get back to our line! What are you doing?' He reaches out. A stick grenade spins through the air behind them. No time to react. Air rips from his lungs. His body is liquid; a wave of sound and light. Everything is yellow. Hot. The earth flips. The field is upside down, folds over, slams into his spine. No sound; one note, like a bell. Black. Grit in his teeth, blood. He tries to open his eyes but grit there too. Something burns against his temple; a bee sting. He stays still. Breathes. Opens his eyes. Smoke flowing above him and clouds; slower. One star in the middle of it all; as still as a crystal.

He's in a shell hole, on his back. His ribs ache. He lies still. Breathes in deeply, lets it out slowly. Moves each limb, bending each joint. He's all right, but head stinging. Cold mud around his legs, in his boots; stinks of rivers and death. Ringing still in his head, in his bones.

The soft earth feels safe. He digs his hand into the soil and squeezes. He wants to stay here, bury himself deeper into the Earth. But has to get up, find Percy. He pulls himself out of the hole and rolls over into the field. He rests for a moment then gets on his feet.

Gunfire oozes back into his head, muffled by the ringing.

He looks for Percy, stumbling at first; legs feel like a memory. There's no one here.

Patches of smoke drift past.

It's quiet now.

'Elphick!' he whispers into the darkness. 'Percy!'

No reply.

He runs along the wire, searching.

A dead soldier here, curled up as if he's sleeping. Alex turns him over. A broken face as if the skull has been removed from under the skin. It isn't Percy. It wasn't ever Percy.

He tries to run back towards the British line. He can't run, has to walk. His head throbs with each step. He has to get back to the men. Regroup, find out what Woodstone needs them to do. His feet look strange, walking; further away than he remembers. Eden will be angry. The wire wasn't cut. What could they have done? He has to walk around the shell holes, not fall in; keep walking. He brought the men in too close. A man died. The one who smoked the good ciga-rettes. What was his name? But they said the wire would be cut. Why wasn't it cut? His head aches. The parapet is ahead of him; He has to keep walking; just a few yards to the trench.

Mustn't lie down.

Keep walking.

22

CONCUSSION

'You've taken a hit from something, Sir,' says Kemmell, leading Alex by the arm towards the officer's dugout. 'We'll get that bandaged up for you.' They seem to be drifting along the trench, past the men who are sitting, exhausted, silent, on the fire-step.

Alex looks for Percy but he can't see him. 'Have you seen Percy?'

'No, Sir. There's quite a few missing. Some of the lads are still coming in.'

'There was a grenade.' Alex can hear his own voice, but it's as if someone else is speaking inside his head. He has to look strong as he goes past his men. He tries to walk normally, but his legs are not behaving; they seem to want him to lie down.

'You're back,' says Charlie. 'I was about to go out and look for you.' He peers into Alex's eyes. 'You all right? You're not quite with us.'

'He's got a cut, on his temple.' Kemmell is talking to Charlie, in the dugout.

Alex is there too, lying on a bed. How did he...? He wants to sleep, but he needs to find Percy. 'Where is my hat?' he says, trying to sit up. 'Kemmell, I've got to go out.' But it's only Charlie now. 'Where is Sergeant Kemmell?'

'He's gone to fetch the medic,' says Charlie, pouring water onto a cloth and wiping blood from Alex's temple.

'It's not my blood,' says Alex, 'It's... What was his name, Ariston?'

'Stay still. It *is* your blood. I can see a cut. You must have stopped some shrapnel. How do you feel?'

'I'm fine, just a headache. Have you seen private Elphick? He was up by the wire.'

'No. But he may still come in. Hopefully more will come in. We lost five, perhaps more. You should stay lying down for a while, get some rest.'

'What the hell are you doing back here?' Woodstone is at the top of the dugout steps. 'You're supposed to be in the Boche trench with Eden. Why didn't you go through?'

'There was no way through the wire, Sir,' says Charlie. 'We couldn't find a gap.'

'What? But Eden—' Woodstone slips and half falls, half runs down the steps, grabbing onto Charlie to break his fall.

Charlie helps Woodstone to an upright position. 'Artillery failed to damage the Boche wire, Sir. They still had functioning machine guns.'

'Ridiculous,' says Woodstone. 'Eden found a gap. Why couldn't you?'

'Eden found a gap, Sir?' says Charlie.

'He thought you were in the trench, so he took his men in. He found a gap.' Woodstone wipes his hair into a parting with the palm of his hand. 'Why are you lying down and what's that?' he says, pointing at Alex's head.

Alex feels his temple. There's a bandage. 'I don't know, Sir.' He doesn't remember anyone doing that. Was the medic here or did Charlie do it?

'Shrapnel. It's a graze,' says Charlie. 'He was out for a while, but he'll be fine.'

'I told you to cut your own gap,' says Woodstone.

'We tried, Sir,' says Alex, pushing himself off the bed and managing to stand. 'But the cutters wouldn't cut.' His head throbs.

Woodstone glares. 'What was wrong with the cutters, Sergeant?'

'The wire was thicker than we've seen up to now, Sir,' says Kemmell, who seems to be back in the room now.

'Did you say Eden and his men went in on their own?' says Alex, starting to feel more awake.

'Yes, just after you lot ran away, Eden got through. They were sitting in the Boche trench with no support!' Woodstone is tapping his cane against his boot. He scans the dugout roof, as if the answer to his problem is somewhere behind the bulging chicken-wire. 'Whole thing's a damn mess,' he mutters. 'No wonder Eden lost most of his men. He had to fight his way out single-handed! Heroic! But *I'm* going to be the laughing stock of the whole damned battalion. Shambles!' He marches back up the steps, throws open the canvas door and climbs out into the trench.

Charlie looks astonished. 'How the hell did Eden get through?'

'I've no idea,' says Alex. 'But that means *we* should have got through the wire too! I promised Eden we'd get into that trench. I promised Percy he would be all right and now I don't even know where he is. I've failed.'

'No one's failed,' says Charlie. 'Nothing was how it was supposed to be. The wire wasn't cut.'

'You did right by the lads, Sir,' says Kemmell. 'They would all have been killed if we'd tried to get through that wire.'

'Exactly, you heard Woodstone,' says Charlie. 'Eden lost most of his men. Is that what you would have wanted?'

Alex doesn't reply.

'I've got to get on,' says Charlie, running up the steps. 'I've got to get my men ready in case there's a counterattack. Alex, get some rest!'

Alex puts on his helmet, loosening the strap to get it over the bandage.

'What are you doing, Sir?' says Kemmell. 'You stay here and rest. We can get the lads ready without you.'

'I'm going out.'

'Out, Sir?'

'Yes, back out. I have to find Private Elphick. I told him it would be all right.'

'You're not thinking, Sir. You've had a bump. The Boche might be coming across the field at any moment. The lad could be anywhere.'

'The least I can do is go and look.' Alex climbs up the steps and stumbles.

Kemmell grabs Alex's arm. 'Wait, Sir. We can send a unit out tonight. There's no time now.'

'I know that but I promised it would be all right. I lost him. He doesn't have any gloves. I'm going.'

'He's most likely dead, Sir!' Shocked, either by his own words or seeing Alex's expression, Kemmell softens. 'I'm sorry, Sir.'

'I have to go,' says Alex. 'I won't be long.'

23

SOUVENIRS

Outside, the men, still bloodied from the raid, are standing shoulder to shoulder along the fire-step. They stare down at Alex like saints on a church wall; green helmet haloes framing faces, serene with exhaustion. He walks past them, trying not to be noticed, until he finds an empty traverse. He takes a shovel; he may have to dig Percy out. Then, checking no one can see him, climbs the ladder.

'Ryan, what the hell are you doing?' It's Eden.

Alex drops the shovel on the other side of the bags. 'Some of my men are still out, Sir. I was going to see if I could find them.'

'It's a bit dark to see anything out there, isn't it? Come down.'

Alex climbs down.

'What happened there?' says Eden, pointing at the bandage under Alex's helmet.

'Just a scratch.' The sky is getting lighter. Alex needs to get over the bags before the sun comes up. 'Captain Woodstone said you made it into the Boche trench.'

Eden is clenching his pipe in his teeth. The glowing embers light up his face; he's smiling. 'Yes, it was fun. You should try it sometime.'

'We did try, Sir. We couldn't find a way through.'

'I found a way. There's always a way.' Eden slaps a canvas satchel that he's carrying. 'I was just coming to find you. I found maps in the Hun trench. Might be useful to someone. Had to shoot a couple of Hun as I went in. Ripped a regiment badge off one of them. So we know who they are now. Also, some things that I think you might like to see.' He pulls out a sheath knife and hands it to Alex. 'It's a good knife. And look at this! A helmet with a spike. Pickelhaube, I think they call them. I wonder if they take them off when they go up in the observation balloons!' He laughs. It's like a game to him, a sport. Men have died today and he's running around with a bag full of souvenirs, grinning.

'I have to go, Sir. I can look at them when I get back.'

'Get back from where?'

'I'm going back out, Sir. I won't be long.'

'Why are you going out?'

'One of my men is missing. I think he might be injured.'

'The stretcher-bearers can go out and look later. He'll probably walk in on his own if you wait. I've seen men crawl in after days.'

'He's the youngest in my platoon. He went missing by the wire.'

'So what?' says Eden, dropping the smile. 'Leave him out there. Look at that sky. You've got no time.'

'I know, Sir... But I made a promise.'

Eden coughs out a laugh. 'A promise? What's wrong with you? You can't risk an officer's life just for one private!'

'I don't think I'm risking anything. I just—'

'Go back and look after your men.'

'I need to find him, Sir.'

Eden looks angry now. 'He's a private! Send out a party after dark tonight. Go with them if you want. If he's dead by then, he wouldn't have made it anyway.'

'Please let me go, Captain. I think I know where he is. I can go directly there and come straight back. There's no Boche out there now. They haven't fired a single shot since we came back.'

'There's no one out there because they're regrouping in their supply trenches, preparing for a counter attack.' Eden taps his pipe out on a sandbag and stuffs it into his pocket. 'So, no, you can't go.

Come with me. We need to get the men up, standing-to. You can keep that knife. I took it for you. Come on!'

Eden marches ahead, turns the corner and starts yelling orders at the men.

Alex slows down until he is alone again. He turns back, climbs the ladder and drops down into No Man's Land.

24

THE WIRE

Clouds hang, ripped and heavy above a wash of blue light. Trees are already visible behind the German line. Alex runs towards them.

He reaches the first group of fallen soldiers, scattered like seaweed washed up on a beach. This morning, these men were singing in the trenches, complaining of the cold. They'll never sing again, never feel cold, or the sun on their backs. He tries to imagine what it would be like to sense absolutely nothing, but he feels the air moving around his body, smells the torn grass, the fresh soil, the sulphur, the death, and he's grateful.

Looking at these corpses, he suddenly knows that Percy must be dead. He will find the body and carry it back. He doesn't want to think of it rotting in the mud like the others. He retraces his steps to where the grenade fell between them. He digs around with the shovel. There's no sign of a body, or parts of a body. Nothing.

He runs further along, to a tangled net of barbed wire, hanging between metal stakes. There's a large, rugged form here, sharp against the sky, that's now brushed with pink along the horizon. Crows fly up, squawking, glide away and fade against the dark earth. The form becomes a pile of men; a face is pressed against the ground, squashed by the weight of a body lying above it. A soldier lies flat against the carpet of wire, his hand folded back in the soil. Another on his back, fallen between the strands of wire, one knee up, arms above his head, fingers searching for a rifle that lies just out of reach. There's a man like a dead bird, ripped cloth fluttering gently. One, on his knees, his rifle under his arm, the bayonet stuck in the soil. He looks like he's praying. Alex could climb over them, walk right across their torn backs and into the German trench.

These are Eden's men! Alex recognises some of the faces. It's too dark to see where the bullets came from but it feels that these soldiers were not advancing or retreating, but escaping *forward*, somehow. It looks as if they had surged, one on top of the other, and got tangled in the wire like terrified sheep.

The crows hop closer, calling softly.

A tick, tick, metallic sound; the button on a dead soldier's tunic, flapping in the wind.

Someone is moving in the field, low in the dirt, on the edge of a shell hole. The Hun could be creeping up already. Alex is only yards away. He looks around. There's nowhere to hide, not without running. It's still dark enough, if he gets down, stays still, up against these corpses, perhaps he won't be seen and they'll run past. He crouches, stays perfectly still, shovel in one hand and revolver in the other.

The figure slowly rises to his feet, holding no rifle. The British uniform is baggy, webbing straps hanging loosely from his shoulders.

Alex walks over. 'Percy, it's me, Lieutenant Ryan. Are you hurt?'

Percy rubs his eyes. 'I was asleep.'

'Keep your voice down. We're close to the wire. What are you doing sleeping here?'

'I don't know.'

Percy's rifle is half-buried in the soil. Alex picks it up. 'We have to go back now, it will be dawn soon.'

Percy stares out across the empty field. 'Where is everyone?'

'Back in our trench. We retreated a long time ago. I think you had another turn.'

'Stubbs too?'

'He's waiting for you.'

'I got buried in the dirt. It was really smoky so I couldn't see which way to go.'

The relief, that Percy is alive and unhurt, feels almost painful. Alex can feel it pushing up from his stomach, through his veins, as though it should burst out of his skin and erupt in a mass of flowers, singing flowers! 'I'm so glad you are all right, Percy. Have you been asleep all this time?'

'No. I was lying down. Then the others came with Captain Eden and he ordered them to go over the wire, into the Hun trench.'

Alex pushes Percy forward and they start walking back across the field. 'Did the captain try to make you go?'

'No, I was lying down, so he didn't see me. He was very angry and he was shooting at them. I didn't know where to go so I just lay down more but then it was very dark and everyone had gone and you said I'm to sit down if I don't know what to do.'

'You mean he was shouting at them?'

'No, he was shooting at them,' says Percy, casually.

'Who was Captain Eden shooting at?'

'The men.'

Alex stops and turns to face Percy. 'The British men or the Germans?'

'The British men, in his platoon. I don't know their names.'

Alex holds Percy by his arms. 'Captain Eden was shooting at the men from *his own platoon*? Is that what you're saying?'

Percy looks ashamed, as if he's said something stupid. 'He was yelling that if they don't get up, he'll shoot them, and then he did shoot them.'

'He shot them?'

Percy nods and pulls away from Alex.

'The Germans were firing at us,' says Alex, letting Percy go. 'Surely *they* did this. It was chaos. You've made a mistake.'

Percy shakes his head. 'The Germans shot the first ones, then the others wouldn't go, so Captain Eden made them go by shooting some of them.'

'Where was this?'

Percy points. 'Over there.'

Across the field, the piled up shapes of the soldier's bodies are turning from blue to brown in the new light.

'Are you sure that Captain Eden didn't see you?'

Percy nods. 'I was lying down. I told you. It was dark.'

'But you saw him shoot the men?'

'Yes! In the flashes, I could see.'

Alex grabs Percy by both arms again. 'Do not tell anyone about this, about what you saw the Captain do.'

'Why not?'

'Because I think he will just say it isn't true, and that might make things very difficult for you. Do you understand that?'

Percy looks as if he's going to cry. He nods, slowly.

'Come on. Let's get back,' says Alex gently.

They walk in silence across the field. Above them, the clouds, bright like embers, ripple across the dawn sky.

Kemmell has seen them coming in and is waiting with Stubbs at the parapet. 'Well done, Sir. I knew you would find him!'

'Did you, Sergeant?' says Alex, handing Percy over to Stubbs.

Kemmell looks sheepish and smiles. 'Well, I hoped you might.'

'Has Eden said anything about me? Did he notice I was missing?'

'He didn't mention it, Sir. The men have been stood-down. Nothing came of the counter-attack. Everyone's at breakfast. But Captain Woodstone has asked to see you.'

'Good,' says Alex. 'I need to see him too.'

Stubbs leads Percy away, lifting him with one arm off the duck-boards. 'Come on little lad. We saved you a bacon sarnie.'

25

THE FUNK HOLE

As Alex heads for Woodstone's dugout, Kemmell calls after him. 'Not that way, Sir. He's not there. Nothing's there. One of our guns was firing short during the bombardment. His servant was killed.'

'Gibbons was killed?'

'Yes, Sir. We've put Captain Woodstone in a funk hole in the Comms trench. He's pretty shaken up.'

Alex rushes along the narrow trench until he comes to a hole in the wall with a corrugated metal sheet for a roof and sandbags piled up around it. The roof is lit by an undulating oval of light; the last guttering remnants of a candle, flickering and spitting at the bottom of an empty condensed-milk tin. An upturned packing crate serves as a table. On it is a bottle of whisky, an enamel mug and an army message book with a pencil lying across it. Woodstone is sitting on a bed made from sandbags stuffed with grass. He's asleep. His cheek, resting against his shoulder, fills like a trumpet player's before his lips vibrate and blow out a little puff of air. His hair, glossy in the mix of candlelight and dawn, falls across his face like a dead bird's wing.

Alex decides to let the captain sleep. He turns.

'What was that?' says Woodstone, coughing. 'Ryan? That you?'

'You're resting, Sir. Should I come back later?'

'Resting? I wasn't. I was just...' Woodstone eases his hair into place with shaking fingers. He opens the notebook on the desk. 'I'm writing reports.' His words are sluggish and soft. 'There's been an... I've lost most of the papers. Most of the things.' He looks up desperately. 'Come and sit.'

There's nowhere to sit. The floor is covered in an inch of mud. Alex crouches with his back leaning against the sandbags.

'Are you all right, Sir? Kemmell told me about the dugout. About Gibbons. I'm so—'

'Yes, Gibbons was... Can't find the damned note book.'

'It's there, Sir. Under your hand.'

Woodstone flicks through the book with one hand as the other seems to crawl across the desk until it finds the whisky. He pours some into the mug and drinks it, gulping noisily.

'I'm so sorry about Gibbons, Sir.'

'I was just outside when it hit. Just sent him in to get... to get... I can't even remember.' He looks terrified for a moment then shakes his head. 'Really must tell those gunners to recalibrate... Will you remind me?'

'I'm sure it's already done, Sir.'

Woodstone pours another drink. The bottle rattles against the mug. Suddenly he looks angry. Pushing the bottle to one side, he leans across the table towards Alex. 'You disobeyed an order.'

Alex, surprised at the sudden change of tone, doesn't speak.

'Captain Eden gave you a direct order but you wilfully disobeyed it. He told you to stay with him and prepare the men for a counter-attack. You were told not to go out! I could have you court-martialled for disobeying, or for abandoning your men!'

'I'm sorry, Sir. I thought...' Alex needs to think. 'I must have misunderstood the order.' He rubs the bandage on his head. 'My head, Sir. I'd been hit. I was confused. I thought the captain told me to go out while *he* prepared the men.' This seems plausible, as long as Woodstone doesn't ask Eden. 'So I went out... for twenty minutes... locating and retrieving one of my men. If I'd known... what I know now, then I would most certainly have not left my men and Eden alone in the trench. I promise, Sir, it won't happen again. I won't leave the men.'

Woodstone looks confused. He drinks more whisky. 'Well, all right then.' He scrapes something from the outside of the mug. 'I'll need a report from you, explaining why your men couldn't get through the wire.'

'Yes, Sir,' says Alex, hiding his relief. 'There was… something… that I'd like to mention to you now though, as I'm not sure if that should be part of my report.'

Woodstone looks up.

Alex tells Woodstone what he's just seen; the corpses of Eden's men, piled up against the wire, seemingly forced to keep moving forward as their comrades fell beneath them. He explains how it appeared that they had been shot, from behind. He's careful not to mention Percy; there's no knowing what Eden might do if he learned that Percy was a witness.

'What are you asking me?' says Woodstone. 'Is there a question?'

Now Alex is confused. 'Well I thought it was shocking, Sir… I thought… I thought you should know.'

'The mission objective, was to get into that trench and gather intelligence. Captain Eden did exactly that. You didn't and no one else did.'

'But his men were forced, Sir, at gunpoint, by the Officer Commanding. The officer who is supposed to be *protecting* his men!'

'If it gets them moving.' Woodstone shrugs.

'Captain, I think Eden might have shot some of his own men!'

'What nonsense! How could you know? Boche machine guns firing in the dark. All the chaos.' He pours another whisky and drinks it. 'This is what I was saying to you the other day. This isn't a game.' He's speaking as if he's remembering the words, reading them from the air. 'Sometimes… actions that would be difficult to justify, or even comprehend in civilian situations, are quite necessary in the heat of battle… An officer's pregograt… prerogative, is to get the men moving, *any way he can*! Besides, no one was there, you see? No one saw what happened.' He combs his hair dramatically with his fingers and points the mug at Alex. 'And you, Ryan, you would do well to stop questioning the actions of an officer who is superior in both rank and ability and try to *learn* something! You need to decide if you are with us or against us. If you want to lead your men or not. You need to decide who you want to be. You need to decide if you want to be here at all. If not, I can write a letter and have you on a boat sailing for England by the end of the week!' Whisky spills from the mug and runs down his arm. He looks around for something to mop it up, shaking his head. 'We could all learn from him. Both of us... Just not good enough, you see? Never good enough... We've lost good people, some damned good men. So now is not the time. War is never the time.' He waves Alex away and closes his eyes. 'You should get yourself some water. Get some sleep. We're being relieved at seven.' He laughs. 'Relieved!'

26

VIEILLE CHAPELLE

Last night a German counter-attack delayed the relief by several hours. Trench repairs and casualties meant Alex's platoon didn't leave the front line until early this morning.

The men are exhausted. During the three-hour march back to Vieille Chapelle, one man peeled away from the ranks; strange, high-footed steps off the road and into a potato field. Kemmell yelled at him to get back, but the soldier was marching asleep. He fell sideways and collapsed, unconscious and groaning.

No one is speaking as they march through the high street and turn into a dark, cobbled lane. The clump and shuffle of exhausted boots is mixed with faint music. A door opens. A burst of lamplight and singing. Three clean officers flow out, clearly drunk. Seeing Alex, they salute theatrically. Instinctively Alex salutes back. The officers turn away, giggling, and stumble down a side street. Alex is enraged. His tunic sleeves are still sticky with Worthington's blood. He has an urge to follow them, tell them everything he and his men have just been through. To tell them about Worthington trying to stuff his own guts back inside his body, about the soldiers hanging off the wire.

Kemmell draws Alex away from the officers and points to the door they've just fallen out of. 'That's the Café de Lion. Run by two lovely sisters. It's for officers, but I've been there on several occasions!' he says, proudly. 'As a guest of Lieutenant Collins, God rest him.'

The men peer in, but nothing can be seen through the closed shutters.

The sun is coming up behind the houses as the platoon reaches the crossroads at the centre of the village. Kemmell says he has to go to the quartermaster to collect new rifles for the men who've lost them.

'It can wait,' says Alex. 'You need sleep as much as the men do.'

Kemmell laughs wearily. 'It's to be done now, Sir. Eden has ordered musket training for this afternoon and they can't do that without rifles.'

'I'll go,' says Alex. 'You take the men back to the billets and I'll send Fenton with the rifles later.'

On his way to the quartermaster's office, Alex sees the same drunk officers up ahead of him in the middle of the road. There's a girl, carrying a milk urn. As she crosses the road, one of the soldiers tries to make her dance. It's Odette. She pushes him away. He lunges at her and the urn falls, clattering and splashing its contents across the pavement and the soldier's uniform. He yells something and moves toward her again. Odette is shouting.

Alex is running, grabbing the soldier by the collar, swinging him around and he falls hard against a wall.

'Alex!' yells Odette.

The two other men come on, fists raised, but now Alex has his knife held out towards them and they stop.

Odette says something to them in French. 'It's all right!' she says in English. 'It's all right!'

The officers seem to notice Alex's mud-caked uniform, or the blood, or perhaps they realise that none of this is worth the trouble it could cause, and they calm. The fists turn to open palms and they step sideways, lift their comrade up by his arms and the three of them stagger away.

Alex puts his knife back into his pocket and turns to Odette. He takes hold of her arm but she shrugs him off, grabs the urn and walks away.

'Odette, are you all right?'

She doesn't turn around.

'I was trying to help you,' he says.

'I don't need your help.'

He follows behind her, not sure how close he should get. 'What's the matter? Why are you angry with *me*?'

'I told you, I don't need your help.'

'I thought they might hurt you.'

The urn clinks and rings as it rubs against her skirt as she walks. 'I can take care of myself.'

'I'm sorry if I've offended you,' he says, coming up beside her.

'I'll see you at breakfast,' she says, coldly. She's crying.

'I can find out who they are and report them to their commanding officer. I think I know which regiment they're from.'

She stops and turns to face him. 'Alex, I know who their commanding officer is! I was bringing the milk to their billets!'

He stops walking. 'I thought... from across the street, it looked like something might happen.'

'It might have, but I said I would report them, and it was going to be all right, but then you came running in with your knife!'

'I'm sorry, I thought I was helping.'

She glares. 'You soldiers, you *all* think you are helping, but all you do is wave knives around and, and shoot people! Your kind of *help* is what is causing all of this.' She looks around, waves the urn. 'All of this!'

All Alex can see is the empty street and a dog, lit by the first rays of sunlight, lapping what's left of the milk from the cobbles. 'I just thought...' He hadn't thought anything. He doesn't even know when he took the knife out. He's so tired. 'I thought I was helping.'

She laughs bitterly. 'You sound like my father!' She starts walking again. 'He thought he *knew* how to *help* and now where is he? Who did he help?'

Alex follows. 'I don't know. But—'

'You think, because we don't try to hurt everyone who offends us, that we can't look after ourselves.' She stops. 'But we can! If we wanted to, we could pick up a gun, just like you men. You know we can.' She jabs her thumb into her chest. 'You *know* I can!' She marches off again.

'Yes, I—'

'Since guns came, the sword even, we could *also* use violence to protect ourselves.'

'Yes. I can see—'

'So why do you think that *all* the women of this village, this country, don't just get some guns and use them to protect themselves from the men who offend them? Why don't we just do that? Have you thought about that? We could! But we don't! Why don't we do that, Alex? Why don't we?'

He doesn't know. 'I don't know. Perhaps all the men have all the guns?' He really doesn't know. She's marching double-time now and his head really hurts. 'Odette, wait!'

'I have to get back,' she says, stopping and turning to him.

'Odette, please. I'm sorry. I think you're right. I just don't see how any of this will change. It's all too... too big. I'm sorry. I'm very tired.' He looks back towards the quartermaster's office. 'Look, I have to get some equipment for the men. It won't take long. You can wait for me, then we can walk back to the farm together and talk more about this.'

Her shoulders drop a little. 'No, it doesn't matter,' she says, her voice softening. She waves the empty urn. 'I have to get back and get more milk. I'll see you at breakfast.'

'Could I at least give you the money for the lost milk?'

'No, thank you. It's all right.' She looks up at him and smiles. 'I'm sorry too. I think I was just trying to finish an argument that I had with my—' She sees the bandage across his forehead and reaches up. 'Alex, what happened? Are you hurt?'

'I'm fine. It's just a graze. Nothing.'

'Thank you for trying to help.' She squeezes his hand. 'It was kind of you.' She starts to walk, then stops and turns back towards him. 'I need to make a pen for the chickens today. You could help me if you want?'

'All right,' he says, smiling. 'The men have training this afternoon. When it's over, I'll come and find you.'

He watches as she walks away, into the rising sun. Her hair looks like a flame, flickering against the dark clouds, and he thinks it might be the most beautiful thing he has ever seen.

27

BREAKFAST

Alex has had no sleep, but he washed and is now wearing his clean uniform, standing in the courtyard of the Berger farm. He doesn't want to go into the house. He can see Woodstone sitting with Eden and the other officers in the dining room. He's late for breakfast but if he waits a while, Eden might finish and go for his morning ride.

Madame Berger is hanging sheets in rows in the sunlight. Her chubby fingers squeeze wooden pegs onto the string. Steam and a tune that she's humming rise from the sheets and drift in the breeze. Her silhouette dances against the rippling white cotton; erotic, like an Indian goddess, then plump and old and back again. She glances at Alex suspiciously from behind the sunlit sheets. He tries to look as if he's simply enjoying the morning air. The sky is pale blue. Smudges of shell-smoke rise gently from the horizon. A dove flaps on the roof, cooing and pacing towards another that sits on the tiles.

She pops her head above the sheets and frowns.

'Bonjour, Madame,' he says.

She frowns harder.

He goes into the house and, managing to avoid eye contact with Eden, mumbles good morning to the officers seated around the breakfast table. He sits, pours himself some tea and reaches for the milk jug. It's empty.

'There's no milk,' says Woodstone. He looks haggard; bags under bloodshot eyes. 'It seems Odette spilt her milk this morning and gave ours to someone else.'

'Did she cry over it?' says Eden.

'No use in that!' says Halsall, grinning.

'How long does it take for a cow to make a jug?' says Woodstone. 'Why can't she just go and get some more?'

'She can't get the cows in,' says Eden. 'A shell exploded on the track by the field. Now they won't go past the crater.'

Alex's chest tightens. How does Eden know? He must have been with her in the lane.

'Damned close, that shell. Woke me up,' says Woodstone, taking a piece of toast out of the rack. 'There was shelling in the village two nights ago. Suspect there's been an aeroplane sniffing about. They know we're here. Might have to move the men if Fritz gets a range on the billets.'

'Should we not move out of this farm too, Sir?' says Charlie. 'If it's going to cause a risk to Madame Berger and Odette?'

'The shell hit the lane halfway between the two farms,' says Eden. 'Whoever they were aiming at, they missed by half a mile. So I wouldn't worry.'

'I worry if it means we get no milk,' says Halsall, unenthusiastically stirring his tea.

'Taking milk in ones tea is uncivilised, if you want my opinion,' says Woodstone, reaching for the butter. 'Something that those chaps who lived in caves would have done. And stirred it with a bone from that animal... like a hairy elephant... Blast it. I forget.'

'Neanderthals,' says Eden. 'Mammoths.'

'I don't think that's true,' says Halsall.

'It is, they were named after the valley where the bones were found,' says Eden.

'No, I mean, lots of people take milk in their tea. I would say, all of the men do. They drink gallons of the stuff every day.'

'There you have it,' says Eden, taking out his pipe. 'According to the scientists, the Neanderthal brain was too small to be capable of moral or theistic conception. So...' He strikes a match, drawing the flame slowly into the pipe. 'So, despite what the regimental chaplain would have us believe, most of the men *must* be Neanderthals!'

Woodstone and Halsall laugh.

Eden puffs out a triumphant column of smoke and leans back in his chair.

'I have found most of the men to be thoughtful and kind,' says Charlie.

'Eden was joking,' says Halsall.

'Was I?' says Eden.

Alex drinks his tea in one go and stands. 'I think I'll go and see if I can help Odette with the cows.'

'One moment, before you rush off,' says Woodstone. 'I have something to announce to the platoon commanders. Does that include you, Ryan? Have you made your decision? Are you one of us? Are you a platoon commander? If not, by all means, run along and help your milkmaid.'

The room goes very quiet. Someone crunching a piece of toast, stops.

Alex takes a deep breath. 'I was unsure if I was ready to command a platoon, Sir... But as an officer it is my duty to protect the men... And in light of recent events, I now realise that the best way for me to protect the men is to lead them.'

Chairs creak.

Woodstone blinks. He glances at Eden. 'Good. Sit down then. You'll stay with 4 Platoon.'

Charlie flashes a questioning look to Alex. They haven't spoken to each other since yesterday's failed mission. Alex hasn't told anyone except Woodstone about Eden shooting his own men.

Alex sits.

Woodstone spreads butter on his toast and straightens his back. 'I spoke to the colonel this morning. There's going to be a push of some sort. All rumours at the moment, but he thinks there's something to it. So we need to get the men on top form. I noticed a lot of —' The toast snaps in half, spraying crumbs over the table. 'We should say something to Madame Berger about this toast. It's far too dry.'

'Do they know when, Sir?' says Charlie.

'What sort of show, Sir? Is this the *Big Raid?*' says Halsall.

Woodstone takes another piece of toast and butters it, more carefully this time. 'Well, they didn't say. It's just a rumour.'

'I hope it's the big one,' says Halsall, scrunching up his napkin with both hands. 'I'm beginning to worry that the kick-off is going to be further down the line and we'll be left sitting on the bench. I can't wait to get stuck in. It was frustrating having you chaps go out with my lot stuck behind.'

'You shouldn't be frustrated,' says Charlie. 'Most of us didn't really achieve anything.'

'Yes, we did,' says Woodstone, indignantly. 'There was some… miscommunication, but the objective was to get into the Boche trench, and both A and D companies achieved that. Captain Eden, here, even managed, single-handed, to secure some valuable maps, despite heavy losses in his platoon. It's already been mentioned in despatches and… ' He raises his chin and spreads a look around the room. 'I've been told there's likely to be *a medal*.'

Halsall smiles. 'Oh, well done, Eden! That's marvellous.'

Alex crushes toast crumbs with the back of a spoon. 'Exactly how many men did you lose Captain?'

Eden turns his chair to face Alex.

'Was it most of your platoon, or all of them?'

Charlie coughs. 'Alex?'

Eden doesn't answer. He puffs loudly on his pipe.

'Although, some of them might crawl back in,' says Alex, slowly running his thumb through the toast crumbs. 'There's still a chance, isn't there? So it won't be a complete loss.'

'Alex!' Charlie taps his knife on the table.

Alex looks out of the window. Madame Berger has finished hanging the washing. A cat is on the roof, creeping slowly towards the doves.

'What are you doing, Ryan?' says Woodstone.

'We *all* lost men, Ryan,' says Halsall. 'It's tragic but it can't be helped.' He turns to Eden. 'What are we talking here, Military Cross?'

'Just serving my country,' says Eden, turning away from Alex.

'He can't get a military cross,' says Alex.

'That's hardly something for *you* to decide,' says Woodstone, glaring.

'Why can't he?' says Halsall. 'He was virtually the last man standing. Positively heroic, as always. They have to recognise that.'

'Like I said, just serving my country.'

'He can't have a military cross or any medal,' says Alex. 'In order to get one, you need to have the action witnessed by a superior officer. There was no one there. No one saw what happened.'

Eden throws an arm over the back of his chair, watching Woodstone carefully.

Woodstone coughs awkwardly. 'Technically, yes, but... But I think it's all rather obvious how rough things were out there. The artillery let us down. There were casualties, but despite that, the captain managed to come back with maps and other things... and besides, I've heard that two officers from A Company are being decorated. And none of them got so much as a Boche boot from the Hun trenches. So I don't think we should nit-pic with the details.'

Eden leans forward, staring at Alex. 'How is your head?'

Alex touches the bandage. 'My head? Fine. Why?' Suddenly he feels ashamed. He wants to get out, go and find Odette.

'Have you seen the doc?' Eden sounds genuinely caring.

'Not yet. He's still at the casualty clearing station.'

'Make sure you do. There can be complications when it's a head injury. It can affect your judgment.'

'He's right you know,' says Halsall. 'I knew a chap in the Lancs. Got bumped on the head with a knobkerrie. He was fine for a week, then dropped down dead during a stressful game of bridge.'

'My head is fine,' says Alex, standing.

Charlie stands. 'We should get going to the parade ground and prepare for this afternoon's drill.' He's glaring at Alex. 'Don't you think?'

They leave the farmhouse and walk between the rows of sheets in the courtyard. The sun is hot and the laundry is warm and stinks of soap. The cat is on the roof above them. A dove hangs in its jaws, head swinging. One wing flexes up slowly, spreads a brilliant white fan into the blue sky then falls back against the tiles.

28

THE KESTREL

'Go on! Kiss it!' says Rowlands, waving his puffy foot in Eggleton's face.

'It's been so long, that's not such a bad proposition,' says Eggleton, rubbing a piece of whale-oiled cloth between his toes.

Earlier in the month, with no chance of drying their boots or socks, too many men had suffered so badly from trench-foot, they had been sent home. Some had even lost their feet when the trench-foot turned to gangrene. So now, D Company sit shoulder to shoulder with their backs against the sandbags, waiting for a foot inspection, followed by the application of Jonah Whale Oil and a clean pair of dry socks. It's been sunny for several days and the mud lingers in only a few corner puddles. Boots have been dried in the sun and the men's feet are starting to look healthy.

'What about that girl at The Pelican? She was only two days ago!' says Rowlands.

Eggleton grabs Rowlands foot. 'She doesn't count. I definitely prefer your foot to that girl!'

Rowlands pinches Eggleton's cheek with his chubby toes. 'Ooh! Come eeer you ansom garson! Kissy kissy!'

'Feet up! Feet up!' yells Kemmell. He and Alex are walking along the duckboards, solemnly inspecting each foot.

As they come to Percy, Alex sees that although one of the boy's feet is pink and clean, the other is brown and wrinkled with grime. 'That does not look like a washed foot, Elphick.'

Stubbs, sitting next to Percy, as always, rolls his eyes. 'He only washed one foot, Sir.'

'The water was too cold,' says Percy, angrily.

'So, you washed one foot and stopped?' says Alex.

Percy shrugs and looks at Stubbs for support.

Stubbs shakes his head.

'When you're done, Lieutenant, could I have a word?' Eden is standing on the fire-step at the end of the traverse.

Alex points towards the water bucket in the middle of the duck-boards. 'Elphick, go wash the other foot. Stubbs, make sure he puts the clean socks on and puts the dirty ones in that bag. I'm not losing him to trench-foot. There'd be too much paperwork.'

Percy hops, on his clean foot, to the bucket.

The men laugh.

Alex climbs up to join Eden.

There's a low ridge between the British trench and the Hun. It makes this section one of the few places where you can look out across No Man's Land with little fear of a sniper's bullet.

A brown bird is hovering over the field. Its head is perfectly still above the broken soil. The wingtips flutter like flames in the sunlight.

Eden is looking through field-glasses towards the German line. 'Division have asked me to write another report on the Festubert raid.'

Alex takes a deep breath. 'Well, you managed to get into the Hun trench, Sir. They must be intrigued.'

'Seems I've been recommended for something. Not sure what.' Eden laughs. 'Something else for Fenton to polish.' He's cut himself shaving. There's a small nick in the dimple behind his jaw, just below his ear lobe. 'Division need more information before they'll commit. I want to be clear that I have all the facts.'

'Of course, Sir.'

'Private Elphick.' Eden over-enunciates the 'k' so that it clicks. 'I had little chat with him earlier but...'

Alex's breath quickens. 'But what, Sir?'

'You brought him in didn't you? Thats why you ran off while your men were standing-to?'

Alex pauses, breathes in. 'He was lost, Sir. I found him.'

'Where did you find him?'

'Not far from the wire. He'd stopped a grenade. He'd been unconscious.'

The bird is hunting. Hovering, hanging on the wind above the soil, folding its wings and swooping towards the ground, gliding up in smooth arcs and hovering again.

'He was out there the whole time?' says Eden. 'During and *after* your retreat?'

'Yes, Sir. Why are you asking? Is that going to affect them awarding you a medal?' Alex runs the sentence again through his head, seeing if he can detect any insolence in the tone. He can see Percy sitting on the fire-step with Stubbs and the others. They're all laughing.

Eden lowers the glasses and follows Alex's gaze, towards Percy. 'I just thought, if he'd been near my platoon when we were trying to get through the wire, he could be helpful about what happened.'

'And was he? Helpful?' says Alex, trying to sound nonchalant. 'When you spoke with him?'

'Well, he's a bit slow isn't he? A bit simple?... But I wondered if he'd said anything to *you*?'

A shrill squeak comes up from behind the ridge in the field. The bird has dived and is fluttering in the dirt.

'No Sir, I don't think he'll know anything. He was unconscious, as I said. And I found him much further over than the place where you went through the wire.'

The bird is standing on something, ripping strips of flesh from under wet fur.

Eden turns to Alex. Suddenly his eyes are burning. 'You don't know where we went through the wire. You have no idea what happened out there! You found some dead soldiers in the middle of a battlefield and made ridiculous assumptions!'

Woodstone must have said something.

'I was asked to make a report, Captain. I reported what *I* saw.' Alex turns to go. 'So if that's all, Sir, I have a foot inspection to complete.'

'It's a kestrel,' says Eden.

'The bird? Yes, I know.'

'That's a rat that was screaming out there,' says Eden, gesturing towards the field. 'The kestrel needs to live. It needs to kill rats. It has no choice. Do you see?'

'Of course, it's a carnivore,' says Alex, dryly.

Eden smiles. 'Which life is more important, the rat or the kestrel?'

Alex doesn't know where this is going. 'I would say they are both equally important, in the natural scheme of things.'

Eden puts the field glasses on the parapet. 'And yet the kestrel is required to take the life of a whole rat, a *whole life*, every single day. How can that be right? How can the rat be equally important?'

'I don't know, Sir.'

Eden nods towards the men on the fire-step. 'Sometimes someone has to die in order for others to live. That's the order of things.'

Alex shakes his head. 'Then shouldn't we officers be proud to die, in order for our men to live.'

Eden laughs. 'No soldier should be proud to die. Be proud to *serve*. You can't do that if you're dead.'

Alex thinks of Eden's men hanging off the wire. 'The men you left out there, the men who were not expecting the bullets to come from *behind*, they can't serve anyone now, can they?'

Eden blinks, expressionless, swallows. 'No, no they can't, but they did. They served.' He pauses to find his words. 'But I wonder... how surprised Captain Kingsman was, when he saw you throwing a grenade at him. He can't have been expecting *that*. He isn't serving anyone now, after your little *faux pas*, is he?'

Alex can't think of any words. He feels sick.

Eden raises an eyebrow. 'Let he who is without sin, cast the first stone.'

Alex's gut twists like he's been punched. He steps down from the fire-step and walks along the duckboards.

Rowlands has turned a sock into a glove puppet and is singing to the men.

The puppet waves to Alex.

Alex doesn't wave back.

29

THE PARADOS

It's a good sketch: Softly feathered lines of the German trenches. White paper showing through for the new barbed-wire, glinting in the sunlight. Sharp vertical pencil strokes for broken trees and posts. Finger smudges make the shell holes and puddles in No Man's Land. Then, at the bottom of the page, are the helmets of the soldiers in the trench below him. The dark ovals give weight to the landscape, add contrast, echoing the clouds at the top. The image is divided into horizontal thirds; Fibonacci's golden sections. Order, balance.

But the landscape in front of him is littered with human bones. There are corpses floating just below the surface of the puddles. Everyone who isn't dead is trying to kill someone. This soil will run red for decades to come, either with the blood of these soldiers or the rust of the bullets that killed them. There is no order. Nothing is balanced. It's a slow, stinking chaos. He drags the pencil diagonally across the page. The paper rips and puckers. He throws the sketch-book down and picks up the field-glasses.

A patrol reported scraping sounds in the night; gravel or cement being shovelled. So before the sun rose and flooded the field with this golden, hazy light, he climbed over the parados and lay down here, to observe. He's in relative safety, obscured by the wall of sandbags and the long grass that's growing behind it. He scans along the German parapet, looking for anything new or unusual.

He notices a broken section, a gap with loose sandbags. There's movement. A German soldier raises his head, looks around and crawls out between the loose bags. Then, sliding through the grass in front of the parapet for a few yards, he sits down in a shallow shell hole, removes his tunic and lies down. What's he doing? Sunbathing in his shirtsleeves! Does he not realise he can be seen? Alex should call for a sniper. There would be a clean shot from up here; no more than four hundred yards.

Perhaps the soldier doesn't care. Perhaps being killed after your damp bones have been warmed for a few minutes in this glorious sunlight is better than living in the dank shadows of these trenches. Alex will leave the man alone. Let him sunbathe.

Two enamel mugs appear on the top of the sandbags. 'See anything?' says Charlie, lifting himself over and dropping into the grass.

Alex shakes his head.

Charlie hands Alex the tea. 'It tastes of petrol again, I'm afraid.'

Alex, peers into the mug. Oily clouds swirl in the grey liquid. 'Why do they bring it up in petrol cans? If they can bring us millions of tins of bully beef, whale oil, ammunition boxes, why not clean water, in clean cans?'

'Just drink it while it's still warm.' Charlie looks out across No Man's Land and sighs. 'What a beautiful morning. Spring is such a tease.'

'What's wrong with spring?' says Alex, still looking through the field-glasses.

'Days like this. You think winter is over and before you know it, it's snowing. Spring is not to be trusted...'

'Just enjoy it while it's still warm,' says Alex.

Charlie laughs, lies on his back. The long grass fans out above his shoulders as it flattens.

'I had a letter from Odette this morning,' says Alex.

'Oh did you? That's topping! What did she say?'

'Nothing really. Something about repairing a fence in the back field. Oh, and one of the chickens has a dicky foot. She asked me to look at it when we get back.'

'That's a good letter,' says Charlie, smiling.

'Why?'

'She's sent you a letter about nothing.'

'I know… Why is that good?'

'Because she's trying to say something else. If the letter was about something, then it would be about that thing, but it isn't, so it must be about something that the letter isn't about. Do you see?'

'I think so,' says Alex, smiling and hiding it by sipping his tea. 'What do you think she's trying to say?' He spits the tea into the grass.

'I've no idea.' Charlie picks up the sketchbook. 'Are you painting?'

'Sketching.'

Charlie runs his finger along the gashed line in the sketch. 'What happened here?'

'It was too… I don't know. Too right.' Alex takes the sketchbook from Charlie and closes it. 'The men love this tea. How do they drink it?'

'It's comforting. Something from home. A little port of sanity in this ocean of madness… Evelina used to make good tea. I've never got the hang of it.'

'You must miss her?'

'Evelina?' Charlie sits up, curls his fingers around a long patch of grass and pulls. The damp stems snap with a muffled thud. 'I feel ill without her, Alex. Diseased. Like I have a lung missing, or an eye. Even out here, where she would never have been, everything I look at seems to have an Evelina-shaped something missing from it.'

Alex tells Charlie about his idea of a silver thread linking the space between lovers.

Charlie is quiet for a while. He picks a piece of grass from his mug. 'I think Evelina cut our thread.'

'Why did she? Why did she leave?'

'She thinks I'm a coward.'

'What?'

Charlie takes a deep breath. 'Evelina's father fought in Africa. Her brothers signed up for this war on the day it started. I'd been at officer's training corps so, of course everyone expected me to sign up too. And I had every intention of doing so, at first. But I didn't. Something stopped me. I wasn't afraid, I was excited about the whole thing. I just didn't go. And we argued. Then people we knew who went out, stopped coming back. And the more I thought about it, the more I didn't *want* to go. I just couldn't bear to think of Evelina and I being separated.'

A shell explodes somewhere near the German line. Black smoke plumes into the air and drifts across the field.

'Then her brother was killed. It was awful. But I thought, now she'll understand. Now she'll let me stay. But she got angry, insisted that I go. To avenge him, she said! I was confused, I wanted to fight, but I couldn't leave her. So I went to see my doctor; a mutual friend. I explained that I didn't want to go. I thought he would understand, see the romance in it. I asked him to make me a certificate that showed I couldn't go, make something up, an illness. I thought he'd done it. Then a group of women came to my office and gave me a box. They said, "This is from Evelina and all of us." I opened it, and there was a white feather. I knew what it meant. I went home and she'd taken all her things. Gone. I never saw her after that.'

They both watch the smoke as it thins and settles in the shell holes.

'I'm so sorry, Charlie.'

'I had no reason *not* to come out here after that. So I signed up and here I am.'

'Does she know you're out here?'

'I don't know. I write. She doesn't reply. I wrote to her father. No one replies.'

'If she knew why you hadn't volunteered at the beginning, she would understand, surely?'

'I don't know. I hope so. I thought, perhaps if she knows I'm here, *being brave*, you know?' Charlie rips up a tuft of grass and throws it into the air.

'Yes, I'm sure of it, Charlie. She just needs time. You should keep writing.'

Clouds are beginning to form behind the German trenches; cauliflower against the blue sky.

'So, why did you come here, Alex?'.

'Similar reasons, I think. But I don't know who I'm proving it to. My father, perhaps? I don't know. I wanted to be a hero.' Alex laughs. 'Like Eden! I wanted to be in the same battalion as him. There was an article in the paper, something he'd done in Loos. There was a picture. He was standing in a garden, next to a very pretty young woman, and I looked at that picture and I thought, *that's who I want to be. Thats the kind of man I want to be.* And I thought, if I could come here and learn directly from the man himself, I could also be… there's no other word for it, a hero!' He laughs again.

'Eden *is* a hero.'

'He's not. Heroes are brave. They do things despite being afraid. I don't think Eden is afraid of anything.'

'He's afraid of failing,' says Charlie. 'He thinks of himself like one of those noble, medieval knights who march loudly into battle, with a fair maiden's kerchief tied to his lance. He's terrified that some nameless peasant archer is going to shoot him in the eye and rob him of his chance to display his chivalric honour. But whether he wants to be hero or not, he *does* heroic things. So he *is* a hero.'

'There's nothing heroic about shooting your own men,' says Alex.

'You can't be sure he shot anyone.'

'Percy saw him do it.'

'Yes, so you said. But you also said that Percy was sleep-walking or something. He might have been dreaming. Perhaps Eden just accidentally shot someone and that's what Percy saw.'

Alex stares at Charlie. 'And if it was that, a terrible accident, if you knew that he'd killed one of his own by mistake, because of the confusion…' Alex sighs and stops.

Charlie turns to face Alex. 'What's the question? Are you asking me what I would think if Eden had *accidentally* killed one of his own men?'

Now Alex is pulling at the blades of grass. 'Yes, if Eden, or anyone... If you knew...' Again Alex can't finish what he wants to say. He looks away.

'I think it would depend. But I think it probably happens all the time,' says Charlie, carefully. 'Men running in the dark, the smoke, the chaos.' He pauses. 'Alex? Is there something...?'

'What? No!' Alex laughs nervously, picks up the field-glasses. 'Someone said to me that the enemy isn't always where you think it is. I'm beginning to realise what he meant.'

The sun is behind the clouds now, but the soldier is still there, his hands behind his head.

'No one knows what we're doing out here, or where we're going,' says Charlie. 'It's just a huge machine.' He flings grass into the air. Watches the wind take it. 'No one's in control of it and none of the parts know what the whole machine is doing. The best we can do is protect ourselves and the men from being crushed by the cogs. But the problem is, we *are* the cogs, all of us, grinding away...' He rips up more grass.

'Charlie, don't throw that grass. Snipers, looking for movement. Are you all right?'

'Sorry, old chum,' says Charlie. 'I was about to ask you the same... But yes, I'm fine. You got me thinking, that's all. I shouldn't do that too often.'

'It will be all right. I'm sure of it,' says Alex, punching Charlie on the arm.

Another shell explodes in the same place as the last. Beams of wood spin up and thud down into the mass of wire at the front of the German line.

'Looks like our tea break is over,' says Charlie, suddenly more cheerful. 'We should get back. Don't be long. We have to prep the trenches for the relief tonight.'

Alex sighs. 'Thank God. A bath, clean clothes and no reason to get up in the morning!'

'Actually, there is. We've got a triple memorial service, early. Kingsman and the others.'

'What? Why didn't you tell me before?'

'I don't know. I didn't want to spoil your tea.' Charlie climbs down into the trench.

Alex sits, watching the clouds grow heavy, until the first few drops of rain tap against the sandbags and the grass begins to quiver. As he climbs down, a gunshot rings out across the grey sky. He doesn't look to see if the sunbathing soldier is still there. He doesn't want to know.

30

THE CEMETERY

The cemetery is in the corner of a walled orchard. Painted wooden crosses lie under rows of skinny apple trees that fade into a thick fog.

The officers huddle together, facing the graves of Lieutenant Collins, Lieutenant Hartman and Captain Kingsman. They listen to prayers recited by the chaplain, but he's said them so many times, they're now devoid of meaning. The consonants drift away and only the vowels echo back, mingled with the lonely cries of crows.

Earlier rains have already started to wash away the mounds of earth above the graves and Kingsman's little wooden cross is leaning. The chaplain tries to straighten it, but it doesn't work. It falls forward, slowly, as if Kingsman is making a half-hearted protest from underground.

Soldiers come into the orchard, carrying three bodies wrapped in blankets. They lay them next to a stack of bloodstained stretchers and leave.

Now the chaplain is talking about the three officers' gallant deaths. Why is he saying that? Who is he talking to? Collins died in his sleep. Hartman died climbing out of a mule cart, three miles behind a front line that he'd never seen, and Kingsman... Kingsman died... None of their deaths were any more brave or heroic than if a bag of flour had accidentally fallen on their heads. The chaplain should be talking about the gallantry of their lives, not their deaths. But although Kingsman was gallant, Collins wasn't. Who knows about Hartman; none of them ever met him.

The soldiers, carrying spades, walk back into the orchard and wait for the service to finish. They light cigarettes, turn their backs on the rows of graves and stare out into the fog.

A ruffled blackbird scrapes against last summer's leaves and picks something out of the mud. It reminds Alex of the flapping black coats. 'Goodbye Doris!' his father had said, squeezing Alex's hand, as his mother's coffin was lowered, alarmingly roughly, into the earth. There's nothing to hope for after you've seen that. He wonders if it's better to see them buried. If Kingsman's wife had been here, if she had stood under these fruitless fruit trees and heard the spatter of soil against the coffin lid, she wouldn't have to hope. Despite the black-edged letter, will she always be listening for the squeak of the garden gate? It must be so tiring to always hope.

When the chaplain has gone, Alex looks around to see if anyone is watching. He walks over to the graves of Kingsman's men. Their row is already three lines back from the freshest ones. 'I'm sorry,' he says, in front of each one. Then he goes to Kingsman's grave, and now *he* tries to straighten the cross, pushing it down into the soil, wincing when the wood grinds against a stone. 'I'm sorry,' he says. 'I am *so* sorry.'

He hears someone behind him and turns to see that Woodstone is also talking to a grave. Alex pretends he hasn't seen but the captain calls him over. 'Gibbons,' he says, as Alex joins him. 'He came out with me from home. He said he had no choice as I would struggle with my tie.' He smiles. 'It was our little joke.' He points to some blue flowers in a milk bottle in the centre of the grave. 'We were in the market in Vieille Chapelle. There was a girl with some of these in a bucket, and he said he liked them.' Woodstone disguises a waiver in his voice as a cough. 'I forgot the name of the flowers, so I couldn't ask anyone. Then yesterday, I was passing and she was there again, the girl. Lucky really, things like that.'

One of the soldiers has climbed into a new grave and is shovelling soil up onto the grass.

'Just look at all these graves!' says Woodstone, sounding almost cheerful now. 'I've got more dead officers under this orchard than I have live ones standing on top of it. We're running out of space.'

'Apparently,' says Eden, overhearing. 'The adjutant is talking to the farmer about buying the whole orchard.'

'At this rate, we're going to need his whole farm,' says Woodstone. 'I'm so short of officers now. It's frustrating. Damned mess with this show coming up.'

'I was wondering, Sir,' says Alex, as they join the other officers. 'Would it be an idea to send some of the sergeants for officer training?'

'The sergeants?' says Woodstone.

'I was thinking that Kemmell might make an excellent subaltern. He has actual battle experience, more than many of the officers and he's very good with the men.'

Woodstone looks embarrassed. He takes his hat off and runs a finger down his parting, smoothing the hair away from it with the palm of his hand. 'Well... Eden?'

Eden shrugs. 'If we send our sergeants off for officer training, then we'll have a shortage of sergeants. No. If he's good at being a sergeant, keep him as a sergeant.'

'Exactly,' says Woodstone. 'Right, I'm off. Lunch with battalion HQ. Captain Eden, don't forget to tell them about the farm raid.' He turns, glancing at Gibbons' grave, and walks out of the orchard, into the fog.

'The farm raid, Sir?' says Halsall, smiling. 'Do tell!'

Eden uses a stick to draw an imaginary map in the grass. 'We're moving up to Givency in a few days. Boche have a machine gun tucked into a farmhouse on the only bit of raised ground for miles. It's been causing a lot of bother. Artillery can't get the correct range, so it needs to be done on the ground. Previous attempts have been done at night but no one seems to be able to clear it.' He grins. 'So I suggested we have a go in daylight, directly up the hill. It should be fun.' He looks at Alex. 'There's no Boche wire to worry about this time, so everyone should manage it. But I'll lead with my men, just to be sure, and you chaps will be flanking with yours.'

A soldier is dragging a corpse by its feet. It falls into the grave with a thud.

31

THE FARM RAID

07.28: Fix bayonets and wait.

A dove, somewhere in the trees.

Nervous whispering.

Wait.

The ticking of his watch.

Breath plumes, white in the cold air.

Wait.

'Dear God,' Alex whispers. 'Let me be brave. Let me be brave.'

07.30: He blows the whistle and runs. The men are with him, through the undergrowth, through the dark canopy of leafless branches, curving down to the fields, towards the sharp morning light beyond the trees.

Voices fill the air.

Whistles.

An acid stench of leaf-rot and soil.

They reach the edge of the wood and beyond it, a green hill. Tufts of grass shimmer, rising up towards a redbrick farmhouse.

Alex stands for a moment in the shade, sucking the coldness into his lungs. He signals to the men and they all move out into the sunshine.

They are striding out, holding the line, steady in the formation they've been trained to hold. 'Keep straight. Don't bunch up!' Charlie is on the right. Eden and his men are in front, running up the hill; black shapes against the bright ground.

A machine gun crackles from the farm.

'Get down!' Alex is on his knees. A snail clings to a quivering blade of grass.

Running again.

Gunshots. Eden's men are returning fire.

Alex leads his men up the hill. He feels the air stings his nostrils, feels life is in his fingers, in his blood, pushing against his skin. He feels it in his men running with him; a glorious line of soldiers running through the cold air. He's laughing.

The machine gun again. Bullets thud in the soil.

Eden's men are crawling. They've almost reached the farmhouse.

An explosion, muffled. The machine gun stops.

Shouting.

The undergrowth is thicker here. Afraid of slipping on the wet ground, Alex takes short fast steps, curving around the tufts of grass. He falls behind, his men are ahead. A small pebble of doubt rattles in his stomach. He looks up towards the farm and pushes harder. His foot slips out from under him and he crashes down, hard, into a clump of low brambles. Blood on his face. Dirt in his mouth.

There's a pale shape under the bushes. A young man's face. The uniform, strangely grey, different from his own. A German soldier!

Both men scramble to get to their feet.

The German looks afraid, yanks his rifle; the bayonet caught in the brambles.

Alex aims his revolver. Holds it with both hands, shaking. He doesn't know if it's fear or excitement; it should be fear but the soldier looks so... so soft.

The German stops, lets go of the rifle and falls onto his knees. He has thin wrists. He smells of soap.

Both men are breathing together, panting little clouds into the green shadows.

Slowly, staring at Alex, the German unbuttons the top pocket of his tunic and opens the flap.

A gunshot. A blackbird screeches and flutters out of the brambles. The German grimaces, places his fingers gently over the hole that has appeared in his tunic and looks down, confused.

Alex turns around.

Eden is standing behind him, holding his revolver by his side.

The soldier, gasping, moves his shaking hand once more towards his pocket, pulls out a piece of paper and tries to unfold it. He lifts it towards Alex.

Eden fires again.

Alex cries out.

The soldier slumps to the ground.

Everything is still.

'I saw him running down the hill,' says Eden, calmly. 'Must have escaped out the back of the farm. Thought I'd see if I could find him. You're lucky I did.'

'Why did you shoot him?' says Alex. 'We could have taken him prisoner.'

'He reached for something. I didn't have time to wait to see what it was.' He reaches down and unfolds the paper.

'He wasn't even holding his gun.' Alex's mouth fills with bile. He turns away and throws up in the bushes. When he's finished, Eden hands him the paper. It's a photograph of a woman wearing a lavish black hat. She's holding her hands up towards it, smiling.

'It's a portrait,' says Alex, spitting and wiping his mouth with his sleeve.

Eden raises an eyebrow. 'Let's hope, for his sake, that this was his mother, and not his wife.'

Alex stares at Eden. 'Why are you so full of hate?'

Eden shrugs. 'This is nothing to do with hate. This is war. We're standing on a battlefield and this is a *German* soldier!'

'But you show so little respect. You have no idea who he was or what he was like.'

'I can guess,' says Eden, crouching by the soldier. 'Look at his face.

He's got that puffy, potato look that peasants always have. He might have bred a few chickens or worked in a saw mill, then got fat and old and drunk, living out his dull life achieving absolutely nothing.'

'You can't say that.'

'Now his name will be carved in stone in the middle of whatever little village he came from. Now his darling mother and some pert little peasant girl will weep for him.' Eden stands, casually dropping the photograph onto the soldier's chest. 'It's a good death. He would thank me if he could.'

Alex glares.

Eden laughs. 'Do you think the Hun would stop to think who you might be? Of course not. You are the enemy and because of that, they will shoot you.' He looks over towards the farm. 'I've got to get back. The farm is secured, but there might be traps.' He kicks the dirt with his boot. 'Look, we'll be in Vieille Chapelle by this afternoon. I was thinking of paying *The Pelican* a visit tonight. Why don't you come with me? We can talk more about shooting or not shooting the enemy. You can ask me questions. It's a rough place, but so are the girls. It will be fun.' He grins.

Alex shakes his head. 'I'm afraid I can't, Sir. There's a dance in the village. I promised I would go with Odette.'

'A dance.' Eden's eyes burn for a moment. 'Right. I've got to get back to the men. Yours are just arriving at the farm now. You should come and congratulate them, when you've recovered… I'll see you at breakfast.'

When Eden has gone, Alex folds the photograph carefully and places it back into the soldier's pocket. The body is still warm and the smell of soap seems stronger than before.

As he walks towards the farmhouse. He thinks of the soldier's body warming the soil under the bushes, then the stillness, and the soil becoming cold again.

32

THE SEWING MACHINE

'What do I do with this? It looks like a silver bullet.' Charlie is sitting at the table, trying to thread cotton onto a bobbin that he's managed to remove from the shuttle of an old sewing machine.

'I've absolutely no idea.' Alex stares at the machine: black lacquered, ornate gold lettering, shiny spindles and a large brass wheel. 'Where did you get that?'

'I was out looking for somewhere we could use as an ammunition dump, in the comms trenches by the Rue du Bois. One of them runs right under this big old house. You can look up from the trench into the family parlour. There's a piano teetering on broken floorboards, sheet music still on the stand. Chairs with cushions and even cups on a table. This was there. No one's coming back for it, so I took it.'

'I wonder if any of the family are still alive,' says Alex, sitting down next to Charlie.

Charlie finds a reel of cotton in a little drawer on the wooden base. 'Aha! This looks useful!' He places it on a spindle on the top of the machine. 'It felt like they'd just left the room. As though the father will come in with a whisky in his hand, and a little girl will sit down at the piano. It made me rather sad.'

Alex turns the wheel on the side of the sewing machine. 'Why did you bring it back? What are you going to do with it?'

'I thought I could learn to sew. I've been getting ideas for making things.'

'What kind of things?'

'Alterations really. In case the weather turns cold again. It's so unpredictable. The men have scarves, but they're usually too long and get in the way.' He grabs his scarf from a hook on the wall and wraps it around his neck. 'I thought I could cut them in half and sew them up, like this, so it hugs your neck but has no bits hanging down.'

'Couldn't their wives or mothers make them and send them out?' says Alex, trying not to smile.

'They could, but who's going to show them? It's so much easier for me to do it.'

'And are you going to make scarves for the whole regiment or just your men?'

'I haven't thought that far yet. I'll start with my men... Why are you laughing? I thought it was a good idea. I just need to figure out how to use the machine. I didn't think it would be so complicated.'

'I'm laughing because the days are getting warmer now. It will be high summer by the time you finish a single scarf. But you make me happy, that's all. You're so calmly good about things. You see a problem and you just get on with fixing it. I wish I was like that.'

Charlie replaces the metal shuttle and closes the flap. 'Why are there so many levers?' He runs the thread up through the machine. 'We had to translate a Greek philosopher at school, Epictetus. Have you heard of him?'

Alex shakes his head.

'Epictetus said we should try to identify the things in life that we're capable of changing, and change them if we need to, but to accept the things that we can't change. That made sense to me.' He turns the handle slowly, watching the levers click up and down.

'But how do you know what things you can change? Sometimes you think you can change something but you can't.'

'Well, that's the trick isn't it? To be good at knowing. But sometimes you don't know until you try.'

'And what if,' says Alex, slowly. 'What if the thing you really want to change has already happened? Say something bad happened in the past. Do you think it's possible to change that, by doing something good in the future?'

Charlie looks confused. 'I don't know. Perhaps every bad thing does have a good thing that opposes it.'

'So the bad thing stays bad, until the good thing happens to cancel it out?'

'I think that's possible. I haven't really thought about it that much.' He reverently hands Alex the needle. 'Hold this. I think it's important.'

'But then how would you know which good things were connected to the bad thing?'

Charlie stops and turns to Alex. 'What's the matter, Old Chap? Are you still feeling bad about the farm raid?'

'No, this is something...' Alex stops himself, holding his breath, holding the words in. 'Well, yes. Yes, it's the farm raid. I messed everything up.'

'You did not. We achieved the objective and no one was hurt.'

Alex sighs. 'I was useless. I wanted to really *lead* the platoon. I ended up sitting on the floor with a German, while my men stormed the machine gun post without me.'

'Eden had already blown up the machine gun by the time they or anyone else got there. There was nothing for us to do.'

'I almost got shot. Eden had to rescue me. Then I threw up in front of him.'

Charlie laughs. 'You told me the soldier was just trying to show you a portrait of his mother!'

'But he was the enemy! I should have shot him, without thinking.'

Charlie takes the needle. 'You should *always* think. Just think fast.' He fastens the needle into position. 'Or you could do what Eden does, and just shoot everyone, whichever side they're on. No thinking required.' He pauses to give Alex a knowing look, then turns the wheel. Oiled levers rock up and down, shiny things slowly rotate.

'I don't think I've made a very good impression with the men, so far,' says Alex.

'On the contrary,' says Charlie, squinting as he threads the needle. 'Your men were very impressed when Eden told them what happened.'

'What did he tell them?'

'I think the focus of his story was how he was required to save you. But, according to his account, when he found you, you were in the final stages of a hand to hand, epic fight.'

'An epic fight!' Alex grimaces. 'We were about to exchange addresses when Eden shot him.'

Charlie smiles. 'The men like you, Alex. The officers respect you and the men trust that. I'd be chuffed if they felt the same about me.'

'Why wouldn't they? You're so kind to them. You knit them scarves!'

'This is sewing, not knitting. But anyway, I don't know if kindness is what they want. They want someone to be gallant, someone who can lead them bravely across the battlefield, don't they?'

'Gallant...' Alex shrugs. 'You're as gallant as any of us. You just do it quietly.'

Charlie turns the wheel again. The machine runs for a moment then the cotton snaps and spirals into a knotted clump. He rests his forehead on the table.

Alex pats Charlie on the back. 'We should ask Madame Berger. She'll know how to do it.'

'Good idea. Go and get her now, would you? We need to fix this machine immediately. Dinner will be ready in less than an hour, and Odette will be serving.'

'And?' says Alex, allowing himself a cautious smile.

'We need to make you a good suit!'

33

THE SKETCHBOOK

The cows move slowly across the field. Insects follow them, catching the afternoon sunlight like sparks above a fire.

'May I see your book of sketches,' says Odette, sleepily. She's lying next to Alex, holding a stem of grass between her teeth.

He shrugs. 'If you like.' He hands her the book. 'They're just rough, quick sketches. Nothing's finished.' They've been drinking wine and the world has grown softer, but he still feels a sting of apprehension as she sits up and flattens out the book against the grass. He watches her turning the pages, gently, reverently.

'These are good,' she says, tugging at the grass between her teeth. She studies the clusters of pencil lines; the drawings that represent his time in France: No Man's Land in the snow, views of the farm, the men cooking breakfast in the rain. 'How did you get so good at this? With your parents being farmers? How did you learn to draw, to be good enough to go to art school?'

'Being a farmer doesn't mean you can't draw,' he says.

She blushes. 'No, I meant—'

'I'm joking,' he says, smiling. 'My mother was an artist, a painter. She was actually very good. Landscapes mainly. Beautiful.'

'Ah, so she taught you?'

'No, I was too young. She died before I was interested. But my father kept her studio for a long time. I would stare at her paintings for hours. I'd examine them; the brushstrokes. A little curve, a point where a line would gently thicken or quiver, and I would wonder if I could feel her breathing there. Did a subtle change of colour signify a different day, or a different mood? And I felt that… it sounds silly now but, I felt that, through her paintings, she was speaking to me, and I could hear her.'

'That isn't silly at all. I understand that.'

'So in a way, yes, perhaps she did teach me. But then we had a maid who moved my mother's things and my father was very angry. Then he cleared everything away. I think he sold them. And then I was really angry with him. And…' He stops speaking, shakes his head.

Odette turns to him. 'What was she like?'

'I don't remember exactly. My father has a photograph of her in his bedroom. It must have been a little high street photography studio. She's leaning against a little table and she's staring out, past the photographer. She's young, in her twenties, perhaps. She looks so out of place, in a silk dress, I think it is. But she has this extraordinary smile, as if she knows that everything will be all right. She seems so confidently calm.'

Odette's face is very close to his and he can smell the sweetness of the stem of grass between her teeth.

'As for actual memories,' he says. 'I just have flashes, from when I was very small. Patches of things; a few sentences, a smile, a smack.'

Odette smiles. She turns back to the sketches: soldiers digging, Charlie looking like a general with field glasses, storm clouds billowing above his head. The soft muscles of her face tighten at a dark image of a horse, stuck in the mud on the Rue Du Bois. Its eye, white and shining on the centre of the page, surrounded by converging lines of rain and reins and the stretched out hands of helpless cavalrymen. She sighs and turns the page to an image of a row of men, asleep and huddled on the fire-step. 'Who is this?'

'That's Stubbs, and next to him is Rowlands and Eggleton, and that's Percy.'

'Is he that small?'

'He is!' says Alex, laughing.

Odette doesn't laugh. She turns the page: a sketch of Eden, sitting at the table in the officer's dugout, pipe clenched in his teeth, candlelit, handsome. 'I don't like him.'

'Eden? I thought... You always seem so... warm to him.'

She shrugs.

'But whenever I see you with him, you're always laughing. I thought...'

'That's not true.' She rubs the drawing with her finger. 'Sometimes he makes me laugh, yes. He's *charming*. But I don't like him.' She picks up the bottle and pours more wine into Alex's glass.

He drinks, watching her, trying to make sense of what she's just said. Alex's childish admiration for Eden the hero, and what he now knows about the real man, is still a conflict; two truths, like clashing paints forming a muddy brown. It seems so easy for Odette to separate the different ways she feels.

'And when you told me what he did...' She shivers. 'Forcing his men!'

Alex takes the sketchbook. 'I shouldn't have told you. I'm not exactly sure if he did that.'

'You should tell someone. It can't be right.'

'I did, weeks ago. No one was interested.'

'Then go to...' She flaps her arms, looking for the English words. 'To the men higher up!'

'The higher up you go, the more they would approve of what Eden did. Some officers will do anything to get the men on their feet. It's accepted, as long as no one talks too much about it.'

'Would you do that?' she says.

'Not intentionally.' He studies her expression so he can see how it changes. 'But Eden and I are not so different.'

She stares at him. 'What do you mean by that?'

'Eden shoots the men who refuse to go. The ones that do go, get

165

shot by the Germans. I want my men to trust me, so that when I ask them to, they all go. And then *they* get shot by the Germans too. Either way, everyone ends up getting shot.'

'But you are not killing them. You are not ordering them to their deaths. You are *advising* them on the best time to take the risks that they have volunteered to take. You order them to go only when they are *less* likely to be shot. No?'

'Your English is very good,' he says.

'Did you listen? Did you hear what I said?'

'Yes,' he says quietly, watching her turning the pages. 'And I think you're right. I hope you're right.'

There's a sketch of her, sitting on a bench in the farmyard. 'When did you draw this?' she says, looking at him suspiciously.

'You were making something with a stick, a tool. It was from the window. I was in the dining room.' He looks away, embarrassed.

She thrusts the book at Alex and stands, assuming a pose like a Greek statue; legs wide apart, one arm up to the sky and a scowl on her face. 'Draw me, now! Like this!'

Delighted, he feels in his pocket for a pencil. 'No, how you were just now, in the grass.'

She giggles and lies down.

He arranges her hair so that it flows away from her like the petals of a flower.

She's smiling.

He doesn't smile. He's being serious; a serious artist. He stands back. She's beautiful. There's nothing that he would change, but he continues to study her in order to give the impression that something more complicated needs to be considered before he can start his sketch. When he feels enough time has passed for her to be sufficiently impressed, he begins to draw. Holding the pencil loosely, twisting it in his fingers as he traces the outline of her body, the oval of her face, marking the positions of her features. He draws the tension of her tendons. 'I heard your father volunteered,' he says, as he follows the undulation of skin across muscle and bone, the fruit-like curve of her shoulder, the softness of her skin.'What was he like?'

She sighs slowly, staring up into the clouds. 'He was strong, like a *cheval de trait*, a horse that pulls carts, you know?'

'Don't look at me, keep looking up.'

'Sorry,' she says, smiling. 'He was a kind man, but angry too. He used to drink. Always shouting about something, politics, the market price of milk, some neighbour's goats in our field, everything; always shouting.' She closes her eyes. 'My mother ignored his anger, if she could. We both did. We were used to it. So when he started to shout about the Germans, we didn't really notice. And then the war came, and one day he left. Are you still drawing me?'

'Yes. Don't move. That must have been very sad.' He sketches the smoothness of her neck, the lightness, the little hairs, silver from the sunlight behind her.

'It *was* sad, for a while. But we managed without him. We used to do most of the work anyway. But it was also... It was peaceful. There was a war, but it was so peaceful. Is this what you meant? Am I talking too much?'

'No, not at all, I'm interested.' He has drawn women before; plump models sitting awkwardly on white cubes in the studios of the art academy. But he has never drawn a woman who he knows, who he likes. And right now, in this field, he thinks he feels closer to Odette than any woman he has ever met.

'Then we had a letter. It said that...' She pauses, breathes in. 'He had been killed somewhere near Arras. The first day of October, two years ago.'

Alex stops sketching. 'Do you miss him?'

'Yes I do. I do miss him. I loved him. I...' Her eyes sparkle. 'Can I move my arm?'

'Of course. I'm sorry. I'm sorry about your father.'

'I need more wine,' she says, wiping the corner of her eye.

'Hold on, I've nearly finished,' he says. 'You have beautiful collarbones.'

She sits up. 'I have what?'

'Now you've moved!' He closes the sketchbook.

'You said I could move!'

167

'I meant just your arm!'

'What is a *collarbone*?' she says. 'I don't understand.'

He points. 'Clavicle.'

'Ah, Clavicule! It's the same. Can I see?' She rolls over to him and reaches for the book.

'Let me finish it first, then I'll show you.'

'Show me now!' she says, moving closer.

'No, if you see it now, you'll think I'm no good.'

Odette leans across him, reaching for the book. Alex takes her hand, firmly. She twists and stretches up towards him. A hundred tiny expressions move across her face. Her chest rises up to the cotton of her blouse. He touches her skin, slides his finger along her collarbone.

'Clavicule,' he says.

'Yes.' She laughs.

He draws his finger up slowly along the curves of her neck, under her chin, towards her mouth. 'Lips,' he says. He waits for her to translate, but she doesn't speak. He holds his finger against her lips so carefully that all he can feel is the warmth from her breathing; steady and deep. A breeze forms in the middle of the field, the long grass swirls and hisses. He kisses her. Her breath tastes of wine and fresh grass. They breathe together, into each other. She raises herself to him and he curves his arms around her. Her hands are warm against his back.

He is falling now, into the ground, between the green grass and the white shoots, down past the earthworms and the tree roots and the stones and soil and the ancient bones and skulls of heroes whose deaths were never written down. He's wrapped in the rocks and the darkness of the Earth and Odette is with him and she's holding him and he feels that he belongs here, feels that he is home.

On the way back to the farm, the cows trudge along the narrow lane ahead of them. The setting sun drips like a broken egg into the trees behind the farmhouse. A haze of insects and the sound of blackbirds fills the warm air. The evening hangs heavily around them and stinks of green living things. She carries her shoes, walking barefoot, carefully, like an acrobat balancing between the pebbles in the dusty path. Each time she steps too hard on a stone she stumbles sideways and grips his arm, and each time she lets go, he feels a momentary grief, lost in the underworld, as if a river of death is raging between them.

34

THE TRAINING GROUND

D Company officers are standing in a semicircle, inside a dome of grey fog that's so thick, they can't even see the hedges that surround the training field.

They face Captain Woodstone, Eden, Lindsey and three training sergeants.

Woodstone is on his horse. 'Division think the Germans are digging a mine in our sector. Aeroplane photographs have shown…' He bends down in his saddle towards Lindsey. Lindsey whispers something. The horse's ears twitch. Woodstone looks confused and whispers something to Lindsey.

Lindsey steps forward. 'Aeroplane photographs have shown a discolouration in the soil, that might indicate the entrance to a mine.'

'Exactly,' says Woodstone. 'Our mission is to find that entrance. So over the next few days, you and your men will be training for the attack and search.' He pulls a sheet of paper out of his pocket. 'I'm splitting you up into units of five to eight men. Three forward attack units with 3 Platoon in reserve. Captain Eden will take Alpha, Pope will lead Beta, Ryan you will be in charge of Ceta and—'

'There is no Ceta!' says Eden, lighting his pipe.

'Why not? I need three forward units.'

'Ceta is not a Greek Letter.' Eden spits a piece of tobacco off his lip. 'If you're using the Greek and you want the third one, then you need Gamma.'

Woodstone looks confused. 'Gamma? That's G isn't it?'

Charlie raises his hand. 'I think, Sir, it's because the Etruscans didn't distinguish between the G and K sounds. The Greek alphabet is derived—'

'Thank you, Mr Pope,' interrupts Woodstone. 'This doesn't have to be a thing about Greece. I just need names for each unit. So Ryan *will be* leading Ceta. Halsall is away on training, so Lieutenant Francourt will be leading 3 Platoon. Telephone lines have been placed—'

'Excuse me, Sir?' says Francourt, raising his hand. 'It's not my place to suggest any linguistic corrections to a superior officer, but should my platoon not be called Delta?'

Woodstone looks confused again. 'Why?'

Francourt flashes a wink to the officers behind him. 'The others are all called something a bit Greek.'

Woodstone shakes his head and waggles the piece of paper. 'No, Francourt. I've spent a long time working this all out. Only the *units* have Greek letters. The *platoons* are *numbered*. You're in charge of 3 *Platoon*.'

No one speaks. They're trying not to laugh.

Lindsey coughs. 'Should we ask the sergeants to take over from here, Sir? If the officers would like to head over to their respective units, please? Your men are already waiting by the training trenches.'

Alex is paired with a training sergeant who seems to be trying to compensate for the dreary, damp weather; leaping around a fifty yard replica of the German trench that, to Alex, looks exactly the same as the British trench. 'Your units will enter here! Tadaa! Work their way along, knob any Boche they meet. Biff! Biff! And dash on!' He pauses and grins. 'All right?'

Alex's men look bored and cold. They stand, silently, with their hands in their pockets.

Undaunted, the sergeant continues: 'Bombers will clear any

dugouts. Boom! Inspections will be made, and if a mine entrance is found, it will be reported back to HQ immediately. All right?'

'I think I saw this bloke in The Pirates of Penzance, last year at the Hippodrome,' whispers Rowlands.

The sergeant sploshes around the waterlogged trench, spraying mud as he goes. 'Artillery! Here come the big boys!' A great sweep of his arms to represent the arc of shells. 'Pow! Kaboom! They'll keep the flanks closed off for a short period of time. They'll try to block anything coming up the support trenches. But this is an *in-and-out*! So you should all be back home before lunch!' He flops over, hands on hips, panting. It's difficult to know if he's feeling light-headed, or if he's bowing, expecting applause.

'Before lunch, Sergeant?' says Alex. 'Is this mission not at night?'

'You'll go out just before dawn, Sir, under cover of darkness, stay hidden in shell holes near Fritz's wire and attack after breakfast. It's new, Sir. No one's tried it in our sector.'

After several equally enthusiastic demonstrations of the raiding technique, Alex is given command of the session.

Stubbs, being the best shot, is ordered to lead the unit. The men wade through the waterlogged practice trenches, throwing grenades, yelling and shooting and thrusting their bayonets into straw-filled dummies.

Percy tries to throw a practice grenade over the parapet. It bounces off the sandbags, clangs onto Stubbs's helmet and falls into the water.

Stubbs glares, wiping mud out of his eye. 'You don't throw the bombs, Perce!'

'But I've got bombs here,' says Percy, showing everyone his satchel.

'I know, but they're not for you. We throw the bombs.'

'Why am I carrying them then?'

Alex is in the field above them, running along the edges, guiding them on. 'You're in rear support, Elphick. You give them to the others when they need them. You're guarding the rear. So turn around and aim your rifle.'

'But there's nobody there,' says Percy, staring up at Alex.

'There might be! You're making sure no one comes around that corner. You have to stay there until the others have cleared the next line.'

'But there isn't! We're the only ones here.'

'Just pretend! Pretend for fuck's sake!' yells Rowlands, laughing.

Gradually, everyone begins to work together. Even Percy finds his rhythm; walking backwards, guarding the rear and handing out grenades.

At the end of a very long day, Alex blows his whistle. 'Back down to our end and let's go one more time,' he says, smiling as he watches his men, *his wonderful men*, fading into the pinkish fog.

35

MUSKETRY

Alex lets his body relax, sinking into the grass. The rifle butt is warm and smooth against his cheek. He flexes his fingers one by one, tightens his grip. The gun creaks gently. He pulls back the bolt, closes his left eye, breathes in and aims. His finger feels the trigger, feels the tension in the spring. Daisies sway in his peripheral vision. A fly buzzes near his shoulder. Birds sing in the trees behind. He tries to let all that go, let the world fade away; everything diminishing to a single, simple point at the centre of the target.

'Fire!' yells Kemmell.

Gunshots ripple across the firing range.

Alex gently squeezes the trigger and fires.

Percy folds his arms and stares at the target. The paper sheet is as white and clean as when it was first pinned to the firing range wall. It dazzles in the sunlight. 'You missed!' he says, triumphantly.

'Well, you get the idea,' says Alex, standing up and brushing grass off his uniform. 'I'm more used to a revolver. And it's, *you missed, Sir.*'

Percy is trying not to laugh.

'What I was demonstrating, is that you don't just fire without thinking. You take your time. Even in the rush and chaos of the battle, you aim thoughtfully, quickly, but take your time.'

'But you missed.'

To Alex's relief, Kemmell orders the men to take up their positions again on the firing line.

'When is the instructor arriving, Sergeant?' asks Alex, quietly, so the men can't hear.

'He's been delayed, Sir. He's coming all the way from the School of Musketry in Hythe.'

'Well I hope he hurries up. I'm not cut out for this. All I seem to be demonstrating, is that I'd struggle to hit a house at twenty yards. The men are laughing at me!'

Kemmell gives Alex a fatherly smile. 'He should be with us this afternoon. But in the meantime, perhaps... if you take a more verbal approach?' Kemmell raises his cane into the air. 'Fire!'

Gunsmoke wafts across the range.

'Well done, Stubbs!' says Kemmell. 'That's another bullseye, by the looks of it.'

A tight cluster of holes has almost removed the circle at the centre of the sheet.

'Stubbs has a method!' says Kemmell, proudly. 'Explain your method, Stubbs. Tell the Lieutenant about your way of thinking.'

Stubbs shrugs his shoulders.

Kemmell nudges Stubbs forward. 'Until this new instructor arrives, it would do no harm to show the lieutenant. Show all of us, about the string.'

Alex beckons for the men to come over and watch.

The men gather round.

Stubbs, awkwardly at first, swivels his feet deep into the grass, swings his hips from side to side, finding his balance. Then raises the rifle to his shoulder and aims at the target. 'Well.' He clears his throat and looks at Kemmell.

Kemmell nods, encouragingly.

'I find it helpful to imagine, Sir... a string, tied from my rifle sight to the target. I line up the barrel so it runs along the line of the imaginary string.'

Percy laughs. 'Imaginary string? You're mad!'

Stubbs lowers the rifle.

'Enough of your opinion, Elphick!' says Kemmell. 'You watch and learn. Continue will you, Stubbs?'

Stubbs raises the rifle again.

'All right then,' says Percy, excited now. 'Shoot it up his arse!'

During the last break, someone drew a chalk image on the wall: a German soldier with his trousers down, arse sticking in the air, looking shocked. It's a good picture.

'May I, Sir?' says Stubbs.

'Why not?' says Alex. 'Go ahead.'

Stubbs swings round and aims at the cartoon soldier. 'So, I align the rifle... Adjust height for distance, accounting for any breeze, as if the wind was taking the string—'

'At the Kaiser's arse!' says Percy.

'Shut it, Elphick!' says Kemmell.

'Imaginary string...' says Stubbs slowly. He fires.

A chunk of brick flies out of the wall, a puff of red dust, and a hole appears right in the middle of the German's arse.

Everyone cheers.

'Very well done!' says Alex.

'Thank you, Sir. It's nothing like what an expert might suggest, just my way of thinking, that I find to be helpful.'

'He never misses,' says Kemmell.

Percy is still staring at the target. He shakes his head. 'Imaginary string!'

'You just think of that imaginary string tomorrow,' says Kemmell. He turns to the men. 'All of you, tomorrow in them trenches, during the raid, when you aim your rifles up those Hun's real arses, you think of that imaginary string being shoved right up there!'

36

GOING OUT

'Eggleton, Rowlands, Wislawa.' Alex is sitting on the parapet, guiding each man over the bags. 'Stubbs, Elphick... Wait. Where's your grenade bag, Elphick?'

Percy looks down, tapping his tunic as if he's looking for a box of matches. He grins, teeth shining in the moonlight. 'It's in the shitter.'

'How? You had it two minutes ago. I checked you. Private Stubbs checked you.'

'But then I had to go. It got caught up, so I took it off.'

'And you left it in the latrine? A bag full of hand grenades. For Christ's sake, Percy, go and get it, quickly.'

Percy climbs back down the ladder and shuffles along the trench towards the latrines.

'Stubbs!'

'Yes, Sir?'

'Hold there. Elphick is delayed. One minute.'

'Well, here's a howdoyoufuckingdo,' says Rowlands from the shadows. 'Here's me thinking that we were sneaking out into No Man's Land on a dangerous mission where we might have our skulls split open by a sniper at any moment, but no, let's just stand here and wait

177

for fucking Percy shall we?… I should've brought a teapot… Dying for a cuppa… Does anyone fancy a nice cup of tea?… I can just pop back and—'

'Rowlands.'

'Yes, Sir?'

'Silence.'

For a moment, there is a kind of silence, somehow it makes the stars seem brighter, and heavy, as if they're pushing the sky down into the mud. There's Ursa Major; the Great Bear; cold and ancient. And there's Kallisto. She made love with Zeus. Something happened with Artemis. Was she blamed for something? Did Artemis turn Kallisto into a bear and throw her up there? Or did Zeus do it? Alex can't remember. He thinks of Kallisto; olive skinned, nubile. She must have been like Odette; beautiful and green-eyed.

Odette is sleeping less than three miles from here. He imagines her curled up in her bed. The chaotic folds of white sheets touching the simple curves of her skin. He wishes he was in that bed, instead of out here in the cold. He could get up and walk right across this field, along a couple of trenches, down a long road to the village, out past the fields into the farmyard, up the stairs and into her bed! Like Zeus with Kallisto; the bearded god's muscular arms lifting her thin waist, pulling her towards him—

'I can't get up, Sir. You're in the way.' Percy is at the top of the ladder.

Alex slides off the parapet, into the damp grass, reaches over and pulls Percy down into No Man's Land.

They move out, single file, between the gaps in the wire, into the open field, through slow curling pockets of mist. Feet sliding through long grass, like boats pushing through a moonlit sea.

A flare goes up, rips into the black sky. The men drop fast but Alex is too late; if he moves now, they'll see him. He freezes, scans the ground in front: no one visible, just posts and a ghostly silver blanket across the field. It's too open; nowhere to hide if he drops. He thinks of his throat, imagining a bullet sliding in below the jaw, parting the oesophagus, burning, crunching into the spine at the back of the neck. The sound; like someone biting an apple.

The flare splutters and goes out. Darkness rushes in; a cold, safe nothingness. He rubs at his throat.

On they go. He's pleased with his men, pleased with the training. They're moving forward, hunched, cowered, fast like foxes at the edge of a city. So quiet he can hardly hear their feet.

The line of German wire is close now; fifty yards.

Alex signals and the six men climb into a shell hole and settle in for the night. Nothing to do but wait. They sit in silence, quick eyes glinting in the blackness, waiting for the dawn.

Alex is so tired. Bone-heavy. An empty roughness in his skull like a finger scraping the inside of a clay pot. He closes his eyes and listens. It's so quiet tonight. From across the field he thinks he can hear men talking in the trenches, boots on duckboards, the clanking of tins, someone stirring a mug of tea? Above all that is the usual rumble of distant guns and traffic from both armies. And he can hear a hissing sound, strange yet achingly familiar. It's new leaves. Even out here, in this rubbled destruction, the poplar trees are still standing, swaying defiantly somewhere in the darkness.

An owl hoots, long and still. It drifts out low across the field and fades into the distance.

Percy is asleep already. His body, lost somewhere in the folds of his oversized uniform. He has a hood made for him by Charlie on the sewing machine. He looks peaceful, protected by the dark. He's safe here, for now, but tomorrow, when the British guns drop hundreds of eighteen pound shells just yards away from where he's sleeping, he will not be safe. Then Alex will order him to stand and run towards the shrapnel, into air filled with red-hot, bone-cracking bullets. Alex will tell him to run towards angry and frightened men who will try to hurt him harder than anything they have ever done in their lives.

All the men are sleeping now. He thinks of what Odette was saying about choosing the time to take the risks. He cares so much for these men. He doesn't know if that's enough to be different from Eden. He's so tired. He closes his eyes.

A soft breeze strokes the grass on the edge of the shell hole, mixing with the silver sound of the poplar trees and he's rising up between them, up into the darkness, floating away across the fields, looking for her farm.

37

THE MISSION

Water, trickling.

Alex opens his eyes. Shockingly blue sky. He stretches out his legs; muscles like cold wire. The sun is up and hitting the soil on the opposite side of the shell hole but it has yet to warm the air. It was a cold night. Everyone's curled up against it; collars up, balaclavas and scarves wrapped around dirty faces.

Percy is kneeling, pissing into the puddle in the middle of the crater.

Stubbs throws a stone, hitting him on the shoulder. 'Quiet!' he whispers. 'The Hun are fifty yards away!'

Percy sits down angrily and scrapes at the soil. 'I didn't say nothing. But you're shouting at me. And what about him doing that?'

Wislawa is snoring gently, gas hood pouch for a cushion.

'That's a good fucking point, Percy,' says Rowlands, kicking Wislawa.

Wislawa sits up. 'What?'

'You were snoring,' says Rowlands.

'I was not.'

Rowlands doesn't answer, he's watching Percy. 'Mate, what have you got there?'

'He's dead.' Percy is staring into the soil by his side.

'Who is?'

A black face has emerged from the dirt with white, half open-eyes; a leather gargoyle.

'This man.'

'For fucks sake, Percy!' says Rowlands, pulling his scarf up over his face. 'Leave him alone. He stinks.'

There would have been a time when Alex would have gagged at a smell like this; putrid meat, rotten milk, something forgotten in an opened jar. But now this is just how the world smells. Although it's not all rancid; there's also petrol, lime, black mud, woodsmoke.

'Let the dead man alone,' says Eggleton. 'How would you like it if someone poked you like that?'

Percy is scraping the soil away from the soldier's ears with a little stick. He brushes around the eyes, flicks grit away from the lip that has curled and pulled back to show the teeth. Fascinated, he pokes the stick into the dead man's mouth.

'Is he German or English?' says Rowlands.

'No idea,' says Alex. 'He might be French.'

'Too new to be French,' says Stubbs, 'French haven't been in this sector for a year.'

'The eyes are still there,' says Rowlands. 'Eyes are the first thing that go. Leave him, Percy. Come over here.'

A fly, shining green like an emerald, wanders across the corpse's face, circles on the corner of the mouth, drops into the plum coloured darkness and emerges again.

'Look at that,' says Rowlands. 'That fly goes in there, then it's gonna fly right across this field and shit in some poor man's cup of tea.'

'Cover him back up and come over here with us,' says Alex.

Percy, without covering the soldier, moves away, sliding around the water. He lies down next to Stubbs. 'What shall we call him?'

'Hans,' says Stubbs. 'Or Fritz?'

'No, he's not German,' says Percy.

'You name him then.'

'David,' says Percy. 'His name's David.'

Stubbs shakes his head at Alex. 'His brother,' he whispers.

'I'm starving.' Eggleton rummages in his pockets. 'Have we got time for a biscuit, Sir?'

Alex looks at his watch. It's almost time. 'No, you don't. The bombardment starts in about five minutes. I need you all up and ready. Get your kits together.'

But before anyone has a chance to move, a scream rips through the air above them. A dark shadow, then another and another. Deafening explosions expand into one thunderous roar.

Stubbs cradles Percy in his arms.

Alex lifts his head above the edge of the hole. The German parapet is damaged and there's a gap directly ahead, ten feet wide. Forty seconds to run it. Smoke drifts over the shell hole. The sky turns grey. Here's the smoke screen, thank God. They've got to go now. He signals. 'Go!'

His limbs are stiff. He has to push hard into the pain. A momentary terror; that his body won't be able to do what he needs it to do. But he keeps going, getting faster. The men are with him. Stubbs and Percy on his left. Eggleton and Wislawa, on the right. Rowlands is behind but keeping up. Others further down. He can't tell if it's Charlie's or Eden's. All, running, through the wire, into the smoke. Everyone, running.

He leaps over broken posts and ripped up earth, heading for the gap in the wall.

Germans appear above the bags. Gunfire. Stubbs firing his rifle. Men falling. Alex fires his revolver, keeps running. He waits for the punch of a bullet. It doesn't come. A nothingness spreads through his body; he's invisible, transparent, as light as air. He cannot die, he can't, he has to live so he can get back to Odette.

They reach the bags. Everyone leaps over and slides down, crouching on the fire-step. They're inside the German trench. Some dead Hun, but no one living.

Alex signals.

Eggleton moves along and throws a grenade around the traverse. A deafening thud, smoke rises up, soil falls like hail.

'Go!' yells Alex.

Everyone goes round. Stubbs fires, again and again: Three dead Hun.

Eggleton and Wislawa, throwing grenades. Stubbs, shooting. Percy, guarding the rear; he's alert and focussed. The unit moves quickly, systematically working their way along the trench: 1: Grenades. 2: Move around the traverse. 3: Kill any Boche left standing.

A German runs forward, firing his rifle wildly, fear in his eyes. Alex shoots. The German falls into his arms; matted hair that smells of sweat and sweet tobacco. They hold each other, chests writhing, hearts pounding. Alex thinks, if they can both just stop, stop at the same time, then... But the German has a knife! Alex brings his revolver up and fires. Bone, blood and hair stinging against his face. He lowers the German to the duckboards, gently cupping the broken head in his hand. The eyes are no longer afraid; glassy, reflecting the clouds. Alex hears himself breathing. He is breathing but the soldier is dead. This is his first kill. He has killed. He is a killer. He runs along the trench to catch up with his men.

Wislawa is crouching on the duckboards. He's been hit in the arm, but he's all right. Charlie is with him. Charlie's unit has made its way along from the other end. No one has found an entrance to a mine. Eden's men are holding the Germans back a hundred yards down. Everyone has to get out before the Hun get through. Charlie will lead them out.

Alex gathers his men. Rowlands and Percy are missing. He runs back, around the traverse. There is Percy, standing in the middle of the trench.

'He won't walk. He's refusing to move!' Rowlands is pulling Percy by his pack straps. 'Move, you fucker, move!'

Together they try to drag him but the boy is as stiff as a board and falls forward into the dirt.

'The others have gone back,' yells Alex to Rowlands. 'Climb out, get as far as you can and wait until dark.'

When Rowlands has gone, Alex turns Percy over and slaps him. 'Wake up! Move!' Percy goes limp, groans, opens his eyes and pulls himself up. He looks afraid, confused. He gropes for the fire-step with shaking hands and sits.

'No time to sit. We have to get out, now!' says Alex. 'Can you walk?'

Percy nods and stands.

Alex pulls him over the sandbags and they drop into the field and run.

Machine gunfire opens up behind them; the Germans are back in the trench already.

There's a deep shell hole up ahead. Alex jumps in, pulling Percy down. They lie on their backs in the soil, panting.

He moves over to the far side, takes out his knife, scrapes soil from the lip of the crater and peers over the edge: the ground goes out flat for thirty yards, then dips away towards the British line. 'We'll have to stay here until it's dark.'

Percy isn't listening. He's staring at the clouds.

'Then we'll crawl out, over that ridge. From there we should be able to make it back without being seen... Percy? Are you all right?'

'How can it do that?' says Percy.

'Do what?'

'The clouds. One lot is going one way, but higher up, the other clouds are going another way. How can it do that?'

'I don't really know. I suppose there are different layers of wind, travelling in different directions.' Alex crawls back to face the boy. 'Percy, do you know what happened back there? You froze again, in the Hun trench. What happened?'

'I don't know. I was asleep, I think.' He turns to Alex, cross-eyed and grinning. A fly has landed on his nose. He watches as it buzzes up into the field and disappears.

'Percy, this is important. I need to know why you froze. What do you think is happening to you?'

Percy sits up and glares. 'I don't fucking know!'

'Keep your voice down!'

'I don't know. Everyone keeps asking me.' His eyes are glistening. 'How the fuck should I know? One minute everything is the way it always is, and then… then.' He shakes his head and a tear runs down his cheek, cleaning a pale streak of skin against the dirt. 'I don't fucking know!'

'Drink some water.'

Percy takes his bottle, shakes it. 'It's empty.'

'Did you drink it?'

'No.'

'Then where's the water?' Alex lifts the bottle. 'Look, here's a hole. That was close. You caught a bullet.'

Percy puts his finger in the hole. 'I could've had a *Blighty*. I could've gone home.'

Alex takes out his own bottle and gives it to Percy. 'Is that what you would like, to go home?'

Percy drinks and wipes his mouth with the back of his sleeve. 'I don't want to go home. Not until all the dirty Hun are dead.'

'That might take a very long time. If you wanted to go home—'

'Mum and Betsy say I should, but my Dad says I'm not to come.'

'Is Betsy your sister?'

'She's a year less than me, but she talks like she's older. My dad says that after what they done to David, I'm not to come home until all the dirty Hun are dead.'

'How old was your brother?'

'Two years more than me.'

'And how old are you?'

Percy lies down. 'Me and David used to work in someone's big garden before the war. There was a glass-house with these massive plants. Leaves as big as umbrellas. We would sit under them and eat our lunch sometimes. I wish… I wish we was still under them big leaves.' He closes his eyes and in an instant, he is asleep.

Alex watches him sleeping for a long time. He watches as the shadows soften and the clouds grow grey and heavy and black. He feels the coldness of the wind. He feels his skin tighten as the blood of the German soldier dries and cracks on his hands.

38

THE CAFÉ DE LION

There's no sign on the outside of *The Café de Lion*, just piano music, laughter and tobacco smoke wafting from an open window into the little lane behind the village church.

Alex is sitting at a corner table with Charlie and Sergeant Kemmell. They're listening intently to Stephanie, who is telling them, in a charming mixture of French and English, how she and her sister had set up the estaminet in the parlour of their family home, after their parents had been killed by the Germans. 'Juste la bière et le vin first, no food. The kitchen, not big. We sell good wine, not diluée merde like they drink in *La Pelican*. We are popular with les officiers. They like us.'

Charlie glances sideways at Alex. It's fairly clear what she means.

She tells them that one thing led to another and before long, the bedrooms were incorporated into the business. 'You have to do what you can do,' she says, resting her head against Kemmell's shoulder. 'You have to manger, to eat, No?'

'Of course you do!' says Kemmell, filling Stephanie's glass and then his own. 'We all do! No one's judging anyone for that!'

She's drunk more wine than the three men put together, and her green eyes, like weeds in a shallow river, glisten. 'So handsome, you two!' She reaches across the table and pinches Charlie's cheek.

Charlie laughs awkwardly and smiles at Alex, who, not wanting to have his cheek pinched, turns away.

Naked women; drawings, presumably cut out of magazines that one might buy in Paris, peer out from the walls. None of them are very good; there's no quality of light. A large mirror, with a crack across one corner, hangs at a steep angle above an open fire. It reflects the crowded parlour, full of officers from the regiment; men that Alex doesn't know. There are tables and a couch against the wall. Some men sit, others stand, singing around the piano that's being played by two officers. They don't appear to be playing the same song.

Stephanie leans back in her chair and yells across the room to her sister. 'Charlotte! Viens ici. Rencontrer les nouveaux officiers. So handsome!'

One of the officers comes over, talks with Kemmell for a while and leaves them with a bottle of wine.

So you've been here before, Sergeant?' says Charlie.

'I have, Sir, yes. Lieutenant Collins brought me along as his guest. I shouldn't really be here, this being more of an officer's place.'

The pianist's efforts have coagulated into *Keep the home fires burning.* Everyone joins in. Stephanie grips Kemmell's arm, enthusiastically singing the few words she knows. Kemmell watches her and leans in secretively towards Alex and Charlie. 'I think they let me in on account of the fact that I'm polite and gentlemanly.' His words slur, rippling with the wine still on his lips. 'I respect them, as I'm sure that, given a different set of circumstances, both these sisters would be earning their keep in different ways, if things were not the way they are now.'

'Are you drunk, Sergeant?' says Charlie, smiling.

Kemmell looks shocked. 'Why? What did I say?'

'It's not what you said, it's how you said it.'

'I'm not drunk, Sir.'

Stephanie laughs loudly and kisses Kemmell on the cheek.

'I'm not!' says Kemmell, rubbing his cheek as if she'd slapped him.

'We should all go home soon,' says Charlie. 'There's a route march after parade tomorrow. Then we have to set up for some concert in the evening.'

Kemmell runs his tongue around his mouth. 'P'raps I should be off. I'm not drunk though, it's this wine. It's making me feel a bit peaky.' He turns to Stephanie and slowly enunciates. 'Peaky! That means ill, or under the weather, in French!'

'We can help you feel better,' says Stephanie with a theatrical pout.

Kemmell strokes Stephanie's cheek. 'I know, my love. You could make a dead man feel better. But as much as it pains me to say, the lieutenant is right, we should all be off to our beds.'

Stephanie turns and stares intently at Alex. 'Charlotte!' she yells. 'Viens ici!'

Charlotte, on the other side of the room, is pouring wine from a jug into the upheld glasses of a group of officers. She looks over and catches Alex's eye.

Stephanie kisses Kemmell, takes a bottle from a shelf and wanders over to the piano.

'They can, you know,' says Kemmell, smiling. 'Make you feel better.'

Charlie leans across the table. 'How can they help exactly? Do they...?' He waves his hand, unsure even of what gesture to make.

Kemmell frowns. 'They're not like the girls from *The Pelican*. These are good girls. They would, in my opinion, bring a man *back* to his wife.' He's swaying noticeably in his seat now. 'These ladies offer a small reminder of the warmth and tenderness that a soldier's wife will offer. They help a man to think of home, to miss his wife and thereby give him the resolve to return to her when all of this is over. In fact, I think they do a great service to the wife.' He looks confused at first, then, satisfied, smiles, drains his glass and places it confidently on the table. 'No, this isn't like *The Pelican*, Sir,' he says, seemingly replying to a question that Charlie hadn't asked. 'Officers don't go there. Except Captain Eden, he goes there. Well, he used to. I think he stopped going after what happened.'

'What do you mean?' says Alex. 'After *what* happened?'

'After what Percy saw. I don't think the lads were too happy to share a drink with him after that.'

Alex sits up. 'I told Percy not to say anything.'

'Everyone's been talking about it, Sir.' Kemmell looks worried now, as if he's said the wrong thing. 'But if it's true, it's not news. There were rumblings from before.'

'What rumblings?' says Alex.

'I don't know, Sir. P'raps I shouldn't say... But there were rumours, about the Battle of Loos. Eden led a unit and got medals for it. At first they thought he was the only one who survived, but some poor soul crawled back in after being stuck in No Man's Land for five days! He was raving on about Eden using the men as shields for himself to get through. The poor man was delirious and died short after, so no one really listened to what he was saying. But others said other things too...' Kemmell shakes his head. 'I dunno. I wasn't there. Just heard it from someone...'

Alex feels like it's the end of something. He feels a soft grief for who he wanted Eden to have been, and who, he and Eden, together as soldiers, might have been.

'But his men seem very loyal,' says Charlie. 'They'll go anywhere for him.'

Kemmell nods. 'They would, Sir, he's got charisum...' He tries again. 'Charism...' He seems irritated now. He raises his voice. 'He's a famous war hero and that is why no one gives a fuck what some small lad has to say, and even if they did, which they would not, the regiment gives more of a fuck about its own reputation than the life of any man!'

'Excuse me!' says a captain, angrily, from an adjacent table.

Charlie coughs and smiles apologetically at the outraged officer.

'Private Percy Elphick is ill with something,' says Kemmell, calmer now. 'He shouldn't be here. That's my opinion.'

'We should get the doctor to take a look at him,' says Charlie. 'If they find he's got something wrong, then perhaps we could persuade them to send him home.'

'I'll talk to Woodstone tomorrow,' says Alex.

'I love the boy,' says Kemmell. 'But nothing would please me more than seeing him go home to his family.' Laughter explodes from the other side of the room. Kemmell stands, steadying himself against Charlie's shoulder. 'I think I should get back to the billets.'

'I'll walk you across the fields, Sergeant,' says Charlie.

'You don't need to do that on my behalf, Sir.'

'I think I should. If Captain Eden were to see you looking... *not drunk*, I don't think he'd be too impressed. Also, I'd like you to tell me more about this *Estaminet du Pelican*, if you would be so kind?' Charlie grins at Alex and leads Kemmell outside.

An older man, a captain, is singing on his own at the piano. It's a funny song, about a girl with beautiful eyes. The men laugh, but there's a softness in the room now.

Charlotte comes and sits at the table with Alex. 'Do you know it?' she says.

He shakes his head.

'It's about you,' she says, as the song finishes. 'The song is about you. You have beautiful eyes.'

He laughs. 'So do you,' he says, awkwardly. But it's true; her eyes are much darker than her sister's, they seem to reflect every candle in the room.

She brushes his hair from his forehead with her fingers. 'Yours are a little sad, I think.'

The officers laugh again and a new song swells.

She puts her hand on Alex's wrist. 'Would you like to come upstairs?'

He looks at her, looks to see if she's mocking him, but she's earnestly holding his gaze. If anything, there's a dignity in her expression. He wonders if she's making her choice in a world where there can't be many choices. What can this be like for her? Sitting on the laps of strange men, in the same room where she must have sat on her father's lap not so long ago.

She leans towards him in a way that he thinks she's going to kiss him, but she tips her head forward and rests against his chest.

He puts his arms around her. She smells of lavender. He thinks about going upstairs with her, but suddenly he knows exactly where he wants to be. 'I'm very tired. I think I'm just going to walk home.'

She sighs and he feels her body fall a little in his arms. Then she pulls away and they're strangers again.

Outside the air is sharp and blue. He stands on the moon-washed cobbles, between the silent houses and the stars, and he listens to the shells exploding at the front. He thinks of the men who are huddled right this minute in the trenches. He thinks of Eden's men, hanging on the wire, and the soldier's button, tapping against the pole in the wind.

The night feels black and cold and empty and he doesn't want to die. He wants to be with Odette. His whole body aches with the fear of not being with her.

He runs out of the village, along the flat fields, through the moonlit darkness sliding past him. He runs into the farm, sees a light on in her room, opens the farmhouse door, runs through the kitchen, up the stairs and now he's standing outside her door, breathless. 'Odette?'

'Yes?' she says.

'It's me, Alex.'

Silence.

'Can I come in?'

'Yes,' she says.

39

THE CONCERT PARTY

Piano music swells. Delicate fingers and ruby nails glint in the sun; a hand stretches and quivers skyward. A crescendo. Then the tune tumbles, the hand collapses, lithe arms caress a tiara of meadow flowers. The piano rumbles with dramatic chords. A grand jeté and allegro follows adagio. The dancer spins around the stage. Slim legs are revealed as a breeze lifts a silk toga.

'There's no fucking way that's a woman,' says Rowlands, standing in front of the stage, holding one end of a wooden bench. 'You can tell by the wrists and the throat. He's got an Adam's apple the size of an...apple.'

Eggleton is holding the other end of the bench, gawping. 'I can spot a woman from a mile off,' he says, eyes smouldering. He licks his top lip and takes a deep breath in. 'I don't know how. It's like I can smell them with my eyes. I'm telling you, that *is* a woman!'

D Company is hosting a concert party and the little troop of performers are rehearsing their acts before tonight's show.

Alex's platoon is arranging benches and chairs in front of a makeshift stage that's been assembled in the parade ground behind the Ferme du Boaze, now called *Booze Farm* by everyone except Eden.

The dancer jumps down off the stage, pulls off his wig and tiara and walks across the grass to the pianist. 'I'm telling you, Henry,' he says. 'That stage is going to kill one of us. No Man's Land has got less fucking holes in it!'

Rowlands stares at Eggleton and laughs.

Eggleton shakes his head solemnly. 'I don't care anymore. He's wearing a dress. These days, that's enough for me.'

Woodstone, standing with Alex on the side of the stage, stares blankly at the dancer, then turns to Alex. 'Tell Kemmell to organise a couple of guards. They need to keep an eye on the men in the front rows during the dancing. I've invited the Battalion CO and we don't want any trouble.'

'I think all the dancers are actually men, Sir,' says Alex, quietly.

'Exactly, I'm worried about what might happen if the men find out.' He slaps his cane against his boot. 'Right. We'll see you later. I need to get on.'

'Before you go, Sir. I wanted to talk to you about something that happened to one of my men during the trench raid.'

'Yes, the raid. That's why I've invited the major. He was delighted with the results.'

Alex was not delighted: No one found any sign of a mine entrance. A few Hun had been killed, twelve by Alex's unit alone, but D Company had more casualties in this raid than during any other action since March. And since the raid, the Hun have done their best to retaliate, destroying yards of the battalion's front line. D Company spent the last two nights shoving sand back into the bags and guts back into the men. He is exhausted. Everyone is exhausted.

'The major wants to meet you,' says Woodstone. 'So I think you should sit with us tonight.'

Alex doesn't want to sit with Woodstone and the major. They will ask him questions to which he has no answers. They will ask him how he thinks the war is going; he has no idea. He wants to sit with his men, with Charlie. He wants to sit with his friends and be surrounded by their laughter.

'You've been mentioned in despatches,' says Woodstone. 'I

thought I would read it to the men when I announce your promotion. They need a bit of cheering up.'

Alex had almost forgotten about the promotion. This is his first command since becoming a first lieutenant; laying out chairs for a concert party.

'I think I'll do it at the beginning of the evening,' says Woodstone. 'Start things off on a positive note. The men are very tired and its going to be a warm night, so we'll need to inject a bit of enthusiasm and energy. And from what I've just seen, I doubt the dancing will help.'

The dancer, having clearly heard, stops tying his ballet shoes and looks up.

Alex smiles an apology.

The warm weather has brought new challenges; the trenches are finally dry, but now the corpses that have lain buried in the cold ground for months are being blown by the shellfire into the spring air, black and swollen. There's a putrid stench of death so strong that it seeps down into the dugouts and clings to the men's clothes, their blankets, their hair. Even here, days later, in these springtime fields, it stays in the back of everyone's throats like a layer of rancid fat.

With the death stench came the flies, swarms of them, over every-thing, like a crawling, crystallising treacle. The men had to scoop them out of their tea, scrape them off their bread. The flies buzzed into their mouths when they yawned, drank the tears from the corner of their eyes, laid eggs in their nostrils when they tried to sleep.

A clown, white face, white gloves and huge red fluffy buttons down the front of his shirt, is juggling coloured balls in the middle of the stage.

'I wanted to talk to you about Private Elphick, Sir,' says Alex.

'That's him there, isn't it?' says Woodstone, looking over to the stage.

Stubbs is carrying chairs into the middle of the field and super-vising Percy, who is arranging them in rows.

'Yes, Sir, the small one. I wanted to ask if we could have him assessed by the doctor.'

'Why does he need a doctor? He doesn't look ill.'

'Not physically ill. I explained in my report about what happened during the trench raid. I think there's something wrong.'

'Ah yes, he was the one who refused to move. That can't be allowed to happen. You can't have a man jeopardise the mission by refusing to attack.'

'No, Sir, it was a paralysis of some sort. That's why I think the doctor should take a look.'

Woodstone glares. 'Nonsense!' He jumps down off the stage, slipping on the grass. 'I've been speaking to Captain Eden about this. He says that if you allow one man to let his fear get the better of him, then it will spread throughout the whole platoon and before you know it, *insurrection!*' He removes his hat and combs his hair back into place with his hand. 'He says your men need to learn about consequences and that Elphick should be punished for his behaviour.'

'Punished? For what? You can't punish him for being ill!'

'He isn't ill. Look at him!'

Percy is on stage now. The clown is showing him how to juggle.

Woodstone turns and waves his finger at Alex. 'You've just been promoted. You need to start acting like a first lieutenant, in charge of a platoon of men, and not like a nanny in charge of a bunch of little girls!'

A cheerful young soldier is holding a roll of coloured bunting in his arms. 'Excuse me, Sir. The pianist is complaining that the piano is sinking into the grass.'

Woodstone stops and stares at Alex.

'Get some planks from the large barn,' says Alex. 'See if you can slide them under the piano.'

'We tried that, Sir, but the—'

Alex glares. 'It's a piano, not a Howitzer! The ground should be hard enough, it hasn't rained for a week!'

The soldier looks shocked, tries to salute through the bunting and runs back to the piano, trailing a line of coloured flags.

'That's it,' says Woodstone, smiling. 'Discipline!'

'Could we at least ask the doctor to look, Sir? To have a chat with him? If he *is* ill, then he can be sent away and there'll be no chance of him ever jeopardising the success of another mission. We might have been able to clear much further along the Boche trench if the boy hadn't been with us. Imagine how pleased the major would have been. So if the doctor says he should be sent home…'

Woodstone thinks for a moment, staring at Percy and the clown throwing balls at each other. 'All right. I'll ask the doc to pop over in the morning. But if he says there's nothing wrong with the boy, then he *will* be punished. Do you hear?'

The men clap and cheer.

Percy and the clown are holding hands, taking deep, exuberant bows.

40

FIELD PUNISHMENT NUMBER ONE

Alex is standing in the lane between the two billet farms, watching a huge column of smoke rising up from behind a row of trees. It's beautiful and silent, billowing gently. Turning from blue to purple to gold as it catches the sunlight and spreads out across the morning sky.

The neighbouring farm was hit by shellfire in the night. No one was killed but the farm has been destroyed. The Germans have better guns now and the shelling is moving further west, beyond the frontline villages to the farms and houses that were considered safe a few weeks ago.

On his arrival at Booze Farm, he sees there is a man tied and hanging over the entrance gate. As he gets closer, a sickening realisation makes him run.

Percy's arms are pulled over the top bar of the gate. His wrists, tied by a rope wrapped twice around his chest. Ropes lashed around the lowest bar pull the boy's ankles up, so that his body arches forward and his naked feet are suspended an inch above the ground; a uniformed crucifixion. His breathing is shallow and fast; little bubbles of spit on the edge of his mouth. His head hangs down, neck stretched out, pink and covered in sweat.

Alex pulls at the knots; so tight he can't get his fingers in. 'Wait here,' he says, shaking the stupidity from himself. 'I'll get them to untie you.'

The farmyard is noisy and crowded with soldiers cleaning kit, polishing rifles, sharpening bayonets. A group of Eden's men, shirt-less and laughing in the sunlight, are burning lice eggs from their clothes with sticks heated on a brazier in the centre of the yard. Seeing Alex, they stand and salute.

'The soldier on the gate,' yells Alex, 'Who ordered it?' He knows the answer.

'Captain Eden, Sir.'

'Where is he?'

A muscular soldier drops his cigarette and twists it into the dirt with his boot. 'He's gone with Captain Woodstone to the quartermaster, Sir. They won't be back until this afternoon.'

'Where is your sergeant?'

'In the parade ground, Sir.'

'Fetch him. The rest of you come with me.'

The soldiers untie Percy and lay him on the grass where he lies face down and panting. They give him water, which he refuses until Alex insists.

'He's supposed to be up for another hour, Sir!' A portly sergeant is jogging out of the yard, red-faced and sweating. 'Field Punishment number one. Two hours a day for two weeks!'

'Who are you?' says Alex, coldly.

'Sergeant Bucton, Sir.' He salutes. 'Transferred from the 13th on Tuesday. I'm now with 2 Platoon, with Captain Eden.'

'Did you do this?'

'Under Captain Eden's supervision, Sir.'

'Is this how you usually tie a man for an FP1? Hanging with his feet off the ground?'

'No, Sir. I usually have them tied with enough rope to allow for sitting, even for the reading of a book. But the Captain was quite specific about how it should be done, and with me being new, I didn't feel it was my place to suggest otherwise.'

'Private Elphick is in *my* platoon. Why was I not informed about his punishment?'

Bucton is confused. 'I thought the lad was with us, Captain Eden's platoon. I collected him from our billets.' He looks at Percy. 'What platoon are you in, Son?'

Percy rubs his wrists. '2 Platoon. Captain Eden's.'

'Since when?' says Alex.

'They woke me up last night and told me to get my stuff and carry it to the other barn.' Percy is pushing the words out through tight lips, as if he might cry. His eyes are burning, glaring at Alex. 'Eden said you told them I disobeyed your orders.'

Bucton lifts a chubby finger. 'Mind how you talk to the lieutenant, Private. You speak respectfully and always address him as Sir.'

Alex waves his hand at Bucton reassuringly. 'I didn't tell them that, Percy. I told them you couldn't move. You were supposed to see the doctor. Did he not see you?'

'Yes.'

'What did he say?'

Percy shrugs. 'Nothing. Why should he? I'm not ill...' He glances at Bucton. 'Sir.'

Alex turns to Bucton. 'Is the doctor still here?'

'He's seeing the lads with ailments, Sir, in the guardroom.'

'Take Elphick back with you,' says Alex.

'But what about the FP1, Sir? He's still got an hour to go.'

'Take him back! Tell them I ordered it. I need to see the Doctor.'

As Alex walks through the courtyard, he feels that there's something deliberate in the way the men stop what they're doing and watch him. A bayonet-practice dummy lurches towards him, carried by two soldiers from the parade ground. Its arms dangle ludicrously, bouncing and flailing accusingly. He has an urge to kick it out of the way or draw his revolver and shoot it in the chest. He wants to yell something, to announce to all of them that he wasn't responsible for what they've done to Percy, but he knows he partly *is* to blame; it was *his* report. Even if Woodstone has misunderstood or Eden has twisted the words, it's Alex who has started this and now Alex who has to do something about it.

Laughter and whistling rise up from the far end of the yard. Rowlands is waltzing around the brazier with the dummy.

41

THE DOCTOR

'Rub that on twice a day and try to let the air to it as often as you can. It's bound to itch, but nothing to worry about.' Captain Noel, the battalion doctor, is sitting at a table in the middle of the guardroom.

A pink-faced soldier, clutching a small tin, salutes awkwardly as he leaves.

Noel smiles wearily at Alex. 'Come in and sit down, but leave the door open, would you? It's stifling in here.' He opens a large brown ledger and picks up a pen. 'Just let me write that chap's details down before I forget. The bullet holes and boils…' He looks up and smiles, swings his pen in the air rhythmically. 'The *bullet* holes and *boils*… that I see in the *billets*… all *become* a *blur*… by the time I get *back* to my *bunk!*' He laughs. 'Well, that's the beginning of a song, don't you think? I should write that down. Oh. But first I should make a note of this chap's…' He stops smiling and writes.

The guardroom must have been some kind of potting shed before the war. It smells of peat and creosote, but now brown bottles, tins of ointment, cotton swabs and tweezers are arranged neatly on the table.

Noel is sweating. His hair clings to his shiny head like weed on a river pebble. 'There!' he says, placing the pen on the table and smiling again. 'How are you? How are your lungs? It's your lungs? Am I right?'

'My lungs are fine.'

Noel looks disappointed. 'Oh, some of the officers are saying the dust is getting to them. What is it then?'

'I'm fine. I'm actually not here to talk about me. I want to ask you about one of my men, Percy Elphick?'

'Ah yes, the little chap.'

'Yes, the little chap. Did you see him?'

'I did.'

'So what did you find?'

'Well, there's nothing wrong with him. Fit as a fiddle, I would say.' Noel smiles, lifts his pen again. *'Percy's penis* was neither *pox-ridden* nor *pustulated!...'* He grins. 'His *gonorrhoea* had *gone to the rear!* No wait!... His *gonorrhoea—'*

'I've just found him hanging by his arms from the entrance gate.' Alex is not smiling. 'They've put him on an FP1. His feet weren't even touching the ground.'

'Oh my goodness!' Noel looks horrified. 'That's not how it's supposed to be at all. But, you know, there's no guidelines in the handbook. I've been asking for them. They should write it down, explain what's reasonable. Sometimes things go too far but you can't do anything about it without guidelines.' He stands. 'Show me where he is, and we'll sort this out!'

'No. I've untied him already. They've punished him for refusing an order, my order. But I wanted you to look at him. I think it was some sort of fit or paralysis.'

'I told you, I *did* look at him.' Noel takes out a handkerchief from his pocket and wipes his face. 'Woodstone asked me to read your report. You wrote that he'd gone a bit doolally-tap in No Man's Land. Well, as soon as I read that, I thought about a thing called *neurasthenia.* It's a psychiatric disorder caused by the stresses and horrors that these poor souls are subjected to in battle. It's quite new, but I've seen it in patients in the hospital in England. The body isn't damaged but the brain is. They're seeing more and more cases of it every month.' There's not a trace of flippancy now. His brow is furrowed in concentration. 'Some of these chaps who are afflicted, some of them freeze in the way you describe, although this, as far as I'm aware, is not so likely in the working classes. Most of the reports are about officers. But the men who are suffering from this have very specific symptoms that last a long time after battle: shaking, stammering, memory loss, that sort of thing. Your chap shows none of those symptoms. No tinnitus, nothing. He's quite normal.'

'He may not show any symptoms now,' says Alex. 'But they come on when he's afraid or excited, in the thick of the battle. He was shaking like a leaf during one of his fits. We thought he'd been hit in the spine.'

'Look, Ryan. I have to go.' Noel stuffs his equipment into his bag. 'I didn't realise it was so late.' He looks under the table. 'I thought I had a coat... But I hope you can understand, I can't speculate on how Private Elphick might behave when I'm not there. That wouldn't be scientific. All I can do is make my observations on what I see right in front of me.'

'But, I *saw* how he behaved. I was *there*. It's all in my report!'

'I'm not here to report on your report. That would be assumption based on anecdote, and that wouldn't do...' Noel looks around the room again. 'Perhaps I didn't have a coat. It's far too hot for a coat isn't it?'

'I wanted you to see him. I was hoping you would have him sent down the line.'

'I did see him and I found nothing wrong. So there's nothing else I can do.' Noel wipes the back of his neck. 'Eden's platoon is going on a raid tonight, as far as I understand. I've asked him to keep an eye on the lad.' He snaps his bag shut and walks out of the room. 'If anything *unusual* happens, I'm sure he'll let us know.'

Alex follows and grabs Noel's arm. 'They've already punished him because something *unusual* happened. And now you've told them there was nothing wrong. So now they think he's a coward! What do you think they will do if it happens again?'

Noel pulls his arm free. 'I'm sorry they punished private Elphick. I didn't know they would do that. I was asked to give my medical opinion. I did exactly that, nothing more, nothing less. I can't worry about any consequences as a result of that opinion. Now, I really must go.' He walks fast across the yard, then turns. 'But let me just say this. As uncomfortable as it might be, if the lad only freezes when he's expected to be brave, then unfortunately, we might have to conclude that he *is* a coward.'

42

ODETTE

He can't sleep. Lying on his side, staring at the floral-patterned wallpaper in Odette's bedroom. The roses look like blood-soaked bandages in the darkness. He thinks about Percy, perhaps right this minute, going out with Eden's men into the German trenches. He'll be afraid. He has no friends there. What if something happens? What if he has another seizure…

'When are you going back?' Odette is sitting up and staring out of the bedroom window. Her cheek is wet and silver in the moonlight.

He runs his hand down the curve of her naked back. 'To the front? In a few days.'

'I don't want you to go.'

'I have to go. I always go. What's the matter?'

'After dinner, you asked me to keep your sketchbooks here. To look after them for you. Why did you say that?'

'I don't have time to sketch anymore, that's all,' he says. 'I don't need to take them with me to the front.'

'Is that the only reason?'

He knows exactly what she means. Often soldiers seem to know when their time is up. He'd told her that last week, Nolan gave

Wislava his wedding ring, *"To look after"*. Three hours later he was vaporised by a direct hit from a 5.9.

He squeezes her hand. 'It's nothing like that. I won't be using them, so I would rather keep them here with you until I get back, that's all. I promise.'

'But I don't want you to go.'

'You know I have to.'

She looks at him. 'Why? Why do you have to do anything? You volunteered. They can't make you go back.'

'They can. I volunteered to *allow* them to *make* me go back.'

'We could run away.'

He sits up. Something surges in him; to be alone with her, without her mother, away from Eden and the other officers, away from the war. They could make their way to Paris and get lost there... but... He sighs. It's a ridiculous idea. 'I would love that,' he says.

'Then let's go.'

'They would catch me and I would be shot.'

'But if you go back, you might be—'

'I won't! I just know, I won't.' But as he says this, he imagines climbing up the ladder, over the bags and into the black. He hears the crack and hiss of bullets speeding towards him. His skin tightens. It's inevitable that he'll be injured. He's not afraid of that. But, just like Charlie and Evelina, like all of the men with attachments, with silver threads stretching out between them and the people they love, the idea of being separated from Odette is as horrific as the circumstance in which it is likely to happen.

He wraps his arms around her, fills his lungs with the heat from her skin. 'Do you remember Percy?'

'The small one?'

'Yes. I tried to get him sent home but it's all got mixed up. They punished him this morning. They've taken him out of my platoon and put him with Eden. My platoon was like a family with Percy in the middle of it somehow. Everyone looked after him. It gave them a purpose outside of the ordinary things. I need to get him back. I need to stay with my men so I can do that.'

An artillery barrage starts somewhere at the front. Faint yellow flashes bloom on the horizon.

'Please,' he says. 'Let's try to sleep.'

They lie down and listen to the guns thud and pulse against the silence of the farm.

'You said, in England, they are forcing men to come here now,' she says.

'Yes, conscription.'

'But not the married ones? The married men don't have to fight?'

'Not yet.'

'So we could get married. Then you wouldn't have to go back.'

He smiles, 'Yes, we could marry.' He kisses her neck. 'But the system doesn't work that way. I'm already in France. It's just for new men, who haven't signed up… But I think you should come with me to England. It's not safe here anymore.'

'England!' her eyes; bright as the shellfire flashes on the wall. 'But what about the farm, and my mother?'

'You could sell the cows and chickens, then you and your mother could come back with me when I get leave. You could both stay with my father, help him on his farm until the end of the war. Then we could all come back here.'

She stares into his eyes for a long time. 'No, I think I should be here, with the people I know. I want to help them somehow.' She closes her eyes. 'I love you, Alex.'

He lies in the darkness, feeling her breathing and her body soften as she falls asleep. And her words flow through him like a moonlit river. And he holds her as if they might both be washed away.

43

DUST

It's hot. Dark clouds rumble. There's shouting coming from the barn. Alex squints against the dusty wind as he crosses the farmyard and pushes open the large wooden doors.

'Stubbs, stop this!' shouts Kemmell.

Rucksacks and helmets swing from nails on the wooden beams. Rifles, wash kits, books and mirrors clatter against the barn walls. A group of soldiers is holding Stubbs.

'Let me go!' He's squirming against their grip.

Flecks of straw-dust plume up and sparkle against the shadows.

'If you don't calm down,' says Kemmell. 'I'm reporting you to Lieutenant Ryan!'

'I'm right here,' says Alex, stepping forward. 'What's going on?'

The men, including Stubbs, stand to attention.

'Nothing, Sir,' says Kemmell, looking shocked. 'Stubbs here's just letting off a little steam.'

'What's happened?'

Stubbs, breathless, pulls his dishevelled shirt into some order and staggers forward. 'They've arrested Percy, Sir. He's in the guardroom. He's no idea what's happening.'

'Arrested?' says Alex. 'What for?'

'For nothing, that's what for.'

'Shut yourself up, Stubbs!' says Kemmell.

The men move forward preparing to restrain Stubbs again, but he waves them off, standing still and raging.

Kemmell turns to Alex. 'Percy was with Eden's men last night, Sir. A trench raid, near Richebourg. We've not been told what the charge is, refused an order or something of that nature.' He lowers his voice. 'Stubbs had the idea to find Captain Eden and ask him directly, if you understand my meaning?'

'He's done nothing,' says Stubbs, calmer now. 'Had one of his funny turns, is all.'

'We don't know what he's done or hasn't done,' says Rowlands.

'We do! I heard it from one of his men. Eden, the cu—'

'Stubbs!' yells Kemmell. 'One more crack like that and you'll be on an FP2!'

Stubbs nods and folds his arms to show compliance.

'Sergeant, make sure Stubbs doesn't leave this barn,' says Alex. 'Tie him up if you have to. I'll go and find out what's going on.' He presses his weight against the barn door and steps out into the wind.

Woodstone is crossing the yard. 'Ryan, I was just looking for you.' Leaves and dust hiss in scratching spirals along the ground. He has to shout against it. 'You need to get your chaps to fill out their wills. The adjutant has given us some forms. I've given them to the sergeants. A lot of the men have lost their old ones or ruined them. I don't know what they do with them. Wipe their arses on them, I suspect. Anyway, do that after you drill your men. Eden's lot are on bayonet drill now. I want yours to start as soon as he's off the field. We need—'

'Why has Private Elphick been arrested, Sir?' says Alex.

Woodstone looks blank. 'No idea. You need to ask Captain Eden. He made the arrest.'

'So you've heard about it?'

The blank expression changes to indignance. 'Of course I have! I just don't know the details.' The wind almost takes his hat. He clamps his hand on it. 'Damn this weather! You need to ask Eden, but I hope it's nothing serious. We won't have time for anything serious.' The indignation changes to intrigue. He leans in. 'Don't tell anyone, Ryan, all very hush, but we're all moving to Hingette in a few days. Whole battalion. As soon as that's in the bag, we've got something coming up in Festubert, and then I think it's going to be something really big. The actual *push*, with all four battalions! This is why you need to sort those wills.' The wind gusts and he gets something in his eye. 'Goddamnit!'

'Can I go and see Elphick?' says Alex.

'You must. He was in your platoon. That's no coincidence,' says Woodstone, one hand on his hat and a finger in the corner of his eye. 'You should take responsibility, sort this out. It's the last thing we need before the big push.'

Alex is already halfway across the yard.

'And be quick about it, Ryan! The men need to be as sharp as buttons for this big show!' The wind gusts again, Woodstone staggers and for a moment, he disappears inside a swirling cloud of dust, straw and leaves.

44

THE GUARD HOUSE

The guardhouse is in the old stable block at the back of the farm. Dusty horse-tack and wood-wormed tools still hang on the outside walls.

Percy is sitting in a pile of straw, his arms wrapped around his knees. He's lit by a small, high window above him. The glass is frosted with old cobwebs.

'Hello, Private,' says Alex, sitting in the straw.

Percy doesn't look up.

The wind lifts the corner of the tin roof. It rumbles like distant thunder.

'Did they give you water?'

The boy nods towards a mug on a shelf. His eyelids are swollen and red.

'What happened? Why are you here?'

'I don't know. Same thing I done when I was with you.'

'Can you remember what happened?'

He thinks for a moment, rubbing his forearm as if trying to clean something off it. 'We finished the raid on the Hun trench and some of Eden's men said they wanted to get souvenirs. They went down into the dugouts and got some. They came up and said that there was one of them helmets with a point on it. They said I should go down and get it. So I went down and… It was very dark…'

'Go on, Percy. You must tell me exactly what happened.'

'Someone grabbed me and it was this Hun soldier. He was still alive. He was holding onto my tunic. He was coughing and blood came out of his mouth when he coughed and he looked at me like I was supposed to help him but he was very angry.' Percy pauses again and looks at Alex.

'Go on.'

'Then Captain Eden came and was yelling from up the steps at me to come out and I tried to get the Hun off me but I couldn't. And Captain Eden was yelling more. And I remembered what he'd done to those men who wouldn't move and I thought he might come down and shoot me…'

There's a fly dying on the window sill. It buzzes and spins in circles on its back.

'So what did you do?'

Percy shakes his head. 'I don't know. I was scared and I couldn't move and I got sleepy. I tried to get the soldier off me but I couldn't stay awake… Then I woke up and they were dragging me back. Eden's men, they pulled me up the steps—'

The tin roof clatters. Percy flinches.

'What happened to the Hun soldier?'

'I don't know. I didn't see.'

'I'll talk to Eden,' says Alex.

'When can I come back to your platoon?'

'I don't know. I don't even know what they're charging you with. Did they tell you?'

Percy shrugs. A fly lands on the corner of his mouth. He slaps it, missing the fly but hitting his own cheek, hard. He lifts his hand to do it again.

Alex reaches out and grabs Percy's wrist.

The boy's eyes glisten with tears. 'I want to see Stubbs.'

'I'll get Stubbs to come and see you. But you have to be patient. I don't know how long this will take. I'll try to get you out of this room. They can't keep you in here.'

'I didn't mean to do it.'

'I know. I'll talk to Eden.'

The dying fly has stopped buzzing. Its legs twitch in the sunlight on the window sill.

45

THE PARADE GROUND

The men charge, stumbling forward, tunics flapping, plunging bayonets into straw-filled dummies that twist and swing in the wind. A chair blows over and a box falls to the ground. White sheets of paper spill out and scatter across the field like birds after a gunshot. Sergeant Bucton, yelling obscenities, chases after them. The men follow and soon the whole platoon is grabbing at the papers, stamping them into the grass, plucking them from the angry sky.

Eden is at the edge of the field, staring at the chaos. 'Hello, Ryan,' he says, without taking his eyes off the men. 'If you've come to parade your platoon, I'm afraid you're a bit early. My little fat sergeant over there was supposed to distribute the wills but, being new, he's a tad keen and seems to have distributed them across half of France.'

'Why did you arrest private Elphick, Sir?' says Alex, coldly.

'Why is it any of your business? He's in my platoon now.'

'He shouldn't be in anyone's platoon. He's ill.'

Eden thinks for a moment. 'Actually, I suppose cowardice is a kind of illness. An infection.' He's speaking quietly, casually, despite the noise of the wind and the shouting of the soldiers on the other side of the field. 'When you identify an infection, you need to cut it out, before it spreads to the whole regiment.'

'What offence are you charging him with?'

'I haven't decided. It could be disobedience or cowardice.'

'Why not discharge him, send him home?'

Eden turns to Alex. 'I can't. He refused to fight an enemy soldier. He refused to move in front of my whole platoon. What kind of message do you think that would send to the men if we send him home? Every gutless man in the battalion will think that if he acts like a coward, we'll send him home to his mother. Soon there would be no one left in the regiment.'

Thunder, high up in the clouds, ripples across the field.

'He freezes with fear,' says Alex. 'It's an illness. You know he isn't a coward!'

'It doesn't matter what I know!' Eden seems exasperated. 'The men saw a wilful defiance of my authority. *They* think he's a coward. So I have to do this, for them!'

This isn't going anywhere, Alex needs to change tack.

The soldiers have reached the end of the field and are plucking sheets of paper off the wire fence.

Alex sighs. 'So what do you intend to do now? You can't leave him locked up in that stifling guardhouse.'

'I know. The battalion's on the move in a few days. We don't want this to slow things down.'

'So why not throw him out of your platoon, Sir? As a demonstration to your men that you won't tolerate indiscipline. He can come back with my men. We can keep an eye on him, confine him to barracks. Cancel his pay for a week.'

Eden smiles. 'This is what will happen, Ryan. Private Elphick will be court-martialled.'

'What? A court martial? For not immediately responding to your command?'

'He's already being punished with an FP1 for disobeying *your* orders. We've run out of options. This is the next logical step. A court can decide on the correct course of action from here. I'm done with it.'

'He did not disobey my orders! The same thing happened then as has happened now. He had a fit!'

'The doctor says there's nothing wrong with him.'

'Woodstone won't allow this!' says Alex, raising his voice. 'The big push is coming. He doesn't want anything getting in the way of training.'

Eden raises an eyebrow. 'Actually, Woodstone seemed excited about a court martial when I mentioned it. Gives him a chance to show the top brass that he's serious about discipline. Trust me, he needs to show them *something*.'

'This is so unfair.'

'It's much fairer than one of us deciding his fate. It's a trial, Alex, not a stoning. And he won't be on his own. He'll have what's called a *prisoner's friend*, someone to help him with his defence. If you want something to do, and if you feel so passionately about it, you could do it. Why not? It looks like Major Babcock will be presiding. He likes you. It might do you some good to show your face with the top brass when you've got a little less mud on your uniform.'

Another clap of thunder, louder.

Eden curls his nose up at the ragged and darkening clouds. 'They might even find he's completely innocent. If they do, you can have him back, I promise. How's that?'

The men have collected most of the papers and are handing them back to the exhausted sergeant.

'Alex, I really must go. But you should think about helping with his defence.' Eden turns towards the field. 'Dear God, where do they find them? Are all the good sergeants dead already?' He jogs towards his men. 'Sergeant Bucton, let's get these men signing those wills before it rains. It's definitely going to rain.'

As Alex walks out of the parade ground, large drops begin falling into the grass.

46

THE BATHS

D Company has marched to a brewery just outside Vieille Chappelle, where the vats have been turned into bathing tanks for the men. Each man strips in the drizzle, throwing his uniform and underwear into a pile in the courtyard and joins the queue for the baths. The shivering men shuffle forward, naked but for the blankets wrapped around them; skinny white legs and bare feet squirming on the wet flagstones.

'This reminds me of a school production of Antigone,' says Charlie. 'Toga-clad boys, confused and bored, wandering aimlessly around a stage.'

'I thought Antigone was a woman,' says Alex, sullenly. He didn't sleep well, thinking about the court martial and how none of this would be happening if he had never mentioned anything about Percy in his report.

Charlie grins. 'She was. Played by a chap called Launcelot Bowman. He was very good. I believe he's a lieutenant in the Warwicks now.' He leans in, studying Alex's face. 'You're miles away. Are you all right, Old Chap?'

'Not really. This thing with Eden and Private Elphick. I still can't believe it's happening.'

'You shouldn't worry. It's so ridiculous, this will all blow over.' Charlie lines the men's boots up against a wall. 'And with you helping with his defence, I'm certain he'll be fine.'

'I haven't decided that I'm helping yet. I need to be sure I could do it without making things worse.'

'Of course you can do it. You know him better than anyone, and you've seen him when he's had these fits. You can explain to the court exactly what's going on. And as long as they get the doctor to explain the medical side of things, they're bound to see that it's just a misunderstanding. And didn't Eden say he thinks you should do it?'

'He did. That's partly why I'm worried. Why would he suggest that unless he thinks I'll fail?'

'I don't think it's that. He probably knows you'll put up a good fight. I think this is a game for him. He wants you to play.'

On Sergeant Kemmell's command, the men drop their blankets in a pile by the brewery door, climb into the vats and ease their aching bodies into the water.

Lit only by two raging furnaces, the room is warm and cosy. Golden flames dance on the walls, plumes of steam hang in the rafters above the great wooden vats and hot water gurgles and hisses from brass pipes.

'Holy Mary Mother of God!' says Rowlands, as he lowers himself in. 'This is better than anything you could pay for at *The Pelican*!'

'That's not saying much,' says Eggleton, scrubbing himself with a lump of yellow soap. 'I'd rather drink this bath than the beer they serve in that place.'

'I wasn't talking about the beer,' says Rowlands, with a glint in his eye.

'Whatever the outcome of this trial,' says Charlie. 'If you don't help Percy with this, don't you think you'll regret it?'

Rowlands waves the soap at Alex. 'Are you coming in, Sir? The water's lovely! Look! Even the fucking lice are doing the backstroke!'

'Excuse me, Lieutenants,' calls a soldier from the brewery door. 'Captain Woodstone has arrived to inspect the new laundry machine.'

'All right, Mr. Pope,' says Alex, picking up a pile of damp uniforms. 'I'll do it. I'll tell Woodstone now.'

'That's topping!' says Charlie, smiling. 'Percy will be back in your platoon in no time, I just know it. Once he's under your protection again, you'll have time to figure out what's the best plan.'

Outside, the soldiers are throwing piles of clothes into a huge horse-drawn, brass and wooden kettle.

Woodstone waves his stick at Alex and Charlie. 'You seen one of these machines before? The quartermaster got hold of it from somewhere. No idea what it does.'

'It's a disinfector, Sir!' says a pink-skinned soldier, swinging the massive round door closed and clamping it shut with an iron lever.

'Is that you, Sergeant Cook Coles?' says Alex.

Coles looks up and smiles. 'It is exactly me, Sir! Nice to see you again, Sir. But I'm not Sergeant Cook anymore. They put me on this a few weeks ago. I am now Sergeant *Disinfector* Coles!'

'We don't have time for this,' says Woodstone. 'I've come here to inspect this thing. So get on with it please, Sergeant.'

Woodstone's horse flinches as the great machine belches steam and smoke. Sykes, his new servant, a wiry man, flapping like a storm-damaged umbrella, leads the horse out of the yard.

Coles clears his throat and raises his arms theatrically, as if he's about to do a magic trick. 'This, gentlemen, is the *Thresh Disinfector!*'

Charlie claps.

'I don't care what it's called,' says Woodstone, glaring at Charlie. 'What does it do?'

Coles climbs up on the wagon. 'Clothing is placed loosely into this iron drum. The door is shut and sealed with this lever.' He's pointing at the levers and dials of the machine. 'A vacuum is created. Then steam from this boiler under here, enters via this valve. This creates a pressure of fifteen pounds. We hold that pressure for twenty minutes, after which time—'

'For God's sake, man!' yells Woodstone. 'I don't have a week! Just tell me what it does!'

Coles slumps. He looks dejected. 'It's supposed to kill the lice, Sir.'

'And does it work?'

'No, Sir.'

Woodstone turns to Alex. 'Damned waste of my time. No idea why they asked me to look at this. I still don't understand what it's supposed to do.'

'It's supposed to clean—'

'I don't care!' yells Woodstone. 'Right, I'm off. Meeting with the adjutant about this court martial.'

'Well, I wanted to talk to you about that, Sir,' says Alex.

'It's going to be quite a show,' says Woodstone. 'I managed to pull a few strings. We've got Major Babcock presiding and Captain Aubrey Merritt, whom you'll remember from the football match in April, the incident with the goat?'

Alex doesn't remember. 'I was wondering if I might be considered for—'

Woodstone isn't listening. He waves for Sykes to bring the horse over. 'Prosecuting officer will be Lieutenant Wanecroft. He's a qualified barrister.'

'Sir, I would like to act as the *prisoner's friend.*'

Woodstone climbs into the saddle. 'No need, Ryan.'

'I know it's not legally required, but I would like to offer to—'

'Not necessary, it's all been arranged. Major Babcock suggested a good chap already, Captain Crabtree. He's also a barrister!'

'But I know private Elphick, Sir. I think I could—'

'That's what Eden said, but Babcock has suggested this Crabtree fellow, so that's good enough for me. We *will* need you as a witness. Your report started this whole thing. So prepare yourself for that. Kick-off will be Tuesday.'

'Tuesday!' says Alex, raising his voice. 'That's in two days time! How can anyone prepare for the trial in two days?'

Woodstone looks confused. 'I don't think we need worry, the major said we can have it at battalion HQ, in Hingette. It's a large house. We only need to move a few chairs. The adjutant will organise catering. Sykes, here, will help him.'

Sykes nods solemnly.

'No, I mean preparations for the evidence,' says Alex.

'What evidence? You just need to answer a couple of questions.'

Alex, without thinking, grabs hold of the horse's reins. 'But, Sir, we need to talk to Eden's men, the one's who saw him during the last raid. We should contact the boy's family doctor, ascertain if there's a history of illness, and we must talk to Captain Noel again. He seems to know something about psychiatric disorders.'

Woodstone looks incredulous. 'Talk to Eden's men? Family doctors? Psychiatric disorders? This is not...' He leans down from the horse so he's eye to eye with Alex. He whispers. 'Look Ryan, the big push is going to be very soon and the major has said, if things go well beforehand, I might have a crack of something at HQ. With this court martial coming up, there's people watching me, seeing how I handle everything on a smaller scale. If I can show them that I can do this trial, and do it well, I might have a chance to stop being sent to places like *this*!' He straitens up, waves his stick at the brewery and jabs it towards the disinfector. 'And inspecting blasted steaming things! Laundry-thing machines! Do you understand?'

'But, Sir—'

Woodstone raises his hand. 'The Major has asked us to get this whole thing out the way as soon as we a can. Nip it in the bud before it gets out. It's not good for us or the men.'

'But if he doesn't have time to prepare his defence, how—'

'All I'm asking you to do is to let this Crabtree chap do his job. It's the best thing for everyone concerned. You'll have a chance to talk to him. We all will. We can have this trial, everything will go smoothly and quickly and we can all get on with fighting this damned war. Will you do that for me, Ryan? And, Ryan?'

'Yes, Sir?'

'Let go of my horse.'

47

CAPTAIN CRABTREE

Captain Crabtree is taking intermittent notes. Each time he makes an upstroke with his pen, the nib digs into the paper, judders and sprays a little plume of ink across his fingernails. His hands look like sea creatures. The knuckles are yellow. Faint blue veins swirl down the fleshy, shapeless fingers and disappear into the speckling of black ink. As his right hand forms the words across the paper, his left hand follows like a mollusc grazing on seaweed. 'Shell... shock,' he says, as he writes the words.

'No, not shell shock,' says Alex. 'The doctor said it reminded him of a condition called *neurasthenia*, but you really should ask him to explain it.'

Rain lashes against the little window of the office at Booze Farm. The oil lamp on the desk between the two men flickers.

'Neur... as... then...' Crabtree's pen scratches. 'Do you know how to spell that?'

'I don't, Sir. As I said, you should ask the doctor.' Alex must stay calm. He strokes the desk, feeling the woodgrain ripple under his fingers. He's been here for half an hour and the barrister has barely written a sentence.

Crabtree strikes out the attempted word. 'It's a court martial for cowardice, not a medical tribunal. We don't want to clog up the proceedings with unnecessary information. They need clear facts.'

'But isn't that the point, Sir? It's about a medical condition that has been *mistaken* for cowardice and our defence... your defence should—'

'Being *prisoner's friend* isn't quite the same as defence,' says Crabtree shrugging. 'It's more of a supportive role. I'm just helping to answer questions on behalf of the defendant.'

The wind rattles the window frame.

'But surely by examining the details of Elphick's seizures we can prove that—.'

'There's not enough time. We only have today to gather any information.' Crabtree spots a hair on the nib of his pen. He picks at it with his thumb and forefinger.

'To save some time, I anticipated what you might need to know.' Alex unfolds a sheet of paper and slides it across the desk. 'I've written this, Sir, explaining in detail about the seizures as I witnessed them.'

Crabtree glances at the paper. 'I don't know why they asked me to do this. I used to work in Shoreditch as a magistrate. The *Summary jurisdiction act, 1895. Married Women* was my speciality. Divorces, separations, abusive husbands...' He watches the rain lashing against the window and sighs deeply. 'I did some work for Major Babcock's cousin a few years ago. That's how he knows me. I lost that case, so it's odd that he thought of me for this. I've never done a court martial before, so...'

'Excuse me, Sir. I really think we should get on.' Alex pushes the paper closer. 'I've written, here, about how Elphick seems to behave quite normally at times, but falls into a kind of sleep during stressful situations.'

Crabtree shakes his head. 'Probably not good to mention that. The sleep thing. Laziness won't help his cause.'

'This isn't laziness.'

'*You* don't think so, but the prosecution will jump on something like that.'

'I see. So we shouldn't use the word *"sleeping"*. We should ask the doctor if *neurasthenia* is the correct term.'

Crabtree winces. 'Lieutenant Ryan, all we're doing here is trying to anticipate what the prosecution might ask the defendant. They might want to ask you about his previous conduct, and they might ask some of Eden's men if they saw anything, but that's all!'

'Well about that.' Alex hands Crabtree another sheet of paper. 'I've made a list of the men who were with Eden during the raid, we should interview them. Some of them would have seen what happened in the dugout, with the German, especially the ones who carried him out.'

Crabtree shakes his head again. 'I spoke to Eden this morning. I don't think I can refute that Elphick refused to obey an order but I could question the assumption that Elphick's actions, or lack of them, were born out of cowardice. I could suggest that his behaviour was due to some other cause: fatigue, confusion, shell shock or, yes, *neuras... nauras...*'

'*Neurasthenia!*'

Crabtree looks as if he's about to write it down, then changes his mind. 'But I don't know if any of those things are admissible defence. I need to look this up.'

There's a knock on the door. Woodstone walks in wearing a rubber poncho. 'I do beg your pardon, Captain Crabtree. I'm...' He's flustered, windswept and dripping. He smooths his ruffled hair into a parting with both hands. 'I'm sorry to interrupt. Lieutenant Ryan, we've just received our marching orders. You're to take the men into Vieille Chapelle immediately. Trucks are waiting there to take you all to Hingette. I'll meet you in the yard in ten minutes.'

As the door slams behind Woodstone, rain gusts in. The sheets of paper drift across the table.

'What about Elphick's age?' says Alex. 'He's very young. I'm sure he shouldn't even be here.'

'I've already spoken to the adjutant about this.' Crabtree drops his pen onto the desk and watches as it rolls in an arc, dispensing little blobs of ink that glitter in the lamp light. He takes out his handkerchief and mops each droplet one by one. 'He's registered as being eighteen when he signed up and that's all we've got. So no luck there, I'm afraid.'

'But that would make him nineteen now. It's obvious he isn't nineteen!'

'Lieutenant, he's not on trial for his age!' Crabtree sighs. 'I need to go and see Private Elphick, ask him what happened.'

Alex glares. 'You mean to say, you haven't even spoken to Private Elphick yet!'

'Not yet, no. Captain Woodstone said I might not get much out of him due to him being a bit, a bit... I thought I should talk to you first. I really didn't mean this to be a detailed examination of the facts. I just needed some background information from you. I need examples of Private Elphick's good behaviour. They'll be looking to see how valuable he's been as a soldier. We need to find reasons why they should be merciful.'

'What do you mean by that? Merciful in what way?'

Crabtree brightens. 'I've looked this up.' He shuffles through the papers, letting the top one slide towards Alex.

There are only a few words, written in capital letters: "ELPHICK", "ROYAL SUSSX", "BRIGHTON", "COWARDICE", "NEWRAS-" struck-through and, curiously, "MARY". Crabtree flips the sheet over. There's a list, with numbers. 'Here it is. Yes. I was hoping the charge might be disobedience, but they've gone for cowardice. So if we assume they find him guilty, and I think that would be a fair assumption here as—'

A tap on the window. Woodstone peers in. 'Ryan! Five minutes!'

'Yes, we should both get on,' says Crabtree. 'If we can show that he's been a good soldier: useful, loyal, hard working, they might show mercy, in which case he might be given a few years penal servitude or hard labour. This could, of course be suspended, so he might be sent back into the trenches until the end of the war and then sent home to serve his sentence.'

Alex can feel sweat forming on his forehead. 'You said, if they decide to show mercy. What will happen if they don't show mercy?'

Crabtree looks confused. 'Did no one tell you?'

'Tell me what?'

'The recommended punishment for cowardice is death.'

48

THE COURT MARTIAL

Battalion headquarters has moved into a little square house, built on the bank of the Canal d'Aire, just north of Hinges. The court martial started two hours ago. Alex will be the last witness. He's been told to wait outside until he's called. He's sitting on a bench in the garden, facing an iron bridge that crosses the canal.

A swan leads three cygnets out from the bridge's shadow. She calls to them and they squeak back in unison. Her feet flash in the after-noon sunlight; rust-coloured in the murky water. The humid air smells of flowers and river weeds.

Eden's voice drifts on the hot air through the open windows; confident and calm.

Laughter.

Alex nervously picks at a blister of peeling paint on the bench. Beneath it, sodden after the earlier rains, is a nest of tiny spiders. He pokes them with his finger. They scatter lazily across the wood and disappear. He walks across the lawn. By the wall of the house, a huge bee is trying to crawl into a foxglove. It's too big and keeps slipping off the petals, recovering mid-air and trying again, over and over. He wants to move the bee away, so it will find an easier flower. He tries to stand between it and the foxgloves. He can see into the windows of the house from here.

Percy is sitting on a chair with his back to the window. He looks bored; hunched forward, rubbing his chin on his shoulder, opening and closing his mouth like a fish.

One of Eden's men, standing to attention in the middle of the room, is being questioned by Crabtree, who is sitting at a desk next to Percy. 'I don't know, Sir,' says the soldier, with a voice like a motor lorry on a cold day. 'But I believe Private Elphick was perfectly able to move. He'd not received no injury. He just would not go on.'

The assistant adjutant has come out from the house and calls to Alex. 'If you could come in please, Sir? They'd like to speak to you next.'

Alex takes off his hat and follows the officer into the coolness of the hallway. It smells of sweet tea and old wood. A door opens, the gruff soldier is dismissed and Alex is led into the centre of the main room.

Percy, on seeing Alex, grins.

There are fewer people here than Alex had expected: Major Babcock and two others, presumably judges, a clerk of some kind and Wanecroft, prosecuting. They face him from behind a row of what appear to be school desks. Everyone looks hot and tired, except the officer sitting to the left of major Babcock, a grey-haired man who simply looks angry. Eden and Woodstone are sitting off to the side.

The clerk hands Alex a bible. It seems strange to be swearing on a religious object while it's decided if it's a good idea to shoot a boy.

The major has taken off his hat. His shiny head is like a dew-covered apple. He looks wearily at Wanecroft. 'Lieutenant, would you like to start?'

Wanecroft fans himself with a sheet of paper. Thin, fibrous wrists, a neck like tensioned rope. He starts by asking basic questions: Where did Alex train? How long has he commanded his platoon?

Alex's voice echoes vulnerably off the walls.

'In one of your reports,' says Wanecroft. 'You suggested that the prisoner should be sent home on medical grounds. Is that correct?'

'Yes, Sir.'

'Are you a doctor?'

'No, Sir.'

'Have you received *any* formal medical training?'

'No, Sir, but on three occasions I witnessed—'

Wanecroft raises his hand. 'As a result of *your* report, the prisoner was punished for insubordination?'

A twig outside one of the windows is brushing against the glass. It squeaks intermittently.

'Yes, Sir, but I didn't report that he'd been insubordinate. I said he'd fallen into a type of trance that—'

'Lieutenant Ryan,' says the major, pouring himself a glass of water from a jug on the table. 'It's been a long, hot day. This court has already been in session for a considerable time. We all have better things to do, and I've a train to catch in less than two hours. So please, only reply to the questions put to you.'

The twig squeaks.

Wanecroft continues. 'Had the prisoner displayed any other signs of cowardice before that trench raid?'

Alex is about to say no, then catches himself. 'He's *never* shown any signs of cowardice, Sir.'

'But he had gone missing during one of your earlier missions.'

'Not voluntarily. He was rendered unconscious by a grenade and left behind during the retreat. When I found him again, he'd been asleep.'

Wanecroft grunts incredulously. 'Sleeping? During a raid?'

'Well, I mean, no. I mean, being afraid causes a kind of seizure.'

'Captain Noel, the company medical officer,' says Wanecroft. 'Has given a very thorough examination of the prisoner, and stated that there are no signs of seizures or *shell-shock* or any other such thing.' He flicks through the papers on his desk with the end of his pen. 'Oh wait.' He looks up, smiling. 'Private Elphick has a cold!'

All the officers, except the angry one, laugh.

Percy grins.

'No further questions,' says Wanecroft, looking pleased with himself. 'Thank you, Lieutenant.'

'That can't be all you're going to ask me?' says Alex. 'I've got so much more to say!'

The angry officer next to the major lifts a finger into the air and lets out a noise like a goose that makes everyone jump. 'Baabp!' He curls his finger down with a flourish and points at Crabtree. 'If Captain Crabtree feels that there have been any omissions that would be pertinent to the prisoner's defence, then *he*, being the *prisoner's friend*, may give *you* the opportunity to elucidate.'

Alex doesn't quite understand what that means. He looks over to Crabtree, but Crabtree looks as confused as Alex.

'Captain Crabtree,' says Babcock. 'What would you like to ask Lieutenant Ryan?'

Crabtree looks startled. 'Oh. Yes,' he says, nodding vigorously. He runs a finger across his notes. 'Thank you. Just... If I may?'

The twig scratches against the window, sounding like a frightened mouse.

'Lieutenant Ryan,' Crabtree clears his throat. 'Would you mind telling us a little more about the previous conduct of Private Elphick? What kind of a soldier is he?'

Finally, a question for which Alex has prepared. 'Private Elphick has always been a good soldier. He's reliable and brave, obedient to his superiors and supportive to the ordinary ranks. He's very trusting, not at all cynical, and that makes him very easy to command. His lack of cynicism does mean that he can be the butt of some jokes from the men sometimes, both practical and verbal. Private Elphick thinks somewhat slowly at times, but he's never rash. He's popular with his comrades because he brings out a fraternal spirit... *paternal*, I should say, because of his age. But it's his age that is the other problem. He can't be more than sixteen.'

'Stick to the questions, please, Lieutenant Ryan,' says the major.

Wanecroft grabs a sheet of paper from his desk and waves it in the air. 'He was registered as eighteen in October 1914. I have it here.'

231

'That's ridiculous, Sir!' says Alex. 'Just look at him! I think he lied about his age so he could be here with his brother.'

'Baabp!' says the angry officer again. 'This is a court martial, and here we deal with facts, not personal opinions!'

Alex looks at Woodstone. 'Elphick shouldn't be here. You have to send him home. He's too young to be here!'

'Ryan!' yells Woodstone from his chair. 'Stop this!'

Alex turns to Percy. 'You have to tell them the truth. If you tell them you're younger than nineteen, they can't keep you here. They'll have to send you home!'

Percy glowers. 'I don't want to go home!'

'Silence!' The angry officer slams his hand against the table. He turns to Alex. 'Lieutenant, you will not address the prisoner directly!'

'Crabtree?' says the major. 'As the *prisoner's friend,* you should be making some effort to control your witnesses. Don't let them ramble on!'

'Of course, Sir. I apologise.'

'Well, do you have any further questions?'

Crabtree looks at his notes. 'I think we've covered most of...' He clears his throat and rubs ink off his fingernail with his thumb. 'Lieutenant Ryan, just now, you said that the prisoner has never shown any signs of cowardice.'

'I did, Sir.'

'But you said that his seizures might be caused by a reaction to fear.'

'Yes, Sir.'

'I must object to that question,' says Wanecroft. 'We've already established that Lieutenant Ryan is not medically trained. His answer cannot possibly be anything more than supposition.'

'Captain Crabtree hasn't asked the question yet,' says the major, pouring himself another glass of water. 'So I don't think you can object to it.' He drinks the water and for a moment, his mouth, magnified by the bottom of the glass, looks just like the foxgloves in the garden. '*Are* you going to ask a question, Captain?'

'Yes, Sir. My question is: was Private Elphick a fearful soldier? Did he appear to be afraid before he had these fits?'

'That's two questions,' says Wanecroft. 'And you can't make the assumption that they are fits,'

'I really do have to catch a train,' says the major. 'So could we just get through this? Answer the question, Lieutenant, just the last one, as briefly as possible.'

'Of course he was fearful,' says Alex 'Why wouldn't he be? We all are, all the time, but that doesn't make him a coward. If you're afraid but still do what is asked of you, then surely that makes you brave.'

'But he didn't do what was asked of him did he?' says the angry officer. 'And one more ramble like that, Lieutenant, and we'll ask you to leave the court.'

'May I ask one question?' says Wanecroft.

The major looks exhausted. 'I thought you had no more questions.'

'I've just realised the flaw in the defence's argument, Sir. I should very much like to explain, if I may?'

The major shrugs.

'Lieutenant Ryan implied that the prisoner's behaviour was caused by fear, but...' Wanecroft waggles his finger in the air for emphasis. 'The prisoner's refusal to move occurred *after* Captain Eden had led his platoon on a successful trench raid. They had completed their mission and were simply wandering down an empty, conquered, German trench. The German soldier, whom Private Elphick had refused to fight, was now dead, shot by Captain Eden himself. There was no danger. So surely, if the prisoner was going to have a fear-caused-fit, this would have occurred at the beginning of the raid, when the fear of death or injury was at its greatest, not after the raid, when there was nothing to fear?' He smiles triumphantly. 'What, Lieutenant, do you say to that?'

'As far as I understand, the German was not dead yet and was actu-ally attacking private Elphick,' says Alex. 'It was this, combined with his fear of Captain Eden that caused the fit.'

Wanecroft blinks. 'Why on Earth should he be afraid of Captain

Eden? We've heard testimony from several of the captain's men here today. He's very popular. No one seems afraid. It seems that they would do anything he asked.'

'Is that because the ones who complain, the ones who *wouldn't* do anything he asked, are no longer here?'

Wanecroft lets out a little laugh. 'What do you mean by that?'

'Ryan?' says Woodstone.

Alex swallows. 'Private Elphick had seen what the captain does to men who don't immediately obey his orders.'

'Goddammit, Ryan!' yells Woodstone. 'What the hell are you doing?'

'Captain Woodstone, please allow the court to proceed and restrain yourself from intervention!' says the angry officer.

Wanecroft seems genuinely intrigued. 'What had Elphick seen?'

The court officers lean forward. Even Crabtree has put down his pen.

'He saw Captain Eden...' Alex pauses and looks at Eden.

Eden doesn't react. A hint of a smile, perhaps.

Woodstone claps his hands, stands and half-bows. 'Major Babcock, I'm so sorry. I'm beginning to worry terribly that you'll miss your train. We've kept all of you here for much longer than any of us were expecting. You really have all been marvellous, but you still have to discuss your verdict. I would feel awful if we don't manage to complete our duties here this afternoon and risk having to reconvene again tomorrow.'

'Captain Woodstone!' says the angry officer. 'I will not tell you again.'

'Actually, Captain Woodstone does have a point.' The major stares theatrically at his watch. 'And I really cannot miss that train.' He stretches. 'Shall we wrap up, take five minutes of fresh air and come back in to discuss the verdict?'

'I think we should let him speak,' says Eden.

The major hasn't heard. 'Thank you, Lieutenant Ryan. You may leave the court. Show him out, someone, please.'

'No, I think we should let him speak,' says Eden, louder. 'We need to hear what he has to say.'

'I really don't see the point,' says the major. 'What anyone saw or didn't see anyone other than the accused doing is of no interest to us in this case. And apart from anything, it's so damned hot in here. What do you think Lieutenant Wanecroft?'

'If Captain Crabtree is happy to move on, then so am I,' says Wanecroft.

Crabtree nods with a shrug and closes his notebook.

Eden stands. He's smiling now. 'But the lieutenant wants to tell us something. Don't you Ryan?'

Woodstone places his hand on Eden's sleeve.

Eden twists away from it. 'What is it, Alex? What were you going to say? What did Elphick see me do that made him so afraid?'

'Is this *really* relevant to anything?' says the major.

Eden takes a step towards Alex. 'This is a court martial. What better place for *both* of us to confess? But first let's talk about you. Why don't you tell the court what happened on your first mission, with Captain Kingsman? Or would you like me to explain?'

The room is silent now, except for the twig, scratching little circles in the glass.

'Nothing to say, Ryan?' says Eden.

Alex stares at the floor. There's an oblong paleness in the centre of the room. They must have moved a rug.

'Perhaps we *have* finished here after all,' says Eden, gently.

The major shrugs and the officers start to pack up their papers.

Alex tries to speak, but all the words are lost in the darkness and rain of that terrible night. If he had just a moment to think, he could figure out what he should say. He wants so desperately to tell them the truth about everything, but he's afraid once they know what he did, that will mean that he's not a reliable witness. But he also knows that it isn't about helping Percy; he's afraid and ashamed for himself. And everyone is staring at him now and waiting and Eden is standing so close that he can feel the floorboards flexing between them. He turns to Percy and suddenly one word does come. 'Sorry,' he says.

Percy shakes his head and smiles; he doesn't understand.

By the time Alex turns back, the judges have started to leave the room. The assistant adjutant is leading him towards the door. The door closes and he is in the hallway and now the garden.

He stands in the middle of the lawn, holding his hat with both hands. The flowers by the wall quiver in sympathy. He walks up to a foxglove and kicks it. The stem spins, spraying purple flowers across the lawn. He walks around the side of the house, into the warm shadows, and throws up in a bed of daisies.

49

THE TOBACCO FACTORY

D Company is billeted in an old tobacco factory, just along the canal from Battalion HQ.

Not a single flake of tobacco remains, but the floorboards and rafters, at once dark and shining in the afternoon sun, give off a pungent, sweet aroma that makes Alex think of home. Something about Sunday afternoons at his father's farm. Rain-soaked dogs and pipe smoke. Or is it something about his mother? A sting of loss and quiet rage as he watches Percy pack his things.

Charlie is here; come to say goodbye, leaving the men parading in the factory yard with the sergeants.

'So I'm not ever coming back?' says Percy, hands shaking, struggling with the buttons on his tunic.

'The provost sergeant is on his way now,' says Alex. 'He's coming to take you to the police station in Hinges.'

'What's a provost sergeant?'

'A kind of policeman. You're to stay there with him until the sentencing.'

'What do you mean, *the sentencing?*'

'It's when they tell you what the punishment will be.'

Percy looks up from his buttons. 'I know what the punishment

237

will be. They told me. They said they're going to tie me to a post and shoot me.'

Alex grits his teeth. 'Who told you that?'

'I don't know their names.' Percy goes back to fighting with the buttons. 'From Captain Eden's platoon.'

'That's not…' Charlie leans against the wall and sighs. 'They won't do that. The court has recommended mercy. Which means they might just send you to prison for a while, in England.'

Percy looks shocked. 'England! I told you, I don't want to go back. I want to stay here and kill the dirty Hun.'

'Percy, do you understand what's happening?' Alex speaks slowly. 'They won't let you go back to fight. They are deciding whether to send you back to England, to spend time in a prison or to… They're deciding if they should, like you said, if they should shoot you.' He makes these last words softer, but they hang in the air between them like gun smoke.

Percy's fingers relax away from the buttons. 'I don't want to go back,' he says quietly. 'I'd rather be shot than go back.'

'You don't mean that,' says Charlie. 'Going home to England will be the best thing. It will only be for a few years and by then this war will be over and you can do anything you want after that. But it's up to other people to decide. We should know in a week or so.'

'Why can't they just tell me now? I want to know how to think about everything.'

'They have to send a punishment recommendation up through the chain of command. Brigadiers and generals will be reading that and adding their own to it. All the way up to old Haig himself.'

'Who's that?' says Percy.

'Field Marshal Douglas Haig. He's the man in charge of everyone and everything.'

Percy looks astonished. 'And he's going to decide if I get shot or if I go to England?'

'Yes, based on the recommendations of the court and all the others,' says Alex.

Percy's eyes narrow. 'What did you recommend?'

Alex looks at the floor. 'I don't make a recommendation. Only the court officers and Woodstone do that. I tried to get them to send you home without any punishment. But I didn't say it right... I should have said something about Eden to the court, but...'

'I'm sure you did everything you could,' says Charlie.

'I didn't. Something happened. Eden knows. I was ashamed and I thought he was going to tell them, so...'

'It was hot,' says Percy. 'Everyone wanted to go home.'

'You've missed out a button,' says Charlie.

Percy undoes his buttons and tries again.

A knock on the door.

Percy looks afraid.

Charlie smiles. 'Don't worry, they can wait. We'll let them in when you're ready.'

When the buttons are correct, Charlie brushes something from Percy's lapel and stands back. 'It will be harder without you, Private Elphick, but we will do our best to get rid of all the dirty Hun. So you mustn't worry.' He swallows. 'Everything will be all right.' He looks as if he's about to say something else but stops and turns to Alex. 'I have to get back to the men.' He opens the door and slips away.

Three policemen shuffle in. Curt greetings from the oldest, the provost sergeant. He has a kind, plump face, like someone who might sell you an ice-cream in the park. Alex gives him the only chair in the room and he sits with his back straight and his knees spread out as if he's playing a cello. He asks questions softly, writing the answers in a book that looks tiny in his big hands.

Percy stands to attention. 'Nineteen, Sir,' he says, proudly.

The provost sergeant looks at Alex and squints.

Alex breathes out slowly, says nothing.

Percy doesn't know what religion he is. His mother went to church. She made him and his brother and his sister go but his father wouldn't. He can't remember if he's been baptised as he doesn't remember much from when he was a baby.

The provost sergeant smiles. 'I'll put down Christian, if that suits? A chaplain will come and talk to you in the next few days.'

'Is it Reverend Clayton?' says Percy. 'He brings us chocolate sometimes.'

'It can be, yes, we can ask for reverend Clayton.'

When the questions are finished, one of the younger policemen asks Percy to stand and turn around. He pulls handcuffs out from his belt.

'Do you have to use those?' says Alex.

'I'm afraid we do, Sir,' says the provost sergeant. 'It's in the book. It won't be for long. The prison cart's just outside and the ride won't take ten minutes.'

They place the handcuffs on Percy's wrists and he stares with an expression that makes Alex think he might struggle, but as they turn him towards the door, he slumps, head down and shoulders hunched, as if the handcuffs are as heavy as a sand-bag.

'Attention!' yells Kemmell as the policemen reach the factory yard with Percy held between them.

Boots thud against brick, hands against cloth.

Alex's platoon is standing in a line that stretches right across the yard. Kemmell is at the far end by the gate. His face, proud and golden in the evening sunlight.

'Well, this is a first,' says the provost sergeant, glancing at Alex for reassurance.

'It's all right,' says Alex. 'This is his platoon. These are his comrades.'

'Carry on, Gents,' says the provost sergeant, nudging his policemen.

With Percy at the front and Alex at the back, they walk along the line. Percy walks sullenly, keeping his head down, staring at the ground, until he reaches Stubbs.

Stubbs salutes. And winks.

Rowlands, next to Stubbs, salutes.

Percy smiles and walks on.

Wislawa salutes, so does Eggleton, and as they move towards the road, each soldier in the line salutes.

Percy is laughing, lifting his knees up, twisting in the handcuffs; chinking the chain in recognition of each man.

'What's going on here?' Eden is in the yard. 'What are these men doing?'

'Provost Sergeant Campbell, Sir. Escorting this prisoner to the police station at Hinges, as requested by Captain Woodstone.'

Eden pushes through the line of men and stands facing Alex. 'Why are these men lined up like this? Why are they at attention?'

'I believe they are on parade, Sir,' says Alex.

'Why were they saluting?'

'As I said, Sir, they are on parade.'

Eden turns around. 'Who ordered this?' He sees Kemmell standing at the end of the line. 'You? Was it? Did you order these men to stand here, to salute?'

'Yes, Sir,' says Kemmell. 'We was just in the middle of salute-drill, to the front and side.'

Eden looks along the line.

Percy looks at Rowlands.

Rowlands winks.

'Lieutenant Ryan, get these men back into the billets,' says Eden. 'Provost Sergeant, get the prisoner into that cart.'

'Sergeant Kemmell,' calls Alex. 'Call off each man to the billets.'

Kemmell marches formally to the front of the line and orders each man, who has already saluted Percy, back into the warehouse.

Again, to Percy's delight, as he passes down the rest of the line, the remaining men salute.

'Stop this!' yells Eden. 'All of you get into the billets, at once!' He grabs Alex by the shoulder and turns him around. 'What the hell do you think you are doing? This man is a damned criminal!'

Alex feels a delicious violence surging through him. He holds it, then breathes it out. 'He's not damned yet, Sir.'

Eden glares. Perspiration glints on his top lip.

'Lieutenant Ryan, I ordered you to escort the prisoner personally onto the cart.' Woodstone is leaning out of an upper floor window, pointing towards Percy and the policemen. 'Why are you not over there, with them?'

'I'm on my way now, Sir.' says Alex, without taking his eyes off Eden.

'Well, get on with it. You march to Festubert tonight. You'll have your men ready in one hour.'

Alex watches as the cart moves away down the lane. Percy is sitting between the policemen, waving with both hands. The sun, an exquisite orange disk, ignites the trees behind them.

50

THE CORNFIELD

There's not much to see from here, just a narrow lane that curves gently out into old cornfields. The corn, unharvested for two summers, rustles in the darkness. Half a mile away, hidden by a small wood, is an old chateau, now occupied by a German signalling corps. Above the house and the trees, clouds, like countries on a vast map, glow silver from an unrisen moon.

An hour ago, at a junction at the other end of the lane, Alex watched Charlie and Halsall lead their platoons out through the corn for a coordinated attack on the chateau. Crouched over, silent and slow like a herd of deer; rifles for antlers, they crept towards the walls on the outskirts of the estate. They should be there by now, waiting for a mortar attack at the front of the house. Then over the walls, through the ornamental gardens and down into the cellars, where specialist bombers will do what needs to be done. They will then make their way along the lane to the junction, where transport is waiting to take them back to Hinges.

Alex is in support, standing in the lane, halfway between the chateau and the junction. His men are behind him, staring towards the trees, waiting for the flashes that will signal the attack.

Boxes of ammunition, a machine gun, stretchers and medical equipment are piled up to be taken forward if needed.

'This is it, lads. I can feel it!' says Kemmell. 'Everyone ready!'

A large explosion thumps out across the field. For a moment, the bright walls of the house shine through the trees; flames reflecting in rows of windows.

Shouting. Muffled intermittent gunshots. A single shot, another, then nothing.

The moon has broken clear of the cornfield. The lane is silent and empty.

A bird flaps in the hedgerow, screeching away into the darkness.

Minutes pass. The corn rustles.

Soldiers now, running along the lane: five, ten, thirty-five men. Alex counts them through; no one missing from the ordinary ranks.

Lieutenant Halsall is jogging behind them.

'Do they need us?' says Alex, handing him a water bottle.

Halsall waves the men on. 'We got in,' he says, drinking the water. 'But it was empty. Fritz must have moved out before we got there. We threw a couple of bombs and got out as fast as we could.'

'Should we go up?'

'No need. We could have handled the whole thing with five men. There's nothing left to do. Woodstone sent a message, ordered everyone, including you, back to the junction. We're not to engage any Boche units that might be wandering about. I'm sure he wants everyone home so he can tell HQ that his mission was a success with not a single casualty. I'm also sure he'll forget to mention that there was nothing in the chateau except for a few dead pigeons and some broken radio equipment.'

'I haven't seen Pope,' says Alex, looking behind Halsall at the empty lane.

'Charlie? Has he not come through? He was with his chaps, just ahead of ours. He must have made his own way back through the corn.'

'We could take a unit and spread out across the cornfield, Sir,' says Kemmell. 'Have a look around, in case he's injured.'

'That's not a good idea. We really must get going,' says Halsall. 'The moon is up and Fritz will be along soon. They're sure to be angry when they come home and find out someone's been eating their porridge!'

'Sergeant, take the men to the junction with Lieutenant Halsall,' says Alex. 'I'm going to wait here for a few minutes.'

'Don't be long, Ryan,' says Halsall. 'I'm sure he'll be waiting for us at the junction.' He jogs away, shouting behind him. 'I'll wait ten minutes, then you'll have to make your own way back to Hinges! Woodstone has laid on a London bus to take everyone back. They have buses here now, would you believe? All the way from London!'

If Charlie isn't dead and the Hun haven't found him, he would have headed for the trees.

As Alex runs along the lane, the sickening thought that Charlie might be dead thuds through his guts with each boot hitting the ground. He'll run as far as he can, turn off into the trees, and start looking.

German voices; soldiers ahead of him. Moonlit helmets, silver-edged bayonets and rifles.

He dives across the road, into the rows of corn.

Torchlight spreading along the lane. Flashes on the corn leaves.

He drops to his knees, peers out between the bristling stems. He's out of breath, tries to breathe quietly.

The soldiers are making no attempt to be quiet; someone is laughing. Faces slide in and out of the torchlight. They're close but no one sees him.

He gets up and creeps towards the trees.

A shape on the ground ahead of him. He dives sideways into the thickness of the corn. They must have seen him. He drops to the ground, listens, then starts to crawl away.

'Alex! Alex! It's me!' Charlie whispers. 'What are you doing, rummaging around in here?'

'I was coming to get you,' says Alex, relief flooding through his bones.

'Well, that's kind of you.' Charlie is out of breath too.

Alex crawls over. 'You're keeping everyone waiting. What are you doing lying down here? Hiding from those Boche? Or was it your usual nap? I really should mention it to Woodstone.'

Charlie is lying on his front, head pressed into the dust. 'Are you alone?'

'I am. Everyone made it back, except you, of course. Are you all right? Let's get back. Woodstone is going to kill me when he finds out I came to find you.'

Charlie doesn't reply.

'Charlie we should move. This moon is getting brighter.'

'I don't think I can.'

'What do you mean?'

'I've been hit in my back, I think. Would you have a look for me?'

'Oh God, have you?' He kneels, runs his hand down Charlie's back. There's blood; a lot of blood. It looks black in the dappled moonlight. 'Does that hurt?'

'No, it doesn't. What are you doing?'

'I'm pressing quite hard. I don't think it's serious, you must have had a graze. You'll be all right. Just shock, I should think. They've got ambulances at the junction. We can get the MO to look at it.'

'All right.' Charlie is quiet for a moment. 'But I'm finding it quite hard to move my legs.'

'Can you move them at all?'

'Not yet… Perhaps in a minute.'

Alex sits back, tries to think what to do, tries to breathe. 'I need to turn you over so I can lift you. Is that all right?'

'You can try.'

He moves Charlie's leg up and pulls him over onto his back.

Charlie groans.

'Oh God, sorry. Does that hurt?'

'Yes, no, sort of. I don't know. Sorry, Alex. I'm not helping much am I?'

'Sorry for what?' Alex laughs, but the laughing feels like bleeding. 'I'm going to try to lift you, all right?' He pushes his arm under Charlie's shoulders and lifts.

Charlie yells out. 'That *did* hurt! You should go back, Alex. Whoever shot me is still in the lane. You can get away if you're on your own.'

'I'm not leaving you here,'

'I'll just stay here for a bit,' says Charlie, calmly. 'I'll come along in a while. I just need a rest, I think.'

'I said I'm not leaving you.' Alex peers through the corn. He can't see any soldiers. 'Let's try again.' He lifts, this time trying to keep Charlie's back as straight as he can.

Charlie yells. 'No! No! Please, Alex.' He's breathing very fast. 'Can we stop?'

He lowers Charlie down. He looks back along the bright rows of corn and the blackness between them. 'I can run to the junction, get some help. I can be back here in ten minutes.'

'You can't go back now, the moon is too bright. There will be Germans everywhere.' Charlie's words are thick and slow. 'Can we just stay here? I want us to look at the moon.'

He removes Charlie's helmet. 'I should try to drag you.'

'No, please, Alex. Please listen to me. I don't want to be dragged across the field. Look at the moon! It's beautiful.' Charlie waves his hand in front of his face. 'Can you feel it?'

'Feel what?'

'The moon. It's protecting us.'

Alex looks up. It *is* so beautiful: the moon seems to be on a different plane, as if it's in front of the sky that surrounds it. A rainbow haze of ice crystals shimmer.

'Just look at that!' Charlie smiles. 'Who gave us that? Who gave us such a perfect thing?'

Alex settles into the dust and gently pulls Charlie's head against his chest and holds him.

'It will be summer soon. We're so nearly there,' says Charlie, 'I was so looking forward to it. I'll hate to miss it. I love the summer. This has been the longest spring, don't you think?'

'You won't miss it. We'll just rest here for a bit and get going.'

'Alex, don't worry about what happened with Captain Kingsman.'

He looks at Charlie. 'What do you mean?'

'It was you, wasn't it? He wasn't killed by the Germans. Sorry if I've got that wrong. But I thought… Isn't that what you meant?'

A little pulling sound squeezes up from Alex's throat. He clears it. 'Yes. How did you know? I haven't told anyone.'

'I thought that's what you were going to tell me, with Percy, yesterday.'

'Yes, I killed Kingsman, and his men. The first night out. I was with Eden. I thought they were Germans. A grenade. The first time I ever threw a grenade.'

'Yes, I thought that's what had happened. I've thought that for some time.'

'Why didn't you say anything?'

'I was waiting for you to tell me. It was stupid of me. I'm sorry. You shouldn't worry, it was a mistake. You *meant* no harm.' Charlie winces, clenches his hand into a fist. He starts to sob. 'I can't believe I'll never see her again. Everything I did was to prevent what is now going to happen!'

'Don't be ridiculous, Charlie. We're going back in a minute. We can—'

'Alex, I need you to promise me something.'

'Yes, Charlie.'

'Would you find my Eva, and tell her that I did all right in the end?'

'We can go together. I'll back you up.'

'No, Alex, I mean it.'

Alex sighs. 'Of course I will. I promise I will.'

'It didn't feel like it would be today. Everything felt quite normal.'

'It isn't going to be today. We can just rest here. Then we can try again.'

They don't speak for a while.

'I'm not in any pain, I'm looking at the moon with my good friend.' Charlie closes his eyes. 'I feel quite sleepy though.'

'Don't fall asleep.'

'I think I *will* sleep for a bit, if that's all right?'

'Try to stay awake. I'll go and get some help in a minute.' Alex brushes Charlie's face with his fingers. 'Charlie?'

A rustling breeze slides along the rows of corn.

'Charlie.'

The name feels different now. The sound of it spreads out across the field and in its place, a silence rushes in.

51

FESTUBERT

Alex sits, watching the clouds thicken in front of the moon. Then he lifts Charlie across his shoulders and carries him along the rows of corn. The dry plants seem taller now and everything is very dark. Charlie's skin is already cold. It smells like pepper and damp leaves. He feels as if he's carrying the body down into the underworld. He tries to remember the names of the rivers: Oceanus, Styx, and what was the river of pain? Acheron. And the river of wailing? He doesn't remember.

The junction with the lane and the road to Festubert is empty. There are deep tracks where the London bus must have got stuck. Ammunition boxes have been broken up and laid down for traction.

He places Charlie's body against a wall while he decides what he should do.

After a few minutes, a motor ambulance stops and the driver and a nurse get out and carry Charlie into the back.

The nurse tells Alex to sit in the front and she climbs in and sits very close. He can feel the warmth of her.

When they arrive at the casualty clearing station at Festubert, the nurse climbs out and takes Charlie's papers into the huts. Four men carry Charlie on a stretcher to a grassy area in front of the huts and place a blanket over him. There are other bodies there too. They are all covered with blankets. In the morning half-light, they look like strange plants.

Someone sends a message to Woodstone and Alex is told to make his way back to the billets in Hinges.

The nurse tells him that Charlie will probably be buried at the cemetery in Festubert. They will send the details and any possessions to the adjutant. She offers to wash the blood from Alex's uniform. But he has to get back.

He kneels down next to Charlie. There is a beetle walking across the blanket. He puts his thumb next to it and it climbs onto his hand. He watches it for a long time until it flies away, low across the grass. Then he walks into the road to find transport that will take him to Hinges.

52

HINGES

When Alex arrives at the billets, his platoon is packing their kit in the yard. They stop what they're doing and move towards him. 'Are you all right, Sir?' says Kemmell.

'It's not my blood,' says Alex, without stopping. 'Where's Woodstone?'

'I didn't mean that, Sir. I meant… He's in his office.'

Woodstone looks up from his desk. 'Ryan, there you are. You took your time.'

'Lieutenant Pope is dead,' says Alex. He can still feel the weight of Charlie on his back, the weight of their two bodies combined, pushing into the soft dark soil between the rows of corn.

'I know.' Woodstone places his pen carefully on the desk and lays one hand on top of the other. 'I received a telephone call from an officer at the clearing station.' He shakes his head. 'What rotten luck. I was just about to send a message to the major, saying we pulled this mission off with no casualties, but now… Rotten luck!' He rifles through some papers on his desk and pulls out a form. 'I've already written something to go into the battalion diary. Best to get these things done while it's still fresh.' He clears his throat. '*The death of Second Lieutenant Pope was a great blow to the battalion and one that was felt by all ranks. This officer was a model of energy and cheerfulness in the perfor-mance of his duty and was always ready to help anyone in trouble.'* He looks up. 'What do you think?'

Alex feels as if he's sinking deep into himself. He has to push back from somewhere to answer. 'It's fine.'

'Good. I'll send that off with the adjutant this afternoon. Get it to the London Gazette for Friday. Did you see him before he died?'

'I did, Sir.'

'Good. Full report then. I don't think he was married. So, letter to parents and all that.'

'He has a wife, Eva. I'll write to her today.'

'Was he? Married? He never mentioned—'

'What about his men, Sir? Where are they? Do they know? I should tell them what happened.'

'I spoke with Eden on the telephone. He's taken Pope's men up to Vieille Chapelle with his own lot. He's informing them now. Will you be all right? You were chums.'

Alex shrugs. 'Yes, Sir.'

'Are you injured? You're covered in blood.'

Alex touches the stains with the tips of his fingers. His tunic looks like his old painting smock: *burnt umber, burnt sienna, perylene maroon.* 'It's not my blood.'

'Right, good. I thought so, but you'll have to change your uniform. We're all going up to Vieille Chapelle this afternoon. You can't go out like that. We'll need to find you something.'

'I've got a spare at the farm,' says Alex, suddenly needing to be with Odette. To be quietly with her. 'We'll be marching past. I can go up ahead and collect it.'

Woodstone looks confused. 'You can't.'

'I can't what?'

'Go to the farm.'

'Why not?'

'It's not there.'

'What do you mean?'

'The farm isn't there anymore. It was shelled a few hours ago.

Boche artillery must have known it was an officer's billets. The women were killed and I think we've lost all our things, including your spare uniform, I shouldn't wonder. Big fire. Captain Eden was damned lucky, though. Arrived moments after it was hit. He said the main house was completely destroyed. Two minutes earlier and he would have been inside and gone up with it. I've got Fenton looking for something else for us in the village.'

'The women,' says Alex. 'What did you say about the women?'

'The women? Killed, unfortunately. They would have been asleep when it hit. Probably best, to go in your sleep. Still, damned shame. We've got people there now, sifting through the rubble. I had a very nice watch, heirloom. I should have left it at home. Doubt they'll find that.'

'Both women were killed?'

'I think so, yes.'

53

HOWITZERS

They had told him what to expect. They told him Odette and her mother were dead. He knew the house had been completely destroyed, and he could smell the burning from half way down the lane. But as he comes through the gate, past the fire engine, over the sooty puddles into the farmyard, what he sees shocks him as much as anything he has seen on the battlefield.

It's as if the farmhouse has been sawn in half. Only the back wall and remnants of a few rooms remain. The roof of the main building is gone. Blackened and dripping beams stick out like the rib cage of a forgotten soldier. Walls have crumbled and cascaded down in piles of rubble that cover the courtyard. The pump is half-buried in bricks and roof tiles. There's a burned window frame with curtains still attached. Sheets of wallpapered plaster from the hallway are strewn across the yard; at once familiar and shockingly strange in the daylight.

A rescue and recovery team is working through the wreckage. Their clothes and faces are smeared with dust and soot. They pull items out of the rubble and place them in piles by the cowshed: kitchen chairs, clothes, the clock that was on the mantel, a teapot. They move slowly; no sense of urgency.

'What are you doing?' says Alex, climbing onto the largest pile of rubble. 'We should be looking for survivors!' He grabs a blackened post with both hands and tries to free it. 'Help me with this!' he yells. 'There could be someone under here. Help me!' He grabs chunks of brick and throws them across the yard.

The soldiers, glancing at their sergeant, move forward in obedience but don't help.

'We've been through all of this rubble, Sir,' says the sergeant; long-limbed, clambering across the rubble like a spider.

'You can't stop now. Someone might still might be under here!'

'No one could survive being buried under this. No air pockets you see?' The sergeant reaches down and picks up half a brick. 'Soft bricks. Everything turns to dust. It was most probably a delayed fuse.' He pushes a wiry finger into the brick to demonstrate. 'There's a mechanism in the shell that causes it to detonate half a second after the impact, allowing the shell to bury deeply into the structure of the building before it explodes.' He crumbles the brick to dust in his hand. 'Even if you could survive being buried in the rubble at first, with the heat from the fire… They probably used incendiaries in conjunction with the high impact—'

'Why are you telling me this?' says Alex. 'We should be digging!'

'This is what I'm explaining, Sir. Everything was burning like hell. We've only just been able to get this close in the last two hours. There's a stream running up behind those trees but it took us ages to get the pumps going. Since then we've turned over as much of it as we could. The adjutant said we should be looking for two occupants, the wife of the owner and a daughter.'

'I know, I was billeted here.'

'Oh, sorry, Sir, I was unaware. I'm telling you what you already know.' He points up at the remains of the house. The safe cocoon, floral patterned walls of Odette's bedroom, now torn open to the sky. 'They were up there on that level when the shells hit. We found one, the wife I assume, thrown across the courtyard and landed against that wall. We climbed up for the other. Nothing. The floors are gone.'

'The wife? Where?'

'We put the body over there, in that old shed.'

The chickens are scrabbling happily next to the body. Madame Berger's feet are sticking out from under an army blanket, thick, strong ankles. Alex lifts the blanket. She looks peaceful, asleep. The brick dust even gives her cheeks a healthy, rosy glow.

He walks back over to the main house. Something is still burning under the rubble from where the kitchen used to be. Grey smoke curls among the loose bricks and drifts free in little surges. 'You didn't find the girl?'

'No, Sir,' says the sergeant. 'She must either be under this lot, roasted by now in the heat or vaporised. Sometimes with the big shells like this, if it's a direct hit, I've seen men disappear, clothes ripped off and the body simply gone. Nothing but a cloud of pink mist where they were standing. I've seen—'

'I've seen what shells can do! Don't you think I haven't?' Suddenly Alex feels so hot he wants to rip off his own skin. Everything seems to turn darker, rushing away from him. He staggers and finds himself kneeling in the rubble.

The soldiers move closer. The sergeant rushes over and lifts Alex by the arm.

Alex pushes him away. 'Are you sure? Are you fucking sure?' he says, quietly.

'About what, Sir?'

'That no one survived!' The air feels as if it's made of thorns. 'I'm just asking you if you are sure!'

'Yes, Sir. We've been here for three hours. We've been through everything.' The sergeant unclips a bottle of water, uncorks it and hands it to Alex. 'Did you know them well, Sir? The women?'

'Yes. I did. I knew them very well.'

'I'm so sorry, Sir, I didn't realise... We've done everything we could. But there's nothing. No one. I'm sorry.'

'Perhaps she was injured and crawled away from the house?' says Alex, feeling calmer from the water.

'I've had my men go around the fields, Sir, in case of that. And your captain, Captain Eden, was here earlier. He said he arrived just after the farm was hit. He would have seen something. There was no one on the road in either direction.'

'Then perhaps she wasn't here at all. Perhaps she'd gone out to do something… With the cows!' Suddenly there's hope. 'The cows are not in the barn! Where are the cows?'

'No, Sir,' says the Sergeant. 'A local farmer came. He took them. Signed some papers. I can show you if you like? We're just trying to find the officers' possessions now. Sort through everything and see what we can save. You should get some rest, Sir, leave all this to us. If I know what to look for and where to look, we can try to find your things and let you know. Where were you staying, Sir? Where was your room?'

Two white doves fly across the courtyard and land on the roof of the milking shed, where Alex stayed with Charlie. They trot daintily along the ridge as if everything is how it used to be. The tiles are unbroken, still covered in a vibrant green moss. But the roof, like the back of a beached whale, sits bowed and twisted on the rubble.

'Well, with your permission, Sir,' says the sergeant, 'I should get along now. Me and the lads should get on. I'll contact you, of course, if we do find anything but…' He shakes his head and goes back to his men.

Charlie's sewing machine is lying on its side in the rubble. Alex picks it up and with all his strength, hurls it onto the roof of the milking shed. The doves arc up and fly away across the fields. The arrhythmic wing-beats fade into a dusty calmness. He remembers the quiet after the fire that killed his mother: the crackling of the burning wood, the hiss of the dust swirling against the flagstones.

54

CECIL HENDERSON

The horse smells like warm grass. It pulls the bathing machine across the pebbles and down into the water. The wheels sound like thunder. Alex wants to run back up the beach to find his father but his mother is calling him. Her bathing suit is striped like the sunlight on the water. She laughs as he climbs down the steps and holds on, feet dangling, afraid to tread on a fish. He lets go and slides below the waves. Grey sunlight, bubbles, salt at the back of his throat.

He reaches out and finds Odette's soft hand. As he lifts her, a wave washes over her head and she screams with delight. He lowers his hand into the water and pulls out a shell the colour of blackberries. She curls her trembling fingers over it and her laughter blends with the cries of seagulls and the hiss of water through the pebbles.

Suddenly a rushing white-water wall of knowing. A green sea-wave tumbling, pushing him over, dragging him down. Ankles, elbows, fingers crushed against the stones. He's choking, coughing up salty bile.

The water recedes. He's on his back, half-buried in the stones. The beach is empty. Odette is gone. Charlie is gone. And now the beach is littered with corpses like fronds of seaweed. 'Alex.' His mother is calling him from far along the beach. Someone is shaking his arm. 'Alex.'

'Alex? You all right?' Halsall is leaning over the camp-bed. He smells of wine. 'You sounded quite disturbed, old chap. I came back earlier to see if you were coming along for supper but you'd dozed off and I realised that must be the first time you've slept for two days.' He strikes a match and lights a lamp that's hanging from a nail against the central tent pole. His face is like an orange moon against the dark canvas. 'You were shouting something. We could hear you all the way from the officers' mess. I thought you'd been attacked by a snake or something. You all right?' He throws the match into the grass between the camp beds. A puff of smoke curls into the shape of a seahorse and drifts away.

Has it been only two days? He'd had no sleep on the night of the raid at Festubert. He'd taken Charlie to the clearing station, marched his men from Hinges to Vieille Chapelle, searched the ruins of the farm while his men were sleeping, then marched them here, the training camp in Pacault. He'd helped Kemmell see the men into their tents and come back to his own to dress before dinner. He doesn't even remember lying down.

Time is measured by hours and days, but it's felt by how much things change between them. It feels a very long time since he was watching the moon with Charlie. It seems like months have past since he last saw Odette. 'What time is it?'

'Nearly ten. I asked Fenton to save you some dinner,' says Halsall, pouring water into a tin bowl.

'Thank you,' says Alex, sitting up. 'But I'm not hungry.'

'You must be exhausted after the bad luck you've had. Woodstone should have given you a few days leave. You should ask him.'

Alex has had no leave since he arrived in France. He doesn't want any. He doesn't want to go home or have to wander alone around some dreary French town until he can get back to his men.

There's a young officer sitting in the shadows, on a camp-bed at the end of the tent, combing his yellow hair with a tiny tortoise-shell comb.

Alex looks at Halsall for an explanation.

'Good God, I'm so sorry!' says Halsall, squinting through soap suds. 'We've been sneaking around in here trying not to wake you. I forgot you hadn't been introduced! This is Second Lieutenant Henderson.'

'Call me Cecil, please!' says Henderson, bounding across the tent and thrusting his hand out as if he's leaning over a low fence.

Alex raises his hand. It's shaken vigorously.

'Cecil has just arrived,' says Halsall.

'The journey was a nightmare. Twelve hours. I was exhausted.'

Halsall grins. 'Nothing a good dinner and a few bottles of red didn't sort out, hey Cecil?'

Henderson mimes drunkenness like a schoolboy and laughs.

'Do you two know each other?' says Alex.

'We didn't,' says Henderson. 'But everyone has made me feel quite welcome.'

'The whole battalion is here now,' says Halsall. 'Cecil has been entertaining us. He can sing and play the piano! What was that song about the dead cow? You should have heard it, Alex. Even old Babcock was laughing.'

Henderson waves his comb in the air and sings: *'In our little wet home in the trench, that the rainstorms continually drench! There's a dead cow nearby with its hooves in the sky, and it gives off a terrible stench!'* He laughs, sits back on his bed and rearranges his expression to something more serious. *'Richard* was telling me that you've just come back from a raid on the haunted chateau. I must say, that did sound exciting.'

Again, Alex looks at Halsall.

Halsall shrugs. 'Well, it *looked* haunted. Dungeons crawling with the corpses of slain Boche! Cobwebs all over the place!'

'I was in support,' says Alex. 'I didn't see the chateau.'

'Is that frustrating?' says Henderson. 'Being in support?'

'We lost a very good officer, Charlie Pope. He was the last man out of the chateau. The Boche shot him in the spine. He didn't mention any ghosts.'

Henderson looks shocked. 'Gracious me, that sounds awful. But even so, it does sound exciting. I hope we go on a raid soon. I rather can't wait.'

Halsall looks apologetically at Alex. 'It is awful about Charlie. He *was* a good officer. A really fine chap.'

'Gosh, that *is* awful,' says Henderson, shaking his head. 'But it's all part and parcel, war and death, isn't it? I have no misconceptions of what to expect. I'm fully prepared.' He raises his fist in the air and gives it a little shake.

Alex doesn't want to reply.

'Cecil is a Scout leader!' says Halsall, filling the awkward gap.

'That's it! Be prepared for anything in mind and body!' Henderson waves his fist again. 'I led a troop in Robertsbridge, Sussex, teaching young lads the rudiments of *Scoutcraft*. Much like we'll be doing here I should imagine. All the essentials: first aid, fire-building, map reading, lighting fires.' He smiles. 'I know it's not quite the same as leading a platoon of soldiers into battle, but you would be surprised how stressful things can get with boys running around forests in the dark. The damage they can cause to themselves and each other is beyond most people's understanding. One lad…'

Rain is drumming lightly on the tent canvas. Alex lets the sound wash over Henderson's words. He thinks of Percy, locked up in the police cell at Hinges. If only he had joined Henderson's Scout troop, instead of going to war. How nice that would have been; camping and cooking in the open air, with little fear of being shot.

'Cecil was telling me that he can light a fire with two sticks,' says Halsall. 'I'll be damned if I could get so much as a puff of smoke from a whole box o'matches!'

It's difficult to tell if Halsall is playing with Henderson or if he's genuinely impressed.

Henderson rummages in his valise and pulls out a long, striped nightgown. 'Should I wear this? It wasn't on the list. What do you chaps wear?'

'We generally wear our undergarments during training,' says Halsall, with a playful glance at Alex. 'Full battledress on the front line. That way you won't get caught with your trousers down if Jerry decides to drop a grenade in your funk hole.'

Without expression, Henderson refolds the nightshirt and places it carefully back into the valise.

'Where did you train?' says Alex.

'Shoreham. Three months.'

'And where were you before that?'

'Well, they sent me to Shoreham as soon as I signed up.'

'But you've been training at the Bull Ring?' says Halsall.

Henderson looks blank.

Halsall throws Alex a concerned look. 'The Bull Ring, the training camp at Etaples.'

'No, I've just come up. We were fully trained at Shoreham. Three months of it, as I said.'

'And that's the only training you've had?' says Alex.

Henderson nods. 'Yes. Although you're worrying me a bit now. But I think that I've come at a good time, with this *big raid about to happen*. I'm so pleased. I'd heard stories of chaps being stuck in the trenches for months without even sniffing a German, but here I am, arriving in France just days before *la gros spectacle!*'

'That's marvellous, Cecil,' says Halsall. 'You'll be over the bags on your very first night in the trenches, by the looks of things. I didn't get to shoot at anything human for weeks after I first arrived. And something big is definitely happening. I took a wander over to the training ground this afternoon. The engineers are building a huge model of the front line that we're going to attack. I think this is it. It's what we've been waiting for.'

Henderson smiles. 'Captain Woodstone said that if I work hard during this week's training, and with my Scouting experience, it's highly likely that I'll be given my own platoon as soon as we get to the front line. I was hoping to watch and learn from your famous Captain Eden, of course. I'm bitterly disappointed that he won't be here.'

Alex's stomach tightens. 'Why not? Where is he?'

'On leave,' says Halsall. 'Lucky blighter is probably spending it at a whorehouse in Amiens. It seems that he doesn't need any of this extra training, unlike us mere mortals.'

'What's he like?' says Henderson. 'I've read so much about him. Is he as formidable as everyone says?'

Alex gets up from his bed and relieves himself in a bucket by the tent door.

'Alex and the captain have had a bit of a run-in,' whispers Halsall, theatrically. 'I'll tell you all about it over a bottle of something tomorrow.'

Outside, the air smells of grass and wet canvas. Hundreds of bell-tents fill the field as far as Alex can see. Soldiers have lit unofficial fires in the paths between the tents. Sparks and laughter rise up into the rain.

55

PACAULT TRAINING GROUND

The battalion is training for the mission that everyone is now referring to as *The Raid*. There are few details, but the rumour is that it will involve the entire expeditionary force, along the whole front line, from the marshes of the River Somme, all the way across Flanders to the Northern Sea. The Southdowns Battalions will be somewhere in the middle of it, doing something that involves climbing breastworks and crossing dykes.

To that end, D Company is on *Traverse Drill*. Replica breastworks, made of canvas and wood, run parallel to a water-filled ditch that's been cut across the training ground. On the instructor's command, the men, in groups of six, run forward, collect a small wooden bridge, drag it over the breastworks and carry it to the ditch. From there, one man wades in, securing the bridge on the far bank and the others clamber over.

Alex's men are excited and, despite heavy rain, everyone throws themselves into the training, and the ditch, with a zeal that hasn't been seen since March.

No one appears to be more enthusiastic than Alex. This has been noted by the training sergeants. But it's not enthusiasm; a few nights ago, woken by the agonising realisation that he would never again touch Odette's skin, he had rushed out of his tent, running blindly through the darkness like a panicking soldier in a gas attack. He didn't get far and no one had seen him. But in the morning he vowed not to let something like that happen again. So in order to not give himself time to feel, pushing against the agony of movement, he is training harder than anything he has ever done in his life. And for the rest of the week, he will not allow himself to slow down. Now, as he hurls himself across the bridge, he slips on a wet plank and falls into the dyke. He sinks into the soft mud and sits submerged up to his eyes in the cold water.

A bright yellow leaf spirals past, suspended in reflected clouds. Behind the shouting and the crunch of boots, he can hear the rain on the water. It calms him, and he starts to feel a little better. The gas-attack panic begins to dull into something like a fractured bone.

By lunchtime, the rain is falling so hard that it's impossible to hear what the instructor is saying and training is abandoned for the day. On the way back to the mess huts, Alex notices that several of the men have cuts all over their hands.

'They had us cut up biscuit tins into little triangles,' says Wislawa. 'Hundreds of bloody tins. We're going to sew them onto the backs of our tunics, for *The Raid*. Little shiny triangles. They glint in the sun and our artillery will see them and know it's us and not the Hun.'

'Bollocks!' says Rowlands. 'Who told you that?'

'It's true,' says Wislawa. 'I was talking to the sergeant.'

'Bollocks!'

'What if it's raining?' says Eggleton.

'That won't make no difference,' says Rowlands. 'We'll be marching towards the Boche, who are to the east of us. It will be early in the morning. The last time I checked, the sun *rose* in the east! So these triangles will be in the shadows of our backs and we'll be silhouettes!'

'For that matter,' says Eggleton, 'It might still be fucking dark!'

'I met her once,' says Stubbs, out of nowhere. He and Alex are walking together at the back. 'At the farm where you were billeted, Sir. The young lady.'

'Odette?' says Alex. Her name, spoken out loud, stings.

'Yes, Sir. I'd been sent there with something, a new saddle for Captain Woodstone, I think it was. She let me in, gave me a glass of milk.'

Alex doesn't speak. He can't.

'With that and what happened to Lieutenant Pope. I just wanted to say... I don't know what I wanted to say... I just... I'm sorry, Sir.'

Alex smiles, genuinely. He feels such warmth after this kindness that he wants to fling his arms around Stubbs and hug him. Instead, he nods.

'Ryan, this is it!' Halsall is running along the path, jumping over puddles.

Henderson is behind him, out of breath, grinning. 'Marching orders! Captain Woodstone says I'm definitely going to be given my own platoon!'

'Isn't that marvellous?' says Halsall. 'We're going into the line at Richebourg. The Ferme Du Bois sector!'

'Actually, D company won't be going directly to Richebourg,' says Woodstone, appearing out of the rain, engulfed by a huge black umbrella. 'We're stopping off at Hinges for a night, join the rest of the battalion tomorrow afternoon.' He turns to Halsall and Henderson. 'Have your units packed and ready to march in one hour.' He turns back to Alex. 'Not you, Ryan. I've asked Francourt to prepare your men.' The wind gusts. He staggers backwards, fighting the umbrella. Alex steps forward to help but Woodstone pushes him away. 'I can manage!' he says, angrily. 'The documents are in... Your chap from the court martial.'

Alex's heart thumps. 'Private Elphick, Sir?'

'Is that his name? Why am I thinking it begins with a P?'

'His name is Percy Elphick.'

'Yes, Elphick, that's it. Well, I've received the order. Haig has confirmed, to execute, I'm afraid. They've asked that we get everything out of the way as soon as possible, before we go into the line. That means tomorrow. D Company will be detoured to Hinges for the execution, then on to Richebourg in the afternoon.'

The rain seems to grow thicker, coagulating into a wall of sound, hissing through Alex's head. 'What can we do?'

'We need to organise the guard, and the firing party. We can use the same chaplain who's there now. He'll know what to do with the religious bit. The burial is ridiculously complicated, there's regulations—'

'No, I mean, what can we do to stop this?'

Woodstone looks confused. 'No, Ryan, there's nothing anyone can do.'

'But isn't there a procedure... for an appeal? I thought the court recommended mercy.'

'They did, but...' Woodstone frowns. 'Concerns have been raised about this company. Things were bad enough before, but now...' He glares. 'I have been humiliated, Ryan. *You* have humiliated me! I asked for your help with the court martial, and then you behaved like a schoolboy. In front of the Major... I was ashamed!' He steps closer. 'Then I heard from Captain Eden about your men saluting the prisoner. He said you failed to control them. Damned near caused a mutiny.'

'That's a lie!' says Alex.

'Ryan, enough! This is exactly what I mean and I won't have it! You have damned near cost me a crack at something at HQ and I will not have it! Do you hear? With this show coming up, the discipline has to be *total*. If there is even the slightest suggestion that any of your men will fail to obey an order, then the entire raid might be at stake. The easiest thing for me to do would be to pack you off to some mapping office and be done with you, but I can't afford to lose any more officers, so we need you and your men to get back in line. They need to be punished. They need to be shown... *You* must show that you have the ability to command them...' The wind tugs at the umbrella again, threatening to turn it inside out. Woodstone gives up and closes it. 'There was a dinner last night at HQ. Eden was there... He suggested...' He clears his throat. 'It has been decided that you will command the firing party.'

It takes a moment for the words to assemble into any kind of meaning. Alex stares, blinking into the rain. Then as he realises what Woodstone has just said, an aching, icy rage floods through him, as if an axe has been driven into his spine. 'No. No. No.'

Woodstone looks as if he knows he's done something terrible and is morbidly fascinated by the result. 'You *will* be leading the firing party, Ryan.' He blinks as if he's expecting to be hit.

And for an instant, Alex thinks he might do it. 'I refuse. The men will refuse or they will deliberately miss.'

'Then your men will be disobeying an order and they will also be shot.' Woodstone has rehearsed this. Eden has probably told him what to say.

'I will resign.'

'I will happily accept your resignation, but not until *after* the execution. And not until after *The Raid*. I don't have the men! And until then, you are under my command and this is an order and if you don't obey it, you will be put into prison and someone else will shoot him, and then you will be court-martialled!'

'Then you should arrest me now.' Alex wipes the rain off his face with his sleeve, stares intently at Woodstone, swallows. 'I killed Kingsman. On my very first night, I killed all of them. I threw the grenade. You should arrest me for that and get someone else to carry out your execution.'

Woodstone lets out a little, nervous laugh. 'I know about Kingsman. Eden told me months ago. Everyone knows.' He shakes his head. 'No one cares, Ryan. No one cares what anyone does out there, in the dark. You should know that by now!' He sniffs loudly, triumphantly. 'So you *will* command the firing party, of which there will be ten men taken from your unit. I've drawn up the list.' He hands Alex a sheet of paper:

CO - Lt. Ryan.
Guard unit Sergeant - Kemmell.
Guard unit - Chandler, Sharp, Bridger, Head, Stubbs, Rowlands, Davis, Eggleton, Wislawa, Lancet.

Alex feels the blood rushing out of his head. He's either going to throw up or pass out.

'A lorry has just collected these men,' says Woodstone, taking back the paper. 'It's going to Hinges, where they will be instructed by the provost martial. You will go separately, receive your own instructions. You will need to interview the prisoner and make sure he has... well, everything he needs. D Company will march to Hinges tonight where there will be a special parade. I will read out the charges. I will do a speech about discipline and you will stand next to me. Then tomorrow at dawn, the prisoner will be taken across the road from the police station and, and executed.'

Again, Alex feels as if he is falling away. Spiralling far back inside himself. He hears his own voice, distant, disconnected. 'I can't make them do this, Sir. I can't.'

'Yes, Ryan. You will. You have to.' Woodstone suddenly looks desperately sad. He speaks softly now. 'We all have to do what we are told. We are all being watched. And, as I've said, if you don't do it, someone else will. Eden will do it, and things will be a lot harder for everyone if he does and...' He pauses and looks up into the clouds. 'Do you hear that?'

Behind the rain is a darker sound, like nothing Alex has ever heard before; continuous, thunderous, like an endless wave crashing on a distant beach.

'You hear that, Ryan?' There is a glinting mixture of wonder and terror in Woodstone's eyes. 'That is the beginning of the bombardment in the Somme! That's fifty miles away! You understand how big this all is? We can't stop this. No one can!'

56

THE POLICE STATION

Percy is standing on tiptoe, looking out of a little barred window that opens onto a yard. Trees dance wildly in the blackness. 'What time is it?' he says, resting his chin on the sill.

'It's nearly eleven o'clock.'

'What time will the sun come up?'

'Four o'clock.'

'That means I get to be five hours older.'

'Older than what?'

'Than now, when I die.'

'When you die,' says Alex to himself. The words feel like blood in his throat. He swallows as quietly as he can. 'How old are you now, Percy? You never did tell me the truth.'

Percy turns around, staggering a little; he's been drinking rum for an hour. 'I promised my brother I would never tell. We never told anyone our secrets.'

'You sound like you were really good brothers.'

'Yes, Sir.' A candle, placed on a chair in the middle of the room, wavers and crackles. 'We were the best brothers.'

They sit quietly for a while, both staring at the candle. A black wisp of smoke twists above the flame.

'Do you want anything?' says Alex. 'They said you can have *anything*.'

'More rum please, Sir.'

Alex pours from a big stone jar and holds it on his lap.

'You not drinking, Sir?'

The provost martial said Alex could, in fact, recommended it, but he doesn't want to. He wants to be fully here, to remember everything.

Percy drinks his rum in one go and wipes his mouth with his shirt sleeve. 'I want to see Stubbs. I want to say goodbye to him.'

'I asked them,' says Alex. 'They said no.'

'Why?'

'I don't know. I think they're worried he might get too upset. I'll tell him you said goodbye. Would you like me to tell him anything else?'

'I can't think of anything. What did he say when they said I was going to be shot?'

'He doesn't know yet. He's being told soon. They all are.'

Percy sits heavily on the bed. 'I didn't mean to do anything wrong! You should tell him that!'

'He knows that. Everyone knows you did *nothing* wrong.'

'I wish he was here,' says Percy, quietly.

'He'll be here in the morning. You just won't be able to see him.'

'He'll be here?'

'Yes, all of us, all your friends.'

'Can I say goodbye to him then?'

'I don't think so. No one is allowed to talk. We have to be silent. So we can't talk to you, but we will all be here.'

'You'll be here when they do it?'

'Yes.'

'Will you do it? The shooting. Will you shoot me?'

Alex exhales, a little gasp. 'No... I have to give the order. I'll tell them when to shoot. Then they, your friends, will do it.'

'Good. I want Stubbs to do it. He's a good shot. I don't want Eden or Woodstone to do it.'

'No, they won't do it. It will just be your friends.'

'What's the order? What do you say?'

'I don't say anything,' says Alex, raising his hand. 'I'll go like this, and when I drop my hand, they fire.' His hand is shaking. He wants to lower it, but the movement feels dangerous, violent. He runs his fingers through his hair and down his neck to disguise the movement.

'Will it hurt?'

'No. It won't hurt at all.'

'But sometimes they yell out. When Arthur got shot by that sniper, he yelled for ages.'

'That was different. That wasn't a clean shot. This is more controlled. They pin a badge on your tunic and everyone aims at that. This will be so quick.' Alex knows this isn't always true. He's heard stories of men, after the shooting, still trying to untie themselves from the post.

Earlier, across the road from the police station, in the garden of an abandoned mill, the provost martial told them that it's unusual for something like that to happen, and if it does, then there are protocols in place that ensure an efficient resolution to such an unfortunate occurrence. He had trained Alex on how to conduct the *coup de grâce:* After the shots, the doctor will check to see if Percy is dead. If he isn't, Alex is supposed to take out his own revolver and shoot him through the heart. He has been given a sheet with printed instructions.

Kemmell, who will be in charge of the firing party until the moment that Alex takes over, asked many questions. When the training was finished, he had quietly walked to the corner of the garden and vomited behind a pile of packing crates.

'Can I have more rum, Sir?'

'Yes, of course.' Alex pours more rum. 'But don't drink so much that you're sick. You don't want...' He can't swallow, he thinks he might cry. He looks away, pretending to struggle with the cork in the jar.

A door opens somewhere in the police station and voices echo along a corridor.

'That's the chaplain,' says Percy. 'He comes every day and brings me a whole cake.'

'A whole cake, every day?'

'Not every day, sometimes… but nice cake, like my mum sent once, but with cocoa and nuts in it. He helped me write to her.'

A motor engine chugs outside. Voices in the yard, shouting, Kemmell shouting orders.

The men have arrived from the camp. Percy's friends will be led away and told that they will have to kill him. They will be locked in the garden, away from the others and trained until dawn by the provost sergeant.

'Is Stubbs here?' says Percy, tiptoeing again to look out of the window.

'Yes, he'll be with them. All of your friends are here.'

'I wish I could see them.'

'I know.'

Woodstone's voice, yelling outside. 'Lieutenant Ryan?'

Alex stands. 'Percy, I have to go.' He grabs Percy's hand. It feels so hot, so alive. He grips it tightly with both hands. 'I want to tell you that I am so very, very sorry. You did *nothing* wrong. I think you have always been very brave. You are *being* so brave! I am so proud to have you in my platoon. All the men are so very proud.'

Percy stands awkwardly. His arm goes limp, as if he's trying not to pull his hand away.

'Percy, I have to go. Try to sleep if you can…' Alex winces, enraged at his own stupidity. 'Of course, do whatever you like. I'll leave the jug for you and the chaplain. He's coming in now, I think.'

'Ryan!' Woodstone again, his voice louder, inside the police station.

'Percy, I have to go.'

'I might have some more rum with the chaplain,' says Percy, his eyes shining as if he's telling a great secret. 'He had some with me earlier!'

'Did he?' smiles Alex. 'Good night, Percy.'

'Good night, Sir.'

57

STUBBS

The night rages. It's midnight. D Company is standing to attention in the garden of the abandoned mill. Overgrown rose bushes lash and scrape against the walls. The execution post has been driven into the ground in front of them. Its shadow bows and flexes as if it's trying to break free.

Sykes holds a lamp with both hands while Woodstone, buffeted by the wind, announces the sentence to the men. His speech about discipline is lost in the rain.

As the men are marched out, Alex pulls Stubbs to one side. 'Will you do it?'

'I'm on the list aren't I?' says Stubbs, taking a cigarette from his pocket.

'I mean, will you shoot?'

'Why are you asking me?'

'Because I want to be sure. I need your help.'

Stubbs sucks hard on the cigarette, struggling to light it, arching his body over the flame. 'Why should I help you?' His eyes glare in the glow.

'You're the best shot. You're the only one I can really trust.'

'I won't do it. I'll miss.'

'I think all the others might try to do that.'

'Rowlands won't have to try. He couldn't hit a fucking horse he was sitting on.'

'I know. Some of them might mess it up. Some of them will *try* to mess it up.'

Stubbs spits tobacco off his lip. 'What would you expect? They're all good men.'

'I know they are. But it could be truly awful if they all miss his heart and all they do is injure him. So I need to rely on you.'

'To kill him?'

'Yes, to kill him.'

'I thought, if he's still alive, then you, as the *commanding officer*, are supposed to make the final shot.'

'I am, but it could all take a horrible amount of time.'

'Is that why you want me to do it, Sir? So you don't have that on your conscience?'

Alex laughs, or sobs, he doesn't know. 'Do you think this won't be on my conscience? Even if I'm not pulling the trigger?'

'What if we all just refuse, Sir, every one of us?'

'Then Eden will do it.'

'But we would have said *no*. That must be the right thing. Isn't it?'

'I don't know,' says Alex. 'It won't make any difference to Percy. He'll still be dead. So I think all we can do is be there with him when it happens. And the closest we can get is if we are the ones who do it. And Percy asked me if you would be there. He wants you to be there. I think this is the only way.'

'He said that? He asked if I would be there? How is he? Is he all right?'

'I think he's all right. He's got a whole jar of rum.'

Stubbs stares at the ground for a long time, playing with the cigarette in his fingers. 'I thought I was brave once. I have no idea if I'm being a coward now or if this is the bravest thing I've ever done.'

'So does that mean you'll help?'

A tin can, dragged across the garden by the wind, clatters loudly, turning and bouncing through the puddles.

Stubbs stamps the cigarette into the gravel and blows out a long puff of smoke that catches in the wind. 'All right.'

58

THE MILL HOUSE GARDEN

'There will be a white cloth where the heart is. If the medical officer tells you that life is not extinct, you are to walk up to the prisoner, place the muzzle of the revolver to his heart and press the trigger. Do you understand?' Sergeant York, the provost martial, is an expert. He's done this before, in Africa and here in France. He shows no emotions, but he is courteous and gentle.

'I understand,' says Alex.

'As soon as I give you command, you are to have your revolver ready, loaded and cocked. Do you understand?'

'I do.'

They are in the middle of the mill house garden. It is still dark. York is standing to attention. He is holding a paraffin lamp, chest height, between himself and Alex. Beyond the reach of the lamplight, the garden, with its rose bushes and stone walls, is black and brooding and sad.

'Are you ready?'

'I am.'

Kemmell leads the men in.

Rowlands walks as if he's falling slowly down a hill. Wislawa looks like he's been slapped awake. Eggleton, seeing the post, the leather straps and rope laid out behind it, grits his teeth and whispers a string of profanities. Stubbs, sharp and calm, looks at Alex and keeps looking as the men are turned about. Kemmell orders them to ground arms. They place the rifles on the gravel and march out.

York holds a box of ammunition as Alex loads each rifle and places it in a different order on the ground. One cartridge has the bullet removed. Alex loads it carefully into the last rifle and places it at the end of the row.

He follows York into the street where D Company is in formation. Woodstone is on his horse behind them. They will not be coming into the garden. They will not see the execution. They will hear it. That will be enough. There's no sign of Eden.

Beyond the soldiers, the grey street is deserted. Puddles and closed windows reflect a hint of dawn.

Noel, the doctor, arrives. He makes no eye contact. He looks as if he's had no sleep. He follows York and Alex into the police station. The door to Percy's cell is open. They all go inside.

The chaplain is standing in the middle of the room. He also looks exhausted.

Percy is sitting on the bed. He stands. He looks so young, so healthy. His eyes are bright, alive and wild.

When the barn was burning, when his mother died in the fire, Alex had tried to open the doors, but he was too small and they caught on the cobbles and they wouldn't open. A huge black horse scraped at the gap between the doors with its hooves. Terrified and angry, its eyes were bright, alive and wild.

'Lieutenant Ryan,' says York, formally. 'Is this soldier Private Percy Elphick?'

Percy looks at York and back at Alex as if there is hope in the question.

'Yes, Sir,' says Alex.

'Pinion his arms please,' says York.

Two soldiers step forward and tie Percy's arms behind his back. Percy says nothing but now he looks afraid.

Alex takes a step forward to touch Percy's arm. York stops him with a hand signal and a shake of his head. Then he steps into the corridor and speaks to the soldier by the door. 'Ask the sergeant to have the men return and take up arms please, Corporal.' He comes back into the room. 'Would you like a blindfold, Private Elphick?'

Percy looks at Alex and says something that's too quiet to hear.

'What was that?' says York.

'He said he would like a blindfold,' says Alex.

York takes out a dark hood from his tunic pocket, unfolds it and hands it to Noel.

Noel looks confused. 'He's to wear this now or when we… when we are at the post?'

York nods calmly. 'No need for all of us to see the post, or the yard. If we can place the blindfold now, this will be best.'

Alex smiles at Percy. He wants him to see a smile; the last thing he will ever see.

Noel, hands shaking, places the hood over Percy's head.

Percy gasps and his knees fold under him. The soldiers lift him up.

'It's all right,' says Alex.

'It's too dark,' says Percy, muffled in the hood.

'Does he have to wear it, Mr York?' says Noel.

'He said he wanted one,' says York. 'It would be best if he did.'

'It's too dark,' says Percy again.

Noel removes the hood. 'Could we use this?' He takes a bandage from his pocket.

York shrugs.

Noel winds the bandage around Percy's head, covering his eyes.

'Is that better?' says Alex.

'Yes,' says Percy. 'Don't go.'

'I'm here. I'll be here all the time,' says Alex.

'We are all here,' says the chaplain.

York hands Noel a small square of white cloth. Noel tries to pin it onto Percy's tunic, over his heart. He's shaking so much, he fumbles and drops the pin. 'Sorry. Do you have another?'

'I'm afraid I don't,' says York. 'That was the only one.'

Everyone looks for the pin. Alex finds it and hands it to York. York pins the cloth onto Percy's tunic.

Alex imagines the nine bullets ripping through the cloth. He wants to pull it away, as if it is the cloth that's dangerous, as if the cloth is the window through which the bullets will break Percy's heart.

York nods. They are ready.

'Do you say anything?' whispers Alex to the chaplain.

'It's all been said.'

The soldiers, with York ahead, lead Percy along the corridor and out into the street, past the platoon, standing in the twilight as still and silent as old trees.

The group walks very fast into the garden. Percy is led to the post and the soldiers pass a rope around his chest and tie him. They tie his ankles with the leather straps. York tests the bindings.

Sunlight hits the edge of a cloud above the garden. 'Stubbs?' says Percy, lifting his head towards the changing light.

The firing squad have their backs to the post. Stubbs turns around. 'Yes! It's me, my lad. I'm here!'

'Silence!' hisses York.

'Imaginary string!' yells Percy.

'That's right, Percy, imaginary string!' says Stubbs.

'Silence!' yells York, glaring. 'Turn your back!'

A wood pigeon swoops up over the wall and drifts down over the firing squad.

York signals to Alex.

Alex is now in command.

He signals for the men to turn and face Percy. Take aim.

The men lift their rifles. Someone is shaking. A gun rattles.

Alex raises his hand and holds his breath to fight the urge to scream. This is the edge of life and the death of so many things. He should walk away, but he can't stop this; it has already begun and it is already ended. He must fall asleep inside himself. He must turn to the boy and not look away.

Percy is breathing life into his body. Breathing. *Breathing.*

Alex lowers his hand.

Shots rip across the garden, chaotic, floundering, reverberating off the walls, fading into the beat of the pigeon's wings.

Percy screws up his face like he's bitten into a sour apple. His knees bend softly and he falls forward, resting across the rope around his chest. The cloth is gone. There is a jagged hole in the tunic pocket where the cloth had been.

Blood comes now, from the chest, the stomach and on both of Percy's arms.

York steps forward. 'Medical officer!'

Noel runs over, pushes his fingers onto Percy's neck. He lifts the bandage and opens an eye with his thumb.

Alex knows. He has seen enough dead men to know.

Noel nods to York.

York orders the firing squad to turn and march out.

The company is marched away.

The two soldiers untie the straps and lower Percy onto a stretcher.

Alex kneels down and touches Percy's lips with the back of his fingers.

The soldiers cover the body with a blanket, throw the ropes on top and carry it out to an ambulance that's waiting in the street.

Everyone has gone and Alex is alone in the garden. There is blood on the ground. The post is splintered on one side. There are four roses on the bush behind the post; three in full bloom, one a little older, softer than the others, darker at the edge of each petal.

59

FERME DU BERGER

The berry pops in his fingers. Juice-wet seeds drip like blood on his bare feet and run down into the cool dust between his toes.

He's walking, as gently as he can, through dusty lanes and sunlit meadows. He places each foot carefully, slowly, watching the grass change colour as he presses through it. The stems turn from green to yellow as they bend. With each step, a silver wave of little crickets flows ahead of him.

After the execution, instead of following the company to the billets, he walked in the opposite direction. He walked to the edge of the village, saw the corn shimmering in the morning sunlight, and kept walking.

Now he's walking to Odette's farm. He'll find what he can amongst the rubble. If her father's clothes are still in the cowshed, he'll dress in those. He'll burn his uniform. He'll rest there; he's so tired. Then he'll go south and west, heading for the forests, avoiding the roads, and walk in the dark through the fields. He'll sleep in barns and take apples from abandoned gardens, steal milk from cows and eat raw eggs. When he was a child, he used to crawl into the safe darkness of the chicken coop and crack warm eggs directly into his mouth.

He'll walk and hide and keep going until he's in Spain or find a boat or just keep walking until all of this is over, one way or another.

He thinks of his hand reaching up to take an apple, thinks of his raised hand this morning; the signal that *he* made. *His* order. The rifles coughing the bullets out, pushing the cloth into Percy's heart.

He clenches the hand into a fist, wishing he could crush it, snap the bones, break the fingers. He yells out; a guttural cry. A bird shrieks, flies up out of the hedgerow, wings battering into the trees.

He walks on. Through a field that he knows is close to the farm. He comes to a wall. He knows it. He lay here once with her. He wants to lie down in the shape of where they had been, but he climbs over. It's difficult. He's slow. His limbs are as heavy as the stones in the wall. He expected this; coming close again to the farm. Images of her, the sound of her voice. He has to push through it. Push the thoughts away.

He crosses the field where he sketched her. A nettle stings his ankle. He doesn't mind. It feels bright and fresh, buzzing on his skin.

He walks around the side of the house and into the courtyard. He tries not to look at the ruins; he wants to remember how it was, before.

The doves are on the roof of the cowshed. They stare at him but don't fly away as he climbs over the rubble into the coolness of the barn. Someone has piled up the milking things into a corner; villagers probably. Everything will be gone soon.

He thinks of her again, crouching on the milking stool, milk squirting into the bucket, the soft little mounds at the back of her neck as she bends.

Her father's clothes are still hanging on the wall. He takes off his tunic, throws it on the floor and lifts one of the jackets from the hook. It's damp and heavy.

'Alex?' Her voice.

He stops all movement, all thought.

'Alex.'

Blood hisses in his head.

'Alex, why won't you look at me?'

Again, he has the urge to close up and fall asleep inside himself, but he turns around. He sees her and blinks. A cold tear quivering on his eyelashes.

She's wearing black. A black headscarf. She looks pale but not like a ghost. She's gripping a burned stick in both hands. 'I heard something. I thought it was soldiers. They've taken most of the things.'

He tries to say her name. He can't. He blinks again. 'I've lost my boots.'

She looks angry. 'I came back to see if I could save some of my things. My uncle is coming with a cart...' She's trying not to cry. 'I still have the cows. My uncle has them... and a few chickens. I came back here to see if there was anything...' Now she cries.

He wants to go to her, to touch her, but he can't move. He stands there, watching her crying.

'Why didn't you come to me?' she looks up; the grey eyes, sparkling and alive, beautiful. 'I waited!'

'Come where?' he says, struggling to push the words out.

'To the hospital. I waited.'

'What hospital?'

'In Merville.'

'I don't understand!' He reaches behind for something to support himself. He won't take his eyes off her in case she disappears.

'Then after the hospital,' she says. 'My uncle brought me to his farm. I thought you would at least have the courtesy to come... to say goodbye if you didn't want—'

He shakes his head. 'I thought you were dead.'

'No, no, not me, my mother.' Her wet eyes, burning. 'She's dead.'

'I know, I'm so very sorry.' He tries to say more but he still doesn't understand. 'We looked for you! Men were here looking for you. I sent people out into the village to ask in case anyone had seen you. We looked in the fields. I called out your name in the streets! I thought you were dead.'

She touches the scarf. 'No! I hurt my head. Captain Eden must have told you! I was in the hospital for three days. He found me and pulled me out.' She glares. 'You know this! It was in the letter! He took me on his horse to the hospital.'

'I didn't see a letter.'

'But I gave the letter to Captain Eden. He said he gave it to you.'

'I wasn't given any letter, I swear!' He sees she has a cut next to her ear and moves to touch it but then stops. 'What do you mean, Eden found you? I don't understand!'

'When the house was hit. He was here. He helped me. He must have told you!' She drops the stick and takes a step closer. 'He came to visit me. Then, when you didn't come, I thought something had happened, but he said you had all moved away for training and perhaps you did not have time to write.'

'He didn't tell me anything.'

'There must be a mistake,' she says. 'He was kind to me. He took me to the hospital and made sure I was all right. He must have thought you knew, that someone else had told you.'

'No, I've seen him. He was with me at the billets. He let me think you were dead. I'll kill him. I'll go back right this minute and kill him. He made me kill Percy and he let me think I'd lost you. I'll kill him for it!'

'What do you mean, you killed Percy?'

'There was a trial. They said he was guilty and he should be shot. They...' He grits his teeth. 'Woodstone, Eden.' He leans against the wall. He's crying now. 'I did what they ordered me to do. That's who I am, when someone asks me to kill someone, I just do it. I killed Percy!'

She covers her mouth with both hands. 'Oh Alex!'

Suddenly he knows he has to tell her everything. He sits on the floor in the corner of the cowshed and tells her about the night he killed Kingsman. He tells her about the court martial, how he was too afraid that Eden would say something to the court and what would happen if they knew.

She sits with him, takes hold of his hands and listens.

He tells her about Charlie, how they'd watched the moon and how he'd carried the body through the corn. And about the execution; Percy calling out to Stubbs, and how brave all of the men had been.

She doesn't speak, she keeps hold of his hands. She doesn't let go.

'You see?' he says. 'You see how I'm no different from them?'

'But they made you do it. You had no choice.'

'I could have said no. I'm part of the worst of all of this!'

'The way you have explained it to me, there was nothing better that you could do. It was the right thing to do when everything else about this was wrong. But now, with Eden, you *do* have a choice. If you go back and hurt him, then you *will* be the same as him.'

He thinks for a moment. 'I don't have to go back. We could both run away, like you wanted us to. We could find a boat to take us to England.'

She reaches up and holds his face in her hands. 'But if you run away, who will look after your men? Surely it has to be you? Surely, the right thing for you to do is to *go back* and *lead* your men, and the right thing for me to do is to let you go.'

They stare at each other without speaking for a long time.

He breathes in the deliciously familiar scent of her hands. 'But how can I go back now, after this? How can I leave you again?'

'I know. I don't want you to go back,' she says. 'My God, I want so much for you *not* to go back, but...'

'All right,' he says. 'I'll go back. But after this, I want you to come with me to England. It's dangerous here now. I can get some leave. I can take you back to my father's—'

'I can't go to England,' she says.

'Why not?'

'I have to stay here now.'

'Why? It's dangerous here.'

'When I was at the hospital, I met an officer who is setting up a...' She pauses, making sure she pronounces it correctly. 'A *telephone operations unit*. He has a team of operators translating telephone calls between the French and the British. He asked me to work for them. I said I would. I will be translating, on the telephones!'

'Where, behind the lines?'

'Yes, of course. I don't know where exactly, they wouldn't say. But I have to go for training at Hazebrouk. I will stay on my uncle's farm in Oblinghem. I think it's safe there.'

'All right,' he says. 'That's good.' A tiny feather curls down from the rafters and lands on her shoulder. He picks it off and lets it spin away to the floor. 'I thought you were gone.'

She slides her arms around him. 'No. No, Alex. I'm here.'

He grabs her waist and holds her so hard that she has to push him away.

He touches her scarf. 'Does it hurt?'

'It's all right.' She unties the scarf and shows him a bandage. 'Some cuts and a cracked bone, here. But it's nothing.'

He pulls her to him and kisses her gently. This time she doesn't push him away. She kisses him. He turns her, so her back is against the floor. Holding her head in his hands, he lifts her skirt, pushes her against the floor with his body as he fumbles with his clothes. She wraps her legs around him and guides him as he pushes into her. She smells of plaster-dust and hospitals.

Later, he walks with her back to the village and they say goodbye, without much fuss, agreeing that he will come to her in Oblighem in the next few days. Then he walks back through the fields. He finds his boots on the banks of a dyke that he doesn't remember crossing.

He reaches the place where the regiment has made a temporary camp. He climbs through a hedge into the field and lies down in the sun-warmed grass next to his sleeping men. The rumble of the heavy guns sounds like storm waves breaking on a pebble beach. There is an oak tree. The leaves glisten green and silver in the sunlight. His body fills with an exhausted, nauseating joy, and he sleeps.

60

RICHEBOURG

'Good morning, Sir,' says Fenton, gently shaking Alex awake. 'They've set up a tent for the officers. I've put your valise inside.' He points to a white bell tent in the corner of the field. Halsall is outside, sleeves rolled up, shaving in the dappled sunlight. Henderson is there too. He sees Alex and waves.

'Should I tell the officers you'll be joining them for breakfast, Sir?' says Fenton. 'It's actually lunchtime, but we're serving breakfast.'

'No. Thank you. I'll be eating with the men from now on.'

Fenton nods approvingly. 'They'll be glad of your company, Sir. I'll get that sorted.' He turns to leave then stops. 'Captain Eden was asking after you. I wasn't sure what to tell him. I noticed you hadn't come back with the others.'

'Where is he?'

'He's gone ahead to Richebourg with Captain Woodstone. The company will follow this afternoon.'

'It's all right.' Kemmell comes over with a bucket of water, places it on the ground and wipes his wet hands on his shirt. When Fenton has gone, he says, 'I made something up, Sir. I hope you don't mind. I told the captain that the adjutant had sent you to fetch a box of gas hoods. I didn't know when you would be back.'

'I didn't know if I would be back at all,' says Alex, quietly. He gestures to a gap in the fence where he'd climbed into the field. 'I came through here this morning.'

'Yes, I saw. Thought it best to let you sleep.'

'Kemmell, she's alive,' says Alex, surprising himself.

'Who is, Sir?'

'Odette, from the farm. I've seen her. She's alive.'

Kemmell sighs. 'Thank God for that. Is she all right? Where did you find her?'

Alex explains everything. When he's finished, Kemmell stares into the bucket of water. Then he shakes his head and says, 'It's not my place to say what I'm thinking, and I need to get this to where it's supposed to be.' He picks up the bucket and walks away across the field without another word.

For the rest of the day, final preparations are made for the march to the front line. Kit is cleaned and inspected. Letters are delivered, read and written. Cakes and biscuits from home are shared. No one mentions the execution.

The men sing as they head out of the camp and join the throng of vehicles on the road to Richebourg. Ambulances rumble past. Smooth-faced nurses stare out. The men sing songs about nurses and everyone cheers. They march past a wood mill. Outside are piles of fresh coffins that still smell of forests. The singing falters. They have to climb around an upturned artillery wagon. Still harnessed to it are eight dead horses. The singing stops.

The road into the village looks like a frozen river; mud and brick rubble oozing between banks of destroyed buildings and dead trees. Alex has seen nothing like this before. Nothing quite so immaculately destroyed. Apart from a few walls and garden fences, the village has effectively been turned to rubble. There's still the front of a shop, ragged curtains flapping in the wind. A single telegraph pole; wires trailing forlornly behind it. A dismembered chimney stack leans inquisitively towards the soldiers as they pass.

It's growing dark as they turn off the road, down a cinder track that leads to the front line.

There's no sunset, just a languid fading of the day.

61

THE BOAR'S HEAD SALIENT

The four junior officers are lined up on the breastwork fire-step, shoulder to shoulder, facing out towards No Man's Land.

Alex is scanning the German breastworks through the field-glasses. In front of it lie two hundred and fifty yards of dykes and shell hole puddles, shimmering in the moonlight.

'Why do they call it the Boar's Head Salient?' says Henderson. 'I couldn't see anything on the map that looks like a pig.'

'It probably looked like a boar's head two years ago,' says Halsall. 'But it must have changed after so many battles, and after the damage our artillery did to it this afternoon, I think it will be hard to recognise anything even from yesterday!'

There's no sign of anyone attempting to make repairs. No lights, no movement. 'It's so quiet,' says Alex, handing the field-glasses to Henderson.

'Perhaps they're all dead and we'll have nothing to do,' says Halsall. 'Or they've all run away.'

'That would be a letdown, wouldn't it?' says Henderson. 'Such a waste of training.'

'All the bombardment did was send them deeper into their

bunkers,' says Francourt. 'They're hiding in supply trenches, behind the front line.'

'If their front line is empty, could we just walk in?' says Henderson.

'The bombardment was hours ago and we don't go over for another two hours. That will give them plenty of time to regroup and bring up reinforcements,' says Alex. 'Their concrete machine gun towers look fairly intact to me. They could be still in them, waiting for us to walk across this field.'

'Then why did they start the bombardment so early?' says Henderson.

'Major Babcock's idea,' says Halsall. 'The Hun expected us to attack as soon as the bombardment ended. But we didn't. Now they won't know what to expect.'

'But isn't there going to be *another* bombardment just before we do go over?' says Henderson. 'Doesn't that somewhat defeat the objective?'

Francourt laughs. 'Welcome to the British Expeditionary Force!'

'The distance we're going to have to run to reach the dyke felt shorter than this on the training ground,' says Halsall.

'It was,' says Francourt. 'The farmer complained that our training area was ruining his crops. So the engineers chopped a hundred yards off the model of No Man's Land. No one told us. So instead of taking two minutes, it's going to be more like five.'

'Does it matter how long it takes?' says Halsall. 'Artillery will be laying down a smokescreen. The Hun won't be able to see us until we're under their noses.'

'The efficacy of the smokescreen is entirely dependent on the direction of the wind,' says Francourt, with a hint of irritation.

'Well, despite all that, I'm still rather looking forward to it,' says Henderson. 'Charging gallantly towards the fiendish foe, swords glinting in the moonlight!'

'They have excellent snipers,' says Francourt. 'The last thing you want is for anything to be glinting.'

Halsall puts his hand on Henderson's shoulder. 'Ignore Francourt. He's just trying to scare you.'

'I *am* trying to scare him.' He turns to Henderson. 'I want you to be afraid. You seem to think that this is going to be some jolly, *Boy's Own* caper. We're not leading a troop of schoolboys to attack a cardboard pirate ship. We're about to lead our men into mortal danger.'

'Francourt, stop it,' says Alex. 'I'm sure Henderson is as afraid as all of us. We all know what we are about to do. We just express it in different ways.'

'Didn't you feel excited the first time you went over the bags?' says Halsall. 'I know I did. But I was afraid too.'

'You need both,' says Alex. 'Excitement to get you up the ladder, fear to keep your head down.'

'Of course I'm scared,' says Henderson, staring at Francourt. 'Not just of what might happen to me, but I think I'm more afraid of letting the men down. I didn't sleep a wink this morning, thinking about it.'

'Captain Kingsman,' says Alex, taking a deep, slow breath. 'He told me that you should care for each man as if they were your brother. I think you can't go far wrong with that.'

Francourt huffs. 'Would you lead your brother across this field?'

'I'm about to lead my platoon across it,' says Alex. 'I can't imagine caring for a brother any more than I care for those men.'

They stare out across the field. Everything looks still and peaceful. The night seems to be holding its breath.

'Well, gentlemen,' says Halsall, looking at his watch. 'I believe it's time.'

They shake hands and wish each other luck.

'See you all in Berlin!' says Henderson.

'Bravo to that,' says Francourt, gently, smiling as he shakes Henderson's hand.

62

RUM

'Put that out, you idiot!' yells Kemmell.

A bright light streaks across the sandbags. Someone is working their way through the rows of soldiers with an electric torch. A hundred faces drift in and out of the darkness as he passes.

'It's your commanding officer,' says Woodstone. 'Let me through.'

Alex thinks he sees some of the men turning their backs as Woodstone approaches, but it's crowded in the frontline. Perhaps they're just moving out of his way.

When he arrives, Woodstone shines the torch in Alex's face. 'There you are. Thought I'd come over and check that you're ready and all that.'

'We're just waiting for the rum, Sir,' says Alex, shielding his eyes.

Woodstone lowers the torch. 'Right. Good. Oh, I have an order from the adjutant. Change of plan. Only eighteen pigeons for each platoon now. And each message must be duplicated. So only use the pigeons if the telephones are down.'

'Kemmell, will you make a note of that?' says Alex.

Kemmell raises an eyebrow. 'I will, Sir. Eighteen pigeons. Got it. As soon as the men get their rum, I'll be sure to write that down.'

'Another thing,' says Woodstone, leaving his eye suspiciously on

Kemmell. 'Artillery will drop smoke to the left now. Wind has changed.' His voice trembles. He might just be cold. 'Keep your men behind it, the smoke. Don't run. Should be a walk in the park… But not a *run*… in the park!' He laughs nervously then, seeing the men are staring, clears his throat. 'Each platoon at fifty-yard intervals. I'll be ahead of you with Captain Eden. When you get into the Boche line, clean up anyone who's managed to survive the bombardment. Shouldn't be many. Then on into their support lines.'

The men shuffle. They know all of this better than he does. They've been training for a week.

'Anyway, good luck, men!' he shouts. 'Do your best everyone!'

The men squint and look away. Someone further back mumbles something that Alex doesn't hear.

'I'm going out with Eden, at the front. The major's orders.' A bead of sweat quivers under Woodstone's chin, sparkling for a moment in the torchlight.

'Are you all right, Sir?' says Alex.

'Me? Of course. I'm just… Well, it's my first…' He sees that Kemmell and some of the men are listening. 'Eden and I will lead, then you and Francourt, then Halsall at the rear.'

'Where's Henderson? Is he not with Halsall?'

Woodstone leans in and whispers. 'Henderson's got the wind up. They might have to leave him behind. I knew this would happen. They've sent me men who've never been over the bags!'

'Should I go back, Sir? Perhaps I could talk to him?'

'No, no time now. Bombardment's about to start and… And our men haven't had their rum!' Woodstone waves the torch. 'They should get their rum!' The nervous laugh again. 'We should all have our rum!'

Alex has never seen Woodstone like this. He might even be drunk. 'Perhaps we should turn that torch off for a bit, Sir? Get the men used to the dark?'

'What? Oh yes, of course. Good!' Woodstone fumbles with the torch and gives up. 'I'll just keep it on until I find Eden.' He covers the lens with his fingers. 'Good. Right. Must get on. Good luck, Ryan.

Good luck Sergeant Kemmell.' He shuffles away, cocooned in a pool of torchlight.

'Christ help us,' says Kemmell, as the trench returns to darkness. 'He's never been over the bags has he?'

'No, I don't think he has.'

There's a pile of ammunition boxes at the end of the traverse. Alex sits and gestures for Kemmell to join him. 'I think this is going to be a difficult night, Sergeant. The distance to the dyke is longer than we thought, and the Boche have concrete towers that still seem to be intact. I don't think we can rely on Woodstone, so we're pretty much on our own.'

Kemmell sits awkwardly, apologetically; upright and with both hands on his knees. 'Woodstone will be with Eden, Sir. He'll know what to do.'

'He will, but I'm not sure that will help us much. We should be all right until we reach the dyke. It will probably get pretty hot after that. Keep the men tight and we can reassess as soon as everyone has crossed the bridges.'

'The lads trained well. I'm proud of them. I do think we *will* lose some tonight though, Sir.' Kemmell looks along the trench towards the men, all sitting quietly on the fire-step. 'It breaks my heart, seeing them beautiful, brave lads. It really does.' He pulls a cloth from his tunic pocket, carefully removes his glasses and begins to clean them. 'I've had them write special letters home. So they're ready in all the ways they can be.'

'Did you write one?' says Alex.

'I did, a long one.' Kemmell laughs. 'It's a lecture. How to live your life! My two boys will fall asleep reading it. I can hear them snoring already.'

Alex smiles. 'You should read it to them when you next go on leave. They'll enjoy that.'

Kemmell doesn't smile. 'I never really thought about death before the war. But here, we've been here, what, four months? I don't think there's been a minute in all that time that I haven't thought about death.' He holds his glasses up to the clouds.

The moon is a shimmering half-disk. Alex remembers Charlie in the cornfield and tries not to think about it.

Kemmell replaces his glasses, adjusting them carefully up and down his nose until they're just right. 'I'm not afraid of death, Sir. I just keep thinking about my boys, my sons. But tonight when you told us the plan, I looked out, saw the distance they're asking us to cross, further now, as you say. The dykes, the mud. I got a feeling like everything that's going to happen in my life has already happened. A strong feeling. Can't really explain it. I'm thinking, is this the feeling of knowing that you're about to die? Never had it before and don't know for sure, but I wonder if this is it? I wonder if *I know*.'

There's cheering and a scuffle along the line. Eggleton and Rowlands have come up with the rum.

'After my mother died,' says Alex. 'Whenever someone walked away from me, I thought I'd never see them again. But I always did. Then, last week, I felt that Charlie was about to die, and he *did* die. And Odette, I felt that she had died, but she hadn't.'

Kemmell is listening intently but looks confused.

Alex sighs. 'I think I'm saying that what you're feeling could mean anything or nothing.'

Kemmell laughs. 'You're right, Sir. All of it probably means nothing. I'm just being daft.'

'No, it means *something*. I just have no idea what.'

Kemmell stands and shakes Alex's hand. 'I know you did everything you could for the boy, Sir, for Percy. We're all very grateful to you for that.' He pulls Alex towards him and they hug. 'Good luck, Sir.'

'Good luck, Sergeant.'

Kemmell looks at his watch. 'Right then. We should get this rum down these lads before there's a riot.' He brushes his tunic awkwardly and walks back to the men.

Rowlands is grinning. 'Can I have a hug please, Sergeant?'

'Do I get a kiss, Sir?' says Eggleton.

'Get out of it!' says Kemmell, lugging a jar onto his shoulder and pushing them both away. 'Help me with this rum!'

63

THE BOMBARDMENT

He swallows. Rum still sharp at the back of his throat. He climbs the ladder halfway and stares out at each man below him. He smiles, so they can see him smiling.

They stare up; flowers afraid of the rain. Eyes glisten in the lamplight.

He looks to Kemmell at the back. 'Lights out please, Sergeant.'

Kemmell nods gently. He's ready. The men are ready. 'Lights out, Lads!'

The lamps go out one by one and faces fade like embers in a dying fire: Watts, Bishop, Rowlands, Saunders, Dorling, Goldsmith, Stubbs, Kelly, Parkhouse, Adams, Wislawa, Barton, Coates, Davis, Kemmell, Reed. The railwayman, the office clerk, the waiter, the stone-mason, the greengrocer, the painter, the gardener. Volunteers from the villages and farms of Sussex. Soldiers now. 4 Platoon. Alex's men.

A clamouring hush: bayonets, water bottles, rifles, bomb satchels, helmets clinking and scraping like scales of a great beast sleeping in the darkness. It breathes, deep and strong; a collective, communal, *platoonal* breathing.

Someone is praying.

Whispers.

The ticking of a watch; his watch.

His heart, pushing blood around his veins.

Silence between the beating and the ticks.

Silence.

Silence.

A tearing scream arcs across the darkness above them. Then two bright, thudding flashes.

More explosions, louder, faster, becoming one black roof of sound. A wailing wave, spreading out across the field. It builds, hanging over the parapet then falls, hot, pushing into his skin like burning sand. The sound is like a train. A dark, metallic, grinding, iron-fire above their heads. A ripping metal hate. The ground shudders. Soil loosens and crumbles from the walls.

The men are crouching against the breastworks, hands over their ears. One man is singing wildly into the sky, mouth open wide. Singing into the wall of sound. Some men are cheering, or is it screaming?

Alex closes his eyes. The sound moves over his body, so thick and powerful, so thunderous that he feels it's holding his body together. If the sound stopped, his body would liquefy and fall apart.

He grips the ladder. Vibrations crawl across his skin, churn his stomach, froth the air in his lungs. 'Good God! Let me be brave! *Let me be brave!*'

Behind him, a sound as if the sky itself is splitting. Then a flash of light above the trench where Halsall and Henderson's platoons are waiting. Sandbags, soil, wood and what looks like men! To his horror, Alex sees *men* fly up in one great writhing mass. 'Get everyone up the ladders!' he yells.

'We're supposed to wait, Sir.' yells Kemmell. 'To be fifty yards behind.'

'They're shelling the comms-trench!' yells Alex. 'We have to get them up so Halsall's men can move out. They'll be blown to pieces if they can't get out!'

Stubbs and Wislawa make footholds in the sandbags with their bayonets. The men clamber up the ladders and over the bags.

Halsall's men are already staggering out of the entrance to the comms trench and filling the front line; falling through thick white smoke that pulses with each explosion. 'Where is your CO?' yells Alex. 'Where is Lieutenant Halsall?'

A soldier, one arm ripped off his jacket, points to an officer lying face down on the duckboards. 'That's Halsall,' he says. 'Everybody's fucking dead.'

Alex turns Halsall over: wide eyes; terror. Slumped next to him is Henderson, shell splinters sticking from his neck and jaw bone. Both are dead.

Alex sits down next to Henderson and watches the boots of the leaderless men stumbling past across the rubble. Fear tightens in his throat like a clenched hand. The whole battalion is being shredded by shellfire. Are they supposed to keep going? Is he supposed to lead the men through *this*?

He runs back through the comms trench, into the severely damaged front line, gathering any uninjured men, ordering them to climb up the ladders into the field. He's behind them, half way up. There's a blinding flash and he's ripped from the ladder. He crashes into the men below him and lands on his back in the mud. Above him, white sparks light a cloud of smoke. Eden is standing on the parapet. He looks down, sees Alex, then turns and leaps away like a crow.

64

THE ATTACK

They're running.

At first, Alex's men move fast towards the wall of smoke. They're holding a line, leaping over puddles, striding across rough and grassy ground, but the wet earth is sticky and soon their boots are heavy with mud. He tries to rip the mud from his boots with his fingers but it's useless. His men are clambering through it, cursing. Shells explode around them. The field vomits phlegmy clods of mud the size of horses. The ground shakes. Smoke and fire lurch up and blossom like giant roses and drift across the field.

Eden and Francourt's men are a hundred yards ahead, silhouetted against the fire. They run into the smoke and disappear.

The rattle of a machine gun; the Hun are firing blindly through the smoke.

Two men next to Alex fall. Not from his platoon, from Halsall's. Nothing can be done; they have to keep moving forward.

The smoke thickens. Grey, gritty darkness.

Some of Eden's men appear, walking the wrong way. 'Where is your Captain?' yells Alex at the confused soldiers. 'Where is Captain Eden?' They don't know.

Explosions, very close. Shrapnel spins past. The sickening thud of metal against flesh. A soldier drops as if his bones have been removed.

Monstrous, elongated shadows of soldiers running in the smoke. Alex aims his revolver and fires, again and again. Men fall. The shadows loom, disconnect and disappear.

He's running into water. They must have reached the dyke. 'Find the bridges!' Bullets fly past his face as he runs along the bank. How can he not be hit? 'We have to find the bridges!'

Men are wading waist-deep in black water. More men arrive, crowding against the bank, pushing others in. A line of bullets slams into the water. Men panic but they can't get up the bank; it's too slippery.

'Get away from the water!' yells Kemmell.

Soldiers turn around but they're too slow. Bullets thud into their backs. Men twist and sink below the oily surface.

'We've been the whole length of the bank,' says Rowlands, carrying a duckboard bridge with Eggleton. 'This is the only one! There's supposed to be *ten*! What the fuck happened to all the bridges?'

Alex and Francourt wade in, pulling the bridge across and securing it to the far bank. The men run across in single file. The dyke seems to boil as bullets and the flailing of injured men churn the water.

Francourt stares at the last of the men filing across the bridge. 'This is all there is, ours and theirs together?' There can't be more than forty. The dead surround them, in the water, on the muddy banks and all across the field where they have come from.

The officers lead the few remaining men away from the dyke and towards the German line. From every direction, groups of German soldiers appear out of the smoke. They seem as lost and confused as the British. Wave after wave, running, falling, dying.

Alex climbs into a hole with Francourt and Kemmell, pulls a map from his pocket. 'There's just one machine gun in front of us now.' He's wet and shivering. They all are. 'There's a ridge about thirty yards ahead. We've some protection from that, but as it starts to get light, there'll be nothing between us and that gun.'

'Eden should be waiting at the ridge,' says Francourt, kneeling at the edge of the crater. 'We need to get to him. Find out what he wants us to do. We can't stay here!'

'I could go ahead and try to find him, Sir,' says Kemmell.

'All right,' says Francourt. 'Take three men with you.'

'I'll go with you,' says Alex, reloading his revolver.

Kemmell begins to crawl out but falls back into the hole as if he's been tied to a team of horses.

Alex rushes over. 'Francourt, help me!' He grabs Kemmell's hand and pulls it away from a hole the size of a fist in Kemmell's chest. 'Francourt, get me a field-dressing, now!'

Kemmell gasps and falls still. Alex waits for the in-breath but it doesn't come.

Francourt hasn't moved. There's a bullet hole under his right eye. He's dead.

Alex slides down into the protection of the shell hole. Feathers of grey smoke drift across the sky above him.

Kemmell's glasses are lying a few feet away. He picks them up. They're not broken. He wipes them with his fingers and places them into Kemmell's pocket. He thinks of Kemmell's wife reading the letter to their sons. He thinks of Odette; wonders if he will ever see her again. He remembers sitting in the dark in No Man's Land not long ago, aching for her. He knows he loves her. He *remembers* feeling it, but now all he feels is cold and tired. He wishes he could sleep. Is that all? Is that all he feels, sitting here with the corpses of his friends?

More machine gunfire. The smoke spirals as the bullets pass through it. Someone running; boots scrabbling on the loose earth. They're running directly towards him. He pulls out his revolver, crouches with his back against the wall of the hole and waits.

65

THE MACHINE GUN

Someone leaps, slides down the opposite side of the crater, lands against Francourt's body and clambers back up the rim. It's Eden.

The machine gun has stopped. At first it feels like silence, but the air is thick with a soft sound, like wolves howling in the distance. Injured men and soldiers stuck in the mud on the banks of the dyke are wailing, crying out for help, crying for their mothers.

Eden pulls out field-glasses and scans the German breastworks. He hasn't noticed Alex is behind him.

Alex lifts his revolver and aims at Eden's back. He glances around. The shell-hole is deep. It's dark and the smoke is still thick. No one can see them from the field above. He tightens his grip on the gun. The trigger creaks as it strains against the hammer. He breathes in, holds it.

'I see Francourt's dead,' says Eden, without turning around.

Alex doesn't move.

'Where's Halsall?' says Eden.

'Dead,' says Alex. He can hardly breathe, let alone speak.

'Where are his men?'

'Spread out in shell holes, with mine.'

'We can't go forward until we stop that MG. I think I can see a way.'

'Where's Woodstone?' says Alex.

'Panicked. Ran into a hail of bullets before I could stop him.'

'Is he dead?'

Eden laughs. 'Very! Are you going to lower that gun?'

Blood rushes into Alex's head so fast, he thinks he's going to throw up. He swallows. 'Why didn't you tell me she was alive?'

Eden lowers the field-glasses and turns around. He glances at the gun and rolls his eyes. Not a hint of fear.

'You lied to both of us,' says Alex. 'Why didn't you give me the letter?'

'Oh, I forgot about the letter,' says Eden, casually. 'I still have it. When we get back, I'll—'

'You let me believe that she was dead! Tell me why!'

Eden shrugs and smiles. 'I was trying to help you.'

'How?'

'She was distracting you.'

'What do you mean?'

'You lost focus. And, as I told you before, I don't think soldiers who have emotional attachments make good leaders. They stop taking risks.'

'That's not true,' says Alex. 'If anything she made me *more* focused, helped me realise what I was fighting for.'

'What? King, country and pretty farm girls? Or just the girls?' Eden shakes his head. 'You got soft. You lost discipline, lost control of your men. And once you moved into her bed, you never got any *sleep*, in or out of the trenches!' He laughs. 'I saw you struggling to stay awake at breakfast!'

'That was none of your business!'

'Actually, as your superior officer, it was. It was a shame, I had hopes for you. You were the first officer they sent us that wasn't a complete idiot. So when I heard that everyone thought she was dead, I thought I'd wait. I was going to tell you, but later, after this raid. I was helping you.'

'You weren't helping, you were controlling me!'

'I've *always* tried to help you, right from the beginning. After you killed Kingsman—'

'You lied to me about that too!' Alex grips the gun tighter. 'They would never have court-martialled me for that. It was an *accident!*' He feels the trigger; smooth and cold beneath his finger. 'It would be easy to *accidentally* shoot someone here, with all this confusion.'

Eden grins. 'Yes, it would! Now I think you're beginning to understand!'

Machine gun bullets stab into the side of the shell hole. Stones spin through the air around them.

Alex ducks, covering his face from the splinters.

'This is a war, Alex!' yells Eden. 'People expect us to kill in order to win it. Do you really think anyone cares *who* we're killing? As long as we get the right result, no one gives a damn!' He crawls to the rim of the shell hole. 'We have to stop that gun. We have to go now.'

'We'll be shot to pieces,' says Alex.

'The Hun can't see a thing. They're firing blind, firing towards the yelling. As long as those injured men keep it up, we can quietly get right up to that gun. Do you have any grenades?'

Alex glares at Eden, then replaces his gun in its holster. 'Sergeant Kemmell was carrying a satchel.'

'Give it to me.'

Alex gently lifts the satchel over Kemmell's shoulders and hands it to Eden.

Eden opens the bag. 'Three grenades. That should do.' He reaches down, grabs Alex's wrist and pulls him up into the field.

Instinctively, Alex tries to take cover but Eden doesn't let go. He pulls Alex so close that they could bite each other's lips. His voice is calm, but his eyes are burning in the half-light. 'I'm going to stop this machine gun, but I need your help to do it. So I'm going to make the charitable assumption that you were pointing your gun at the Germans. Do you understand?'

Before Alex has a chance to reply, Eden lets go and points. 'There's a ditch running from here to the wire. It's shallow but should give us enough cover to get under and through. From there, it's an exposed slope of about ten yards to the breastworks. Once we're under it, they'll only see us if they look directly down. We can shuffle along until we're under the gun. I'll throw the first grenade while you pull the pin and hand me the next. Five seconds for each, so pull the pin, wait three seconds and hand it to me. That way, no time for them to throw them back. Repeat with the third. Understand?'

'I think so.'

Eden stares.

'Yes,' says Alex. 'Yes, I understand.'

They drop down into the ditch and crawl on their elbows until they reach the wire. Eden turns on his back and slides under, pulling the wire over his head and across his body, holding it up for Alex until they're both through.

With smoke swirling at its base, the breastworks looks like an ancient castle, looming grey in the pale light above them.

No sign of any Hun.

Eden runs up the slope, throwing himself against the wall.

Alex follows, trying to run, but his legs are weak from the cold and the anger about what's just happened with Eden.

The ground is so churned up by shellfire that after a few strides he's clambering through loose soil and discarded food tins. His foot catches on something. It rolls down the bank, clattering. He freezes, holds his breath. Heart pounding.

Eden signals for Alex to wait. Then beckons.

Alex lunges, landing next to Eden against the wall.

They shuffle along until they are directly below the gun.

They hear German voices, the sound of metal hinges, and someone pouring water; the MG crew must be refilling the gun with coolant. There's a higher voice, younger than the others, and someone giving orders. Then footsteps receding.

Eden takes the grenades from the bag, handing two to Alex. Then, with his back against the wall, he pulls the pin, counts to three and throws the first grenade. It arcs up over his head, over the breastwork wall. Alex pulls the pin on the second grenade, counts to three and hands it to Eden. Eden throws, and again with the third.

For several heartbeats, it seems like nothing will happen.

A flash. A sound like mountains splitting. Stones. Soil. Grit. Darkness. A heart thumping. Eyes open. Clouds edged with dawn light.

Alex is on his back. He stays still, collecting the shape of his body in his mind. All of his limbs seem to be still attached.

'Lieutenant?' A stubby face peers down from the broken parapet. Smoke rising behind him. 'Lieutenant Ryan?' says Major Babcock. 'Is that you?'

66

CAPTAIN

'Did you do that?' says Babcock, standing over Alex with his hands on his hips. 'Are you injured?'

'I don't know.' Alex's head aches. 'Are *you* all right, Sir?'

'Well, the fighting was pretty much over by the time we came through, so nothing too dramatic. MacFarlane cut his thumb. Didn't you MacFarlane?'

A very young looking officer appears next to Babcock and shows Alex his thumb.

'We heard nothing from Woodstone. All the telephones are down,' continues Babcock, when it's clear that Alex has nothing to say about the thumb. 'So we had to come up ourselves, all the way from Vine Street trench. Took an age, had to climb over dead Boche all the way. They've abandoned this whole section. That is, all except this blasted machine gun here. It was slowing everything down. No one had a clue what to do with it, then you came along and blew it to smithereens! Good job, Ryan! You'll get a mention for this in despatches of course. If not *something more*.' He motions for MacFarlane to give Alex some water.

'It was Eden, Sir,' says Alex, still lying on his back. His ribs ache. He should try to sit up.

'What was Eden?'

'He was here. He threw the grenades.'

'Eden was here? Where is he?'

Alex sits up slowly and looks around. A few missing sandbags from the top of the breastwork wall is all that shows from the explosion. There's no sign of Eden. 'I don't know where he is, Sir. He threw the grenades. I must have been knocked out by the blast and... Well, he's gone.'

'Where are his men?'

Alex points towards the shell holes in the field below. 'They're with mine and what's left of Francourt, Halsall and Henderson's.' His voice cracks. 'There's hardly anyone left.'

'Where are the other officers?'

'All dead, I'm afraid, Sir.'

'Even Woodstone? Is he dead?'

'I believe so.'

Babcock stares back towards the British line; the sky is growing pale above it. 'How many men do you have?'

'About forty came over the bridge, but the MG was strafing. We must have lost a lot. I'll go back to them now. We need to get back across the dyke before it gets light.'

'What?' says Babcock. 'You'll do no such thing! You'll get them up and bring them here. You're going into the Boche trench!'

'Why? With what objective, Sir? I thought you said the Hun have gone?'

'They've had a damned good bashing from us today, but they're reforming already. Swarming into those back lines like a nest of angry hornets! Our mission was to occupy their front line. We can't say it's been a success if the Boche have just *moved further back* during the bombardment and we haven't actually gone into their trenches!'

'But we've so few men, Sir. They're exhausted and out of ammunition. Surely—'

'No, no,' Babcock interrupts. 'It was my idea to have an earlier bombardment and it was a damned hard job to persuade Command to let me do it. It all turned out rather well, I think.' He looks at MacFarlane.

MacFarlane nods earnestly.

'But it will be more clear,' continues Babcock. 'If I can show them that we have achieved the specific mission objective and at least one unit of the 12th Battalion has entered the Boche trenches.'

'But, Sir, if the Boche are already back in their supply trenches, we have no hope of holding the line once we get in.'

'You don't need to hold it, Ryan. Just work your way along. You only need to stay for twenty minutes or so, just long enough to make things... *legitimate*. Then get back to our line and prepare for the inevitable counter-attack. It's a shame we've lost Eden. The reports would sound better if the men were led by a captain.' He thinks for a moment. Then turns to MacFarlane. 'Make a note of this, would you? *Captain* Ryan to lead them in.' He turns back to Alex. 'I'm going to make you acting captain, and with Woodstone dead and Eden missing, that makes you *acting commander*, D Company.'

Alex doesn't speak. His head is beginning to pound.

'And when this is done, Ryan, I'll see you get some leave. A month should do it. Give you time to get back to England for a damned good rest.'

Alex sighs. 'Yes, Sir.'

'So off you go, Captain, fetch the men and get on with it. Dawn is coming and so are the damned Boche. You need to get in and out before they do.'

67

DAWN

D Company has made its way through the enemy front line trenches, searching the abandoned dugouts and funk holes. They find nothing of any importance, no surviving Germans. Alex's men are exhausted and hungry and no one is in the mood to look for souvenirs. They've done what Babcock needed them to do, so after building a rough barricade across the entrance to the German supply trench, Alex sends everyone back across the dyke to the British line.

Just as the last few men climb up the ladders into the field, they hear a gunshot coming from a traverse behind them. Alex takes a few men with him to investigate.

Eden is sitting on the fire-step, aiming his pistol at a pile of canvas that's leaning against the breastwork wall. 'I was hoping you'd turn up,' he says, keeping his eyes on the canvas.

'The explosion knocked me unconscious,' says Alex, walking over. 'When I couldn't find you, I thought you might be dead.'

'Sorry to disappoint you.' Eden glances up at Alex. 'I needed to do something. I did check to see if you were hurt before I left, but I had to get on.' He's holding his gun so tightly that his hand is shaking. 'Where've you been?'

Alex feels a surge of anger, but also a strange relief at seeing Eden sitting almost casually. Apart from the gun, it reminds him of the few times they drank whisky together, in the officers' mess, before anything had happened.

'Babcock ordered me to occupy this trench. We came through here five minutes ago but didn't find anything. We were just heading back but heard a gunshot.'

Eden motions towards the canvas with the pistol. 'Here's something you missed.'

Crouching underneath the canvas is a German soldier. Younger than Percy was; just a boy. He's aiming a pistol at Eden, gripping it in both hands, clumsily as if he's not used to holding it. 'Kamerad!' he says between gulps of air. 'Kamerad!' Terrified brown eyes, wide and wet with tears.

Alex's men come up and peer around the canvas to take a look at the boy.

'He's just a lad,' says Rowlands.

'Must have been part of the MG crew, left behind when the trench was abandoned,' says Stubbs.

The boy's helmet is too big for him; like Percy's. It wobbles on his head as he turns frantically from Eden to Alex and the men. 'Bitte lassen Sie mich gehen. Ich will nach... Hause,' he whimpers.

'What's he saying?' says Wislawa.

'Unless he's saying, I surrender,' says Eden, 'I really don't see why it matters.'

Rowlands reaches out his hand.

The boy flinches and tries to retreat further under the canvas. He takes one hand off the pistol, spreads out his fingers towards Eden, then presses them against his own heart.

'I don't think he wants to shoot you, Eden,' says Alex. 'He's afraid of you, that's all. Try lowering your gun.'

'I can assure you he *does* want to shoot me and I will not lower my gun.'

'We could try to rush him, Sir,' says Rowlands. 'I could jump on the canvas, wrap him up in it, while Wislawa grabs the gun.'

'Why should *I* grab the gun?' says Wislawa. 'You or Stubbs should grab the gun!'

'For God's sake!' yells Eden. 'Someone shoot him or *something!*' For the first time that Alex can remember, there seems to be a quiver of fear in Eden's voice.

'No one is going to take any shots!' says Alex. 'We're going back. We'll confiscate his gun and take him with us.'

Eden looks incredulous. 'You're not going back, you're going *forward!* You can't drag a prisoner with you, so you've got to get rid of him.'

Rowlands looks pleadingly at Alex. 'We could just let him go. Or send someone back with him. Couldn't we, Sir?'

'If we let him go, he'll end up back in these trenches,' says Stubbs.

'He doesn't *look* like that would be much of a threat,' says Wislawa.

'I don't mean that,' says Stubbs. 'I mean, if he ends up back here, he's bound to get hurt. It's a miracle that he's survived this far.'

'If we take him as a prisoner,' says Alex. 'They'll put him in a camp in England. He'll be safe there.'

'We don't have time for this!' says Eden. 'We have to keep going, occupy the support trenches. I got into their comms trench. It's empty. I was coming to look for you and regroup the men when I ran into this... problem.'

'No, Eden,' says Alex. 'I met Babcock. He said once we get into this trench, it's over. I've already sent most of the men back.'

Eden blinks slowly, as if he's trying to understand, or trying to focus. 'Babcock said that? Where is he?'

'He came out looking for you and Woodstone. He's gone back now, everyone has. We built a barricade. Enough to slow the Hun, but not to stop them. So we have to go now. You should come with us.' Alex turns to the boy. 'Give me the gun! We won't hurt you.'

The boy doesn't move. He's covered in oil and someone's blood, down one side of his face. Snot smeared in the dirt across his upper lip.

Stubbs steps forward and slowly, deliberately, places his rifle on the ground and steps back with his hands held out in front of him.

The boy, understanding, stands, letting the canvas drop from his shoulders. He holds out the pistol.

Alex takes it, drops it into his pocket and moves between Eden and the boy. 'Eden, put down your gun. He's our prisoner and unarmed, so you can't shoot him.'

Eden laughs. 'No damned bullets anyway.' He lets go of his Luger and it clatters onto the fire-step. 'I'm in a German trench and ran out of German bullets!' He looks down and lifts his arm. Something drips from his elbow. His lap is soaked in blood.

'Did the boy shoot you?' says Alex. 'Was that the shot that we heard?'

Eden slowly unbuttons the lower half of his tunic. His fingers are weak and shaking. He tugs at the shirt; blood, dark and glistening.

'We have to go, Eden. The Boche will be in here any minute.'

The boy tries to sit down. Alex pulls him up and leads him away from Eden. He gestures for Rowlands and Wislawa to join him. 'Take the boy back. Make absolutely sure that he's treated very kindly. Keep him with you and don't let anyone take him away until I've handed him over to the adjutant. I'm relying on you.'

'Give him a cigarette, Rowlands,' says Wislawa.

'I've only got one left.'

'Give it to him!'

Rowlands pulls out the pack from his pocket and hands it to the boy.

The boy, unsure, looks up at Alex for reassurance.

'It's all right,' says Alex, smiling. 'Freund. You have to go with these men. Kamerad!' He smiles.

'Freund! Freund!' says the boy, eyes wide and hopeful.

Rowlands puts his arm around the boy and smiles. 'That's right, Freund!' He gestures over his shoulder towards Eden. 'What about him, Sir?' he says coldly.

'Don't worry,' says Alex. 'You get going. Stubbs will help me.'

'Leave him for the Hun, I would,' says Wislawa.

'Off you go,' says Alex. 'And when you get back, tell Eggleton to put the kettle on for us, would you?'

Rowlands shakes his head. 'I haven't seen him for a while, Sir. Not since the dyke.'

'I wouldn't worry,' says Alex. 'He knows the way back. He'll be all right.'

'He's probably still asleep in one of those shell holes, lazy bastard,' says Rowlands, as the three of them move away around the traverse.

Alex goes back to Eden. 'I should take a look at that wound.'

'No need. I know what it is. A nine-millimetre bullet has made its way somewhere between my stomach and my kidney. There's nothing you can do.'

'Do you want morphine?' says Alex.

Eden shakes his head. 'Got to keep my head clear.' He seems to be diminishing, sinking into his uniform. He looks up at Stubbs. 'Do you have any water?'

Stubbs hands his bottle to Eden.

Eden drinks. There's blood on his lips.

'We can slow the bleeding,' says Alex, pulling out a dressing from his pack and ripping it open.

Eden picks at the edge of the bullet hole with his finger, takes the dressing and presses it against the wound.

A clattering sound wafts over the wall from the German supply trenches.

Stubbs slings his rifle on his back. 'We'll carry him out together, Sir. Get him as far as the bridge. I can cross and find stretcher-bearers, or get some lads back to help bring him in.'

'The hell you will! I'm not going back.'

'Eden, the Hun are about to re-enter this trench!' says Alex. 'If they find you in here, an officer, you don't know what they'll do to you. We have to leave now!'

Eden pulls off his helmet and rests his head against the sandbags. 'They can do what they like. I'm not retreating!'

'This isn't retreating, Eden. It's over!'

The noises get louder; the unmistakable sound of soldiers congregating in the trenches behind them.

Stubbs climbs onto the parados and glances over. 'We have to go, Sir. I can see the tips of their bayonets. If they know we're in here, they only have to lob a grenade and we're done for.'

'You shouldn't leave the sails rolled up like that, Henry,' mumbles Eden. 'You'll get mildew. We should lay them out in the sun.'

'He's not making any sense,' says Stubbs. 'Who's Henry?'

'I think it's his brother,' says Alex. 'You go on, Stubbs.'

Stubbs doesn't go. He looks at Eden, then back at Alex.

'Go on. Get back. We'll be along in a minute.'

'You sure? Is that what you want?'

Alex sighs. 'Yes, you go. Get back before it gets too light.'

'All right. I'll try to get help and wait for you at the dyke for as long as I can.' Stubbs climbs the breastwork and without looking back, leaps down and is gone.

'You should get going yourself,' says Eden.

Alex sits. 'Why don't we try to get into a shell hole on the other side of this wall?'

'I was in their comms trench.' Eden is breathless now. 'No one in there. I would have gone further, but I ran out of... The Hun must have found our bridges, taken them. I thought we could cross the dyke, but the mud... Then the wind changed and I lost a lot of men, I mean, actually lost them, in the smoke...' His voice fades to nothing.

'Eden?' Alex takes Eden by the arm and tries to pull him to his feet. 'Come on, let's go.'

Eden twists his arm away. 'I tell you, I'm not going! I'm not crawling back into our trenches on my fucking hands and knees.'

Distinct German voices now. Thuds, and sheet metal being pushed over. The Hun must be breaking through the barricade further along the trench.

Eden doesn't seem to hear it, or he doesn't care. He fumbles in his pocket and takes out his pipe. It's still lit and glows after a few puffs. 'Tomorrow, in the South, in the Somme valley, they are about to do something marvellous. Tens of thousands of men will be marching across No Man's Land into the German lines and probably on all the way to Berlin. It will be glorious.' He takes a deep, rasping breath. 'We were supposed to be part of that. We were the first wave of the big wonderful push.'

'I don't think what we've done here ever really mattered,' says Alex, handing Eden his water bottle. 'I think this was only ever supposed to be a diversion. A way of keeping the Hun away from the Somme.'

Eden ignores the bottle. 'This whole thing, France, was a diversion.'

'From what?'

Eden shrugs. 'It all used to be so clear. I don't understand who they want me to be anymore.' He turns to Alex, his eyes suddenly burning. 'I did it! I got into that comms trench! You go back and tell them that. Tell them that with a few more men I could have *kept* going and held that line! Will you tell them that?' He grimaces as he grips the dressing against his stomach. The blood looks very red now, soaking through onto his hand. 'Not just a diversion, we could have done something that *really* counted! Could have been part of history. *The battle of the Boar's Head Salient.* Something that people talked about for a hundred years!' He coughs and it seems to really hurt.

'Babcock says you'll get a mention in despatches for what happened with that MG. I told him it was you.'

Eden smiles. 'A *mention!*' He shakes his head. 'It was never about...' He closes his eyes. 'I'm going to rest here for a moment. You decide what you need to do.' His breathing slows. He seems to be sleeping.

The shadows are growing pale.

Alex pulls out the boy's Luger, turning it over in his hand. The little dents and scratches glint in the half-light. The wooden grip is marked with cross-hatched lines. He watches the pattern it makes in his palm; pinched white, then fading as the blood rushes back into his skin.

He's killed a lot of men this morning, but this one, if he does it, will be so much harder; he *knows* this man. He looks at Eden's hands,

swollen now and dark with cuts. He can remember how they held a
pen or a cup of tea. That bruised mouth, creased with dried blood,
still holds the remnant of a smile that he'd once courted. He reaches
out to wipe the blood but stops himself; he mustn't wake him.

Knowing them shouldn't make any difference. He thinks of the
men who came staggering, floundering towards him through the
smoke. *He* didn't know them, but every one of them was known and
loved by *someone*. That should have been enough to stop the killing,
but it wasn't and it never will be.

He slides off the safety catch. He looks at the clouds above the
sandbags, warmed and made plump by a hint of dawn. It will be light
soon. If he does it, he must do it quickly. But he must be sure. He
must do it *well*.

He takes a deep breath, holds it, slowly lifting the gun and placing
the muzzle against Eden's temple.

Eden's eyes move beneath his eyelids, but they don't open.

If Alex does this, it will be *murder*, and Odette will hate him for it.
He thinks of how she said, if he does it, he'll be no different from
Eden. But this isn't about revenge. She wouldn't understand.

He can hear the soldiers coming along the trench. If he does it, he
must do it *now*.

Odette doesn't have to know. He doesn't have to say anything.
He'll never mention this to her, or anyone.

He presses harder, feeling the softness of the flesh and the hard-
ness of the bone. A guttural, primordial spasm of anger, love and hate
spews up and surges through his arm and fingers, squeezing the
trigger.

Eden's head jolts, pulling his body sideways and it lands with a
soft thump on the fire-step. A neat hole. Blood rises but nothing
spills.

Insects spin in silver circles in the air above the body; Captain
James Eden's body.

Alex sits very still until he hears the Germans' mumbled voices
and boots on duckboards. Then he stands and climbs over the breastwork into No Man's Land.

The sun is rising. A thin feather of cloud, distorted by tears, is catching fire above the field. Mist, like a shroud, is lying across the corpses of both armies. There must be a throng of ghosts here. If they had voices, there would be a scream so long and loud that people could hear it echo through the centuries to come. But the field is almost silent; only a single cry from one of the living, lost somewhere in the mud.

He crosses the bridge, past men as still as leaves in the dark water. He stumbles over the torn earth, through the wire, over the bags and into the British trench to regroup what's left of his men.

HISTORICAL NOTE

This is a work of fiction, but Alex's battalion and their movements is inspired by the war diaries of the 12th and 13th Southdown Battalions (Royal Sussex Regiments) and their activity in France from the beginning of March to the end of June, 1916.

The battle in the final chapters, known as the Battle of the Boar's Head Salient, took place on 30th June at Ferme du Bois, near Richebourg. It was intended to be a diversion from the Battle of the Somme, which would take place the next day.

The battle was a disaster. The 11th Battalion sustained 116 casualties whilst supporting the attack. The 12th lost 429 men, either killed or wounded. The 13th lost over 800 men, killed, wounded or captured. In total, the three Southdowns Battalions suffered 366 killed and over 1000 wounded or taken prisoner. For more information on this, please take a look at the excellent book by John A. Baines called The Day Sussex Died.

Percy represents some of the 306 soldiers of the British and Commonwealth Army who were shot at dawn by firing squad for desertion or cowardice. Many of them were teenagers. The first was Private Thomas Highgate, who was shot on 8th September 1914, aged 17. The youngest is believed to have been Private Herbert Burden, who was also 17. The law was changed in 1930, banning the death sentence for the offences for which the 306 were shot. They were all 'pardoned' in August 2006.

For updates and further information, please visit my website at http://pdsherrard.com

ACKNOWLEDGMENTS

Thank you so much for reading this book. If you enjoyed it (or even if you didn't) please take a few moments to write a review. Thank you!

To leave a review on Amazon, please click on this link: https://rebrand.ly/amzlongestspringreview

To leave a review on Goodreads, please click on this link: https://www.goodreads.com/review/edit/190115807

To Tiff, who spent almost as much time in these chapters as I did. Thank you for your patience and thank you for listening, day after day after day...

And to all the people who inspired, taught and guided me through the various stages of this project, including: Moe Atkins, Dianna Aurisch, Sally Beare, Clive Branch, Dani Glazzard, Cat Knight, Rachel Mayers, Shannon Messer, Alison Powell and everyone at Bristol WriteClub, Johanna Spiers, Toby Willems, and lots more. Thank you.

For updates and further information, please visit my website at http://pdsherrard.com

Made in the USA
Monee, IL
06 February 2024

53044593R00192